The Girl from Ha Giang

Martin Love

Those to whom evil is done
Do evil in return
W. H. Auden

ProseWorks Media
Chapel Hill, NC
www.proseworks.us
Facebook: The Girl from Ha Giang
Twitter: @girlfromhagiang

Cover photograph by Benjamin Vu.

This book is a work of fiction. It does attempt to depict accurately aspects of contemporary Vietnam and of Israel/Palestine. The places described are real, but the characters, while they could in spirit depict real people, are works of the author's imagination and any resemblance to actual people, living or dead, is entirely coincidental.

The publisher is not responsible for websites (or their content) that are not owned by the publisher.

ISBN: 978-0-578-10726-4
v. 1.0.2pb

This tale is dedicated to Sean Reed Love and to friends and acquaintances near and far who wage their own battles in their own ways against ignorance and cruelty, obfuscations and cant.

Map of Vietnam

1

guyen Song Tao was her complete name, though a few she befriended could have added sobriquets. So might a dead man we both had known, if the dead could speak. But hers was not a remarkable name. As was customary in Vietnam, the family name came first, and almost half the country of some 80 million carried that same family name despite blood that had no relation. The last, Tao, was her given name, and by that, she was simply called.

My first sight of her was on one of the cushioned, wicker chairs on the top deck of the *Emeraude* -- the finest vessel taking anyone with enough *dong* out into Ha Long Bay for a weekend cruise -- before we slipped away from the dock. I had not noticed her on the bus that carried 60 or so passengers, expatriate members of the American Chamber of Commerce in Vietnam and their wives or partners, from the Ha Noi Hilton to the long dock and our boarding on a hot Saturday noon near Ha Long Bay, whose peaks loomed in the distance like the triangular fins of mythical dragons thrusting upwards from the Gulf on Tonkin. Ha Long meant, after all, the "Bay of the Descending Dragon." Nearby, at the mouth of a small river that emptied into the gulf, was where Tran Hung Dao -- the namesake of the Ha Noi street where *Vietnam News* had its offices and where I worked as an editor -- in 1288 placed iron tipped stakes in the riverbed, sinking most of an invading Mongol fleet. I was not surprised that the Vietnamese had been so enterprising in warfare.

I was too distracted talking to a childhood friend, Dar Williams, who had invited me along, and his Viet wife, named Huong and half his age, on the bus as we scanned the passing scenes of rural Vietnam -- the green rice paddies surrounding villages -- to take much notice of the other passengers, and not yet Tao, whom I had not noticed. But chef Bobby Chinn was boisterously unavoidable amid the talk with Williams across the aisle in the bus. Chinn was enjoying his companions. A young Californian of Chinese and Egyptian extraction with an alleged British education -- a description which could have won most anyone's second glance -- he owned a mildly famous, overpriced restaurant across the street from the southwest corner of Hoan Kiem Lake in Ha Noi. Sporting a ponytail and a gold chain around his neck and looking every bit like the rock star he was not at age forty or so, he had apparently nominated two twenty-something Vietnamese girls to go with him aboard the *Emeraude* and share the same cabin. Williams and I could do little but wish we were not so relatively old. Chinn's young ladies, or whatever they were, snuggled up to him and giggled in their seats, which included Chinn's lap, for it was certain that in no other capacity would they have had the opportunity to board the *Emeraude*.

Once aboard, reportorial instincts went into gear after I found my own cabin and had thrown my bag on the well-turned bed of white linens and grabbed complimentary chocolates on the pillow -- the latter a nice touch. I headed to the bridge and there spoke with the Vietnamese captain. The vessel had been launched in 2002, he told me. It was a modernized revival of an earlier, French, paddle wheeled steamer of the same name, adorned with varnished woods and brass fittings and air conditioning in each of its 37 cabins. It was a modern echo of a bygone, more elegant era long before air conditioning. Useless brass fans were attached to the walls in the cabins.

I wandered back to the crowded bar on the top deck laden as it was with a buffet of seafood and pasta. And that's when I first saw Tao, when she caught my eyes. She was sprawled in the wicker chair, her bare feet on a low table. Oddly, the first thing I noticed were her feet: small and not the least bit ugly as feet can be, her toenails unadorned with paint or polish, and also her slim but sturdy looking ankles. Not even fancy sandals would have boosted the appeal, and I had no fetish about feet.

A handsome boy of four or so with big, black eyes, obviously her child, gamboled around the table, grabbing at plastic Lego pieces that spilled across the table and onto the teak deck. But otherwise she seemed alone -- that is, without a man friend -- and I went over and began casually helping the boy the squeeze together Lego blocks into no resemblance of any particular object, as I had done with my own son two decades earlier.

"I am Marshall McLean," I said, holding out a hand to shake hers.

Tao seemed intrigued with my assistance with the Legos, watching me curiously. "I am Tao. The boy is Tung."

"Are you with Amcham, a member?" I asked, referring to the American Chamber of Commerce branch in Ha Noi.

"No," she laughed, sweeping back her black, straight hair with a graceful hand. "Do I look American?"

"No."

"But I know some Americans in Ha Noi. I studied in America, too," she offered.

"Do you know Dar Williams? He's a longtime friend of mine."

"No. So you are not an Amcham member, too?"

"I am working for the newspaper, *Vietnam News*. I am an editor there, but I haven't joined Amcham. Not into business. Dar Williams invited me along for the ride. You are young," I said, quite aware that I was nearing 60, had a son deep in a medical career in the US, and had been a widower for over a decade.

"Thirtyish," she offered casually, paused and then asked: "How would you like to go for a swim when we get out into Ha Long Bay?"

The query was a surprise, and the first among more later, mostly my own borne upon an abomination: the memories of a friend unexpectedly dispatched to some Heaven, perhaps even the Islamic one, if only I believed in a Heaven.

"I imagine I would like that, if there are no sharks about. Are you sharkish?" I was thinking she might have a predatory bent. It was not a stretch to assume many smart, attractive younger women did. My gut already told me she could be. What exactly she sought after became the question, especially weeks later.

"I don't think so," she said, but then she stood, and peeled off her shorts, then her T-shirt with a flourish aimed at attracting eyes, at least my own. She was wearing a turquoise blue bikini under her street clothes. It was for sure not a thong, but it was revealing enough. *Why*, I wondered. The *Emeraude* was at least an hour away from any kind of anchorage, and we were just leaving the dock, leaving behind a horde of souvenir hawkers who had followed us out onto the long wharf to the boat like flies, or like remora following a real shark. We had hardly gotten past a basic introduction, not to mention that I expected no such summons from any female half my age. I was fast becoming a Taoist of sorts.

Aside from her feet, she was slim, well proportioned, wrapped in velvety skin, a young woman who at just over five feet had no particular feature that made her stand out in some utterly striking way, but neither did she have any feature that made her in any way unattractive. She looked completely harmonious, at ease with herself and her body, natural. Her small breasts, for example, were unremarkable. Youth, relative and real, was what stood out the most. I was both flattered and charmed, and the latter was not because of the sudden invitation to a specific activity, to a kind of intimacy where, if we swam together, we would perforce be dependent on each other to assist if either of us got in some kind of trouble, or spotted a shark. Rather, enveloping her was a penumbra of pure energy. At my age, I could almost imbibe such energy like an old sponge that for too long had been tossed unused into a drawer.

"So, you like to swim, are a serious swimmer?" I asked.

"Of course. I like it," Tao said.

"And what about dragons? Do they inhabit the bay?" I asked, remembering what the name of the bay meant in English.

"We may find out," Tao said playfully.

"And what else do you do? Do you work, too? I see you are a mother, which is work enough."

"I research," Tao said. "I am documenting residual Agent Orange and UXO. That's 'unexploded ordnance'. I work for the Ministry of Defense, for one thing. The aim is to help expose the problem so my government can appeal for US aid for more clean up."

"That's a noble effort. A friend, Dar Williams, who is here and who initially invited me to visit your country, told me he goes to Danang, that his wife has relatives living near China Beach, near the huge American air base operating during the war. He says the site is still heavily contaminated with dangerous chemicals like PCB's, closed off behind miles of perimeter fencing and barbed wire."

"That is true." Tao reached into her handbag beside her chair and handed me a photo of a map. I dropped the Lego pieces onto the table.

The photo depicted Southeast Asia, and most of it on the map, especially Vietnam, Cambodia and parts of Laos, were covered completely in red. Farther west towards Thailand, there were just red dots.

"Each dot represents a place where bombs fell during the war. You can see that the dots converge and then disappear, that almost all of the map is just red," she pointed out as I scanned the map.

"Not surprising, but to see it like this is startling. I was in college and then graduate school during the war."

"Not surprising? Most Americans still don't realize the destruction of the war. It is hard to believe once you know. But you say you were in school during the war? Were you not part of the war machine that attacked and occupied my country? Now, I am surprised, and you don't look that old," said Tao.

"Thanks, but what do you think? I hope you don't think I supported the war. Many young men then did not, like me. Even many who were inducted into the military. Perhaps they were misguided or lacked strong beliefs. The war was not good for my country, too. It was insane, I think."

"But you were not drafted? How was that so?"

"I found a way not to be," I said.

6

"Why? You did not like your leaders?"

"Look," I said somewhat defensively, knowing I did not want to drive away her attention, "I didn't like what my 'leaders' were doing. I gathered what was going on. It was all over the newspapers. The carnage. I protested the war, wrote letters, marched in Washington. It was a difficult time. Many young people like me then were dying. I bet you were not even born then?"

"Protesting I don't think would have meant you could avoid the draft. Am I wrong?"

"No," I said.

"Were you ill? You don't look ill now," Tao said with a smile. Maybe she was lightening up a bit.

"Thank you again for looking at a man much older than you and not seeing obvious signs of serious decline." I smiled back at her.

"So, really, how did you avoid the Army?"

"I went to Divinity school."

"What is *that*?"

"Training for the Christian ministry. The draft board in my hometown in the Carolinas apparently believed I was destined to save souls, as if that were ever possible, and was sincere about trying. I concluded it was because I had written some articles about life in the Holy Land, or in Israel, from a *kibbutz* one summer for my hometown newspaper. But I did give the ministry some thought, of course, as a career, but it was not really for me. I aimed eventually to work in print media as a reporter or editor."

"I see," said Tao. She frowned. "I give the ministry a lot of thought myself."

"The ministry? You?"

"The government Ministry I work for," she said.

"Ha. You fooled me with that word, 'ministry'. Why were you frowning?" I had to ask.

"I am not religious," she said.

"No? You are a Communist. Right?"

"Yes, my government..."

"But isn't Communism, or any ideology, a sort of religion, too, for believers, as perhaps you are?"

Tao's face flickered with mild irritation again, and I quickly figured I had better shut up about "religion", or suggesting her creed was just that and not much more. I hoped she did not see me as someone who had merely come up with an effective ploy to evade conscription, as a poseur, an insincere former student devotee of the Divine.

"A valid 'ministry' in Christian circles at the time at the school I attended could be seen as something as simple as serving 'peace' by protest against, or a refusal to directly participate in, a war," I went on after a lull. "That was part of it, but I was also interested in learning about Islam, and even some Arabic language."

"I am glad you did not personally battle my country or harm Vietnamese," said Tao.

I was relieved at her relief, but then she added: "I would have fought for Ho Chi Minh's beliefs if I had been of age to do so. I would have died for my country to evict American occupiers. But why did you study Islam?"

"I had friends who were conscripted and one of them told me the Marine Corps had mock ups of Middle Eastern villages for practice assaults," I said. "When I heard that, I figured the military was looking far ahead to the next designated enemy, beyond Communist Vietnam and its allies."

"That is fascinating," said Tao. "Middle Eastern villages back then?"

"Yes, right in the Virginia woods somewhere near that Marine base outside Washington. Quantico it's called."

"Not Vietnamese-like villages there, too?"

"I imagine they existed, too, for practice assaults. I aimed to get a leg up understanding a future designated foe, Muslims. But I think generally that any government or country can be wrong in its actions and policies, and not worth dying for. Can you see this is possible?" I asked.

"Not any government, because my government is good," Tao said coolly and with a tone of somber conviction. "But I guess you wonder exactly when I was born?" Tao asked with pride.

"I do."

"I was born the day the NVA took Saigon. That was April 30th in 1975. That day our tanks crashed the gates of the Presidential Palace compound there and Saigon fell."

"Quite a day to be born on!"

"Yes, a serious victory for Vietnam," said Tao.

"A victory for North Vietnam, wasn't it?" I tried to correct her, hoping I wouldn't lose her attention.

"No," she countered. "It was one for the entire country."

"But not for all Vietnamese. What do you think? Ho Chi Minh's successors mandated harsh measures against many in the south after the war ended, did he not?"

"They had gone astray. They needed to become true patriots, true Vietnamese," Tao said sharply.

"I don't know, but maybe you do," I said. Actually, I did not agree with her. One was Vietnamese by blood, by simply being Vietnamese, not by political affiliation.

"You just don't know what it is to live in a country that's being occupied and bombed by foreigners."

"That is true," I said. "I have not experienced that, nor have any Americans, except those who revolted against the British over 200 years ago and thus literally became Americans, not British subjects."

"The aim here was the eviction of foreign occupiers. Who has any right to occupy and exploit a land and people not their own?"

"I understand your perspective. But now you can be friends with Americans? I am impressed at your forgiving nature."

"Winners can be forgiving, don't you think? I like America anyway."

"It's much harder for losers to forgive, it seems. Perhaps because they have nothing to show for their efforts."

"We now have our independence. No foreign occupation. Anyway, I spent half a year in Washington."

"Doing what?"

"Learning more English mostly. My government sent me."

"Just to learn English? A long way to go for that?"

"It was a scholarship. I studied some other things, too."

I wanted to ask Tao about some man I presumed she must have somewhere, if not on the boat, but refrained. Why remind her of another? I had no partner on the *Emeraude* for the excursion into what was arguably one of the most dramatic seascapes on the planet. I was getting some attention and I was disinclined to deflect it by an attempt to fathom her personal situation. I turned to the boy and waved at him to stand in front of me.

It was time to teach him a game I had often played with my own son when he was a child. The game was to see if he could withdraw his hands, resting atop mine, fast enough to avoid my turning my hands over and slapping the tops of his. If he succeeded, he could have a turn at trying to slap my hands. I showed him what to try to do, and once he figured the game out, I moved my hands to slap his, but so slowly that he managed to withdraw most of the time and avoid a slap. And then, when he had his turn, I let him win with a slap time and again, feigning with gestures and expressions of pain, as if I had dipped my hands in boiling *pho*, that he had delivered mighty, stinging blows. This produced peals of glee from the boy.

Tao watched without objection. She was evidently pleased to see an adult stranger take such an interest in her boy, even though I was by turns slapping the tops of his hands. Nearby on the deck the Amcham crowd gorged on piles of squid and shrimp from the buffet, sipping gin and tonics and other libations, including bottles of native Tiger beer. The boat was moving along at five or so knots out into the bay towards the first rocky islands, an outboard powered tender trailing behind in the wake, secured by a line at the stern. Gusts of wind danced and spun like Sufi dervishes across the deck and I was pleased to be breathing fresh air after a few weeks of not in Ha Noi. Dar Williams, my old friend, and his wife, Huong, then wandered over.

"That boy is having some fun," Williams remarked.

"I am, too," I said, glancing up. "Do you know each other?" I pointed at Tao.

"Don't think we've met," Williams said to Tao with his usual warmth and enthusiasm.

"Not until now," Tao said.

"I'm Dar Williams and this is Huong. Marshall here I've known since childhood. He's a newcomer to Southeast Asia but he's spent lots of time in West Asia. When he was younger he was a reporter in the Mideast for a while."

"I am Tao. Your friend was telling me he studied about the Middle East at a divine school," Tao said to Williams, and then she turned to Huong and spoke to her in Vietnamese.

"Hey," Dar teased Tao, "didn't you know that only English is allowed among passengers here? This is an American party."

"Huong is telling me secrets," Tao said, teasing back.

"Like what?"

"Huong says you have been married a year and a half. That you met in Ha Noi."

"Hardly a secret," Dar said. "When I first came to Vietnam I was up in the mountain villages near Sapa. I was begging for donations from the States and using what funds I could get to help build some rudimentary health clinics in the mountain villages. When the money dried up I came into Ha Noi and wandered into a shop next to the Lucky Hotel on Hang Trong Street. That was where I met Huong. It was her shop, and her mother and sister worked there, too."

I had heard this before when staying with Williams and Huong in Saigon, where I had first landed in Vietnam, and where Williams had suggested I look into something like the editing job I landed in Ha Noi. He had also recounted that he was sleeping then in the cellar of a rotten tube house in the Old Quarter in Ha Noi for almost nothing and often woke to the sounds and sometimes the sight of rats scurrying up among the rafters. He had three changes of clothes and had accepted relative poverty, having divorced a former wife and abandoned a big house and a lucrative job in the Carolinas. His previous marriage had soured and he had recounted unhappy scenes on return home from business trips overseas, one in particular that first took him to Vietnam and then when he arrived home he found his former wife strung out on Percocet amid reports she had been driving her Mercedes *Gelandewagen* dangerously fast on the winding Blue Ridge Parkway and quite possibly entertaining other men when he was away. That there were no children from the union was something I reckoned fortunate.

Out in Ha Long Bay on the deck of the *Emeraude*, it occurred to me that perhaps Ho Chi Minh's prime maxim, that there was nothing so precious as freedom and independence, was not so simplistic after all if one were capable of embracing it in multiple lights: not merely freedom from foreign occupation and control and from the *imposition* of "democracy" which in itself was an oxymoron, but the freedom and independence from surfeit inherent in not wanting, and not caring about, any material things but essentials. The choice of relative poverty, however, escaped the Viets. They seemed to be abandoning an ancient culture based on wet rice cultivation and replacing that with a culture of industrialization and materialism rushing towards consumerism.

"Rats," I said, musing aloud. I was curious.

"Rats?" asked Williams.

"I wonder if rats are lurking on board?"

"I think this may be the one tourist boat in Ha Long Bay that is not plagued by rats. If any showed, it would completely demolish the appeal, the ads about just what the *Emeraude* is," said Williams.

"I imagine any paying passenger who saw one would certainly broadcast it," I commented.

"I second that," said Tao. "Northern Vietnam had a rat problem last year. So many were breeding out of control in the rice paddies that they were hurting the rice yield. But this year Vietnam is exporting rice," Tao beamed.

"I remember, too," said Williams. "The government put a bounty on evidence of killed rats. The peasant farmers went to work. They killed zillions of rats and brought their tails into Ha Noi as proof of successful executions, collecting a few thousand *dong*, a few cents, for the tail of each rat killed. That tells you how desperate people can be for a little extra income. But rice yields did rally."

"Rutting rats rendered!" I said.

"What?" asked Williams.

"Just some alliteration," I said, but I was thinking of what the CIA had apparently been doing to alleged Muslim terrorists, to as many as they could scoop up, almost willy-nilly. Almost any so-called towel head was at risk. "Rendering" them, or going for rendition, was often tantamount to killing them. I went on: "Well, there's still a problem in Ha Noi. A new friend of mine, at the newspaper, a New Zealander, one Cain Hamilton, was working late one night in the newsroom and a big rat was spotted amid the tangle of wires and connections behind a row of computer terminals, and then disappeared. I keep my shoes on at *my* terminal there." I might have added that I kept my knees covered, too, recalling a harsh warning from the managing editor, one Phuc by name.

"Enough of rat talk," said Tao. "You might scare Tung." He did speak some English, as I had observed. She swept the Legos into a shopping bag and headed to her stateroom with the boy. "I will see you in a bit," she added. "I will try to get someone to watch Tung."

I had a few minutes to stroll about the deck and look around. And little did I know then that at least one dangerous and different kind of "rat" was in fact on the boat -- some one who would eventually betray what in general I valued most, and what most sustained my spirits in Vietnam.

The *Emeraude* was well into the scenic part of Ha Long Bay. A couple hundred meters off the starboard rail, between two towering islets, I spotted a huge yacht. Her engines must have been running because she was moving along at crawl speed, effortlessly, but with no sign of exhaust exiting from her funnels. I hurried back to my cabin, donned a bathing suit and grabbed a pair of binocular to try to get a closer look at the mega yacht. The yacht's superstructure was clean and clear cut -- completely at odds with the junks and other craft in the bay but for the *Emeraude* -- with dark, impenetrable windows along the hull above the waterline. Behind the funnels on a pad rested a Eurocopter 135 sporting an "F" registration. It was a French helicopter on a yacht of nearly 100 meters. Had I not read in the marketing literature about the *Emeraude* that foreign yachts were not allowed in Ha Long Bay? Something about the Vietnamese being at odds with the Chinese over claims to the nearby Spratly Islands, around which under the seabed allegedly laid untapped deposits of oil and gas? I focused the binoculars on the bridge. There were quite large letters, in gold, about 50 centimeters high. They read *Geneva Princess*. Scanning back along the deck I caught a view of a cluster of people lounging about. The sun was strong, casting just the right angle of light on the stern. Pedigree escort chum, it seemed: Top notch pleasure babes with some Vietnamese and Western men. The Viets looked like a covey of ministerial level officials, like Communist Party officials I had seen in photos in the newspaper. *Vietnam News* had recently carried a story about the government's consideration of a so-called 'Memorandum of Understanding' with the Airbus consortium for 10 aircraft, with options for 20 more. The deal was worth more than six billion Euros. I wondered if the cruise had been staged to help ensure the Vietnamese signed the contract with Airbus. But very soon the yacht vanished, navigating away from the *Emeraude*, slipping out of sight behind one of the islets.

2

Back in Ha Noi I had been walking to Tran Hung Dao to the job at Vietnam News. I did not know right off that the street bore the name of a 13th century military hero, a Vietnamese poet and scholar who had been summoned from his desk to repel the Mongols from his country, but war or talk of war had lost grip in Vietnam even as reminders of war lingered. Tao was correct. Thirty years on since the fall of Saigon to the North Vietnamese Army, only some quarter of thousands of tons of unexploded American ordnance -- UXO -- had been unearthed and cleared from the land, and over those three decades almost as many unlucky Vietnamese -- roughly 45,000 -- had died from post-war explosions as Americans during the long war. This was allegedly what most concerned Tao in her work, whatever it exactly involved. The Vietnamese, accustomed to carnage, had taken yet more suffering in stride. They were too busy trying to make a dong (or even a declining US dollar). Some were becoming as successful at that as their ancestors had been at killing and demoralizing Americans, just as, in lesser numbers, American soldiers and mercenaries were getting picked off or blown up by relatively disorganized Muslim groups and suicidal individuals amid military occupations.

Tran Hung Dao was wide and so were its sidewalks, lined with tropical trees, many of them the *xoan* or China Berry with leaves that twirled to the sidewalks like yellow confetti. Beyond the sidewalks still stood French colonial mansions, many of them refurbished as offices, embassies and restaurants amid various stores and food markets and larger office buildings. Most of the streets immediately south of Hoan Kiem Lake, Ha Noi's heart, were like that, but my humble lodging, an apartment of three rooms, was to the north of the lake, in the dirtiest, oldest part of the city amid the warren of ancient market and residential lanes comprising Old Quarter where Williams had for a time tried to fend off rats.

The walk to work took only half an hour and if one avoided getting maimed or killed crossing streets by the swarms of motorbikes, it was a pleasant enough stroll, especially down along Hoan Kiem Lake, a stagnant oval hiding artifacts and treasures centuries old that whetted an historical imagination. Ho Chi Minh's prime warlord, General Vo Nguyen Giap, was still alive, inhabiting a modest home nearby, not far from Ho's grim, Soviet-style mausoleum in Ha Noi. We were almost neighbors, which astounded me because I recalled reading of him during the war.

I had learned that in the north the Vietnamese pronounced his name "zap", which seemed fitting inasmuch as he had literally zapped many thousands, including South Vietnamese who had more or less cooperated with American forces by helping prop up the weak, perhaps more corrupt government in the south. Giap's survival, I felt, lent a certain historical depth to a Ha Noi that was throwing off the burdens of the past and old traditions to focus on *Doi Moi*, the name the Vietnamese coined for the economic liberalization program under way for almost two decades.

By the time I met Tao on the *Emeraude*, I had been working at the paper for just over a month, but already I was ruffling sensibility there because the lady who managed the domestic news flow did not know horseshit about proper reporting. This was Anh, who perched a few seats away in the steamy newsroom four floors above leafy Tran Hung Dao. She figured I was somewhat inclined to shirk the job which, along with a couple other Western colleagues, involved rewriting into decent prose reams of often garbled, messy and incomplete copy that had been badly translated from Vietnamese and slated for the morrow's edition. My job description at the paper was "editor", but this title amounted to no status because I worked as mere copy editor and rewriter, helping put out a paper aimed exclusively at presenting Vietnam in gleaming light to expatriates and to those Viets who wanted to read the news in English.

It had been easier than I had imagined it might be to get the hang of the job: show up in the afternoons at two at 12 Tran Hung Dao, casually wave to the guards in the booth at the entrance to the building as if I owned the place to avoid some kind of challenge, go up the stairs and find the newsroom staff in languid disarray. I often discovered the couple score of mostly female, young Viet reporters just rousing themselves from naps on cheap office chairs they had pushed together and draped prone over in front of their computer terminals for what was a midday siesta. It looked like the tail end of some kind of lubricious orgy with young bodies sprawled in awkward repose on the chairs. But once work cranked up again, I likened the scene to a view inside a hothouse swarming with exotic butterflies engaged in a sort of Brownian motion, for almost any one of the ladies delighted my almost 60 year old eyes. This scene of busy, lambent pulchritude was by far the best part, and maybe the only good part, of the ambience at the paper. Maybe I should have been satisfied enough just to see with spectacles on my nose, but I had expected more before and for a few days after my start at the newspaper.

Because experienced Western editors were essential to shaping a readable, if dull, English language newspaper, I figured we might be treated to an elevated status, that we might have some access to whatever inner sanctum there was of the Communist Party power brokers among the media. We were by the simple execution of our skills minor mandarins of a sort, but I had not seen The Editor, a reclusive lady, who allegedly inhabited a suite of offices on the floor above. Nor had I literally seen anyone else in charge except Phuc, who was proving to live up to what his name sounded like in English.

Phuc said enthusiastically, "Welcome to *Vietnam News*," the afternoon he showed the way to a seat and a computer terminal, but that was the last of any words of welcome. I readily noted his smile. But within days it seemed odd because it was perennial, as if his facial muscles had become frozen under the bald pate he tried to cover by drawing grayed strands of hair across the top of his head from one side to the other. After that first day, we had had few words for a couple weeks until one afternoon he came to my seat and leaned over my terminal so closely that I could have smelled his breath if I had had a notion to sniff it out. I did not have any such notion.

"You are *not* welcome here," Phuc said sharply.

I was shocked. He had just recently uttered the same affirmatively. My thoughts for a moment scrambled wildly for traction. I wondered if he was going to accuse me of trying to grope one of the young females, something I had no compulsion to try -- without a clear and unequivocal invitation, which I knew I'd never get. I wondered if Phuc had spotted me glancing at the young ladies: there was little else to do between stories to edit. Maybe he thought I aimed to grope one of them in the hallway one night. I had no such interest, but perhaps he just wanted to grope the young ladies himself, and was projecting.

"Not welcome?" I said. "You just recently hired me. What have I done wrong?"

"You are not dressed for work," said Phuc.

"I am dressed and pressed," I countered, snapping a couple fingers across a clean, pressed shirt.

"Your pants!" Phuc whispered with astonished urgency.

I looked down at my pants, especially at the zipper. It was closed. (No dong was in sight, as much later two kinds of dong, the physical one and the monetary *dong*, I would see spilling from a dear colleague's pants on a dark street at the end of an evening of pleasure and fun in Ha Noi.) Actually, that day, I was wearing short pants. "What's wrong with my pants?"

"Your knees!" snapped Phuc. I could almost imagine he had spotted, with sudden super inhuman vision, a spot of *ebola* virus on my knees.

"My knees? They still do their job. Well enough for jogs in the mornings around your lovely Hoan Kiem Lake," I said, hoping he'd back off by my calling the lake not only lovely, which it was, but his, too, which it was not.

"Do not show them! If you do again, you are fired."

He seemed insane. And my irritation with him surfaced.

"But the females here get to show *their* knees if they want. I didn't know the newspaper had an invisibility code or mandate just for men's knees? Is this not discriminatory?"

"You are arguing. Do not argue with me," Phuc admonished. "I say again: show your knees here one more time and you are fired." Still, he was mostly smiling. But dead serious he obviously was, and I was not ready to be fired, did not welcome that then, though during my coming weeks in Ha Noi, I finally did welcome getting fired as a relief from gross oppression marked by neglect and more. I knew when to shut up, in most circumstances where this made sense anyway, and held back further protest. Challenging Phuc about wearing shorts, I figured, might well prove to be a wasteful expenditure of the scant and precious ammunition I might need to employ later if I stayed long enough at the paper. I assumed there could be other, more important issues to object to in a newsroom dominated by subservience to shaping the news, or omitting parts of it, into what really amounted to soft propaganda. Phuc made his point and wandered away. I would no longer don shorts for work. "Okay, Phuc. Okay! Sorry," I conceded.

I had words with Anh, too, early on at the newspaper a few days after my exposed knees offended Phuc. I wondered if I had offended Anh, too. She directed the domestic news flow into the paper, and one evening, as usual, she was perched nearby at her terminal, looking far too serious -- like someone with the codes for a launch of nuclear missiles -- than I thought appropriate for a mere newspaper so bereft of substance it could be the source of a good laugh.

I sauntered over to her with some hard copy in my hands. "Anh, Phuc has warned me about wearing shorts here, showing my knees. I wonder if you have a personal problem with this, too?"

She looked me over, down to my knees, giving away nothing. "I am busy," she said.

"Are my knees ugly?" I asked with a smile.

"I am not interested," she said.

"Okay," I said. "But I have a problem with this copy." I laid the paper on her desk.

"What?" she asked coolly.

"If you want me to rewrite this, I refuse unless we can also add just what the report claimed to the story," I said to her.

"You refuse? It's your job. Why?" she asked.

"Because the reader might want to know, to read about, what the Prime Minister is calling 'lies'. It is not enough to claim the report in question is wrong, just because the Prime Minister says it is."

This exchange with Anh arose from a fresh Western analysis on human rights claiming Vietnam remained grossly unenthusiastic about allowing political expressions antithetical to the Party. The overall apparatus and actions of the government had to be reported as squeaky clean, and even if there were a few deviants within the government or the society, they would likely get their comeuppance -- perhaps time in a prison in some remote mountain province to the west.

"I will report this refusal to Phuc," she warned.

"Go ahead, but I'll argue same to him. An editor in anything but name will see my point, I think."

"I will give it to someone else to handle," said Anh, "as I want it to be edited now."

I could tell she had fast decided not to go to Phuc, and I was relieved.

Anh seemed tough, for lack of any better first impression, but I usually valued intellectual breadth more, which she had not yet demonstrated. I figured she had to have been tough working at Vietnam News Service for 20 years. At roughly my own age, like about all Viet women, she still had a tight body and smooth skin. Even so, she was not much attractive. A large mole stood out above her lip near her flat nose -- like a drowned, or thoroughly inebriated, horse fly in a party punch bowl. I wondered why she had not had it removed. As for the tight body, maybe she got up early every morning and did group exercises.

I had already figured out the best place to jog in Ha Noi, and the best time, which was just before dawn around Hoan Kiem Lake. There, every morning, I could count on seeing three score or so of ladies of various ages at the lake's southeast corner, arranged in tidy rows, waving their arms and twisting their bodies about to the same music blaring from a boom box booming on a sidewalk. Was it not Doris Day half a century earlier singing *Que Sera, Sera?* There was a modern message in the lyrics, I discovered: Trying to rock the boat won't matter, what will be is independent of one's will, and often counter to it. I had already made a mental note to look for Anh around Hoan Kiem at dawn light, but anyway she wasn't about to agree with my view regarding proper editing of the report the Prime Minister had condemned. Worse, she was not even remotely interested in what the report detailed about human rights abuses.

To Anh it was axiomatic that if the Party or its top officials revealed anything, what they said had to be true even while such an assumption was based almost solely on faith, like any belief in a god. But I refused to rewrite the story, and she could do nothing but glare at me with contempt and soon pass it along to Cain Hamilton, a colleague at the paper and a New Zealander who had been at work there several months prior to my arrival after stints in other Asian newsrooms in Kuala Lumpur and Hong Kong.

There was much more that Anh did not well understand yet amid a burbling energy that was prying away a Leninist economic clamp so fast that many Vietnamese were dreaming of achieving lives of affluence. There was, for one thing, an occasional buzz in the newsroom about the rocketing, nascent market for Vietnamese stocks amid expanding government moves to privatize parts of large segments of the economy atop growing inflows of foreign investment, which necessitated shifts from public to at least partial private ownership of many state enterprises new and old. A few days after the unpleasant knee display *frisson* with Phuc, Anh handed me another story to rewrite about the equities market into which investors, the report suggested, were piling like lemmings. She also then expressed a desire to dive into the boiling stockpot with her own scant savings.

"I would not buy in right now," I warned her. "The time to buy any stocks is when no one wants them and people are depressed about prospects."

"Why would I want to buy anything that is unpopular?" Anh countered.

"Because," I said, "when something has become popular, its popularity is already largely reflected in its price, and therefore you are probably buying an overpriced asset. You are not getting a bargain, most likely." But she merely shook her head as if to suggest mine was not quite attached properly, giddy with the delusion that making money in financial markets was easy.

I failed to impress her and edited the piece. Later that same evening, with the newsroom windows flung open impotently to grab for relief, to suck in the polluted air that seemed to find a home in the lower reaches of the Red River, Anh was, as usual, in total charge of the well-hidden device that commanded the air conditioning system and wielding her small power by refusing to use it. Some relief then arrived when my cell phone came to life with a ringtone.

It was Williams, calling from Saigon, what the Communists had renamed Ho Chi Minh City, 1200 kilometers directly south.

"Hey, buddy!" said Williams through my cell phone at *Vietnam News*. "I've got the fever -- dengue. Been feeling bad, but I'll get over it." Despite the illness, he still projected a randy enthusiasm. Making a living asking for money, which was somewhat akin to asking for sex, required enthusiasm.

"Damn! I am sorry you are dengued up," I said sincerely. "But at least you haven't been killed on a *xe'om* yet," referring to the proffer of rides, for a dollar or so, or 16,000 *dong* at the prevailing rate of exchange, on the backs of motorbikes. I had early on suffered that fright in Saigon.

"I'm getting better. Been ill, up and down, since a week after you left Saigon for Ha Noi, referring to my arrival and subsequent stay for a few days in Vietnam's prime city and *entrepot*. "Where are you now?"

"Tran Hung Dao Street. At work at the paper, singing the praises of the Commies. That's the job. Why didn't you call me earlier about getting sick?"

"I didn't want you to worry about me while you were getting settled in Ha Noi."

"I guess I would have," I said.

"I am sending you an e mail right now. Take a look at the attachment. It might interest you, and I want a translation."

"What is this attachment?"

"A photo of very fine gem," he said. "Just take a look when you can. I am feeding your interest in the Arab world. I stumbled across it on the Internet. I haven't been working, just amusing myself at the computer. I thought of you when I came across it."

"Okay, I will."

Williams then literally coughed up the invite to the *Emeraude*.

"But tell me, is this proposed boating weekend going to be like the International Ladies Club luncheon we went to down there?" I chided him.

"No. More fun. Real fun."

"I accept and will also look at what you are sending me."

Before meeting Tao, I had not yet had much "fun" in Vietnam, though being in the country had so far seemed a unique experience for someone my age, someone who had refused to flat retire and passively await decline back in the US. I did not aim to go all that gentle, as one Welsh drunkard poet had lyrically advised, into the eternal night.

Working away after the phone call from Williams, I recalled flying into Saigon's Tan Son Nhat airport after a 30-hour journey, bleary with jet lag. The sultry air on the way into the old terminal building (a new one was under construction) was almost suffocating, and striking the scene across the lighted tarmac: rows of arched concrete and rusted steel shelters where US warplanes had parked in the heydays of the Vietnam War, which the Viets called the American War. Williams and his new family were at the airport to greet me with a borrowed car. It was a straight, 10 kilometer shot across the city and over the Saigon River to *Quan*

Bon, Saigon's District Four, to the east of the downtown commercial district. We pulled into the driveway of a shoddy, 12-floor apartment building with an open, bisecting breezeway where three guards wearing the neon green uniforms of Vietnamese "security" shifted around between broken chairs, doing nothing. Adjacent slum shanties and a branch channel off the Saigon River that demarcated the western perimeter of District Four reeked of excrement and random garbage. But there was much more to learn.

Williams, for one thing, seemed to know many of the Westerners in Saigon, or aimed to, as they, not the Vietnamese, had most of the money to give his employer, an NGO implementing "sustainable development". These expatriates were the current vanguard, those who literally boasted of "getting to Vietnam before McDonalds" even though on the promenade along the Saigon River, where the evening cruise boats docked, lay the ruins of a McDonald's of late 1960s vintage. The "golden arches", though long bereft of any golden luster, much of the original paint gone or smothered by some kind of nasty fungus, still stood there, a reminder of the *hubris* and transience of imperial overreach.

Anyone from afar had to admire the Western businessmen relocating to Vietnam. They were all about helping establishing the initial business footprint of Western corporations in the post-war economic vacuum -- banks, insurance companies, technology outfits, furniture makers and garment manufacturers. But their wives were the ones suffering. They were like the unlucky fish hauled up with bamboo poles and crude lines from the Saigon River. They often flopped about desperately in an environment where they feared their husbands might desert them if they stayed long enough.

Insecurity was evident in Saigon when Williams took me, along with his Viet secretary at the NGO, to the monthly luncheon of the "International Ladies Club" in an office tower downtown, where he outlined one of the NGO's programs and appealed for support. Dar told them that something like 40,000 Vietnamese children had been born with congenital heart defects that would kill most of them before puberty. However, he added with a smile, waving the microphone before the crowd over dessert like a snake charmer, that these heart defects were easily repaired by surgery, performed locally by Vietnamese physicians for only $1500 each.

By the time coffee arrived, many of the Western ladies, many of them American but also Australian and British, had pulled checkbooks from their handbags. I took this as much a sign of generosity and care as one of calculation, inasmuch as I had been marveling at how easily most all of them were upstaged by Williams' striking Viet secretary, who had been the subject of darting, pained glances throughout the luncheon. With some wicked amusement, I wondered if their readiness to give might signify some kind of prayerful pact they would never embarrass themselves by proposing aloud to Vietnamese femininity: *I will help save your ailing children if you promise not to try to steal my husband.*

In Saigon and then later in Ha Noi, it was easy to observe that Viet women seemed to do most of the serious work -- such small but important jobs as sweeping the streets and tending the flower beds in city parks -- that allowed the cities to look reasonably if not spectacularly inviting, but no place in Vietnam was as yet shiny and bright as, say, Hong Kong or Singapore, or Kuala Lumpur or Bangkok. I also gathered the impression that women were largely responsible for what social cohesion and harmony existed in the country. Men, on the other hand, dominated transport and the government, the Party apparatus, which of course included the military. Vietnam seemed a safe place to live, as Williams claimed it was, but this later proved to be only a superficial, initial impression.

Even at the newspaper I was surprised by the absence of a "police beat" -- standard at almost any US newspaper covering a particular town or city -- and absent from the paper were reports of serious crime, murders, incidental violence, robberies, or domestic disputes. I asked Anh about this once, but she merely shrugged and said: "We don't have that in Vietnam." This was, of course, a lie -- the mote of a swarm of lies that I eventually encountered in Vietnam, and many of the later ones impacted me personally, and also one unusual friendship that had been developing ... in the worst possible way.

3

Dragons or sharks, they did not much matter, given the allure of jumping off the *Emeraude* with Tao at mid afternoon with the boat anchored between several unnamed rocky eminences at a distance of a kilometer or two. The water was calm, the sun strong. I found Tao dragging a plastic kayak off a rack at the stern.

"I thought we were going to swim?" The question was no protest, because I was feeling some relief that maybe we did not have to, that having assented to her earlier invitation, maybe it was not necessary to jump in the water to keep my end of the engagement.

"I'm just getting this ready," said Tao. "We can paddle it later."

"Okay, if you like." The swim was fine, but the prospect of extending time alone with Tao even better, I thought, paddling anything or not.

Tao put the kayak down, smiled at me, turned and dove into the bay with hardly a splash. Dithering was impossible, and I jumped in after her with a real splash. A couple of the crewmembers were pulling the outboard tender alongside the stern and setting a gangplank. A crowd of Amcham members, none prepared to swim, were gathering to get aboard the tender and head for one of the islands that contained a large, open cave where the crew was prepared to set up an open bar. When I caught up with Tao, who had swum off towards the island, we stopped and turned around, treading water, to discover no one else apparently wanted to get wet, except at the wet bar on deck.

"I guess we are the only ones brave enough for this?"

"Who can come here without a real swim?"

"Let's head for the island where the tender is going," I suggested.

Tao did not object and we stroked off again. After a while, almost a kilometer of swimming, the tender, fully loaded, passed us, and some aboard stared at us as they went by. I was comfortable in the sea, having spent my youth in coastal Florida. I recalled getting my diver's certification a couple years before Lyndon Johnson had launched his war against North Vietnam and the Viet Cong in the south. Amcham members waved at us from the launch, and by the time we got to the shore of the island, the crowd was already mingling and drinking in a cave that opened up after a short climb from the shore over sharp rocks.

"Tao," I asked, "where did you learn to swim so well?"

"Ha Giang."

"Ha what?"

"My hometown. North of Ha Noi, up in the mountains near the Chinese border."

"No sea there."

"I know. But there's a river. It's called the Lo. It runs right through Ha Giang, where I was born. It's a major tributary of the Red River."

"So that's where you learned?"

"Yes. Children played in the river. There were swimming holes and pools and it was safe when there were no floods."

"Sounds like Mark Twain, like his life on the Mississippi."

"What?"

"Nothing. I guess kids are the same everywhere."

"My childhood was pleasant," said Tao, "even if we were hungry and poor in Ha Giang, except when the war came it was less nice."

"Which war? The war was over the day you were born, when the NVA rolled into Saigon, you said."

"The war with China. China invaded. Soldiers came right across the border near Ha Giang in 1979. But they lost. They lost thousands of soldiers and then they withdrew. Many more Chinese dead than Vietnamese. I was just four and my town was badly damaged," Tao said, stepping out of the water among the rocks and climbing up the embankment towards the cave that was echoing with the chatter of American merchants and their wives above and beyond our landing spot.

I could barely make headway coming out of the sea. The rocks underfoot were sharp, and I moved forward slowly, leaning over and distributing part of my weight onto my hands. But Tao was undaunted, standing straight up and moving easily, her feet apparently immune to pain, as if shod in moccasins. Her movements were clean, natural, as if she had been scrambling barefoot among sharp rocks forever like the fishers of the bay hunting for food along the shores and in the island shallows. Like, I imagined suddenly, she could do almost anything she set her mind to, because of the childhood in Ha Giang, because in Ha Giang then for children and adults alike, survival and even play was adaptation and improvisation, like swimming in the Lo River that dropped into Vietnam from central China.

Up in the cave I caught up with Tao and found Williams and Huong.

"That lady can move," I said to Williams, pointing at Tao.

Tao laughed and said to Williams: "Your friend swims well."

"You mean for an old guy like me?" Williams said.

"Thanks, buddy," I said sarcastically.

"Just have to remind you now and then."

"A reminder I could do without. But hey, you better start getting some exercise yourself. Got a gut there, Dar. You said you had become Vietnamese, but the Vietnamese don't have guts literally, just in the other sense. Huong does not like the gut."

"Okay. Okay. I should not tease you," Williams said, and then he turned to Tao: "Marshall tried to get me to run with him around District Four in Saigon right after he arrived in Vietnam. I went a couple times, but I made him walk. I really should do more of that, and maybe jog, too."

"You should," said Huong. "I'm not ready to become a widow."

Later that afternoon back aboard the *Emeraude* most of the passengers, returned by the tender, had retired to their cabins before a buffet dinner in a couple hours. Tao allegedly went off to check on Tung for a few minutes, but insisted I wait for her to come back, because she still had kayaking in mind. I wasn't about to pass on the invitation.

The kayak was just large enough for the both of us. I took up the stern position and paddled, with Tao dipping her paddle in occasionally to assist, but then, as we got farther from the *Emeraude*, she lay down on her stomach with her legs running along the lip of the kayak on either side of me. I kept paddling, not sure what to make of her position, not sure what, if anything, her body language was telegraphing, but her butt was just a couple feet from me and her legs were apart and the view was compelling, she in her blue bikini.

It was easy to wonder if she was suggesting we head for a secluded cove, and just as easy to think she meant absolutely nothing by her position inasmuch as it was at least reasonably comfortable, and I was doing all the paddling. But still her position was perplexing. Invitation or not, I decided not to try to head for any secluded cove with Tao. It seemed like quite enough good luck to be in Ha Long Bay in a kayak with her, and I did not want to spoil the moment by presuming she might be provocative. I imagined that if we were to become friends in Ha Noi, or ever meet up there, I'd get a deeper measure of her.

"So, tell me, Tao," I asked, stroking the paddle and trying to exorcise whatever spell she might have been trying to cast, "what does Tung's father do?"

Tao turned around and looked at me for a second as if I had deliberately splashed water on her. Then she turned back, facing forward, and said: "I don't want to talk about him. Okay?"

"If you say so," I said, staring at her bottom.

"Go there," Tao said, pointing towards a small boat half a kilometer away.

In a few minutes we pulled up beside a wooden boat topped by a sort of shed made of posts and plywood and draped in greasy, random pieces of canvas. Two were aboard, a man and, apparently, his wife, both middle aged. They were cooking a fish on a small brazier hot with charcoal embers. Tao said a few words to the couple, apparently asking if she could board as immediately she did, conversing with them further.

"Who are they exactly?" I asked Tao when she again splayed herself atop the kayak, not offering to relieve me with the paddle.

"They live on this boat," Tao said. "They survive eating what they manage to catch."

"Subsistence farming, but from the sea," I commented.

"It's what many still do in Vietnam," she reminded me.

"So where to now?" I asked. "Don't you want to ferry *me* around, to paddle some?"

"No," said Tao. "I'd rather just let you paddle and sightsee myself."

I did not tell her she had been giving me a sight to see, even though I had to earn the view by providing the energy to drag us forward.

"Where to now?" I asked again.

"It's getting late. Let's go back to the *Emeraude*. Tung needs me probably."

"Who's looking after him now?"

"Another passenger volunteered," she said casually.

"That was nice," and I dropped further query. It seemed a reasonable answer, and, in fact, I imagined there were any number of Amcham members who might have been willing to watch the boy for a while, and it did not seem at all important to know just who.

I paddled us back to the *Emeraude*, a distance of about two kilometers, saying almost nothing more but again enjoying the view of her especially. I wanted to know much more about her, more about where she had come from, how she had managed to get as far as already she had. She was from a poor family in one of the remotest provinces in Vietnam, and yet with her at Ha Long Bay I felt she could hold her own in any company.

When we got back to the *Emeraude*, we stowed the kayak and then she disappeared. I went to my stateroom, showered, rested an hour or so and later dined with Williams and Huong. Tao did not appear in the dining room. A bit later, in the calm bay, the

Amcham guests clustered in chairs on the deck and watched the film *Indochine* with Catherine Deneuve, set partly in Ha Long Bay and depicting an ill-fated love affair between a young French soldier and a Vietnamese girl. It was all very romantic and tragic, the hardships of young love between unlikely couples in perilous times. I thought of Tao, who was not with the crowd watching the film.

At almost midnight, with most all of the guests retired to their cabins, I lingered along the railing, enjoying the darkness and silence, the stars, a gentle breeze, and noticed a flash on the opposite side of the deck. A lighter it was, stoking a cigar. I crossed the deck to find a man that, oddly enough, I could not recall seeing, neither at the Ha Noi Hilton or on the bus, nor until then aboard the boat. He was not much taller than Tao, but stocky, all thick bone and muscle, dressed in a loose Madras shirt, pressed trousers and, I managed to note, a pair of Israeli-made *Noat* sandals.

"You got a smoke? Mind if I bum one?"

"If you don't mind *Vinatabas*," replied an accented voice that, in the languid instant, I failed to place. "The Cohiba's expensive."

"*Vinataba* is okay," noting that the fellow wasn't offering me one of his expensive cigars. "Seventy five cents a pack in American money. I get them from an old lady on my street in the Old Quarter in Ha Noi. She squats in the same place every day and most nights with a box filled with cigarettes."

The man drew a pack from his coat pocket and handed me a cigarette. "I don't think we've met."

"Marshall McLean. Thanks." I offered my hand to shake his, but he didn't offer anything but a cigarette.

"American?"

"Yes. But not with Amcham. A friend invited me along. I've been in Nam a few weeks. I am an editor at *Vietnam News*," I said.

"Ah, some kind of journalist then?" he commented with some sarcasm.

"More editor now than writer. Your name?"

"Jabotinsky," the man muttered. I got the impression he was only giving me his name only because I had given him mine. I noticed that he jerked his head slightly at the end of each sentence he uttered, that he had some sort of involuntary tic of punctuation.

"You have a familiar accent but I cannot quite place it exactly. Your name...."

Before I could finish the sentence he shot back, "East European."

Jabotinsky scrutinized me as if he were measuring me for a suit in one of the inexpensive shops in the Old Quarter. He was a tough fellow, by all appearances, maybe a decade younger, with a square face of sharp angles and a boxy, muscular frame. I noted an ugly scar running down from under an ear into his shirt collar.

"You know another Jabotinsky?" he asked.

"No. Read of one, though. Where are you from?" I asked.

"I came from Ha Noi to the boat dock."

"I didn't see you on the bus. Then you are from Ha Noi? You are not Vietnamese. I was asking about your origination," I said, believing surely he knew what I had meant.

"Let's say I am from one of the few democratic countries in Asia. Does this help?"

"Not really. I sort of thought you might be from Israel, but Israel is not all that democratic. I saw you are wearing *Noat* sandals. Made in Israel!"

"Why would you say that about Israel? Not democratic?" Jabotinsky asked. His head jerked upwards again.

"Because it allows no democracy in some areas it claims," I said. "In particular the West Bank and East Jerusalem. Do Arabs, even Arab citizens, really have a vote on anything? Like where new settlement construction occurs?"

I had always been a bit outspoken and habits, at my age, were virtually impervious to change. I had also been a reporter, and getting information from people was something I figured I had learned to do relatively well, which sometimes involved stating a view that might be contentious merely to provoke a response.

"You have been there?"

"I have."

"And why was that? Another tourist?" he said with evident contempt.

"My last time in the area I was consulting at a new, American-financed school in the West Bank. I was looking at its longer-term viability in a Palestinian town called Tubas. That's a town in the northern West Bank between Nablus and Jenin."

"I know where Tubas is," Jabotinsky said. "When?"

"But tell me first, you are Israeli, right? Few who are not, except the Arabs, would know of Tubas."

"Yes," Jabotinsky said with a tone of reluctance, but I was pleased I had pinned down his origins.

"I have Palestinian friends in the US. One of them is a Tubas native, now a successful businessman, who was financing the school from afar, from the US."

Jabotinsky shrugged, but I could sense he was interested.

"The Palestinian diaspora," said Jabotinsky, "even wherever you are located in America. I hope they are well settled there."

"They want to return to Palestine eventually. It's always on their minds and in their hearts."

"They should be well settled where now they are, but not in Israel," said Jabotinsky. "They must be. And there is no such place called 'Palestine'."

"Why?" I asked. I already knew the answer but I wanted him to say it.

"Because they will not regain entry. Maybe for a quick visit, but that is all."

"I wonder," fast realizing our differences, "if that's fair. Didn't many Jews return to Palestine over the past 100 years? So why not the Palestinians in the next hundred?"

"They are animals. It is not a matter of fairness."

"Well, your name is historically famous." And not just that, I thought, but fitting, as the Jabotinsky I was thinking of had changed his first name to "Ze'ev", which in Hebrew meant "wolf", from Vladimir. "That other Jabotinsky whom I have read about adopted a hard line about Israel's future composition. He was a driving force behind Jewish terrorism against the Brits and the

Arabs before 1948. Well, I am sure you know this, but I know it, too."

"Do you think you are clever?"

"No," I said, "but more informed than most Americans, even many Jewish Americans, who visit Israel." I did not, of course, have to say anything more. He knew that having been in Tubas, I could not hail the occupation of the West Bank and East Jerusalem and particularly the Jewish settlements, which by international law were deemed flagrantly illegal. "I do wish Israelis would lighten up on the Palestinians. Long term, I think that would be a good thing. What do you think about that?"

"Terrorists," Jabotinsky responded with irritation.

"I met many Palestinians who are not disposed to violence. You might have peace with them at least."

"Impossible," Jabotinsky said, and I realized that the conversation was going nowhere, but it was he who changed the subject. "Tell me what you do here again?"

"I work at the English language newspaper in Ha Noi."

"Your name again?"

"McLean. But what brings *you* to Vietnam?"

"Business," Jabotinsky said in the same, flat tone. Maybe he was marketing *Noat* sandals, but I wasn't buying even if they did beat the tire treads many poor Viets wore after they had cut them to shape their feet.

"Okay. So where did you come from in Israel?"

"A farm. Then I joined the IDF at 18."

"I guess that was mandatory for you," I said. "I managed to avoid the US military during the Vietnam War. But I did not mind going to a militant place for a summer during the war."

"Where was that?"

I decided to test this Jabotinsky. I cited a place in Arabic: "*Kaukab al-Hawa.*"

"*Star of the Wind,*" muttered Jabotinsky, translating my words quickly.

"That was fast," I said. "You know Arabic."

"You?"

"I can read it. Spoken is very weak."

The place I had mentioned was also called *Belvoir*. It was actually the stone ruins of a defensive fortress, one built by Crusaders on a mountaintop overlooking the Jordan Valley from the west. One could easily see the Sea of Galilee to the north from its ruins. The view was spectacular, as its French name implied, deep into Jordan beyond the border in the valley below.

"*Kaukab al-Hawa* is not militant," said Jabotinsky. "It's a site for tourists."

"But it was," I said. "A long time ago. I guess one would now have to go down into the Jordan Valley to find the militants, such as the IDF and settlers. Perhaps even at one of the nearby *kibbutzim* along the border?"

"Do you know them?"

"I know one. I actually visited this one for a couple days when I was leaving the area after the work in Tubas."

Jabotinsky coughed up some smoke from his Cohiba. Maybe I had hit a nerve. I was vaguely trying to hit something, but not too hard. I felt like challenging him, but not so much to drive him immediately away there on the deck of the boat in the cool night. "Which one?" he asked when he had cleared his throat.

"*Ashdot Yaakov Ichud*," I said.

With that, Jabotinsky smiled slightly and his head jerked a bit, and he had not even said anything. I seemed to have hit some sort of nerve.

"Yes," I went on, "I had been to this place before. It was my first time in the Middle East. Several weeks one summer I worked as a volunteer there. That was in 1969. I was in college at the time."

"You are not Jewish," said Jabotinsky.

"Did not matter. Not every volunteer was Jewish, or had to be. But I was very idealistic, and I think one needed to be that there."

"And now?"

"And now what?" I asked.

"Are you idealistic now?"

"Rarely, but one must perhaps try. Are you?"

"I am a realist."

"But the 'reality' you might claim to see is still subjective, or subject to your political and cultural and even religious biases. Is this right?"

"I know what is right and you are not right," said Jabotinsky with irritation.

I imagined he had not often dealt with anyone who could, or would, fence with him about the Palestinians, with anyone who more or less appeared to empathize with them.

"What you say is right just looks like might to me. Well, *my* bias is simple: fair play and inclusiveness for all, including the Palestinians. They've been shoved around for too long."

At that point Jabotinsky laughed. His laugh was weird sounding, too. I had the distinct perception he was laughing at me, derisively. I did not like it but then he wasn't walking away, not yet anyway shoving me aside as an infidel or sorts, as one not enthralled with the Israeli hard right agenda of the Likud and associated parties that dominated his government's policies.

"Isn't peace a goal?" I pressed him further. "Isn't that the fundamental goal?"

"The Arabs don't want peace. We must pursue peace by other means," said Jabotinsky.

I knew what he meant, and recalled the Roman historian Tacitus who wrote about the Roman conquest of Britain: *they make a desert and call it peace.* Domination to the point of complete submission if not utter eradication of alleged enemies was the sole route to the 'peace' he, and many like him in Israel, envisioned. I knew there was no way to change his thinking, but then he changed the subject. Even as I was utterly annoyed by his posture, this was literally the first time I had had direct contact and conversation with an Israeli of his kind. I was rather pleased to have the opportunity and didn't want to waste it.

"Interesting what you say about working at that *kibbutz*," said Jabotinsky, as if he were talking to himself, calculating something.

"Why interesting?"

"That is where I was born," he offered.

"So perhaps we have met before!" I exclaimed. "It was a small community in 1969. But everyone ate together in the community dining hall."

"I can't recall you," said Jabotinsky.

"Nor do I remember you. It was long ago. Now, it's changed quite a lot."

"You discovered?"

"That it isn't now like in 1969. Still lots of bananas that needed picking back from the Jordan and the Yarmuk rivers, the border," I said. "But I found it was privatized, with residents owning their apartments. There was even a small factory there turning out plastic containers for pharmaceuticals. It just seemed like a gated community, not any longer the idealistic socialist experiment it had been."

Jabotinsky seemed vaguely amused with my description. Perhaps he was just reminded of the changes. He took a long puff on his cigar, but without the cough this time. "Realistic changes have occurred all over Israel."

"You may have been a child in 69?" I asked, because he looked younger than myself, and rougher, too. "I was 21 then."

He did not have to answer the question.

I imagined I had literally *seen* Jabotinsky before, but given the years since I could not recall him specifically and anyway he was changed, an adult. That our paths would cross again in such a place as Ha Long Bay seemed bizarre, unlikely.

"It seemed distressing on my return visit there to note that the workers in the factory were Thai," I said.

"Why so?" Jabotinsky asked casually, blowing a couple fast dissipating smoke rings into the dark over the sea.

"Because it seems absurd and perhaps even cruel to call in workers from Thailand when there are so many Palestinians nearby who have been without work, and dirt poor."

"The Palestinians don't belong," Jabotinsky said. It seemed he had no other response to any mention of Arabs. They were not humans, not even human enough to work for Israelis. Just terrorists. Just, I could not help recall the German word, *untermenschen.*

"But Thais do belong?"

"They are not a problem."

"I spent that summer pruning banana plants in the fields, and spreading chicken manure. It was hard work. I do vaguely recall being sent out to do the work sometimes with a youngster, a lad of about ten or so. I guess the *kibbutz* staff did not want volunteers from overseas working entirely alone in the fields near the border. The Palestinians were sometimes lobbing *Katyusha* rockets over the Yarmuk River into the fields, even getting themselves into the fields on rare occasions, usually at night. The lad raked the spaces between the banana plants and piled the dead fronds into a cart, carting them away. He spoke almost no English, and I don't speak Hebrew. But he was helpful," I said. "Actually, although I am uncertain, I think the boy's name was 'Moshe'."

"Moshe?"

"Yes, I think that was it."

"My first name happens to be 'Moshe'."

"Might you and I have worked together there?" I asked, stunned by his remark.

"I don't know," Jabotinsky said.

"This may be an amazing coincidence!" I said, virtually begging for a return of the same, or at least some, of my sentiment.

But then suddenly he flipped his half-spent cigar into the bay. "Shalom," he said, walking quickly away. I had just enough time before he rounded a corner on deck and disappeared to say loudly enough back: "Salaam." I rather savored responding to him with the same word in Arabic, the language of millions he apparently despised.

Given the encounter, my impression was that he might be just a hardcore colonialist, or merely a rude sort walking away as he did. But I had hardly given him reason to warm to me by challenging his views. But businesslike, I thought he was, sentimental about nothing, and he had said his business in Vietnam was "business". Maybe that was why he, like Tao, though neither being Amcham members, was aboard the *Emeraude*. But I still could not figure what Tao's business was except that she was concerned about UXO and worked for her government. I had failed to get her to divulge exactly why she was aboard, except that she had spoken of studying in the US and her English was almost perfect. I finished the *Vinataba* and went to my stateroom, remembering what I could of *Ashdot Yaakov Ichud* in my youth.

Mostly I recalled young *sabra* females in skimpy cotton shorts and T-shirts, with dark eyes and curly hair and a cool sexiness. I recalled embracing one on them one night atop the *kibbutz* water tower and being interrupted by a *Katyusha* that landed and exploded into the kibbutz lawn, and occasional nights underground in shelters with other volunteers, women and children and elderly adults. The danger vivified the summer and stoked the idealism of my youth. But meeting Jabotinsky made me uneasy as it stirred up decades later memories of the dangers of proximity to Israeli soldiers and settlers marauding around in the West Bank.

In Tubas I had lived literally at the top of a small apartment building near the school for several winter months, sleeping in a single room shelter off to the side of the open, flat roof. I had space enough that winter, but it was the largely the space of the heavens: an uncovered flat roof perch exposed to cold winds and sometimes fast moving storms that whipped over the building and swirled around Tubas at nights. But the stars were magnificent even if the town at night was not so, so battened down: a few scattered streetlamps and the late calls of the muezzins from the town's couple mosques, and also too often the late night crackle of gunfire through the shallow valley where lay the town, and in the mornings no clear explanations.

Bundled up to ward off the winter cold, I often sat on the deck of the roof. Over the balustrade I occasionally spotted the headlights of convoys of Israeli military units headed through from Hamra Checkpoint in the Jordan Valley to set up a flying roadblock up the road towards Jenin, sometimes firing their weapons to scare up the locals, to make sure they knew who was in control. For the Arabs, nothing to do in Tubas but eat, sleep, tend children and cling to each other behind very closed doors. Nothing much existed to entertain: no cinemas, no bars, no alcohol, no money and no place to go, not even Jerusalem, only 90 minutes way, which most in Tubas had not seen in decades. Not just Tubas but all of the Palestinian areas of the West Bank outside the settlement blocs had long been virtually an open-air prison, but the air was clean and fresh, the daytime views over fields of olive and almond trees breathtaking, and the children at the school, like children anywhere, precious and fun to take on picnics in rocky meadows in the hills with the local teachers. I recalled in Tubas Palestinians claiming they would build me a small stone house for a pittance on the side of a hill amid ancient olive trees. Be there, I thought, help with the autumn olive harvest, help advise the school and just by that be thrust into a nationalist struggle that had been waxing for 100 years. But the school had closed after just one academic year, fast a victim of mounting uncertainty and poverty in the West Bank.

I found my stateroom. Given the sea frolics with Tao, my imagination was running hot, but I was tired, too. I went to bed with the door cracked open. Minor as this was, I could only think that many pleasant moments had been obviated or missed by failure to send the right message, or by a lack of preparation for them. Maybe, I imagined, Tao would wake and take a walk on the deck and pass my cabin door and, finding it ajar, come inside? It was a vain presumption. I had not even mentioned which stateroom was mine, for one thing, but maybe she had been bold enough to find out on her own. That night she never appeared and somehow I managed to sleep past dawn, then dressed and strolled to the *Emeraude's* dining room for breakfast.

The boat was crawling back to its berth at Ha Long City. In the dining room I at least saw Tao and Tung, but she barely acknowledged my presence. All I got was a polite "good morning" across the breakfast buffet. Then I found Williams and Huong at a table and sat with them. I remembered something I had promised to research for Williams.

"I translated the Arabic etched on that emerald photo you emailed me," I told Williams over a plate of eggs and a cup of bland, American-style coffee.

"I have forgotten about that," Williams said, "but tell me."

"It was an inscribed blessing to one Ja'afar as-Sadiq."

"Never heard of him," said Williams.

"He was the sixth Shi'a Imam. A notable one. Lived in Baghdad in the eighth century. In part because of a dispute over which son ought to be his successor, the Shi'as eventually split into different sects. One of them evolved into the famous Ismaili sect. He also was notable for developing a doctrine called *taqiyah*. In essence, this was a practice that allowed the Shi'a to lie about actually *being* Shi'a in a political environment where *not* being a majority and orthodox Sunni Muslim was often dangerous, where sectarianism was condemned as seditious."

"You are way over my head. I don't know about these things," Williams said. "Too damn complicated."

"Don't worry about it. It's complicated for me, too. But think about being a closet Christian or Buddhist human rights activist here in Vietnam. Same thing maybe to declare no faith sometimes but in the government, to keep out of trouble with the government. So, there's your answer. Thanks for sending me the pic of that fine emerald. Wish I owned it!"

That morning aboard the *Emeraude* I had no clue whatsoever that in Vietnam I'd be addressing the topic of Ismailis eventually with yet another expatriate upon whom tragedy for him and danger for me later descended. But then, of course, one could ask rhetorically, who could ever know the future because sure knowledge of it was a chimera.

After two hours the boat was tied to the long dock at Ha Long City and I was, with Williams and Huong, walking off the gangplank into the same swarm of souvenir hawkers on the long dockage, and looking to see where Tao might be. I wanted to say *something* to her, if just to remind her I existed and had enjoyed meeting her. It was just half a minute later, halfway down the dock to the shore, that I spotted her on the shore some 80 meters away.

Tao and Tung were climbing into a SUV with, it appeared, Jabotinsky, and a couple other men. Both of the latter two looked Vietnamese. The SUV then sped away back in the direction of Ha Noi.

"Damn," I said to Williams and Huong, "I wanted to say farewell to that lady, Tao, that we met. She just got into an SUV. Maybe it was some sort of cab. I wonder why she's not going back to Ha Noi on the bus with us?"

"Don't know," said Williams. "Maybe she needed to hurry home, or maybe she just wanted to get away from you," he jested, slapping me on the back.

"You are *some* friend!" I said, also in jest.

"I think she got in that vehicle with someone else I met on the boat late last night after you had retired. You and Huong were probably asleep. A fellow who is an Israeli!"

"I was not aware of expatriates on the boat from anywhere but the US," said Williams as we tried to avoid not getting shoved off the narrow dock by the crowd.

"I hardly expected to meet an Israeli this weekend. We had some things in common, and some viewpoints that were starkly at odds. I was not shy about expressing myself, my own views."

"You never have been", said Williams. "Maybe the guy was a friend of the president of Amcham here. He's Jewish, too. I probably should have introduced you to him. Sorry I didn't."

"I had a fine weekend. Just inviting me to come along with you was kind. That Tao was especially interesting, though. Superlative female scenery amid superlative geographic scenery."

"You know what I think of Vietnamese women," said Williams. He threw an arm across Huong's shoulders and gripped her warmly.

As for Tao, whom I yearned to speak with again, she was gone. I figured I would not again even catch sight of her unless by accident. But then I thought at the margin that accidents could turn out to be the most substantive part of one's life -- when they did not mark the end of it.

4

I had slowly gotten familiar with my neighborhood in Ha Noi, and perhaps vice versa. Another Anh, not the one at the newspaper, might have gotten more attention if I had not met Tao. She worked close to my small apartment, which was two flights up in an anomalous, almost modern building of six levels that rose above the narrow, low, tube-like domiciles and shops of the Old Quarter. The building seemed secure, which was one reason I chose to live there. A guard literally lived in the undercroft and kept an iron gate locked at night. This was on Hang Giay Street near what had been a water tower, now just an empty shell of stone and mortar, built by French colonialists a century earlier. Nearby was a park where, as at Hoan Kiem Lake, other cadres of earnest women did exercise routines or even played badminton in the early mornings, but if one wanted to hear Doris Day, too, they evidently had to go to Hoan Kiem.

Coming out the apartment building, in one direction, I could walk 300 meters to ramp onto the Long Bien Bridge over the Red River. Going the other way, it was 200 meters to the Dong Xuan market, Hanoi's oldest and largest, where vendors on foot and bicycle and motorbikes brought their wares and foodstuffs across the Red River over the Long Bien Bridge to spread out inside and around the market building and adjacent streets. The three-story Dong Xuan market building, a new version because a fire a few years earlier had destroyed an older structure, was crowded with more than 100 stalls selling a variety of mostly household items and various vegetables and fruits hauled in daily and fresh from the countryside.

In between and beyond in the Old Quarter stood a random collection of other shops -- hairdressers and washers, clothing vendors, florists, groceries, house ware vendors, eateries and the like -- and above and at the back of those shops the rooms where the owners lived with their families. Across the street from 2 Hang Giay I had found one family, making a market of fake Lacoste and Nike sport shirts, that did my laundry for a pittance.

On towards Dong Xuan market was a café with crude tables and plastic stools spilling out onto the sidewalk between the omnipresent motorbikes, which had no place to park but on the sidewalks. This forced pedestrians mostly to walk in the streets, dodging vehicles. This food and coffee place, the Maitre Café, I had earlier begun to visit to grab Vietnamese coffee early in the mornings after a jog around Hoan Kiem. There, I had been pleasantly served by a slender, pretty young woman, the other Anh.

After some time, she seemed to make an effort to give me her best seat on the sidewalk, smiling in such a way, and with such a modest demeanor, that she was as warming as her coffee. We had been casting glances at each other for a while, and finally she queried me, a few hours before I headed to meet the Amcham crowd at the Ha Noi Hilton and cruise off into Ha Long Bay.

"Where you from? Few foreigners come here," she said directly. Her English was okay while my Vietnamese, but for *cam on*, "thank you", did not exist. I had decided not to try to learn another Asian language. Some Arabic and a few Hebrew phrases were hard enough not to forget. My mind had reached the limit of its absorbent capacities, I figured.

"America," I said. "And you? Originally from Ha Noi?"

"Here. I been here all my life."

"All your life? That's okay. It is very nice, Ha Noi," I said.

"*Cam on.*"

"And your coffee is good."

"I am Anh."

"I know another Anh. She works at the newspaper," I said. "I am Marshall."

"You work at newspaper?"

"But you are more pleasant than the Anh I know at the newspaper. Yes, I work at *Vietnam News*. Do you read it?"

She laughed, a slight, delicate sound with the timbre, if such could be visualized, of fluttering confetti, or *xoan* leaves, and she seemed to blush. "No. I read no English. It's Vietnamese coffee you like."

"I do like your coffee. But you have been kind. I don't know many people here. I am alone mostly, just working."

"You not married man?"

"Not now."

"You still young," said Anh, as if to suggest I should be married.

"That's nice to hear," I said, failing to tell her I was almost 60. (Perhaps I was practicing Jaafar as-Sadiq's *taqiyyah*, recalling the photo of the emerald Williams had sent me.) But I went on with Anh: "I was married long ago. I have a son, too. He's grown now, on his own. He's become a young doctor. His mother died a decade ago."

"Very sorry. But you a lucky man having doctor son," said Anh. "How long you stay in Ha Noi?"

"I don't really know."

"How you coming to work at paper here?"

"I have an American friend in Ho Chi Minh City who invited me to come to Vietnam and who told me I might find a job here for a while."

"That good," said Anh.

"Do you have children?" I had to ask her. It was an oblique way of maybe finding out whether she was attached.

"Not married. No children," said Anh. "All people who come eat here, they my children," she smiled gently.

"You take good care of us," I said.

"You like my country? I see you like my coffee," she said, standing back and scrutinizing me with her hands on her hips after she had delivered the coffee onto the table. I noted her fine hands and long, slender, delicate fingers.

Vietnamese style, the coffee arrived in a cup too small, with a crude, second aluminum cup laying on top from which hot water filtered down through tiny holes that usually clogged with grinds and did a poor job filling the ceramic cup at the bottom. The coffee, probably grown in the Central Highlands west of Danang and Hue, was strong and tasty, but the awkward technology of deliverance left but five or six swallows before it was gone.

Had I any mind for business, I could readily have imagined operating a Starbucks franchise in Vietnam and charging the Western rate for *frappachinos*. Starbucks were all over neighboring China. I recalled dinner with Williams and Huong and Hung in Saigon weeks earlier. The only fast food franchise originating in the US that so far had found a foothold in post-war Vietnam was Kentucky Fried Chicken, upon whose greasy wings and breasts the boy Hung, despite the after school exercise with ball and bat round the apartment building in District Four, was fast becoming chubby.

"As far as Asia goes, it's better than the Middle East. I was in that part of Asia just last year for several months. It's peaceful here, not there. I like Vietnam."

"Not peaceful where you were?"

"Not in the West Bank. I am sure you know of the Arab-Israeli conflicts. They are political and maybe even religious, but most of it is about control of resources, land and water."

Anh frowned. The world about which she was familiar, it seemed, extended only so far as the Old Quarter of Ha Noi and perhaps even just along Hang Giay Street. I thought to change the subject but then she responded.

"Bac Ho against religion," Anh said. "It make trouble."

"The opium of the masses. I believe Karl Marx called religion that," I responded.

"Uncle Ho" or "Bac Ho" was the way many referred to the long deceased Communist leader. It was a title of respect, even reverence. Ho's primary dictum, carved on his grim mausoleum standing before a broad, rectangular parade ground called *Ba Dinh*, two kilometers away, seemed almost too simplistic and obvious to stand as a central, defining thought: *Nothing is more precious than independence and liberty*. But then what often seems most precious is what one doesn't have and out of such simplicity and single minded focus emerged victory for the northern armies, but that six years after Ho's death.

What he had won for Vietnam by his leadership, the evisceration of a corrupt government in the south, the Americans fleeing in defeat from a peasant army, was never true liberty. Frightened Viets in the south scrambled away on overcrowded boats, many of them to drown, while others came back ashore. The Communist regime forced them and many others from the south into "re-education" camps designed to compel subservience to a tiger's jaw of tendentious, Communist ideology. Had Ho's successors not been drooling for revenge against many who had lived in and supported what had been South Vietnam's so-called republic, the Communist regime might not have been so reviled in the West. Not even the Viet Cong in the south, who had supported the northern armies with their blood, were later given much credit for their own sacrifices.

"A few Muslims here," Anh said, apparently aware at least that the dominant religion in West Asia was Islam. "There is a place where they pray."

"A mosque? Here in Ha Noi?"

"Here in Old Quarter," Anh said.

I was surprised. It was Sunday and I knew, as I had already seen, that the government had not literally succeeded in extinguishing religious observance even though its expression was monitored to try to prevent it from becoming a medium for political dissent. As I fiddled with the coffee, I knew Christian worshippers would be overflowing in and around St. Joseph's cathedral just west of Hoan Kiem Lake for the Sunday Mass. I had not yet gone inside the gothic revivalist cathedral built by the French more than a century earlier, but I had often taken lunch nearby at a French-style café serving fine pastries. The cathedral, not kept up all that well, sported courses of stone masonry wearing dark stains of moldy growth like splashed blood. In front stood a fair statue of the Virgin with an inscription, *Regina Paces,* and I had wondered how many times the Virgin had seen American B-52s high overhead, usually out of the range of anti-aircraft batteries that during the American War had put the metropolis under a kind of siege. Reams of flak blasted skyward as the American aircraft carpet bombed in but mostly around Ha Noi. There, in the sunny square in front of St. Joseph's cathedral, with beatific Mary firm and frozen in bronze and entirely unfazed amid the buzz of motorbikes and tourists snapping pictures, hung all round the bright red Vietnamese flag with its central yellow star.

The cathedral's bells dutifully tolled a summons to worship and the time, but they had to compete with the omnipresent loudspeakers placed on almost every utility pole at intersections in the city amid a spidery maze of rotten, exposed wires, any one of which seemed precariously anchored and about to fall and electrocute pedestrians. The loudspeakers, as regularly as the cathedral bells, blared rapid-fire government propaganda, Communist slogans and exhortations to duty and Party fidelity that, of course, I could not exactly understand. Though far less eloquent and haunting -- in part because Vietnamese had nothing for beauty of sound like Arabic -- they still faintly reminded me of being almost anywhere in town or urban environment in Muslim Asia, of hearing the daily *adhans*, the prescribed calls to prayer amplified by loudspeakers.

I caught Anh's attention, pointing to the street, Hang Giay. "Please tell me, how do I say it properly?"

"Hang Giay," she said quite properly.

"Hang Giay?" I tried to reproduce her tones, but failed, and she laughed again. Falling confetti, or lovely *xo'an* leaves. Occasionally I had hailed a cab late at night to take me back to the apartment, telling a driver: "Hang Giay." But not yet had I achieved giving proper directions, and every ride involved pointing the way through Ha Noi's intersections until I arrived in front of the apartment building. It was frustrating not being able to get the tones of the language right. The slightest error could suggest something unintended or nothing at all.

"Maybe you can try to teach me more sometime."

"I try if you come back."

"I live just there," I said, pointing up the street at the apartment building that towered over the tube houses and shops of the Old Quarter. "I will come for coffee for sure."

I rose and paid the bill, a few *dong*, less than a dollar, and left double the amount of the check on the table. Tipping was neither required nor expected anywhere in Ha Noi, but it was quite naturally appreciated.

"By the way, you mentioned a place where Muslims pray?"

"I think," Anh said. "Try Hang Luoc, over there." She gestured with a hand in a kind of arc in the direction of my apartment building, as if to suggest the location was over and beyond it. I pulled a city street map from my bag and spread it on the table. I found Hang Luoc Street, and in fact it was the next street west and parallel to Hang Giay.

"OK. 'Giay' means paper," I said, as I had learned before. "What does 'Luoc' mean in English?"

Anh ran her fingers through her hair, and then she did it again. "Don't know English word. Like this," and then she repeated the movement a third time. "What you use," she said.

"You mean 'brushes', street of brushes?"

"No, not that."

"How about 'comb'?" I curled my fingers and ran them through my hair.

"That, I think, comb," Anh said, apparently speaking the noun for the first time in English.

"Ah, now I teach you some English."

"*Cam on.*"

"No. I owe you all the thanks here. I will go have a look at the Street of Combs." I finished the last of the coffee and walked away with a wave.

I decided to head for the apartment first to grab a treasured, unusual piece of paper received on my last day in Israel after the months in Tubas. This document amounted to credibility anywhere in the Muslim *umma*. It was an official ruling, a *fatwa*, giving me lifetime access to the *Haram esh-Sherif* in the Old City in Jerusalem, and it even stated I was "Muslim" when, in fact, I eschewed any religious label.

I had tried several times that morning of my last day in Israel to get inside the *Haram* from different gates, but the Israeli police each time had barred my entrance. To them, I was nothing but an ignorant tourist, and an old one at that, and rather unkempt in jeans and T-shirt and casual jacket. But then, on a sudden whim, with a last ditch effort at one gate, I demanded to see the Grand Mufti at his nearby office in a corner of the *Haram* complex. An older gentleman passing by the gate inside heard me, stopped and volunteered to take me to the Grand Mufti's offices. The Israeli police reluctantly let me pass with the escort. The Mufti happened to be in his offices, and there I discovered one potential fomenter of terror -- he was in fact a Palestinian nationalist and did occasionally deliver fiery sermons at the al-Aqsa mosque -- in Israeli eyes was a bearded, warmly kind, grandfatherly eminence. We talked a while about my stay in Tubas and calmly, mutually condemned the military occupation of the West Bank and the growing Jewish settlements in the West Bank and East Jerusalem. After a half hour he scribbled a note and handed it to one of his attendants. After another half hour the Mufti handed me the Arabic document neatly typed and officially stamped. I was startled to read it claimed I was Muslim, for I had claimed no such thing to the Mufti. But I knew what he must have thought: that having expressed opposition to the occupation and the settlements, and a desire for social and political justice, this was as good to him as stating I was Muslim in spirit if not in fact.

Islam, from its beginning in the seventh century, was a religious system which more than anything else attempted to promote social justice and concern for the disenfranchised and poor. Muhammad himself had been a poor orphan, though from a very noble tribe. I spent the rest of that cool, sunny winter day on the *Haram* at the shrine of the Dome of the Rock and in al-Aqsa mosque. Knowing some Arabic and expressing interest in learning the correct sequence of postures in Muslim prayer, barefoot on the lush carpets in both of the magnificent buildings, kept at bay any possible suspicions among truer worshippers.

At any rate, I imagined any official at the mosque in Ha Noi might be impressed with the document and carried it with me as I headed back outside to Hang Luoc Street. I soon found the mosque Anh had mentioned. It stood behind a white wall of ornate stucco and an iron gate leading to a small courtyard. Above the compound jutted a single minaret, but unlike any kind of minaret I had ever seen. Hanging from the lintel of the entrance in the wall along the sidewalk was a green sign with Arabic script: *Masjid an-Nur*, "mosque of light." I went into an empty courtyard and wandered about amid some potted greenery until I stopped, bemused and a bit horrified. A lizard as neon green as the garb of some Vietnamese security personnel, and almost a foot long, with a prominent snout that looked like the reinforced lower bow of an icebreaker, was lapping up with a sticky tongue a huge, struggling cockroach on a stone step to the portico that led inside to the prayer hall.

Clearly, the roach was no match for the lizard and had no defense but flight, which it could not muster. Yet the lizard seemed in no particular rush. Out went the tongue over and over, cutting off escape until, after a minute or so, it finally lunged forward and gripped the insect in its jaws. The lizard's head jerked back and with that, the roach was gone. The head movement reminded me of the way the Israeli, Jabotinsky, had jerked his head back as a kind of sentence punctuation aboard the *Emeraude*. Involuntarily, I shuddered a bit. But that instant I was startled by a voice at my back and turned my eyes away from the reptile and its luckless prey.

"May I help?" came words in a matter of fact, heavily accented voice. I turned around and there stood a much younger man with lean, sharp features, like that of Bedouin I had seen in travels in the Middle East.

I introduced myself and said that I was an American working in Ha Noi. I also looked down again to where the lizard had been, but now it was gone. Perhaps it had fast scurried out of sight behind one of the potted plants on the steps.

"'Abdullah Hamadi," he said. "I manage the mosque."

"This is a fine little mosque. I've seen many but none quite like this. Unusual minaret."

"It is based on an Indian design. Many mosques you've seen?"

"In the Middle East, yes. Where are you from?"

"Ha Noi."

"No," I said. "I mean originally?" He clearly was not Vietnamese.

"Helmand," he said, probably assuming I had never heard of the place before. Most Americans could not locate Afghanistan on an unlabeled map if their lives depended on it, much less a province in that bloody land.

"Ah, Afghanistan!" I responded.

"You know?"

"Some geography at least," I said. "Never been there. My name's Marshall McLean."

I decided right then to see what effect the document from the Grand Mufti in Jerusalem might have, and pulled it from my pocket, handing it over.

"What is this?"

"Arabic. You do read Arabic?"

"I recite the *Qu'ran*. My first language is Pashto."

He handed the document back to me. He was apparently an Arabic memorizer, not a speaker and maybe not even a fluent reader. I figured as a youth he had memorized most all of the *Qu'ran*, perhaps at some Islamic *madrasa* inside Pakistan, maybe in Waziristan, near the Afghan border. Afghanis were not, after all, Arabs, and could not be expected to know much Arabic beyond memorized recitation of the *Qu'ran*.

"I am sorry. That paper is a decree by the Grand Mufti of Palestine and the Holy Land giving me access to the *Haram esh-Sharif* in Jerusalem. I believe that is the third holiest site in Islam," I explained.

"You are welcome here," he said.

"I was working in the West Bank. Palestine," I went on. "I understand the difficulties native people face under foreign military occupations."

"Then you are a rare American. My country is occupied, too."

"I know. I regret that, but do many come here to pray?"

"Not many," Hamadi said. "Not many Muslims in Ha Noi."

He proceeded to show me around, pointing the way inside. We went into the empty prayer hall. It was clean and tidy, with a carpeted floor laid out in parallel bands of green and white so that if any of the faithful did show up, they could line up in rows to perform their prayer prostrations. On the wall over a recessed *mihrab*, indicating the *qibla* or the direction to Makkah, in black paint on the white wall, was inscribed the *shehada*, the Muslim creed stating unequivocally that there was no god but God (Allah) and that Muhammad was His Messenger. Along one wall was a wooden bookcase, its front covered by glass, filled edge to edge with *Qu'ran's*, and a marble chair, a *minbar* of sorts. The hall was so tidy that I imagined the mosque had to be reasonably well financed, if not by the few Muslims in Ha Noi, then by the embassies of Muslim countries in Ha Noi or Islamic foundations, *waqfs*, elsewhere.

"I won't bother you further," I said to Hamidi, "but thank you for showing me around."

"You are welcome," he warmly said again, and I recalled Phuc welcoming me to the newspaper, and then the harsh un-welcome because I had shown my knees in the newsroom.

The brief look around ended and I was headed for the portico and beyond when through the door of the prayer hall appeared a tall, clean-shaven, olive skinned man in a finely tailored sports jacket. But the moment he saw us, he raised his hands without a word and with a look of irritation, he disappeared as quickly out the door and left the mosque compound altogether. "Did I interrupt a private meeting? Forgive me," I said.

"Not really," said Hamidi. "That man will probably return."

In any case, thanks," I said, and soon left the mosque compound, too, emerging on to traffic-choked Hang Luoc Street. But I was curious about who had appeared and then disappeared so suddenly. The man looked strikingly debonair.

5

The next day it was back to the weekly work routine. I was not looking forward to it, and still, I could not get Tao off my mind, or the blue bikini. Perhaps it was the taste of luxury on the *Emeraude*, too, the contrast with the apartment. The few items of furniture were covered lightly with the dust and soot of Ha Noi. The traffic noise was bothersome. I was disappointed that Tao had hardly spoken after our kayaking in the bay together even while I recognized there was no sound reason for me to have expected further attention: I was old enough to be her father.

Cain Hamilton, the New Zealander and colleague, was in the newsroom early the next afternoon. When he spied me dropping my bag on the desk in front of my computer terminal, he came over. We had been sharing the *Vinatabas* and more for weeks on the stairwell landing between the third and fourth floors, and breaking the monotony of the stream of stories to edit with idle talk about the young ladies in the newsroom and rants about Phuc's mannerisms and opaqueness. Cain was in his early thirties, a dark complexioned fellow who claimed he had some Maori blood, and whose verbal cynicism about the work was a source of counterpoint relief to the suffocating conformity of Communist Party rhetoric and other demands. He liked to call me "mate", and I was not bothered by the appellation, as such seemed all about assuming friendship and collegiality.

"Want a weed, mate?" he asked when I followed him out to the stairwell. And when we were out of earshot to the newsroom, he continued: "Phuc has outdone himself. I'm about to tell him to shove it."

"What now with Phuc?"

"You know Edmond Miller? The Brit here who edits features for the weekend edition?"

"Hardly. We've spoken just a few times and I'm not here on weekends." I knew he had for a couple years been married to a Vietnamese. He was a quiet fellow who came in only a couple days a week and who had managed to find happiness with a local girl.

"Well," Cain went on, "Eddy comes in late. But no more than 15 minutes late. No big deal, I think. But this past week his wife drops by here. She's pregnant and about to burst. Phuc sees her and takes her aside. He won't even talk to Edmond, and he tells his missus that she won't have food to feed the baby unless her husband gets in here exactly on time."

"Nasty," I said.

"That's Phuc."

"I suppose that's the worst thing you can say to a Viet woman. Threaten her unborn baby with starvation." Starvation had been a concern for millions of Vietnamese for almost two decades after the end of the American War. The US, augmenting the internal Vietnamese problems of integration, had imposed a trade embargo on the country, frozen hundreds of millions in Vietnamese assets, denied diplomatic relations, done whatever to make the Vietnamese squirm and suffer for having won the war. Rice production had plummeted, too. "I think it's going to be a long week," I added.

"You can count on that," Cain said, "but at least we have the *Tet* holidays coming up next week. Next week will be shorter. Two extra days off. What have you been up to that I don't know about?"

"Well, for one thing, I spent a day and night in Ha Long Bay with a bunch of Americans. Even spent a couple hours swimming with a Viet. She was quite attractive. Just around thirty."

"You said you were with Americans?"

"Yeah, them, but there was this one, seemingly unattached Viet female there. I don't know why because the American Chamber of Commerce here rented the entire boat for the excursion."

I did not tell Cain about Jabotinsky. I figured I'd never see him again and wasn't looking to.

"Ah, but did you get attached?" Cain asked with a grin.

"Not in the way you think. But I am sort of attached to the memory of her that day. I would like to see her again."

"There are so many," said Cain.

"Many?"

"Good looking girls."

"But few that interest me like this one did," I said. "But tell me, what are you doing here? There are better places to work as an editor. Singapore, Taiwan, Hong Kong...."

`"Been there, mate. As scruffy as Vietnam still is, it's like being on the ground floor in an elevator that's rising faster than most any other."

"But I still must say it must be boring working here, for someone your age. You ought to bust out of here and do something else. I am probably not going to stay long myself, but I'm waiting for the war fever to abate in the US, if that's possible, before I head home."

But just then the domestic editor, Anh, appeared in the stairwell. "I have copy to edit," she said coldly.

"I hope it's not drivel," said Cain.

"Not what?" she asked.

"Nothing," Cain responded. It was apparently not worth explaining to her what "drivel" actually meant.

Before the *Tet* holidays, I did tackle the rewriting of several stories. I also served up professional complaints to Anh about some of them, and even when she seemed to loosen up at the margin and claim to accept a few of my expansionary edits, none of them actually appeared in published copy the next day. One involved Chinese medical technology adopted by Vietnamese physicians whereby silica and coal dust was flushed from miners' lungs, after they were anaesthetized, relieving them of some of the symptoms of their mounting ailments. To flesh out the story, I added a final paragraph to note that if these miners continued their work, it was likely they would be back to undergo the same treatment. Coal mining was inherently an unhealthy occupation, and prospects for mining might be better advised to consider alternative employment opportunities unless, of course, wages, which were lower than Hades, rose as high as Heaven. What mattered solely to Anh was the existence of the novel, imported treatment for ailments after the fact of exposure to Viet mining operations. The message was that the Authorities were looking after the miners. Fat chance. About the same chance that the Bush Administration and FEMA had pulled out all the stops to assist the poor in New Orleans after hurricane Katrina's wrath.

In another story, one of Anh's aspiring twenty-something female minions took it upon herself to write an "opinion" piece about the war in Iraq, a topic I for once did not hesitate, and in fact relished, tackling as an editor.

The author had dished out blandness, devoid of nuance but not of error. For example, she had written that some modest reductions in British forces around Basra, the city at the head of the Shatt al-'Arab where the Tigris and Euphrates meet before emptying into the Persian Gulf, might be an indication that the conflict, at least in southern Iraq, had abated. But the Brits in fact had really begun to lose any semblance of control. Things were deteriorating for the Western occupation -- in the same way that deterioration and then utter failure, that no lies could smother, sparked the rush for the exits by American forces in Vietnam in April 1975. I edited in the suggestion for the writer. This revised and expanded copy I took directly to Phuc. It was around the time the usual swarms of bats began zipping about outside in the dark over Tran Hung Dao Street that midweek evening.

Phuc was at his desk opening up a small, cubed package of folded banana leaf containing a fatty square glob of chopped pork and spices on his desk. He carefully unfolded the banana leaf holding the glob, but not before taking a pink ribbon off the entire parcel. *Tet* was just a few days away and this was, in fact, a traditional holiday food, though it hardly looked festive to me, rather more like, bereft of its packaging, something to induce indigestion if not worse. Phuc did not seem to mind, though, when I interrupted him and handed him the revised copy, bypassing Anh.

"You know, Phuc," I said, looking for acknowledgement before I handed him the copy, "I have spent time in the Middle East and know the region rather well. You had my resume when you hired me and you could see that."

Phuc just smiled, as if I had just told him the toilet in the men's room wouldn't flush, and often it would not. I figured he was trying to be cagey behind the smile, but then, he seemed always to be smiling. I could never have managed to do that.

"Well, I think my revisions here reflect my knowledge. The paper might be well advised to run with it as it now is," I said with as much authority as I could muster, pointing to the copy I had deposited on his desk. But Phuc said nothing and I returned to my desk. Over the top of the computer, I glanced occasionally at him, his glasses resting low on his nose. He finally started reading the proposed, revised article. After a while he wandered over.

"We," he said, with the emphasis on the first word, meaning most all Vietnamese, "know all this," and he pointed to the part of the copy where I had added that the Americans would ultimately have to leave Iraq essentially as they had left Vietnam.

At that instant, I rather liked Phuc.

"Are your saying that because this is allegedly widely known here, or expected, that it's not worth putting in the piece?" I asked.

"Yes."

"But this is supposed to be an opinion piece by one writer, that writer's opinion. She has signed off on my changes," I said. I felt frustrated.

"We can't use them," Phuc said flatly.

"But your argument is that the changes I have made are 'known' and therefore not to be printed. So, if you delete my editing, then you are back almost to the original draft. Now, tell me, what is in the original draft that is not 'known', too? I don't think anything. And therefore the entire piece, by your logic, offers nothing fresh for a reader and shouldn't it be canned."

Phuc took a minute to digest the comment. He stared at the copy as if he was reading it again, but he wasn't. He was trying to find a way to tell me to fuck off without saying exactly that.

"We will run the story mostly as it was originally written. Your job was to smooth the writing and correct errors, not change it."

"Then perhaps, by your logic, you are putting something in a hole on the page that is just junk, of no particular value to any Vietnamese reader?"

"Our readers are not primarily Vietnamese, but foreigners in Vietnam and nearby."

"Even so," I stubbornly continued, but knowing my point did not impress Phuc, "this paper is the national English language paper, the paper of record for this country's government in English. So why fill it with just any filler?"

"I cannot help you," said Phuc. He was conclusive. Holding the copy in one hand, he slapped it resoundingly into his other hand and strode off back to his desk.

Phuc had made it clear the paper was not about infuriating anyone, and particularly not the US Embassy staff in Ha Noi, which would have to object to any suggestion by the official Vietnamese paper that the Iraq "democracy" project was doomed, not to mention the Afghan one as well. The embassy would have to raise a stink about it even if some of the embassy staffers agreed, because they were hamstrung by having to ape whatever line or policy the Administration promoted, and the Vietnamese were hamstrung by their addiction to the flow of American dollars to investments in Vietnam. I ran all this by Cain in the stairwell later that evening, and told him of the conflict over my editing of the article.

"Even if you don't like Communism as an ideology," he said, "you can see that the Party here is not really that. It's an oligarchy of old men and some of their appointed offspring hanging on in a fast economy, and doing relatively well. They are anxious to suck up to other countries for more investment. They surely don't want the boat rocked."

"Yeah, I said. "Communism in name only, I suppose, and the fact that it's the sole political party allowed here."

"Like in China," I said. "But in the end...."

"In the end?"

"In the end the Party can't remain in power unless the lives of the People are improving. Right?"

"It's happened before. Counter revolutions or just collapse," said Cain. "Thinking of collapse, remember what happened in the former Soviet Union."

"So you might say Phuc has a point," I suggested.

"I don't know. Maybe. But even if he does, that's not the point for us," Cain said. "We are editors. We are not supposed to have any axe to grind but that of free expression, strong writing and thorough coverage."

"An independence of the press that we can't promote here."

"Right," said Cain, drawing deeply on a *Vinataba*. So deeply, in fact, that at the moment I rather imagined he might soon be a candidate for the Chinese lung flushing procedure, like Vietnam's coal miners.

"Whatever," I said, "but I rather like the notion of drawing attention to analogies between the American experience of defeat here and the eventual exits from Iraq and Afghanistan."

"Your country has been begging for serious trouble for years."

"In ten years American power could be exhausted, and Americans reviled as has-beens. I agree."

Cain laughed. "Possible, mate."

6

By the end of the week, marking the beginning of a few days of off, the Lunar New Year, *Tet Nguyen Dan*, was beginning in Ha Noi. I was reminded that I had not actually seen the moon in many a moon, so thick the air was with smog and lambent cloud cover. Along the streets and lanes of the Old Quarter and especially around the Dong Xuan market the commerce and crowds were especially intense with preparations: the buying and laying up of gifts, incense, food, firecrackers and decorations.

I left the newspaper late one night a couple days before *Tet's* formal commencement, and was planning to walk all the way back to Hang Giay and got as far as the Opera House when I heard my name called. I stopped, looked around and spotted a cab, one of ten or so, idling before the steps leading into the Opera, with an arm waving me over from the driver's seat. It was Tan, and I recalled that a couple weeks earlier I had hailed the same cab from Tran Hung Dao on leaving the newsroom and ridden across the city to the apartment.

That earlier evening, our first meeting when I had first jumped into his cab, he said immediately: "You are American. That's good."

I looked him over, what I could see of him from the backseat. He was a lean, lanky fellow, with thick black hair he combed straight back from a perfect hairline above a handsome face and pearly teeth. He might have been a Viet cinema star, for all I knew, except that he was driving a cab and most likely not.

"How do you know I am American? I could be Canadian, or even Dutch," I said.

"I can spot Americans. There is nothing to it but instinct after a while."

"What? Some unique look that identifies Americans? You know, there are Vietnamese Americans. Quite a few of them. I bet if I were an ethnically Vietnamese American, you would not know the American part right away."

"I am Tan," he said warmly, throwing his arm over the front seat to shake my hand. "You might be right."

"Well, I *am* from America," I said.

"I love America," he said.

"I'm not sure I do right now. That's part of the reason I came here. Name's Marshall McLean. Nice to meet you."

"Where do you want to go? Tan will take you anywhere you want."

"Two Hang Giay Street. Just past the Dong Xuan market."

"No problem," said Tan, and off we went that evening.

"You are good," I said. "Every other time I have gotten in a cab no driver has understood my pronunciation of the street name."

"I figured it out," he said.

"I must be making some progress here," I muttered.

"What you do in Ha Noi?" asked Tan.

"I work at *Vietnam News*. I'm an editor there," I told him.

Tan laughed heartily. "That's a newspaper?"

"It's supposed to be," I said. "Why do you question what it is?"

"A real newspaper always works to report truth and expose lies," Tan explained forthrightly. "I am a writer. I love to write, except that I am unpublished. Perhaps my writing is honest, but I can't find audience here."

"What do you write?"

"Real things I have witnessed and heard and poems, in Vietnamese. My written English is not good."

"But your spoken English is good enough. What exactly do you write about?"

"Things I come across. Sometimes things that bother me. Bad things I hear," Tan said.

"I bet you hear much as a cab driver. Passengers talking on their phones, or to each other."

"True," said Tan. "But I act like not listening. Mind my own business."

"I've tried myself to get some things in the paper in editing copy. They were unacceptable."

"Then you know," said Tan.

"More interesting to me is the apparent fact that you know the difference between an active and independent press and one that is not."

"Yes," said Tan, "I know."

It was pleased to have found a driver who not only could maneuver his cab adroitly though nighttime Ha Noi traffic, but who also seemed to have critical faculties and might even have some writing talent, at least with his poetry, but in a language I could not read. Almost immediately, I felt I could trust him -- more than I could Anh or Phuc at the paper anyway. When he soon let me out in front of the apartment building, I jotted his phone number on the cover of a book of matches and also took his business card and tossed both on the desk in the apartment.

I imagined that if I ever needed a driver for a serious excursion beyond Ha Noi, that he might be my man, or, as one would have said in the Middle East in an English corruption of the Arabic word for guide, my dragoman. He also seemed intent on an honest business, not rigging the meter in the cab with a hidden switch that bumped up the rate for foreigners. I tipped him double the meter charge.

So, I was pleased that our paths crossed again, and surprised that he remembered me, unless the earlier, big tip alone had made an impression. Given the usual lack of drama in moving between points in Ha Noi, aside from the congestion, Tan's recognition was a reminder that foreigners did not go unnoticed, that they did not exactly blend in. I walked across the wide roundabout in front of the Opera House. Tan was probably waiting for the performance to stop inside. The National Symphony of Vietnam, I noted on an advertising poster, was performing that night some pieces by Bela Bartok and Brahms, and had I known, I would have gone. I made a mental note to try to attend a future symphonic performance.

"Mr. Tan," I said, "how are you? Happy *Tet*!"

"Thank you," Tan said. "*Tet* always nice. Where are you going now?"

"Hang Giay, again," I said, and squeezed up close to the cab window to avoid getting clipped by passing vehicles in the roundabout.

"You want ride?"

"Not tonight. It's a fine evening just to walk and I don't have to work at the newspaper for a few days."

"Street closed from Hoan Kiem up to Hang Giay," Tan informed. I had forgotten. It was a Friday night, and as usual Hang Duong Street, which ran in front of the Dong Xuan market before it became Hang Giay Street in the Old Quarter near the apartment, was closed to motorized vehicles so vendors could sell more of their wares in the open air, in the middle of the street under long canopies or from the sidewalks.

"Then some other time I will call you. You're my driver if I need a serious ride. I still have your number and business card."

"You call me anytime you have need. I help you," said Tan.

I shook his hand and headed off. I had a premonition, wading through the motorbikes and cars across the asphalt in front of the Opera, that I had not seen the last of Tan. Later, just beyond the Dong Xuan market, I stopped at Anh's café.

The crowd was so thick on the sidewalk, many Vietnamese sitting on tiny plastic stools with wooden chop sticks shoveling down *pho* or rice and noodles or slivers of pork cooked on small braziers, that I could not tell who exactly was serving whom, but there was Anh, in the black, loose trousers often worn by peasants and a white, simple blouse darting in and out of the café carrying a tray. I caught her eye and she made a point of going inside and finding a spare stool, setting it down on a narrow space on the sidewalk. "Sit," she said, and I did, and then she went back inside and a few minutes later brought me a cup of tea and a bowl of steaming *pho*.

"This is for free," she said, handing me the bowl and a set of chopsticks. "Where you been?"

"I'm sorry I haven't stopped by in a while," I uttered.

"No problem. You visit mosque?" she asked. "Last time you here we talk about that. I tell you the way." She stood above me, her long fingers on her slender hips.

"I did," I said, "right away. Good directions you gave me to the Street of Combs!"

"Something happen at mosque," Anh said. "Nothing much I think, though. But I keep eyes open for you."

"My eyes open for you, too," I said, and then I thought she blushed just a bit. "What about the mosque?"

"Police go to mosque I hear one day since I see you last. I hear they go inside, look around. Three police cars on the street. Cars blocked from passing on street for half hour."

This story sounded like some kind of unannounced, impromptu raid. Perhaps it was just standard procedure for the police to check in on religious establishments from time to time. They did, after all, exist solely at the discretion of the government in Vietnam.

"It's a peaceful place behind those walls. Serene and decorous," I said, and I was thinking of 'Abdullah Hamidi, the Afghan, whose welcoming demeanor seemed to set the tone at the small compound. "Do you know why police went there? Hear anything about that?"

"Don't know. I think just checking. Make sure everything okay, no problem."

"What might not be okay?" I wondered aloud, recalling that 'Abdullah Hamidi didn't seem like the sort who would be a threat to anyone.

"Not sure," Anh said. "Maybe police just worry sometime. It Muslim place, you know, but no Muslim terrorism here in Vietnam I hear of."

I assumed Anh correct about the absence of "terrorism". For one thing, little or no copy had come across my terminal at the newspaper to suggest anything like it, and especially such based on Islamic visions of *jihad*, in Vietnam. I figured this would be something *Vietnam News* would readily report, if it existed, to remind the People that the government had the power to ban congregational religious observance outright. The national authorities did cite "terrorism", however, from time to time. This was aimed almost exclusively at some hapless *Viet Kieu*, Vietnamese living overseas and having perhaps US citizenship, visiting the country and maybe blabbing that they belonged to a group in the US aiming to undermine Communist Party control. They could be charged with "terrorism", summarily tried, jailed for a year or two and then sent home. In general, though, with Anh's report and experiences at work reading all sorts of copy, I was beginning to get a sense of widespread control and oversight in Vietnam even though it was not readily discernable. But it was a control that could come rushing almost instantaneously to the fore at any target, institutional or personal, around just a suspicion of subversion.

The authorities, I reckoned, kept a watchful eye on any mosque given the worldwide concern about Islam's surging hostility towards Western meddling and military actions in Muslim lands.

"Anh," I said, "except for the traffic police at some intersections and guards at the entrances to important buildings, like where I work, I really haven't seen police here. Do you often?"

"I know round here only. Not know much other place in Ha Noi," Anh responded. "Police everywhere but hard for someone not been here long to know this. Some police not in uniform. They look like normal men, not dressed up. But I can tell them."

"Tell them?" I asked. I wasn't sure exactly what she meant.

"I know some are police even if they not tell me. Many on street here know, too. We here all the time and see everything, know almost everyone," Anh said. "I know man who lives in your building is police. I don't know name."

"Does he come by here for coffee or to eat?"

"He has, but I not like him," she laughed. "He never leave me tip like you."

"Is he unpleasant, too?"

"Not really. He say little. Always staring a people. He act like he expect people to move and give him seat when café full. I see that, but he got good job. Secure job with government. Lucky man."

Tao was lucky, too. She also had some sort of secure job with the government. As for whomever it was Anh mentioned in my building, an asshole, I thought. Another government flak acting as if he were a big shot. But I did not say this to Anh.

"I hope when I come here you will tell me of anything unusual you see. I am trying to learn more about your country each day."

"I will," said Anh.

I dismissed the raid on the mosque as probably a routine occurrence. And also, there that night in front of Anh's café I looked around, too, cradling my warm cup: pretty Anh serving drinks and *pho*, the glowing braziers, the families out to stroll or to shop along the street, young lovers arm in arm, and above all, a strong perception based on what was simply visible: No one seemed afraid of anyone else in Ha Noi.

Cain and I often bitched (because it was one easy way of letting off steam) about the limitations of our jobs at the newspaper, and about Phuc and anything else that on the surface seemed objectionable about the Communist Party's grip on Vietnam, but it was often difficult to object to the results of a sort that could be seen all around: Ha Noi seemed a safe place to live where Westerners and natives could do much as they pleased at least to survive which, in Anh's case anyway, simply meant serving drinks and food tasty enough to corral patrons.

The overall formula, I thought, might not be so bad and maybe better than many elsewhere: on the one hand, economic liberalism by and large, and this was expanding, and on the other, a monolithic political system that forbade dissent and had so browbeat the People to avoid it that they, the People, largely focused on social harmony and community I had rarely witnessed elsewhere. The red flag with its bright yellow star hung up and down Hang Giay in the festive night, and Anh's attentive cheerfulness grabbed faithful attention and, along with Tan's earlier friendliness, created an hour of comfortable repose.

"Anh," I suggested in a deliberately off-handed way, "maybe I should take you out to dinner sometime? An evening together when you are not working, if sometimes you aren't?"

She was grabbing a dirty bowl off the stool opposite me, stooping over, and then she stood straight and halted. "I'm too busy girl," she claimed, shaking her head. 'Very busy girl."

"Okay," I merely responded.

Perhaps I should have been bolder and insisted on a date, but then I was still thinking of Tao, whether I'd ever see her again. I was almost pleased Anh had not assented to my suggestion. Anh anyway looked hard at me and said: "I think maybe you think too much," and then she turned and moved away from my spot on the sidewalk.

I finished my bowl of *pho* and emptied the cup of tea and waited a bit, wondering if she would come over to me again, and then I sensed maybe I had disappointed her because she did not. I returned to the apartment, stopping on the way at a unit of a small, almost modern grocery chain called Hapro that had recently sprung up in Ha Noi to compete with traditional, fresh food markets that existed in chaotic emporiums like nearby Dong Xuan. Foreign foods and beverages were worming their way into Vietnam's gut. The sweet, mild fish sauce I had come to like, and which the Viets had been refining for centuries, perhaps was losing appeal at the center of national taste.

Several days off, and *Tet*, lay ahead. I wondered how I might fill the time, but did recall that Cain had suggested meeting somewhere by Hoan Kiem Lake to witness traditional *Tet* fireworks. As for the next day, I planned to walk around the West and Truc Bach lakes, the latter virtually a large pond, the former the largest anywhere near Ha Noi, and the two separated by a dike upon which a causeway carried city traffic. The circuit was 15 kilometers from the apartment and back.

7

The area around the two lakes, through which I passed the next morning, comprised a particularly desirable residential and even business area of Ha Noi: multi-story condominium and apartment buildings sprinkled along the shore between small shops where the better off and many Westerners and Asian foreigners lived. Truc Bach Lake was almost a kilometer northwest of the Old Quarter. The name meant "white bamboo" but none of that plant was visible in the prime neighborhood, Ngu Xa, or around the adjacent lake, the smallest of Ha Noi's eleven, sporting inky black water. It was said to be the most polluted lake in the city, and it was also the same small lake future US Senator John McCain splashed into after anti-aircraft batteries severed a wing of his fighter jet in October 1967.

Farther along around West Lake past shoreline apartment buildings and businesses and Buddhist pagodas draped by pink and purple bougainvillea, thirst came calling, and halfway around, on the north shore, I stopped at a café beside the premises of a rowing club and ordered fresh squeezed orange juice. Young Vietnamese, crews of both sexes, were out stroking away in "fours" and "eights" on the lake, rowing shells of a vintage that would have long ago been mothballed along Boston's Charles or Philadelphia's Schuykill rivers. Then, I heard my name, in a suddenly familiar voice. I almost leaped from my chair. It was Tao.

She was astride a Honda Dream motorbike, in skin-tight jeans, red blouse and Nike sneakers. She pulled up on the sidewalk by my café table, her black hair spiked by the wind, the strap of a leather bag slung across her chest. "I spotted you," she said, "fifty meters back."

"Do I stand out that much to you?" I asked. "At my age? You were not keeping your eyes on the road."

"You did," said Tao.

I was flattered and also pleased to see a familiar face after the hundreds of unfamiliar ones I had already passed on the walk. "What are you doing up here on your motorbike?"

"What are *you* doing here?" she shot back.

"Just walking. Around West Lake. Now, as you can see, I'm having a drink of orange juice."

"The whole thing?" Tao asked, pointing to the orange juice and sweeping an arm around in a circle to indicate West Lake.

"Yes, the whole walk and the whole glass of juice. Why not?"

"That's a long walk."

"Yeah, where I come from, it's otherwise known a *fer piece*."

"A what?"

"That's what William Faulkner might have said."

"Who?"

"Don't worry about it," I said. "Yes, it's a long way. I'm killing time. What else is there to do on a Saturday morning?"

"Lots."

"So where are you going?"

"Lunch. I am taking the long way to get there, though."

"Where's your boy, Tung?"

"At the American Club playing. My father is looking after him. This is my free time."

"American Club?"

"Yes," said Tao. "It's along Hai Ba Trung Street south of Hoan Kiem Lake, not far from where you work. It was the US consulate before 1954. Then it was home to the Fatherland Front, an organization that helped coordinate resistance to the US during the war. You can eat hot dogs and other American food there, and there's a huge playground. Safe place for children to play outdoors, too."

"Interesting."

"Get on," Tao said.

"On?"

"Here," she said, patting the extension of the seat behind her on the Honda. "I'll take you to a good lunch."

"Maybe I need to walk all the way to build up an appetite?" I said in jest.

"No. I'm hungry and you will like the place. Good food." Tao twisted the throttle, revving the bike's motor, as if she was instantaneously going to bolt away.

I fast left a wad of *dong* on the table. Ho Chi Minh's visage on the bills, a benign smile, stared back, and then we were off together into the flow, another corpuscle in the bloody thick stream of traffic along the lakeshore. I had never liked being at the mercy of anyone else's driving, particularly on a motorbike, but Tao seemed confident and deliberate, not fighting the traffic, not trying to maneuver around it like a *xeom* driver. The seat was just long enough to contain the both of us. That, and the wind whipping about, with her hair flying in my face, I almost felt like I had slipped into a warm bath, as on our swim in Ha Long Bay. "Where are we going?"

"Vines," she said. "From here, it's halfway back from where you started in the direction you were walking. Near the Sheraton."

I looked across part of West Lake and could see the hotel some five kilometers south on the lake's east shore.

"I have something to tell you," Tao said. "But wait until we sit down."

"Okay," I answered, wondering what surprise she had in store. She was the sort of woman who would often surprise, I thought. The question was whether the surprise was to good or ill effect.

I calculated, as far as surprises went, being with her was like gambling with roughly fifty-fifty odds, but odds that in fact were better than a casino's. If you tried to push your luck, you were doomed to disappointment. But if you stood by patiently, or even forgot about her, there she might be, like in the kayak with her blue bikini, or on her motorbike: a surprise. Evidently, she had not forgotten me since Ha Long Bay.

"This is an almost new place," Tao said, referring to Vines, our destination, as she wheeled the Honda off the main road that ran between the Red River and the east side of West Lake atop what was a dike to help hold back the occasional Hong Song (Red River) floods that inundated parts of Ha Noi. "It's caught on fast with foreigners and even my Party officials here in Ha Noi," Tao added. I took note.

The side street was called Xuan Dieu. I assumed the "Dieu" part did not refer to "God" in Vietnamese, but it was clear that Vines certainly worshipped another god, Bacchus, with an extensive, climate controlled wine cellar in the basement also stocking boxes of fine Cuban cigars going for about 20 million *dong*, which amounted, I tallied, to about a year's wages for the average Ha Noian.

After securing a table on the second floor beside a window from which we could see the Sheraton down Xuan Dieu on the lakeshore, I ordered a salad, pizza and a glass of Chianti. Banal as such fare was, I was rather tired of *pho*, even if there were prospects of having it handed me again by Anh at her café. Soon, Donald Berger, the owner and manager, sauntered over and introduced himself. He was from Montreal, about 45 or so, and had been, he said, in Asia at various locations for about a decade running other high-end eateries before he launched Vines in Ha Noi. He claimed a lot of Vietnamese officials, even Party leaders, lunched at his restaurant and spent heavily on the wine, cigars and food, as few other Vietnamese could.

"So," I reminded Tao after Berger moved on to other patrons, "what is this surprise you have earmarked for me?"

"Maybe there is more than just one," she said playfully, "but there's a new magazine starting up, I heard, here in Ha Noi. It might be interesting and maybe you'd like to check it out?"

"Tell me more."

"I think maybe you don't like working at *Vietnam News*?"

"It's not a thrill. How do you know that?"

"You are an experienced editor, right?"

"I imagine so."

"The newspaper is what it is. I think you've figured that out."

"Yes, I have. So what do you know about this magazine?"

"It's not come out yet, but it may soon."

"What kind of magazine? Do you know?"

"It may be some kind of high-end 'lifestyle' thing. Not exactly sure."

"If so, it must be something aimed at the expatriates here," I commented.

"Whoever's involved might be looking for people to help. People good with English, with experience," Tao said.

"So how do I check this out?"

"What I can say is that there's an office not too far from where I live. I rode by there the other day. There was a sign, 'Hong Song Publications' on a three-story house."

"You never mentioned where you live when we were at Ha Long Bay. I don't have the faintest idea. Where do you live?"

"Fifteen minute walk directly east of Hoan Kiem. Across the dike down near the river off Bach Dang Street."

"I've never been in that neighborhood."

"Not as safe for one of your walks. It's very poor. Some drug trafficking, too." Tao went on to mention the area directly along the river north and south of the Long Bien Bridge, which I had already jogged over and back several times. This area of Ha Noi, being closest to the bridge, which carried only pedestrian and bike traffic and the train in and out of Ha Noi, was the first stop for villagers across the river bringing food and small wares to sell daily into the city, and the first place most migrants to the city lingered.

"It's an old area. Sometimes we are flooded. My father owns a house there, down an alley that goes almost to the river."

"Why do you live in such a poor part of the city? You've got a good job, I imagine."

"Because its inexpensive. It's not bad."

"Must be nice to have parents near?"

"Just my father. My mother is dead. He helps with Tung. But maybe I have another surprise or two." She seemed to be calculating something, and not just the time: "I don't have to be back to the American Club for two more hours. Come," she said, snatching her bag and standing up from the table with a mischievous grin.

"Okay." I called the waiter over and paid the bill. I could have lingered at Vines all afternoon with her, but as long as Tao would have me go with her, I was going.

"You don't know the fun of my city yet," she said. "It is clear. A nice Saturday and you were not doing anything but walking."

"You can't argue with walking just as you would not with swimming or kayaking, and anyway, I was thinking about a number of things."

"Good, but you can't think all the time," Tao said. Maybe, like Anh, she thought I thought too much.

Tao proceeded across Xuan Dieu Street in front of Vines to her Honda, which I could not have located among the myriad other bikes, many of them Honda's, on the sidewalk. I followed her, half euphoric about another ride to somewhere else with her, but was struck again by the way she moved. Of course, I noted, she moved like anyone else, one foot ahead of the other sequentially, except that at the margin, there was something else about the way she moved: lithely did not quite capture it. There was the hint of a skip in the tough, fine little feet that had breezed over sharp rocks at Ha Long Bay, something like an anticipatory playfulness of arrival at the location of the very next step and those well beyond, as if even in the deliberation of present movements (and it seemed obvious that she knew what she was doing, or not) she had already arrived, fully engaged.

I thought that if I had ever had the opportunity to pick just one person among Ha Noi's multitudes to draw me into the particular energy of the city and show me around, even without explicitly aiming to do so and even without saying much, she had to be the best choice. It was *her* Ha Noi: she seemed to possess the city.

I straddled the Honda again feeling even more comfortable than before. "Someone else said the same thing about thinking too much," I muttered.

"Who?"

"A lady who gives me coffee on Hang Giay in the mornings sometimes," I said.

"You are making other Vietnamese friends?"

"Slowly," I said.

Slowly, she drove us south along the dike boulevard, past the point where most of Ha Noi's public transit buses departed from on routes around the city, past the entrance to the Long Bien Bridge. Then, she turned off the main road and scooted into a narrow alley near the Old Quarter and then through a gate into a dirt parking lot. Nearby was an almost crumbling, one-story building with an open portico in front of several doors along its length. Tao stopped and parked.

"What this?" I asked.

"The best massage."

"What *kind* of massage?" I asked.

"Just a massage," Tao said with a laugh. "What did you think, thinking too much?"

"I dare not say!" I responded, knowing that Tao knew exactly what I was thinking.

"What do you take me for?" Tao teased.

For some reason I just then recalled an alleged conversation George Bernard Shaw had enjoyed with a comely lady at a British dinner party. He had asked her if she would sleep with him for five Pounds. She responded, horrified, and slapped Shaw. Unfazed, Shaw then asked the lady if she would sleep with him for a million Pounds? With that, she wavered, and asked him the same question Tao had just asked me. Shaw replied that he thought her wavering had more or less settled the matter about what she was, and that they were merely haggling over the price.

"Are *you* going to be my masseuse?"

"Not now," said Tao, emphasizing the last word. I wondered if she was suggesting she might eventually do me the honor. I was reminded of how she had splayed herself on the kayak in Ha Long Bay: suggestively.

"Not now?"

"I'm not a professional. Wait," she said, ignoring my question, and then she disappeared into one of the doorways off the portico.

I stood in the dusty parking area. It was mostly empty but for a few other motorbikes. A few healthy looking coconut palms swayed a bit in a hot breeze above the tin roof of the ramshackle building. After a couple minutes Tao emerged from inside. "It's all arranged," she said.

"What's all arranged?" I asked suspiciously.

"The massages."

"I hadn't planned on it."

"You don't like a massage?"

"Who doesn't? But massages cost and I only have a few *dong*. Do they take credit cards?" I asked half in jest. This particular apparent pleasure emporium, I could see, was not a place that would likely be featured in the high-end "lifestyle" magazine Tao had suggested at Vines that I check out, perhaps for extra work as an editor. It was crude and very pre-modern and might have existed centuries earlier just as it appeared, I imagined.

"No!" said Tao emphatically. "Plastic impossible here, but this will cost you all of the equivalent of three US dollars in cash *dong*," Tao said.

"Naw," I said with incredulity.

"That's right. It's the best bargain. You will see. I have come here many times."

"Is this legitimate?"

"Of course. Whatever something is, if it really is, it's legitimate. No?"

"Tao, you know what I mean!"

She just laughed, but I followed her inside the low building. It looked like a converted barracks of some sort inside and out, except that sections of space were separated by curtains hung on rusted wires, and in each section stood a wooden table draped with sheets, a ceramic wash basin and a chair laden with towels. Two young women stood by, apparently ready for work.

"You take that table. I'll take the one next to you," Tao said.

One of the women, I thought with some fumbling, drew the curtain between our respective tables. "Now we disrobe," Tao instructed invisibly.

"All the way?"

"Most all the way will do."

I took off my clothes and drew a towel around. The young woman had turned her back to me, which I then learned was entirely unnecessary.

"The catch, to use your term, is this," Tao said from the other side of the curtain. "These girls are poor and need to make some kind of living. They might not otherwise be able to survive. They are blind."

This was yet another instance of the Vietnamese, however poor or worse, handicapped, finding a way to survive, even do something useful and, in this particular Ha Noi location, something pleasurable. Tao had brought me to a garden of Epicurus, not the one in classical Athens, but something like a Viet version of it. Epicurus had said the aim of life was pleasure, that pleasure was the highest good. The young woman started with my feet and worked up over the next hour to the top of my head, her expert, skilled hands kneading, rubbing and uprooting stress like weeds from a yard. I was not about the challenge Epicurus, and meanwhile, Tao drew back the curtain.

"Have you ever heard of one Epicurus?" I asked her. "He was a Greek philosopher."

"No."

"He built a house in Athens in the third century BC, around a garden, and surrounded himself with friends in the pursuit of pleasure. The garden seems here, with you, right now."

"Massages are nice," said Tao flatly.

"Yes," I went on, "but Epicurus was often misinterpreted, as if he was merely a hedonist, someone who sought nothing but bodily pleasures. He didn't. What he was really aiming at was the absence of pain, perfect composure, the absence of desire for what was not at hand or unattainable. This he called *ataraxia*, perfect mental peace, the absence of pain borne of unfulfilled desire."

"That sounds like something Buddhist to me. An enlightened state?"

"Maybe there are parallels. Perhaps Taoist, too?"

"But you have a problem with this," Tao said.

"How so?"

"What if a person hurts because they still wish not to be dislodged from that state of mental peace they have attained? There could be some anxiety about that? The fear of losing it?"

I looked hard at her, at the pleasing contours of her back, whatever I could see, exposed. Her arms hung languidly off the table towards the rough, swept floor, and I thought she was clever.

"But in that case they never attained an enlightened state. Have you attained such?" I was probing indirectly for some concrete revelation from her about her personal life, as if I were trying to get a good look under the white sheet that covered critical parts of her body. The blue bikini at Ha Long Bay left little to be imagined, but it was not the same, not as charged, if I should see more of her there on the table.

"I don't think so," Tao said. "I am sometimes stressed. Why do you think I brought you here?"

"Because it's unusual?"

"Yes, that's a reason, but also because here one can forget about worries -- except that you are reminding me now -- and let it all go for a while. That's what this is for, a massage like this among these blind people."

"I'm sorry," I said. "I have maybe ruined this for you?"

"Be quiet," Tao said. She lifted her arm far enough to take hold of my hand and squeeze it slowly, with some warmth. She had trapped me, I thought, or bewitched me with her youth and energy. Part of it was simply being at that spot in Ha Noi, too. The blind girl had climbed up on the table and straddled my back. It seemed like she was about to do a handstand, pressing down so firmly. For a few minutes I drifted off into a near trance of relaxation, and then queried Tao again.

"You told me just a little about Ha Giang, your childhood there, when we were at Ha Long Bay. I liked that part about swimming in the Lo River. I would like to hear more."

"Not now," Tao said, "but I will tell you one interesting thing about the river. During the war with the Chinese in 1979, they built rafts upstream on the Chinese side of the border and loaded them with consumer goods, even things like refrigerators, and then floated the rafts downstream into Vietnam and by Ha Giang."

"Why in the Hell would they do that? Free gifts for the enemy?"

"It was an unusual kind of propaganda. We were so poor back then. No American can imagine. The Chinese were sending us a message. Something like, 'look what we have and you don't, we are superior to you, our country is superior because we have all these things, relative to what you have'."

"China was hardly an industrial nation then like it is fast becoming now."

"True, but they were still far more advanced than we were, and if still poor themselves, far richer than we were," Tao explained.

"So I guess everyone in Ha Giang was pleased to have these more or less free gifts even while the war was going on, and from the enemy, too. Must have been quite a scene, the people in Ha Giang retrieving what was on those rafts when they floated by in the current. Maybe it looked like some kind of feeding frenzy, who got to whatever first?"

"Not at all," said Tao. "Nothing much was ever taken."

"I can't imagine that."

"There was a rule. The local Party cadre leaders decreed that anyone taking things off the rafts, if caught, would be summarily executed. I think some in Ha Giang were, but my parents did not tell me about that. They just told me and my friends not to touch anything we found in the river or on the river banks."

"Incredible."

"To take the goods coming from China was a severe breach of discipline. I think it was also seen as some admission of the Party's failure to provide more for us Vietnamese. And perhaps it was also an admission that the Chinese were superior, if only in terms of development. See, in our long history, we have often been at odds, or even at war, with our neighbors to the north."

"China is a colossus sitting atop Vietnam. A huge weight."

"Yes, that's how it has been," Tao said. "Many centuries. When I was a child the Chinese were supporting the Khmer Rouge in

Cambodia. Vietnam did not support that bloody regime. The brief war was related to that, to dislodging the Khmer Rouge."

When time was up with the blind girls, we set off again on the motorbike. It was well past noon and Tao said she had to go on to the American Club. I was hungry again and she dropped me at the southeast corner of Hoan Kiem Lake where, nearby, was a *Pho 24*, part of a chain of small restaurants that had been sprouting up in Vietnam's cities serving the country's most basic fare.

"Tonight at ten I might go see a film at the *Cinematique*. It's near the American Club, just a couple blocks from here. 22 Hai Ba Trung. If you want to show up, do so," Tao said as I swung off the Honda.

I was stung a bit by the "might". Was she inviting me or, more precisely, would she be there if I showed up at the theater, I wondered. "Any particular film?" I asked.

"No, but I like theaters and most any film. My father will be there, too."

"Good. I will enjoy meeting him. But I won't recognize him unless you come."

Tao smiled broadly, which I took as an affirmation that she would be there, and then she sped off, merging into the traffic, just one of a million at least on motorbikes. I stood at the corner near the lake for a minute before crossing the street to the restaurant, but she was quickly out of sight. A crowd walked around the lake in no particular direction, but it was afternoon and long gone was the morning phalanx of women at that exact spot in orderly rows doing their exercises to Doris Day's *Que Sera, Sera*. What it was exactly I could not precisely fathom about Tao that captivated because it was essentially everything in concert: the tilt of head, the dark eyes, and her small, strong wrists. Such a petite figure she cut, but it seemed like she might be as tough as any Viet Cong guerrilla in black pajamas guarding a cache of Kalashnikovs or grenades in a rice paddy. Our nascent friendship seemed to be warming, and with that Ha Giang rang in my ears, an exotic ring, so remote even from Ha Noi up near a stretch of border with China where few Westerners, and even fewer Americans, had been. *The girl from Ha*

Giang, no less. I wanted to go there, and perhaps someday I might, but not without her. I wanted to jump in the Lo River and let its flow southwards carry me through the town as they had carried Chinese rafts laden with what the Vietnamese had lately been acquiring and even making themselves.

8

"You meeting me?" asked Cain when I answered my mobile phone in the apartment.

"You mean for the fireworks at Hoan Kiem?"

"Around eight thirty if you like, mate. I'll be at the red bridge to the pagoda at the lake. That good?"

It was already almost eight. I had walked back to the apartment after having some chicken *pho*. It had been a lively day, thanks to Tao spotting me from her motorbike along West Lake. I had been invigorated by the massage by the blind girl and by Tao's company and was eager to extend what had so far been my best day in Ha Noi. Flitting about with Tao acting as cicerone was just the thing to spike up my spirits.

"I'll see you there, Cain," I answered, and closed the clamshell device and headed for the shower. I was still vaguely sticky from whatever emollient the blind girl had applied.

The famous offensive during *Tet* of 1967 that I read about in US newspapers at the time had been a bloodbath. Nearly 50,000 Viets killed and several thousand Americans. Uncle Ho and General Giap probably knew beforehand it would be a bloodbath. But they probably figured it would also be a huge down payment in blood for eventual unification of north and south in Vietnam. Almost a decade later, it turned out to be just that in retrospect, the apparent turning point in the American War. It had been a moment when the American public began to realize the price for "liberating" Vietnam, or rather forbidding the Vietnamese to work out their own future without interference, was too steep. I headed out to Hoan Kiem an hour later.

The crowd was already immense and increasing the closer I got to the lake, but it was orderly, respectful. The vicinity of the pagoda Cain had designated as our meeting place, called Ngoc Son, stood on a small island connected to the shore by a red, wooden bridge. Shaped like the inverted arc of a woman's back, it was passage to an ancient shrine to one Va Xuong. Xuong was a literary deity in charge of designing the various trials and tests required to become a Vietnamese mandarin.

One question that amused me as I waded through the crowd and rounded the northern end of Hoan Kiem was whether, since Cain and I, as editors at *Vietnam News*, were the alleged masters of English anyway in Ha Noi, why were we not considered mandarins of some sort ourselves, and at least allowed to wear shorts in the newsroom? Phuc, however, thought otherwise, and in fact, I suspect we might have been considered hacks working at that newspaper. But any job in Ha Noi that paid the rent seemed good enough and I found a bench by the lake near the red bridge to Ngoc Son. The branches of a tamarind overhead drooped languidly into the water. To my left loomed the dominating facade of Ha Noi's main post office building topped by a huge, square clock. I was lucky to have found a place to sit, and after a while, I spotted Cain coming near and called him over to the bench.

"I might not stay long," I told him. "I have a sort of date at the *Cinematique* at ten."

"That's good, mate. You haven't had that kind of company since you've been in Ha Noi."

"She's led me around the city most of the day and I'm having some serious fun for a change here."

"Who is she exactly?"

"Viet, but she's half Western in attitude. Smart. Does stuff for the government here. War related research, she said, involving unexploded ordnance and getting it disposed of."

"She does not sound like my type," Cain said. "Too serious."

"When I was your age, she wasn't much my type, either."

"Mate, you are not old."

"Well, this Tao doesn't seem to think I'm enfeebled enough to avoid me entirely, at least not today and one day earlier."

"Earlier?"

"I met her in Ha Long Bay aboard the *Emeraude*. An American friend invited me to go along. This Tao and I met on the boat and swam together and went kayaking."

"And...."

"That's all, but it was quite lively to be around her. She was somehow with the Amcham crowd on the boat."

"Amcham?"

"American Chamber of Commerce."

"How so?" asked Cain. "Can't imagine she'd be a member."

"Well, I think she must have a number of American contacts, maybe close ones, but I don't know who they are. She's been in the states. She's connected somehow. But beyond that, I just don't know."

Soon there came the wild whistling of rockets darting up from a crude barge set in the middle of the lake, and then thunderous bangs overhead accompanied by intense flashes of multicolored lights. In those flashes, one could see the entire scene around the lake, packed with bodies 40 meters deep right down to the water's edge, but not all standing, many sitting as we were, but on the ground, looking skyward as the fireworks lit up the dark heavens.

"This is okay," I said to Cain. "I think if this were Central Park in New York, there'd be gangs roaming through the crowds, harassing and mugging. You wouldn't want to be there. What is it about Ha Noi that makes this place feel safer?"

"Dunno, mate. Maybe there's pride."

"Yeah, or a essentially unified culture with which all identify?"

"Maybe. I think there's a sense of shame here, too," Cain observed. "The Party apparatus is pretty good at shaming those who have screwed up in its view, and punishing them. Shame extends to whole families for the actions of a single member."

"Well," I said, "shame can be a powerful disincentive to crime and a lot more, even adultery. We've lost all sense of shame in the US. It's a grubby free for all, mostly for money and things."

"You know," said Cain while we watched the fireworks, "we get these stories to edit at the paper once in a while. Some very low-level government worker mucking about in graft and bribery. Then the bloke is tried and thrown in the slammer. I bet we'd find a few more of those stories in Viet language newspapers, if we could read them. Kind of like warning shots to the People to stay in line."

"Ah, the mysterious lady, The Editor, she must drop suggestions for these stories down to Phuc once in a while to make sure the foreigners who read the paper realize that they best be not trying to scam their local business partners, too, some of which are State owned. And this leads me to another question: who is The Editor? Have you ever seen her? You've been working the job longer than I have."

"All I know, mate," said Cain, "is that there's an office she inhabits in the fifth floor, and the entire floor is locked from the stairwell. She's like some remote queen bee. We drones aren't supposed to see or know what's up there, and I've never seen anyone above Phuc in the managerial hierarchy of the paper on the fourth floor."

"Neither have I. It's just us and Phuc and mostly a lot of girl reporters and then a couple battle axes like Anh. I have to say, I'm disappointed. I thought, given that the paper would be gibberish without us, that we'd have some real standing there. That we might even be wined and dined a bit by higher ups and get a real look behind the scenes."

"You're dreaming. They pay us a bit more than the rest of the staff but that's all the recognition we're ever going to get."

"I rather imagined that maybe the mysterious lady would be older and might hook up with a older, reputable Westerner like myself for a nice drink or maybe a performance at the Opera?" I asked, but in jest, like someone fishing for a grand marlin with a bamboo stick.

Cain laughed. "If you manage that I'll give you a month of my wages and tell Phuc to kiss his ass. Or maybe I'll kiss it."

"You are on."

"But what do I get if you don't succeed? You won't."

"Nothing but a picture of my complete humiliation," I said. "But really, I wouldn't even know where to begin. It's not possible, I know."

"We are in agreement on that."

The fireworks continued for a while. I eventually glanced over my shoulder through the leafy splendor above the heads of the crowd to "BUU DIEN HA NOI", the inscription under the square clock above Dinh Tien Hoang Street that ran along the lake's east side and the shore park where we were sitting. It was close to ten, time to find the *Cinematique* where Tao claimed she would be. I wasn't going to miss anything by the lake. The fireworks were sputtering out and even they had not brought the famed turtle to the surface. "Cain, I'm moving on to the cinema."

"Don't blame you."

"What are you doing?"

"I'm going back to my place and have a drink. Maybe three drinks."

"Well, I'll see you in a couple days at the office. Back at the *Tet*-less grind."

"But not a teat-less office," Cain quipped.

I laughed at his remark, slung my satchel over my shoulder and waded off through the crowd.

How many times I had walked down one or the other side of Hoan Kiem in the weeks in Vietnam I could not count. The walk was getting awfully familiar, but at least I was headed to a place I had not even heard of in Ha Noi until Tao had invited me to meet her there. Many of the street names in Ha Noi had some historical significance, and while I had not yet walked Hai Ba Trung a couple blocks south of the lake, I had earlier read something in the newspaper about the Hai Ba Trung legend, referring to two long-celebrated sisters.

The Chinese had forever, it seemed, been, or been trying, to control Vietnam. In control at about the same year Roman soldiers and a Jewish mob crucified Jesus outside the city walls of Jerusalem, the Chinese in an act of intimidation killed a prominent Vietnamese landlord. His wife, one Trung Trac, was defiant. She and her sister, Trung Nhi, organized an army and staged a revolt against the Chinese overlords, which led to a Chinese expulsion, setting Vietnam free for the first time in over a century. The two sisters were made queens, but Viet independence was not to last. A few years later the Chinese sent another army and crushed the revolt. The Trung queens, seeing the strength of the Chinese, drowned themselves in a tributary of the Red River rather than face capture. They became inspirations to Vietnamese revolutionaries forever after against foreign occupation and rule. I could not help thinking of Jewish zealots who had committed mass suicide rather than suffer capture or death at the hands of a Roman legion at Masada.

I also thought about the two sisters as I headed towards the theater, and also the madness and futility of the past American effort to maintain control and hegemony in South Vietnam. I'd have wagered that almost none of the American generals directing what the Viets called the "American War" had heard or read anything of the Trung sisters, legendary or not, nor did they adequately realize that the Vietnamese, given more than a 1000 years of frequent resistance to foreign occupations, would wind up forcing the Americans out, whatever the mayhem and cost in blood. Vietnam's women had often been the backbone of the culture from top to bottom, and it pleased me enormously that I had already enjoyed quite a day with Tao, whom I imagined might have acted like one of the Trung sisters during their time had she then been alive.

But my thoughts were interrupted. I was moving in the crosswalk at the south end of the lake headed south towards Hai Ba Trung. Streetlights flooded the intersection, the traffic light flashed red -- in a part of the city where more likely than not vehicles obeyed traffic signals. But then exactly in the middle of the street a black Chevrolet SUV bolted through the light into a narrow gap between oncoming traffic. If I had not reacted, drawn back suddenly, the SUV would have hit me.

In a blast of anger, I turned towards the vehicle and shouted loudly: "Fuck you!" And I gave it the finger.

A face then quickly appeared from the back seat window, glaring backwards. A familiar face, I thought at once, and then I realized it was Moshe Jabotinsky, the Israeli I had met on the

Emeraude. It seemed bizarre: flipping off a vehicle carrying someone who maybe had assisted me in the banana fields at *Ashdot Yaakov Ichud* almost 40 years earlier. And he of a nation I had once loved at the *kibbutz* and later came to abhor for the way it treated Palestinians.

I also thought of how I had come across Tan, the cab driver, which seemed just as unlikely in the crowded city as a near miss from the vehicle carrying Jabotinsky. It all felt surreal and disconcerting and particularly slow: as if in a dream, time seemed to stall as I recalled the scene of the SUV passing, the details, even the details of the faces of those on the curbs, but especially the details of Jabotinsky's face fast receding as the SUV raced ahead beyond the intersection.

Then I realized that I had maybe seen the same vehicle before: leaving the *Emeraude*, looking for Tao, and at a distance seeing she and Tung and Jabotinsky and others get into a black SUV. I wondered what it meant, if anything.

Just the facts that I had come across him in Vietnam, and also that we maybe had discovered a previous time together decades earlier, at least in proximity, at the *kibbutz* in 1969, was startling enough. But I also recalled that I'd have stayed longer at the kibbutz, perhaps skipped a year of college, if I had not gotten a sweet letter from my future wife, my son's eventual mother. I walked faster towards the *Cinematique*. My chest was heaving some, as if I could not get enough air, and I was sweating. Fear did not enter my mind, but something was amiss. A rush of adrenalin? I hardly broke a sweat on morning jogs around Hoan Kiem Lake, nor did my breathing become labored. I was in swell shape for my age. But I soon put the near miss, and Jabotinsky, almost out of mind as Tao crowded in: I was soon to see her again for yet more entertainment.

Tao's father, Pham, looked about five years older than I, which was a depressing realization given that I was charmed by his daughter, who was young enough to be my own. He had a handsome face, though thoroughly lined, mirthful eyes and a wide smile. He was slight, with not an ounce of girth, and he sat with a couple friends who apparently spoke no English round a table in the open courtyard of the *Cinematique*. I could see a source of Tao's agility. He seemed to have already thrown back quite a bit of something alcoholic from a shot glass which he filled repeatedly from a bottle on the table, and I wondered why he simply did not get a bigger glass, but then there was a flourish he seemed to relish in the motion of refill.

Pham spoke not a word of English, too, and it did not matter, for he communicated quite enough without words, stretching his hand across the table repeatedly to shake mine, seeing that Tao had introduced me to him and told him I was from America and that she and I were there to see a film. There was no way to respond but smile back and allow him to shake my hand.

"He comes here on weekends," Tao said.

The courtyard and theater lay well off Hai Ba Trung down an alley. It was private. The traffic quickly became a distant memory, and one had the sense of having arrived at another unusual place in Ha Noi, a fact Tao underscored. "This cinema has some rules."

"Such as?"

"The government forbids money changing hands for seeing foreign movies. The bar here makes up for that."

"Forbids charging?"

"The movies at this theater would probably be censored by the government. We don't buy tickets to the shows. There are only invitations to see them with a suggested donation of about 50,000 Dong."

"Cheap. That makes it four bucks, but that's more than a massage."

"Massage is different. Not censored."

"Well then, what do we get to see here that might otherwise be censored? X rated massages?" I quipped. I could hardly think of anything more boring than that, and probably with some ridiculous music in the background amid sounds of heavy breathing.

"Haha," Tao said. "Not so funny."

"Sorry. I tried to amuse you."

"Try better," Tao said, but I could tell she was not at all offended. She called a waiter over and ordered two glasses of red wine.

I wondered what Tao's father thought of his daughter hanging out late at night with a foreigner not much younger than himself. He gave no hint that he questioned Tao's judgment. Maybe he thought me incapable at my age of interest in Tao as a woman.

Whatever, the wine appeared and Tao seemed eager about a film. "The movie will begin," she said, and she pointed towards a door off the patio that led inside to a small theater. "Bring your drink," she added.

"We can drink alcohol in the film?" I rose, shaking her father's hand for the tenth time. I had counted.

"Yes," Tao said.

"Very nice. This would be rare, as you know, where I come from. We only get stale popcorn and flat sodas at cinemas at home."

"Welcome to Ha Noi!" Tao said. "City of wonders!"

"I should say," I remarked, and we strolled inside.

We found well-cushioned seats up front and settled back. Tao seemed to lean against me, or perhaps it was just my imagination. And by that time the red wine was having a warming effect such that a hundred blind girls and 200 hands massaging me would not have relaxed me as much as that moment with Tao in the theater. "Hey," I whispered, "I don't even know what we are seeing?"

"French movie, old movie I think," Tao said. "It's called 'Claire's Knee'."

"I know this film," I said with surprise. "A well-known French director made it. Eric Rohmer. It was made in the 70s."

"Is it good?"

"It's okay," I said, "but I want you to look at the scenery, the location."

"Why?"

"I think it's one of the nicest places on the planet. Talloires. It's a small village on the shore of Lake Annecy near the French Alps in a region called Haute Savoie. I have been there. The lake is the cleanest in Europe, too. Cezanne even spent some time there painting, too."

"Cezanne?"

"An important French painter some time ago."

"I haven't been to Europe," Tao said. "So, I will look at this place."

"In the film, an older guy is obsessed with the knee of a much younger, pretty woman."

"Sick," said Tao. "But just one knee? Does she have only one?"

I laughed. "I am sure he likes both of them. But it's not sick. It's really about the attractions and friendships of a sophisticated crowd in summer in a lovely place. It's not pornography. It deals with the complications and worries of mid life for this man. You will see."

"I wouldn't know about them," said Tao. "Not there yet."

"But I have been," I remarked. And then Rohmer's film flashed up on the screen.

Tao watched raptly: the calm, blue lake dotted with boats in summer, the lush, grassy shores, Talloires climbing the hillside beyond, hang gliders, what the French called *parapente*, wafting on thermals high above, and so the tale spun languidly along with such as backdrop. I had already seen the film, remembered it. Already I had seen young Claire's knees. There was not much fresh to hold my attention but Tao's immediate proximity and the enforced silence in the theater.

It was a delight to be off the streets, beyond the cacophony and, above all, beside her. And I thought she was deliberately leaning against me. It was like it had been riding on Tao's motorbike, but without any fear of traffic. When the film ended, too soon I felt, and Talloires and Lake Annecy had vanished from sight, it was near midnight. We walked out of the theater. A couple patrons remained sitting at a table on the patio. A bartender was packing booze into a cupboard, apparently closing up. Dead leaves blew around the legs of the tables and over the pavement making a crackling sound, scooped by a stiff, late night breeze.

"Tao, can we sit for a minute and talk some more?" I asked her.

"It's late but okay."

"Not for long," I said. "It's closing time."

"What?" asked Tao, and she took a seat.

"Did you like the film?"

"It was nice scenery. Yes."

"Good. But I am wondering. I didn't get a chance to speak to you and Tung when we left the boat at Ha Long Bay. On the dock, I was looking for you, but you were far ahead of me. And you did not get back on the bus to return to Ha Noi?"

"I was in a hurry," said Tao.

"But I believe I did see you," I said. "I saw you and Tung getting into a big American-made vehicle with some others. Was that a taxi?"

Tao started twisting a bracelet round a wrist and farther up her arm. She was silent for a good half minute, and had cast her glance away from me, staring at the rustling fronds of a palm tree over our heads planted between the flagstones on the patio. Then she answered my question, I thought reluctantly: "No, not a cab. It was a vehicle sent from my ministry."

"Why was that sent? To pick you up?"

"It was pre-arranged," said Tao. "I was not expecting to return on the bus. I had some work to do that afternoon."

"UXO reporting? I saw nothing of that in Ha Long Bay."

"Not your business," said Tao sharply.

"I am sorry," I said. "Don't mean to pry, but you must understand I am an editor and a reporter. It's just natural for me to want to know whatever I can find out. And you know I like you and want to know more about you. Why not?"

"I understand your interests, but you must respect mine even if I cannot tell you everything."

"But you and Tung got in that vehicle with several other people. One of them I met on the boat. You were not on the deck then."

"Who?" Tao asked, with some alarm.

"An Israeli. He said his name was Jabotinsky. We had a conversation. Our views clashed, but then I learned something strikingly coincidental."

"That was?"

"Turns out many years ago, when I was in college, I spent a summer working on a *kibbutz* in Israel. Jabotinsky claimed he was born and grew up there. I might have met him then, decades ago. Isn't that amazing? And in Ha Long Bay, too, to come across him again?"

"Might be," said Tao.

"So do you know this man?"

"No. But I saw him before, too. He was at the ministry where I work a while back. I saw him in the lobby there. I don't know why he was there, but foreigners come and go."

I believed what Tao said.

"So that vehicle came for you and Tung, and then there was Jabotinsky getting the same ride back to Ha Noi, and some others. Who were the others?"

"I don't know. But now we must go. This talk is over," she said with irritation, lifting her handbag violently from her lap and rising fast from her seat.

"Okay. Okay," I conceded. "Sorry to pry," and I meant it, but still I was curious. I followed Tao beyond the patio into the dark alley that extended some 50 meters to the street. Tao's Honda Dream was there parked.

"Would you like a ride to your place?" Tao offered. "To Hang Giay?"

"Would you come in and stay a while? I have some wine."

"Maybe some other time," Tao said, smiling faintly. "I have to go home. It's late."

"Okay," I said, but I was bemused at what she had said. *Some other time.* She had already given me a grand day of *Tet*. She also knew where I lived and I figured she knew she could come by anytime she liked.

"I can drive you home if you like."

"No, but thanks for asking. I will walk," I said. "I guess your father went home some time ago?"

"Yes," Tao said. She started the motorbike, rolled it out of the alley, climbed aboard and sped off. Gone, I thought, gone with the wind. I started out on foot, coming back to Hoan Kiem's shore, but this time walked the west side of the lake through the narrow park between the street and the tamarind trees that lined the water's edge.

Still, there were people out and about, but most of the *Tet* merrymakers had disappeared and it was blissfully quiet. Across the lake, the front facade of the central post office was lit up, its image reflected in the calm lake. The clock on the roof pointed well past midnight. I wondered if it was possible to have such a fine day again in Ha Noi, that due to apparent coincidence: Tao spotting me from her Honda. The sole annoyance had been the near collision with the black SUV in which I had seen Jabotinsky peering out a window backwards at me.

When I reached the apartment building the guard was sitting in his chair behind the gate at the entrance. He was an older man, dressed in stained khaki trousers secured to his waist by length of rope, and a T-shirt. He opened a padlock attached to a chain and let me inside. I did not know his name, but often we had exchanged waves. In the undercroft of the building he had the chair, a very old television and a crude cot to sleep on. When I passed by the television, it was tuned to some local channel, some official report or commentary, and I paused on my way to the stairs to my apartment, because on the blurry screen was a clip of the burning towers of the World Trade Center, 9/11, before they collapsed.

It had been years since, and I could only wonder what commentary accompanied the scene. However, I had read somewhere that in villages around Ha Noi on that day one could have witnessed makeshift rockets of celebration, like the ones I had seen above Hoan Kiem Lake earlier that night in celebration of *Tet*, shooting up into the heavens. And this even while the Vietnamese government was issuing official statements of condemnation for the attack in lower Manhattan and condolences for the victims, not mentioning the fireworks.

Yes, I realized, pity for the victims, because Viets knew what it was like to be bombed. The American War had leveled a quarter of Ha Noi and forced the evacuation of nearly half the population, and the countryside, all over from north to south, had suffered worse. An estimated 20 million bomb craters left behind, more explosive tonnage than had been dropped on all of Europe during World War II, more than 130,000 Viets dead each month during the long war, not to mention many more maimed and wounded. Celebrating 9/11 was as genuine as the condolences for the victims, because the American empire which had devastated Vietnam, and was devastating other Asian lands, was under attack.

9

The magazine was to be titled *Orient&Occident*, but the first edition had not yet come out. The week after *Tet*, I had returned to the routine of the job, the *Vinatabas* with Cain on the stairwell landing, the arguments with Anh over defective copy, Phuc's obtuseness and all the rest, but I detoured one weekday morning on the way to the newspaper across the dike near the shallow bank of the Red River into one of Ha Noi's poorest residential neighborhoods.

I was responding to Tao's suggestion to check out the publication, a suggestion she had reiterated a couple times over the phone since I had seen her at the *Cinematique*. I had hoped she might come by the apartment, but she had not and yet she had me in such a grip of anticipation that I might have swum across Hoan Kiem's slimy green waters if she had challenged me to try with the proffer of some reward.

That suggestion to visit the magazine's offices came tucked in a flurry of communications consisting of scores of text messages on my cell phone at literally any hour. Often, I had been asleep, or trying to sleep, and yet another message would come in with a beep to which I responded like some abject Pavlovian dog. As much as an interruption such untimely messages could be, it also felt flattering and intimate at odd hours, as if -- such was the fantasy -- she could not sleep for thinking of me, unable to stop the maintenance of contact, pushing the momentum of a huge wave of interest upon which I was eagerly surfing.

"Are we having fun yet?" she might write well before dawn, or she might say that her son wanted to play more games with me, recalling the play on the *Emeraude*, or she might write, without setting a time, claiming that we would dine again soon, or whatever. I wondered if she might show up eventually at the apartment at Hang Giay, and I had been reserving a bottle Merlot in the fridge for just that possibility.

However it was, my mood, up or down, was becoming too contingent on the sheer number of messages Tao was sending even if I was not getting sound sleep. They had almost assumed the force of an addictive substance. I usually responded at some length, but she gave little information herself such that I failed to fathom exactly what was driving her to shower me with such attention, even if it was hardly direct. And she was sucking up considerable information, because I had certainly been forthcoming. I told her about my son, other places I had worked in the distant past. I told her about my son's beloved but long departed mother. I told her about my adventures in the West Bank. I told her about home in the Carolinas. Going to the offices of *Orient&Occident* was also something soon to report back to Tao about, grist for further correspondence that included observations and questions about the changes under way in Vietnam.

I had, in any event, called the magazine's offices from work and been invited over by the alleged editor, a woman who introduced herself on the phone as Kristen Andre. She said she was French and I wondered if she had knees almost as shapely as Eric Rohmer's Claire in summery Talloires. She said she might eventually be looking for additional talent to assist with the launch of the publication.

When I reached the office, a three-story house converted to offices at a corner along Bach Dang Street just 200 meters from the Red River, I was pointed upstairs by a young Viet woman to a meeting room with a conference table. There, Andre soon appeared -- a nicely dressed, pretty brunette of 35 or so along with her assistant, whom she introduced as Trang. Trang left the room and Andre asked to look at my resumé. I imagined she might be impressed, but after I handed it to her and she looked it over she dropped the paper on the table like a bit of distinctly bad news.

"I don't think we can use you," she said, "because you'd expect payment. I cannot pay you anything. We are just starting up."

I was a bit put off. She was three decades younger, it appeared, and I had the editorial experience she may never know, experience that commanded some payment.

"I did not primarily come here looking for extra work," I lied. "I am working full-time at *Vietnam News*. But I did want a glimpse at the venture here. Maybe it's newsworthy, or a possible feature in the paper, this new magazine?"

"We don't want publicity. The first edition has not been published."

"So, what's your aim with this magazine?"

"We are hoping to sell dreams," Kristen Andre said flatly.

"Dreams? I thought you wanted to sell a magazine."

"Vietnam is shifting to a market economy," she said, as if she were quoting something she had read somewhere, "and some people are going to become wealthy. The magazine will show them what they might do with their money -- the stuff that dreams are made of."

"And what in your view is the stuff of dreams?" I had to wonder aloud. The stuff of *my* dreams that day involved merely hoping for another day with Tao sometime, anytime.

"We intend to focus on luxury. Luxurious things, luxurious travel destinations, luxurious vacation spas in this part of Asia, luxury gadgets. Even if only a few Vietnamese can afford such right now, there are a growing number of expatriates here who probably can and who will want to know what's going on and where in Vietnam and elsewhere in Southeast Asia," Andre said crisply. "Have I answered your questions?"

"More or less," I said. "Thank you. But does the magazine intend to focus any on serious journalism, social and political matters?"

"One must tread lightly, but I think what we plan to feature may be serious enough."

"You mean the 'luxury'?"

"The good life."

"I haven't quite found that yet," I said. "I still think a feature article in the paper about the magazine might help your launch?"

"Not now, but I will inquire. We don't have a high opinion of the newspaper where you are working."

"Neither do I as far as newspapers go but I'm learning some things about Vietnam there. You are the editor here. Who else might make decisions here?"

And then, my question was answered, for there appeared in the conference room, coming through the door, a tall, slim, olive complexioned man of about 40 attired casually in a cashmere sweater and pleated trousers. He looked vaguely familiar, too.

Around his wrist prominently, I could not help noting, was a gold Breitling aviator's watch with gold band. "Ah," he said in perfect English with a slight accent and a smile, "you must be the man from the Communist newspaper?"

"All the newspapers here are Commie controlled," I said, "but I'm just Marshall McLean, a man without a creed and little more than a sorry job here."

"And I am Marcel Mossadeq."

"You are…" I said, "you might be from the Middle East?"

"My father is Persian, or, if you like, Iranian. My mother is Swiss. I am Swiss by birth and nationality."

"Very good," I said. "I have spent some time in the Middle East, in the Muslim world, so you understand why I wondered. Your name is famous."

"Famous?"

"Might you be related to…."

"There are many with that name in Iran," he responded quickly, "if you were about to mention the Mossadeq who was briefly Iran's Prime Minister in the early 50s before he was deposed in a *coup d'etat* by your CIA." He bent down and reached across the table to pick up the resumé I had brought with me. He took a seat opposite, scanned the document and smiled.

"I like this. You have familiarity with aviation and airplanes?"

"That's just a footnote," I said, "but yes, I have knowledge of the craft."

He had noted at the bottom of the resumé a line that I had a Commercial License for small single and multi-engine aircraft, as well as an Instrument Rating, which allowed me to fly in bad weather.

"I like what you say," he said. "You call flying a craft. Those are my sentiments, but I would go farther. I would call it an art when done well."

"Yes, exactly. I see you are wearing a fine Breitling," I said.

"An excellent chronograph, made for pilots," he said, glancing at the gold timepiece on his wrist.

"I once owned a stainless steel Breitling. So you are a pilot, too?"

"I don't have a license to fly but I have flown a number of planes from the right seat and even simulators of Boeing and Airbus."

"I've been at it off and on for decades," I said.

"I would like to hear more, but unfortunately I do not have the time right now," he said. He looked over again at Andre, the editor, and said: "Why don't you come to our place the day after tomorrow for dinner, say around six. I would like that. We can talk more about our favorite art."

I had been wandering around too much alone in Ha Noi and quickly embraced the invitation to dinner. "So, where do you live?" I asked. "I look forward to it."

"Ngu Xa. Do you know it?"

"Not sure."

"You know Truc Bach Lake?"

"Yes."

"Ngu Xa is the little island in the lake on the east side. Two little bridges, less than ten meters long, connect it to the rest of Ha Noi."

"I might have been by there but I did not know it."

"Ngu Xa village was notable for it's bronze and copper workers, and their artistry, in centuries past, and its several pagodas. Now it is just a relatively quiet residential area but with some places along the shore selling street food like stuffed rice noodles and other simple, but very good, local delicacies," Mossadeq said, evidently proud of his location in Ha Noi. "We have a house there, on Nguyen Khac Hieu, on the corner with Ngu Xa Street."

"A house. That's nice. I just have a small apartment in the Old Quarter and it's noisy all the time."

"We were lucky to find it. We managed to obtain a seven-year lease for $700 a month."

"That's fortunate," I said. "I pay $500 a month for very little, relatively speaking."

"Do come over then," Mossadeq said.

"Thanks," I responded, and realizing the meeting would continue in two days, I got up to leave and asked: "How long have you all been here?"

"Just a few months. I met Kristen last summer in Europe. I asked her what she might want to do if she could do anything she liked, and she said she would start a magazine a Vietnam."

"Why Vietnam?" I asked, turning to Andre.

"An exciting venture here at this time," she said.

"Of course." I might have added that I thought the entire idea of meeting a lovely French woman -- a sturdy Gaul with a fine face, brunette hair, slim legs and blue eyes -- and hitting it off with her and soon leaving Europe for Vietnam to start a magazine, and finding a house in Ngu Xa, seemed romantic and serendipitous. But they were young, far younger than I, and youth had its advantages. So did the easy presumption that Mossadeq had some money. Starting up what was aimed to be a slick publication was not exactly cheap, although they were doing it as cheaply as possible, angling for free editorial talent.

The elderly Vietnamese lady had said nothing during the meeting, but I imagined she also was an investor in the magazine unless she was merely a censor the government had sent over to keep an eye on the publication. Whatever, I was curious to know more about this Marcel Mossadeq. I envied anyone's Swiss citizenship. His was not a modern country that started wars or joined them. I had harbored fantasies of living in a lake villa at Interlaken or Lucerne and riding a real motorcycle, a BMW, not some shrill Japanese motorbike like Tao's, around the Swiss Alps.

I headed out of the offices of the magazine towards Tran Hung Dao and the newspaper early that Friday afternoon. It occurred to me that I may have seen Marcel before, but I could not place when or where. I looked forward to the prospect of dinner in Ngu Xa with apparently sophisticated Europeans. When I arrived at the newsroom, I found Cain pacing the stairwell landing and looking rather agitated.

"Good to see you, mate," he said.

"You look a bit nervous. What's happening?"

"Same shit," he said. "Defective copy, but I had a row with Phuc about it. Page One story, too, they wanted me to edit."

"Did you do it?"

"I refused. And it wasn't because it was a garbled translation, either. The content was the problem."

"So what happened?"

"Anh was pissed and went over to Phuc and bitched. I suppose she told him I had refused to do the job."

"So Phuc came at you?"

I could easily see it. Phuc dropping his half moon spectacles on his desk, or pushing them father up towards the bridge of his nose, rising from his seat and sliding like a small snake, but one with a smile, that ever-present smile of rectitude and certainty without a hint of warmth.

"Yeah," said Cain, "he came over to my desk. He had the copy in one of his hands and he was flapping it about like a live fish. He stands in front of me and drops it down in front of my terminal and says I must edit it, sign off on it, my responsibility."

"And you refused again?"

"Yeah, mate. I looked him right in the eye and told him I would not do it. Then he said I was fired. I told him well if I was fired I would just leave right then, but there was a lot of unedited stuff laying around."

"Then what?"

"He backed off. He said he would *think* about firing me. He wants to but they need us, you know, or else the paper would be unreadable. Anyway, the newsroom got quieter than I imagine it's ever been. I came out for a smoke. Actually, several so far," Cain said, and the butts lay stomped out cold on the landing.

"What was so offensive in the content?"

Cain pulled crumpled copy from his back pocket. "Here it is. It's bullshit."

"Let me get to my terminal. I'll take a look."

"How'd it go the other night with the Tao lady at the film? You've not reported to me on that. Good time?" Cain asked.

"It was cozy, I thought. Ever since then I've been getting non-stop text messages on my cell phone from her. I mean, at all hours."

"Very good. Close the deal, mate. Tell her to come over to your apartment, that you need a translation of something that's in Vietnamese. Something you need right away. Tell her anything, but get her over."

"I did suggest she stop by, but she hasn't."

"She's what, 30 or something? That's almost old around here. Go for it, mate."

"Maybe she's just trouble."

"She may be fun trouble," Cain said. "There's trouble-trouble and then there's trouble that's worth the trouble."

"Yeah, maybe. She knows her way around, like it's almost her city here, like she owns it. Want to go back in?" I asked, changing the focus.

"I guess we have to," said Cain, flipping another cigarette butt onto the landing.

We walked up the half flight of stairs and turned the corner into the newsroom. Phuc was at his desk, still smiling. He ignored us but most of the young ladies looked our way, or at Cain, and he raised an arm with his fingers spread into a V and flashed a grin. It went unreciprocated. The Viets wanted to keep a low profile, which meant keeping their jobs, and I couldn't blame them because they had coveted jobs for Vietnamese, despite the paltry pay. I went on to my terminal and took a look at the copy Cain had handed me.

My first thought was of Leon Trotsky. Trotsky telling the Mensheviks that they were headed for the "dustbin of history" because, somewhat like Cain, I imagined that could be where the old Communists and their younger minions in Vietnam were headed. Cain was right to refuse the copy, for which a headline had already been written, that the "nation" was in "deep reflection" about the Bolshevik's October Revolution in 1917 and about its impact on "development" in Vietnam and elsewhere. The entire "nation" in "deep reflection"? As far as I could tell, many Vietnamese reflected mostly about getting their hands on a motorbike, or if they already had one, they dreamt of a car and further material enhancements.

One could not blame the People for wanting to better their material lives, but the Communist Party leaders in Vietnam sweepingly called the past revolution a new era of development for mankind, an absurdity since the only real development for centuries had been merely technological. Human nature had not changed. Worse, the Party stated unequivocally in the story that the economic gains under way (in my view reflected by the burgeoning motorbike population) almost 90 years since the Soviet revolution in Russia were the direct result of Communist Party rule in Vietnam. Balderdash. Rather, it was more like the fact that Vietnam still had about the cheapest labor pool in Asia, a dollar a day factory jobs, and remained a relatively poor country. The exploitation of cheap labor by multinational corporations joined with state-owned enterprises had merely boosted GDP from an extremely low base. But the worst part of it remained that I had been working for a paper rigged to Party rhetoric. Phuc was not about to become a serious editor and threaten his own livelihood.

Set before a variety of palms and other tropical flora in a park near the Army Museum in Ha Noi, facing the street, stood a statue almost four meters high of Vladimir Ilyich Lenin, dressed in an unbuttoned frock coat, his chest jutting forward, his visage stern, very unlike the usual image of fellow Leninist Ho Chi Minh, whose images radiated the kind of warmth and good cheer one hopes uncles would. It was the sole public memorial to the old Bolshevik,

Lenin, in the city that I knew of, and I had passed by there many times, often in a cab in the middle of some past day when around the walkways leading into the park a few Vietnamese might be exercising or strolling about. It had not been desecrated, toppled or destroyed like so many other statues of Lenin around the world when the Soviet Union disintegrated some ten years earlier. After work, late, when the piece about the October Revolution that Cain wanted to desecrate was about to be printed on Page One of the newspaper, I walked a longer route back to Hang Giay and stopped by Lenin's feet.

The small park seemed emptied out but for innumerable bats foraging about in near darkness, and I might have kept going but took a seat on the stone pedestal under the statue. Aside from Lenin, I was thinking of Tao, that I had not actually spoken to her since seeing a bit of Talloires on the screen at the *Cinematique*. There had been maybe a hundred text messages of little substance, mostly vague words aimed at drawing me out. I figured if she did not want to talk, she'd simply see that I was calling and not answer, and I was a bit surprised when she did. But Tao seemed not to keep regular hours, at least not regular sleeping hours.

"Where ARE you," she said in a husky voice, as if to suggest vaguely that she would fly to meet me as swiftly as the bats were apparently scooping insects into their tiny, nasty jaws. The action reminded me of the vile lizard I had spotted on the steps near the portico of the mosque Anh at the café had given me directions to.

"I'm communing with Vladimir right now. Stopping on the way back to the apartment."

"Is that a new friend?"

"Hardly. He's about twice my height and frozen in a pose of immortal, maybe immoral, rectitude. He can't converse."

Tao was silent for a few seconds. "Who is this Vladimir?" she blurted.

"Come on, Tao, surely you must know!"

"No, I know no Vladimir."

"LENIN," I said. "The fellow who led the Communist Revolution in Russia almost a century ago. The idol of the Vietnamese Communist Party, aside from Bac Ho Chi Minh."

"Then you must be..."

"Yes," I said, knowing how well she knew her city, "I'm in front of the Army Museum in the park under Lenin's statue."

"I was thinking so."

"I just took a much longer way back to Hang Giay from Tran Hung Dao and work. I wanted to see Lenin up close. Confer with him a bit about how he'd have done less damage had he simply retired to a monastery in his youth."

"He was an inspiration," said Tao.

"Have you ever read anything he wrote?"

"No."

"Then how do you know he was inspiring? How could he have inspired you?"

"Because my government says he was an inspiration."

"So you take that for Gospel truth?"

"I believe," said Tao.

"Well, perhaps he was an inspiration. If you are speaking of carnage and mayhem."

I was then in no particular mood to humor her. Somewhere at the margin of my feelings lingered the memory of her getting in that SUV with Jabotinsky, her unwillingness to ride back on the bus with Williams and me and the other merrymakers just departed the *Emeraude*. As for Jabotinsky, he already had two strikes against him: his right wing, murderous, xenophobic ideology and the fact that the SUV in which he was riding had almost flattened me like, I recalled, young American Rachel Corrie was literally flattened into the sands of Gaza by a Caterpillar D9 bulldozer used primarily for flattening Palestinian homes.

"Are you having fun?" Tao asked in a tone far less playful than I imagined she had in text messages on my phone. She was ignoring my comment about Lenin.

"I would not call it fun, but it's relatively quiet here at this hour and that's a good thing because I especially did not like work tonight."

"O," Tao said, evidently at a sudden and unusual loss for words. "Why are you calling?"

"I was thinking I need someone to go to dinner with me the day after tomorrow. A couple has invited me to dinner and I think you might enjoy meeting them."

"What couple is this?"

"One is a French woman just a bit older than you and the other is a Swiss fellow. They live together, it seems. They are the two who are starting the magazine, *Orient&Occident*, which you suggested I check out. I went by there today before work, by their office, over near where you live I think and met them. They invited me to dinner."

"I knew that," Tao said. "Yes, I will join you for dinner with them," she added without any hesitation.

"How did you know that?" I was immediately compelled to ask. I was also surprised she had so readily accepted my invitation.

Tao uncharacteristically stammered a bit and avoided my question. "I think you must be a good editor. Maybe they *should* know you."

Her flattery made me forget any inclination I had to question immediately the source of her prescience.

"So where do we go and when exactly?" she asked.

"They live at 38 Nguyen Khac Hieu, Truc Bach. I think around six we should be there. Do you know where that street is?"

"I know where everything is in Ha Noi," said Tao.

"That gives me confidence here."

"Nice," Tao said.

"What do you say to picking me up at Hang Giay on the Honda? I can be outside."

"That is okay," Tao said.

"We should bring some wine."

"Fivimart is on the way. We can get a bottle there. It's near Nguyen Khac Hieu, just opposite across Truc Bach Lake."

I had passed through Fivimart before, unimpressed but still buying a few essentials for the apartment. Staples were available there, even some wine and hard liquor, but if it was Vietnam's answer to a copy of a Western grocery, the answer was poor.

The litmus test at Fivimart was in the checkout line where teens behind cash registers took an interminable amount of time entering the prices of items on the registers by hand, punch by punch. Scanning items was out of the question. Geared towards expats, high prices prevailed, but for those living nearby in the more upscale housing around Truc Bach and West Lake, there was no convenient alternative with equivalent numbers of offerings.

"I know," I told Tao. "So I'll be outside my building on Hang Giay Sunday evening at 5:45. That okay?"

"OK," said Tao. "Enjoying Lenin?" she asked.

"Not much going on here in the dark. Lots of foraging bats, though. Lenin remains mute."

"I am not far from Hang Giay," Tao said suddenly.

"What are *you* doing out this late?"

"An errand. Tung is asleep. My father is home with him."

"An errand at this hour?"

"I had to leave something at my workplace."

"Open at this hour?"

"It's always open," said Tao. "So we have firm plans to meet this couple and find out about the magazine, over dinner?"

"We just made the plan," I said. "Yes."

"How far are you from your apartment?" Tao asked.

"You should know, but anyway ten minutes, maybe fifteen. I'm on foot," I said.

"Then I shall meet you outside your building."

"Really?"

"Yes," Tao said. "If you walk fast."

"Fine," I said and closed the connection.

I left Lenin and headed at a faster than usual pace back towards the apartment. The air felt heavy, and along the shore of Truc Bach Lake, it smelled sweet and putrid at the same time, like a rotting corpse, or dead fish on the sidewalk, or something. Perhaps I just noticed the smell because at the hour there were far fewer motorbikes on the streets to provide some cover with their exhaust. I noticed in passing a dark figure squatting on the stone embankment -- a man taking a public shit, his trousers bunched around his feet and ankles. I thought that whatever decorum existed anywhere, it was just a veneer, and awfully thin at that, like a diaphanous shroud that easily fell apart to reveal something raw, if not gross.

But Tao had been decent on the phone, and in a few minutes I might see her, and my mood was improving. Still, I was a bit surprised that she "knew" somehow about the dinner invitation, or had suggested she might, before I told her about it and invited her to come along. Also, that surprise set me to wondering what lay behind the attention she had showered on me over the previous days -- so many messages, all with so little real content, so little real information about her whereabouts or activities, that it seemed like she might have been thinking of little more than just maintaining contact. I had no clear answers. I wondered if she was simply enthralled by the new friendship, or whatever, we had started aboard the *Emeraude*. I could not dismiss this possibility. I valued friendships as the least conflicted of connections. Perhaps she just wanted to push our friendship along a bit farther.

Back on Hang Giay around midnight the shop fronts along the street stood locked down and dark. But there, in front of my building, was Tao. Already she had pulled her Honda onto the sidewalk and shut off the engine, and was sitting sideways on the seat.

"Hello, Marshall," she said warmly when she spied me.

"Surprised to see you. This is the first time I've come back from work late and found someone to greet me."

"Do you like it?"

"I like it that you are here. Will you come in?"

"For a bit," said Tao.

"Come along, then," I said, and she followed me into the undercroft of the apartment building after the guard unlocked the gate and then up two flights of stairs to my door. There, I discovered, to some surprise, the door very slightly ajar, unlocked. I was sure I had never left the apartment without locking the door, unless I was to go out for a minute to stuff some laundry into a washing machine in the undercroft where residents kept their motorbikes parked and where the guard lived.

"This is odd," I said, putting my keys back in a pocket.

"What?"

"That the door is unlocked."

"You just forgot to lock it," said Tao.

"I don't think so."

We went inside and I quickly took a look around. Nothing seemed to have been disturbed. Even so, I'd have been disturbed, except that my thoughts were on Tao. She unwrapped a scarf from her neck and flung it on to the sofa. Her presence in the apartment gave the place a notable energy I had not until then discovered there.

"I am sorry for the humble lodging, but it is shelter, a place to sleep at least."

"My place is humble, too, but much larger, for Tung and my father," Tao said, not seeming to mind.

"What will you have? I have some red wine in the fridge. Will that do?"

"Fine," said Tao. And then she went to the sofa, dropped her shoes and sat, putting her feet on the low table in front of the sofa.

"You look just as you did when I first saw you, on the *Emeraude*," I said.

"How so?"

"You were sitting in a wicker chair then and your feet were up on a table. You seemed relaxed, as now."

"I was and I am, sort of."

"Ha," I laughed. "I don't suppose you are still wearing that blue bikini."

"No, of course not. Nothing."

"Nothing?"

"I mean, nothing under the clothes you see," Tao said with a grin. I moved to the kitchen to get the bottle of wine and a couple tumblers. Her comment seemed something I needed to digest, but without any uncomfortable indigestion.

"I am assuming you might want some wine? All I have is red," I called to her from the kitchen and uncorked the bottle.

"Good," Tao said.

Back in my living room, such as it was, I put the tumblers on the table and realized I had no place to sit but on the same sofa with her. The apartment was sparsely furnished: the bed in a room beyond the kitchen farther back, the living room with just the sofa and low table and a wooden chair that was coming apart. Tao slid over a bit and I took a seat beside her. We sipped the wine. I was feeling a bit awkward, but nonetheless, she was there. "You said you were just 'sort of' relaxed."

"My neck is sore. Riding the Honda makes it so. Would you massage it?"

The answer was clear, but I did not vocalize. I began massaging her neck and she turned so I could also massage her shoulders. She leaned back farther towards me and I kept on, kneading her neck and shoulders with mild pressure. This went on for a couple of minutes. "You are a bit tight," I said.

"But I am already feeling better," said Tao, and then she turned around completely, looked me straight in the eyes and said: "I don't have a long time to stay. It's late, but would you like a quick massage? I might even do it better than the blind girl."

"Okay," I said, and turned my back to her.

"No," Tao said. "Lie down. You will like that more."

"Where?"

"Here, on the sofa," she said, and stood up.

I lay on my stomach on the couch and she swiftly sat on me, straddled across my thighs. Her weight was pleasing, and like the blind girl, began rubbing and massaging my back, and after a couple minutes she began lifting my shirt to my shoulders. Nothing but those fine, strong, hands of hers -- hands as fine as her feet -- on my flesh.

"Do you like this?" she asked in a playful tone.

"Yes. You should let me do you this way," I said.

"No. This is for you," and then she reached under my stomach and slid a hand inside my trousers. I tried to get up, pointing, to indicate that perhaps we ought to go into the bedroom. Tao, with her other hand, pushed me back into the sofa. "Would you like another sip of wine before I proceed?"

"Why not," I said, and she handed me one of the tumblers. I emptied the glass. Evidently, the manipulation was not to be a mutual affair, and she had moved so quickly.

The last thing I heard from her was: "Are we having fun yet?" I had read the same words before, on some text message.

I imagined I must have at least muttered that I was "having fun" given where her hand was moving around, but her words was all I remembered. Next thing I knew I was still laying on the sofa, but under the blanket that I had been using in the bedroom. It was some six hours later, still dark outside, around five in the morning. The apartment was dark, too, and the door was shut and Tao was gone. I also had a bad headache and I was puzzled, wondering how I could possibly have fallen asleep with Tao there and she doing what she was doing. The bottle of wine was on the table beside the couch. I picked it up and put my nose where the cork had been, wondering if it was bad wine, wondering if something had mistakenly been added to it by the bottler, something soporific. No, it only smelt like wine does. For half a second I even wondered if Tao had dropped poison in my wine, but this did not seem like something she would have done and I dismissed the thought. My age, or aging, I imagined; that was the reason I had fallen into deep sleep, but it was the first time anything like that -- in circumstances like that -- such a critical misfortune had ever befallen me. Even though I very much wanted to see Tao again, and would shortly, I knew I was going to feel some embarrassment.

10

Marcel Mossadeq had the French editor, Kristen Andre, for company in the large house they occupied together 100 meters back from Truc Bach Lake on Nguyen Khac Hieu Street. It was a decent place to live: a relatively quiet neighborhood and the house of three stories, each floor sparsely furnished, but everything clean and tidy, and on the roof, a tiled patio under an awning and comfortable chairs, a wet bar and something of a view between other houses to the lake, which was fast becoming a dark blotch rimmed by street lights and traffic around the far shore just a kilometer away.

Marcel opened the door when Tao and I showed up after we had bought a bottle of wine at Fivimart. He was dressed in a white shirt and tan trousers. His dark, short hair, peppered with gray, was brushed back, rather shiny, perhaps anointed with some kind of hairdressing. Kristen Andre was in the first floor kitchen preparing dinner. She appeared in the doorway to the kitchen and seem about to utter a greeting, but when she saw Tao she just waved her hand and turned back into the kitchen without a word.

"This is Tao," I said, introducing her to Marcel. He looked her over thoroughly, and perhaps pleased with what he saw, he smiled broadly, shook her hand and urged us up three flights of stairs to the rooftop patio. Tao, light on her feet as usual, almost bounded up the steps, looking around as she ascended. Reaching the roof, I said to Marcel: "I met Tao on the *Emeraude* in Ha Long Bay a while back."

"And Tao, you are from Ha Noi?" asked Marcel.

"Yes," said Tao. "But I was born in the north, near China."

"She's been around," I offered, trying to make a point that she was no ordinary young Vietnamese woman, "but she comes from a place called Ha Giang."

"I don't know it," said Marcel.

"Most foreigners don't. It's a provincial town far away in the north," said Tao.

"A pleasant backwater by the Lo River," I offered.

At that moment, however, I was thinking of Anh and the Maitre Café on Hang Giay near the apartment. Tao had come on her Honda to pick me up a half hour earlier. I had been waiting outside on the sidewalk, and after I had seated myself behind Tao on the bike, she sped off into the traffic, passing by Anh's café.

Anh was outside wiping tables, and though I wished she had not, she looked up just as Tao and I passed. Our eyes met for a couple seconds and I could do nothing but wave, but she did not return the wave: her eyes followed us as we passed. Of course I had no need to explain myself, and riding the back of Tao's Honda looked innocent enough, but still, I wondered what to say to Anh the next time I went by her café for coffee. She had only seen me alone before. Perhaps, I wondered, Anh might think of me like she could easily think of many Western men who came to Ha Noi: out for a good time with a much younger female. But I had not expected any such thing, nor was such directly sought, except that Tao had appeared on several occasions not summoned and had tried once to give me a "good time", which I could not recall but for a few minutes, and then waking up hours later in the dark in more ways than one and finding her gone from the apartment.

I had seen ragged Western geezers sitting on benches around Hoan Kiem Lake with attractive young girls, and the girls acting like they had fallen impossibly in love. I had long determined not to be or be seen as such. Unlike Tao, I doubted Anh had ever been more than 50 kilometers from Ha Noi. But, oddly enough, I felt befriending her was tantamount to befriending all of Vietnam, which was not something I could say exactly about befriending Tao, who was some kind of hybrid persona in a still poor, largely peasant country. She had spent months in Washington and absorbed knowledge of the West that was far out of Anh's reach. It seemed that through Anh I might get a sense of the entire country's fundamental spirit, and through Tao, just Ha Noi's.

"Tao's spent time in the US," I said to Marcel as we turned out onto the rooftop patio.

Marcel went immediately to the bar and poured himself a tumbler of Johnnie Walker Red Label, throwing in some ice cubes from a bucket. He turned around and looked directly at Tao, flashing a smile. I was almost sure he was wondering what she was doing with me. I was almost twice her age. "What will you have?" he asked Tao.

"I will have a gin and tonic," I said.

Marcel ignored me and asked Tao again: "What will you have? Ladies first."

"Red wine?" asked Tao.

"Of course, a fine Bordeaux," said Marcel, grabbing an uncorked bottle and pouring a glass for Tao. He then prepared my drink. "So what were you doing in the Great Satan?"

"I studied for several months in Washington."

"What?"

"International relations. My government sent me. I was offered a kind of scholarship, but it was mostly to get proficient in English."

"And now? Do you work?"

"The government calls on me to do something sometimes."

"So you know Party leaders?" Marcel asked. "They show up at Vines for lunch and rack up big bills."

"I know some important people," Tao said evasively.

"She's a mother, too," I interjected. "She's got a son. But Marcel, you said 'Great Satan'?"

"I am sure you know that is what Iranians and some Arabs may call the United States."

"I know. Do you believe that?"

"Who else is so much focused on military action in the world now: the US first and then Israel, it would seem?"

"It would seem," I said.

Marcel took a seat on a sofa opposite Tao and pulled a pack of Marlboro Lights from his pocket. He lit a cigarette and inhaled deeply, leaning forward in the chair towards Tao. "This is very nice, no?"

"Very nice," she responded.

"Quite a place to live in here in Ha Noi," I said.

"Kristen found it," said Marcel. He could not take his eyes off Tao, but he spoke to me. The two of them had hit it off, I thought, and I had mixed feelings about that.

"So you must be excited about the magazine?" I asked.

"Quite," said Marcel.

"And what kind of articles are on tap?"

"A full range, eventually. The magazine will feature stories about art and artists in Vietnam and Southeast Asia. There will be travel stories. Pieces about the new resorts and spas in Asia. It will have calendars detailing what's going on in Ha Noi and Ho Chi Minh City and elsewhere. The best places to shop. The latest gadgets to buy. We will also feature photographers' work from this region. Interviews, too. Maybe we will eventually feature critical stories about the situation in Vietnam."

"That's quite a lot. The situation in Nam?"

"Problems here. Social, political."

"That I'd be curious about," I said.

"But we have to establish ourselves first," said Marcel. "I myself will have a couple stories in the first edition."

"Are you getting advertisers? I should hope so."

"We are courting luxury brands and stores. Rolex, Omega, even Louis Vuitton, which you may know has a shop at the Metropole Hotel here in Ha Noi. Airlines. Resorts. And many more like that. High end."

"I wish you luck," I said. "You should talk to Donald Berger at Vines restaurant. I'm sure he would advertise."

"I know Donald Berger. He may contribute articles about some of the good wines he stocks."

"You must have some background in journalism," I suggested.

"On the contrary, I have none but Kristen as advisor and editor. I am mostly in a marketing role."

"Well, what exactly is your background?" Tao asked Marcel.

"It is complex. I have been a banker in Europe. I was one of a few directors of a prominent investment bank based in London where I focused on the financial needs of some Eastern European and Central Asian countries, among other things."

"Are you still involved with banking?"

"Marginally. But I don't want to get into that right now," said Marcel.

"Your father is the Iranian?" asked Tao.

"Yes, but he has died."

"Muslim?" I asked.

"Of course, but Shi'a of a special order, unlike most all Iranians. He was Ismaili. I am not religious myself. I have little if any personal identification with anything religious."

"I don't know anything about Shiites," said Tao.

"The Ismailis are interesting, historically anyway," I offered. "But there is a coincidence here. An American friend of mine in Saigon whom Tao has met e-mailed me a photo of a large emerald upon which some Arabic was etched and asked me to translate it. It turned out to be an invocation of a blessing upon Ja'afar as-Sadiq. Ever heard of him?" I asked Marcel.

"Eighth century, I believe," said Marcel. "There's probably not one Westerner in a half million who knows anything of him."

"Precisely. What else do you know about Ja'afar?"

"Not much, except that he was an important Shi'a Imam. I believe he was the sixth in the line."

"That's right. But the question in the eighth century was over the seventh Imam. Ja'afar apparently had a son, Ismail, who predeceased him, and another son, Musa al-Kazim. The Ismailis accepted Ismail, even though he was gone, as the seventh Imam, while other Shiites accepted Musa. So there was a split in the Shi'a community that prevails to this day. But it is all very complicated historically, and there are other Shi'a sects, too," I said. "Most interesting, though, is the fact that a branch of the Ismailis were the first organized terrorist group, both in Iran and Syria, back before the Mongol conquests in West Asia. The Mongols destroyed the Ismailis in both Persia and Syria."

"Ah yes," said Marcel. "The amazing Assassins!"

"Right. Their leaders would send out real assassins from remote castles they inhabited, one in particular in what is now Iran, called Alamut, and another at Masyaf in Syria," I said to Tao. "They wielded poisoned daggers, I have read. They killed a lot of Sunni notables and even some Christian Crusaders. They were much feared at the time because they did not fear death themselves. They had been promised Paradise and believed in it."

"Paradise? I don't believe in that," said Tao.

"Well, I did read that Alamut had all the elements of what a human paradise might be like. Splendid gardens, flowing water, nubile virgins soon to lose virginity, food delicacies of all sorts, fruits, luxury. Young men were brought there and had a taste of it, then they were taken before the leader at Alamut, one Hassan Sabbah, and told that if they went on some mission to kill a political figure, even if they died in the effort, they would wind up in such a place as fine as Alamut -- Paradise. A bit of hashish was persuasive, too. That's where the word "assassin" comes from originally -- hashshisheen, referring to the assassins."

"Ismailis still exist, too," added Marcel. "Maybe 20 million scattered around the world now. They consider the head of their community the Aga Khan. My father knew the Aga Khan, Prince Karim Hussaini. The Aga Khan is head of an organization that dispenses many millions to poor people in Central Asia and Africa annually through various projects, health and education oriented. Much assistance has recently gone to Afghanistan."

"Some of his children went to Ivy League universities in the US," I said to Tao, recalling something I had read about the Aga Khan's family in the distant past.

"But enough of this," said Marcel as Kristen Andre appeared on the patio. "I am hungry." She had prepared plates for each of us: steak and vegetables. She handed us the plates but did not sit down with us. And she said nothing. I suspected some kind of disagreement between Marcel and her. Aside from preparing dinner, she was not engaged, it seemed. We moved on to a discussion of aviation, a topic of shared interest of Marcel's and mine.

"What have you flown?" he asked.

"I few years ago I was often flying a Mooney, a small single engine plane with a retractable gear," I said. "I owned it for a while with another pilot and put about 1500 hours on it, flying all over the US, parts of Canada and even the Bahamas." I pulled out my cell phone in which I had lodged some photos. One was taken over the Hudson River above the World Trade Center complex. I showed it to Marcel. My son, then a college student, had taken the picture.

"When was this?" he asked pointedly.

"About a year before 9/11," I said.

"Great shot," Marcel said. He ran downstairs and came back with a laptop computer. With a few clicks he had a video on the screen of what he said was the latest Russian Sukhoi fighter. It was doing impossible loops and sudden, dramatic turns at startling angles of attack.

"That Sukhoi warplane is still in development," Marcel said. And then he added after a pause: "I know the owner of a bank in Moscow which helped the government finance the development of this aircraft. I am invited sometime next year to a military airfield in Russia to fly this airplane."

"Fly it? Yourself?"

"From the backseat, with a test pilot in front," Marcel said, as if he were talking about nothing more than a ride on a *xeom*. "Russian fighters don't have the advanced electronic and computer technology of American warplanes, but this gives them an advantage sometimes. They are tougher, less dependent on fallible computer chips."

The prospect of anyone getting a ride in the latest Russian Sukhoi impressed me. Just 40 or so, he seemed by this assertion alone to be as well connected as anyone I had met, if he could be believed. He gave off an air of such sophistication that it almost seemed a bit surreal as the evening at the house in Ngu Xa progressed.

After a while, I again brought up the topic of Islam, because the more exposure I had that evening to Marcel, the vague notion that perhaps I had seen him before the meeting at the magazine's offices, returned. It occurred to me that someone whom I had glimpsed for an instant had certainly looked like Marcel: this was the crisply attired man who had entered the mosque courtyard on Hang Luoc during my only visit there after Anh had pointed the way from her café.

"Marcel," I asked, "you say you are not religious? Not a Muslim, or at least not an Ismaili Shi'a Muslim like your father?"

Marcel laughed. "Never."

"Have you ever been to the mosque on Hang Luoc Street?"

"I have stopped by there," Marcel answered, but then changed the topic. "So you have been at *Vietnam News*?"

"Yes, as you know."

"What do you think of it?"

"Not much," I said.

"I agree."

"There are stories sometimes about some official getting caught doing something wrong. Getting sent off to hard labor for a spell," I said. "But it's not really reporting the news exactly. It's more like some kind of warning, on the one hand, and on the other, an effort to convince Western readers that Vietnam is a safe place to invest."

"That is minor, however widespread it may actually be," said Marcel.

"Minor? Explain."

At this point Tao, I noticed, was especially alert, on the edge of her seat, and looking hard at Marcel.

"I have heard recently," said Marcel, "that the wife of a one of the highest officials in the Communist Party was in Hong Kong recently with her husband on a visit and she bought herself a couple million dollars or so worth of raw diamonds. He has no obvious source for such spending. He is a long longtime Communist in the highest levels of the Party. I can tell you no more except that I believe it is a fact."

"Who is this?" I asked.

"I am sorry, I promised the source who works in the Swiss embassy. And even he gave me no specific name. You must simply understand that this sort of thing is what is occasionally going on here in Vietnam. Some at the top are skimming off whatever they can, but giving the impression to the People they are clean. This while the average Vietnamese is abandoning traditions, their former livelihoods, however meager, in the villages and rice fields, to embrace the false promise of work in sweatshops and factories. A couple years of that and maybe they can own a motorbike and a mobile phone and they think they have made it. But they will get no farther in most cases."

"And why do you think not?"

"Because the serious gains are largely accruing to the Party leaders. They are like rapacious CEO's, but these people have no real hand in business management. The Party's prime aim is simply to perpetuate itself and maintain control. Control is rewarding."

"Might I suggest that you consider an expose in the new magazine if you can nail the story down?"

"We cannot rock the boat initially or we will be out of business before we are even *in* business. Maybe in time we can address such matters as I've suggested."

"Well, Tao, what do you think of this?" I asked her.

"I am uncomfortable with this discussion," Tao said flatly, wincing. She had been picking at the food on the plate in her lap, and when she spoke she demonstrably dropped her fork onto the china and barely said another word for the next fifteen minutes while I spoke with Marcel more about flying. Afterwards, Tao and I bid Mossadeq and Andre adieu.

After we left I was trying to figure how or if Marcel and I might become real friends. I did not expect to make much headway with Kristen Andre who, aside from preparing dinner, had remained aloof and almost seemed relieved when we left. If Marcel had been of like mind, he at least had been courteous enough not to show it. Tao and I sputtered us off towards Hang Giay and the Old Quarter on her motorbike and when we got there she motioned for me to get off quickly.

"Did you not have a nice time?" I asked.

"Nice time," Tao said like a faint echo.

"What's bothering you?"

"What he said."

"Who? Marcel?"

"Yes," said Tao.

"Said about what?"

"That story about diamonds. I don't believe it."

"He said his source was good. One might trust the Swiss."

"My country has come a long way."

"I don't dispute what you say, relatively speaking. But anywhere you go, there are always a few bad apples proclaiming one thing and doing another."

I had stated such an obvious, general truth that any challenge was absurd, whatever the veracity of Marcel's report, and Tao, astride the idling Honda on relatively empty Hang Giay, seemed irritated.

"Maybe we should discuss this further. Care to come up?" I truly did want another massage: her hands on me and mine on her. And I was not going to drink anything beforehand.

"No," said Tao. "I must go home. Tung is there."

Whatever Tung's needs, if any but sleep at that hour, I could not fathom, but I knew she did not want to revisit the apartment. She seemed eager to move along. But I had to query her further, because I had been quite confused about what had happened earlier and was trying to discern what it meant, and had until then said nothing about it. Also, I was gravely, if marginally, embarrassed, for I had almost inexplicably fallen asleep at the very moment when I ought to be been aroused and very much awake.

"I'm confused," I admitted. "What happened the other night? You were, ah, giving me a rather close massage. I remember the first part of that, and then the next thing I knew, hours later, as if I had awaken from a coma, you were gone."

"It is as you know. I was giving you a massage," said Tao slowly, with an air of carefully choosing her words. "But you fell asleep, and I left you to your sleep. You began snoring, too," she claimed.

"No one ever told me I'm a snorer. That's awful news."

Embarrassment was acute. *Snoring*. Snoring like an old man I was, or was becoming, which was not what I wanted Tao to perceive me as. Though I had not expected the kind of attention she had given me, nor had explicitly asked for it, and could only recall a couple minutes of pleasure while she was fondling me on the sofa and sitting astride my legs, the fact that I had apparently done nothing but fall asleep seemed like something I had to expiate for. I felt I had lost her even while I knew I had never had her.

"I am sorry," I said.

"What? That you went to sleep?" Tao asked.

"That I fell asleep, as you claim, with you giving me a massage like that."

"It's okay," Tao said. "I wanted to comfort you. I think I did. You slept!"

"But I did not get an opportunity to return the favor."

"I did not want you to then," said Tao. "And anyway, you did take the soreness from my neck and shoulders."

"I hope so."

"You did and that was that. I wanted nothing more for myself."

"That was then," I said. "But what about now?"

"I like you, Marshall," Tao said.

"Then will you come inside again?"

"Now, I cannot."

"I am sorry about Marcel Mossadeq, too. He upset you, I think."

"I must go," said Tao. She did not bother to say anything more about Marcel's allegations pointing at high-level corruption in her government.

"But I hope we can plan to meet again," I muttered wistfully.

"Perhaps," Tao said, and before I could speak again she twisted the throttle and was off, disappearing around the corner on towards the Red River.

I could not blame her for being a bit angry about Marcel's story. All her life the alleged rectitude of the regime had to have been drummed into her, even by the blaring loudspeakers that hung on utility posts at almost every corner of Ha Noi. And then there was Bac Ho's example, and as I walked up the steps to the apartment, I recalled that Ho Chi Minh had said to the Americans a few years before his death, and several years before the war ended, that he would spread a red carpet for the US to leave Vietnam upon, and he added that once the occupiers left he would invite them back because an independent Vietnam would need American assistance.

Indeed, in the late 1940s Bac Ho had sought American assistance and extended his hand to America, but was rebuffed. I did wonder what exactly he meant by a red carpet. Did he mean one soaked in blood? In any event, in April 1975 when the last swarms of American helicopters were airlifting frightened personnel from Saigon and elsewhere in the south to ships offshore, the American pilots noted on their radar equipment in their cockpits that North Vietnamese SAM missiles locked onto and tracked the choppers as long as they remained over Vietnamese soil, but no missiles were fired at the fleeing aircraft. Such tempting targets and yet such discipline, I thought, and Ho had been good to his word and perhaps had not meant carpets colored red by blood, at least not when it was clear the NVA had finally won the war with its capture of Saigon and the Presidential Palace there on the day Tao was born.

I also thought as I dropped onto my bed about the welcome I had received from Vietnamese generally, for while they had despised the American military presence, they also had heard about the protests against the war in what the Bush Administration decades later had dubbed the "homeland" in its imperial pretensions. The word reminded me of something the vile Nazis might have employed. The Vietnamese anyway had rarely blamed the American "people" for the carnage in Southeast Asia. But the lack of gross animosity had deeper roots, because the Viets had a history that spanned thousands of years and for much of that time had they been battling one invader or another. The American War, perhaps to many Vietnamese, seemed just another of many horrific blips of violence given their long historical perspective and their realization that, eventually, every foreign occupier ultimately had been beaten back.

I went up the steps to the apartment, locked the door behind me, and before getting on the bed stared into a mirror in the bathroom, despondent about the aging image and feeling like a failure with Tao.

11

Tao's "perhaps" about my suggestion to meet again I began to interpret as nothing more than a "no", or a "no more". My spirits were sinking, for there was little I had relied on more in Vietnam than at least the prospect of expanding friendships and deeper contact with the people I had already met, especially Tao. And given my work routines, I knew there was scant chance of easily meeting additional prospective friends. Not only had I not seen Tao, but I was also realizing the absurdity of sleeping beside my cell phone, because I was receiving no further calls or text messages from her.

Several times I sent her a text message, but no reply. I was becoming restless and even possibly a bit reckless, trying to alter at the margins the routines I had adopted. One routine, usually five days a week, was the jog at dawn around Hoan Kiem, but even that was getting old, and one morning I set off running an entirely different route, a dangerous one across the Red River over the Long Bien Bridge, comprising a span of almost two kilometers. The bridge's girders and rivets actually looked in sections like the metalwork of the Eiffel Tower. Not surprising, because Gustave Eiffel had designed it. The bridge had survived repeated bombings by American aircraft during the war when it was the sole link across the Red River connecting Ha Noi to Hai Phong on the coast and to the remote northwest, to Lao Cai. But I had never seen anyone running on the bridge.

It was anyway early enough so that there was relatively little traffic of motor and pedal bikes, and only a single train came clanking along the badly welded rails that bisected the parallel lanes of the more than a century old span.

A viscous fog, despite a brisk wind that morning, raked through the shallow depression of the Red like the hand of the blind

masseuse Tao had taken me to weeks earlier, and not only was I
initially in the dark, but in fog, too. It really was no place to run,
because the pedestrian path across the bridge was just a half a
meter wide and the makeshift railing was merely knee high and of
dubious strength. A misstep or a sudden gust of wind could have
meant a plunge into the river, or onto one of the sandbars off the
main ship channel some 30 meters below.

Though I was little inclined to acts of conscious self-
destruction, the latter did not seem like the worst that could
happen. Worse was losing all grasp of Merton's or even Epicurus'
serenity of mind. Or getting so decrepit I could no longer run. Or
dream with any sanity whatsoever about actually being with Tao.

The river's channel was less than a quarter of the entire span, so
one had small chance of just tumbling into the water and
swimming to a sandbar. So I ran, challenging the wind to send me
over the railing. Light began to suffuse the fog and when I arrived
halfway across I encountered, tied to the railing, two lengths of taut
fishing line. But what was unusual was that the lines did not drop
into the river, but rather ascended vertically. There, I stopped,
trying to figure just what could be defying gravity and lifting the
lines, and peering up through the fog as sight through it waxed and
waned, I caught glimpses of two Vietnamese kites some fifty
meters overhead: one brightly painted, a phoenix with a wingspan
of a meter and a half, and the other a square design, all black. I
grabbed one of the ascending strings and gave it a tug. The phoenix
dipped momentarily. And then I looked around, wondering whose
kites they were, who had set them, but while motorbikes passed by,
there was no one. The untended kites were sudden lifting marvels,
for not since the dinner at Marcel Mossadeq's house on Ngu Xa
had there been much marvelous to note.

I had been reluctantly going to work at the newspaper,
wandering around the city, going to Vines occasionally for a decent
meal, talking with Cain on the stairwell landing, trying to avoid
conflict with Phuc. But I had no momentum, and like the sharks
neither Tao nor I saw in Ha Long Bay, I needed more forward
motion to avoid despond. At the same time, I began to wonder

whether it made sense to stay much longer in Vietnam. Going home to the Carolinas, as relatively empty as I recalled it, clinging to Williams' invitation, began to appeal. But at least I had seen Marcel again and I liked the notion that I might prove useful to him.

Marcel had called me to lunch at Bobby Chinn's restaurant at a corner opposite Hoan Kiem. He intrigued me: as one man looking at another, he seemed perfect, even enviable -- utterly sophisticated, knowledgeable, well spoken, handsome and charming. Perhaps too perfect, I thought, as if for him, the stuff of life's forward motion always fell into perfect alignment, that he was one who always got what he wanted, and if what he had wanted was found wanting, he would easily move on, easily attaining what next seemed to him optimal, perfect. If I had not been flattered some that he thought me potentially useful, and I felt needy for more friends in Ha Noi, I might well have dismissed him as someone so slick he could not be up to much good, like a salesman of snake oil. I wanted to figure him out, if I could, and even though I was 20 years older, I was curious about what made him so successful, even with women, while, at the same time, I was smarting some over Tao's disengagement.

So it happened that Marcel and I met one cloudy noon and took a seat on the long couch behind yellow silk curtains at the back of the restaurant, lit up one of the hookahs, ordered beers and what the Viets called ca kho, fish braised in a clay pot. I also spotted Chinn darting from bar to kitchen, remembering him from the *Emeraude*.

Marcel had a sheaf of papers in a Louis Vuitton bag, and had shown up outside the restaurant riding his Russian made replica, carefully restored, of a German BMW motorcycle. On the black paint covering the gas tank was a decal of the Vietnamese flag, bright red with the yellow star, and the logo of the new magazine, a stylish flourish of "O&O" – *Oriente&Occident*. Even the cycle seemed "perfect".

"I wonder if you could help me?" said Marcel after the beers arrived. He pulled papers from his bag.

"You ordering more?" I asked him.

"Beer is fine for now, and the fish. The food here is often mediocre and overpriced. Bobby's a showman chef."

"So how can I help you?"

"These are a couple stories I have written for the magazine. Perhaps you could look them over and even edit them a bit, if you think they need some work?"

"OK. I'll have a look." I took the papers from him.

"Final copy is due in two days. Then we are going to press in a couple weeks."

"I'll look at the pieces tonight return them to you tomorrow."

Marcel looked relieved. "We have to make a splash with this first edition. I'm not a professional writer...."

"Glad to make a contribution to an entrepreneurial effort. But I do have one small request." I was slightly irritated he had not given me the pleasure of refusing some payment for the work.

"Yes?"

"Just curious, but why Vietnam? Why did you land here?"

"I may have told you already. It was Kristen's idea. After I met her I asked her what she would do if she could do anything she wanted."

"So this is it? The magazine here in Ha Noi?"

"That's what she wanted, and me, too."

"But you must have had to cut some major ties to do this?" I wondered aloud.

"I had planned to leave banking. I had made some real money and tucked it away. And then I had a problem and felt like getting out of Europe altogether, too. Kristen and her dream were the vehicles."

"Problem?" I queried, given that I could not imagine he had faced notable problems. Relative youth, or at least *his* relative youth such as it appeared, looked like no problem at all.

"Two hears ago when I was still a banker I was in Spain for a few days, in Andalusia, on business, and met a young woman who said she was Greek. Whatever she was she was a very beautiful woman. We got involved that day."

"That does not sound like a problem to me," I interrupted. "Especially being in al-Andalus."

"al-Andalus?"

"What the Arabs and Berbers called their civilization, along with the Jews and a fewer Christians, in Spain. Perhaps the brightest, most tolerant, inclusive realm in recorded history, but 1,000 years ago."

"Let me finish," said Marcel. "I will be brief. We parted. She said she had business in New York for a month, and once she may have gotten there, she called me. I really did not know where she was, but she told me she was pregnant. Being Greek Orthodox, she claimed, she also claimed she could not under any circumstances have an abortion. It was against her faith, she said. I was quite baffled. I more or less panicked, and she was threatening. It was complex, the back and forth, but to make a longish story short, I caved and wound up giving her money to go away. Three hundred thousand Euros when all was said and done. Later, I discovered, it was indeed a scam. She was not pregnant. She was in league with some very shady characters. I eventually assumed she had done this sort of thing before. She was very good at it, very smart. And she was beautiful enough to pull it off."

"That's a bitch in more ways than one," I said.

"But what's most interesting," Marcel went on, "is that I saw her again. After she had sort of, as you Americans might say, taken me to the cleaners and I had been unable to track her down, she found me. She claimed she felt badly about what she had done and aimed to apologize. Two months ago she came to Ha Noi, in fact to the Metropole, for two days. I saw her there one night. There was not much to do but fuck her one last time. That was the end of it."

"Well, she sure as Hell fucked you, too. Kristen knew about this?"

"I had to tell her something when this woman suddenly showed up in Ha Noi. I didn't tell her about the tumble among those fine sheets at the Metropole."

"You could have just told her you had to go out for a while? Although I don't recommend lying, however necessary it can sometimes seem to be."

"Not for hours into the night. I told Kristen a distant cousin from Europe was in Ha Noi. I got back to the house at three in the morning. Kristen did not question me since she thought it was a family thing."

I wondered what else Marcel might be inclined to lie about, but still, I liked him enough. He was amusing, as were his tales.

"So that was the end of the affair, or debacle?"

"Yes," said Marcel. "But had she been sincere from the start, not part of some racket, who knows what I would have done with her. She was hot, if you know what I mean. I'd never have taken up with Kristen."

"Of course."

"And very beautiful."

"But rotten," I said. "And I should add, not very smart."

"Not smart? She managed to take half my wealth. And then, apparently, spent it or shared it with her accomplices. I got nothing back but her ass and an apology."

"No," I said, "not smart, for if she hadn't pulled that stunt on you, you might have taken care of her nicely and she'd still have you."

"But perhaps she did not really want me," said Marcel.

"I guess you might say, then, she did not love you?"

With that, Marcel broke into a broad grin sprinkled with exasperation. "What is love? I don't know it."

"Its manifestations can be myriad," I said.

"Love is often costly," Marcel said flatly. "Or rather, sex often is. I can't distinguish between the two."

"They do often go hand in hand. Maybe you will have children someday, or at least one, as I have. I hope so. Maybe with Kristen."

"No," said Marcel. He almost sounded scornful of the idea.

"I don't know what to make of your life with the ladies. I was for some time married, and I married young. She was my son's mother. She was very kind and warmhearted and I loved her dearly, and then she died of cancer in her prime, in our prime. We were happy. I really haven't been happy since before she became ill," I said.

"That's too bad," Marcel responded flatly, taking a puff on a cigarette.

And right then, I knew him better, I felt. That, as impressive as he seemed, he did not care deep down about the same things I did. That perhaps he was one who crafted his persona to be the perfect vehicle aimed at satiating himself, grabbing what he fancied easily and discarding just as easily what eventually annoyed him. Of course, I also thought, he occasionally got snagged himself by someone even craftier than he was -- like the Greek siren he had just described.

I also thought of the two most important women I had met in Ha Noi: Tao, and Anh at the Maitre Café. Tao might easily find Marcel appealing, but Anh, I imagined, would not: she was cut from a different cloth as if from another world. Their spirits were like oil and water, immiscible. *Anh was closer to my beloved former wife, when I had first met her decades earlier, than anyone I had met since.* The sudden realization warmed me: that there on Hang Giay Street I had re-encountered my deceased wife's spirit, or aspects of it, in a Ha Noi café girl. I had to change the subject with Marcel. I had to absorb the realization later, and it beckoned me to do that, like a fine woman, or the remembrance of the spirit of one, waiting for me at the apartment on Hang Giay.

"I enjoyed dinner at your place."

"And did Tao, too? I have…" Marcel said, halting mid sentence.

"You have what?" I asked, wanting Marcel to finish his thought.

"No. Answer my question, please."

"I imagine Tao did enjoy meeting you, but I haven't heard from her lately. There was a period when I heard from her many times a day, but lately there's been nothing. It's a bit strange." I did not tell Marcel about Tao's distress over his story about corruption.

"Yes," said Marcel. "Tao has a captivating energy and she can turn it on. She can really turn it on if she wants."

"How do you know that?" I asked.

Marcel did not answer directly, but only with a question: "Is it not evident?"

"I guess so. But I have a question."

"Yes?"

"At dinner and afterwards, I felt that maybe Kristen had been offended? She hardly said a word when Tao and I were there. You did the entertaining, all of it, but for the cooking."

"There are always problems."

"Perhaps I should not bring this up," I mused aloud.

"Not a problem," said Marcel. "I do not ever plan to marry Kristen anyway."

"She's attractive. She's a good cook!"

"She troubles me. I did not expect her to be troubling when we met. She complains about my habits. Drinking. Smoking. But it goes beyond that. She can be clenched about things in the bedroom. She may be a good cook, but she's not good with cocks," Marcel laughed.

"Cocks aren't everything."

"I cannot ever marry this woman."

"Have you told her that? Wouldn't that be fair? I don't know what her expectations are, but she's single and not getting younger and must be wondering what's ahead, whether she'd ever have a family?"

I was thinking that she was not happy. And that perhaps this was the reason she had been so aloof at dinner, unwilling to join the conversation.

"Maybe someday I will tell her. But not yet," said Marcel. "I do want the magazine to work."

"Well, in any case, I hope the magazine is successful, too. I will look at what you wrote."

"Very good."

A few minutes later I watched Marcel vanish into the swarm of traffic on his rare BMW replica, but when walking out of Chinn's restaurant, past the bar, there sat the Israeli, Jabotinsky, on one of the bar stools beside a jowly, heavyset, Vietnamese man in a tailored suit sporting oversized gold rimmed sunglasses that made him appear buffoonish, like some caricature of a Third World drug lord's bagman.

His face looked just slightly like that of Gen. Phuong Quang Thanh, the head of Vietnam's Defense Ministry and a member of the elite Communist Party Politburo, whose photo and caption I had seen in the newspaper several times. No way, though, it was in fact General Thanh, who was literally one of the top three men in the country's power hierarchy and a person very unlikely to be easily seen in public except at some official function, whatever the appeal of Bobby Chinn's restaurant. They were conversing, but keeping their voices low. I had to wonder, though, if Thanh had been aboard the mega-yacht *Geneva Princess* in Ha Long Bay.

Anyhow, I was both startled and even disappointed to cross paths with Jabotinsky again in any venue, but decided to make the most of it. Outside, after Marcel had vanished, I glanced back through the window into the bar area and caught the Israeli leaning back on his stool and looking my way. I went back inside, feigning to look for something. Passing by the bar, I turned my head and looked at the Israeli.

"What a surprise!" I said to Jabotinsky. "It's been a while since we met on the *Emeraude*."

The Vietnamese man he had been conversing with had vanished.

Jabotinsky seemed to pretend he did not recognize me, but I imagined he already had. "You are?" he responded.

"McLean," I said. "You might recall I bummed a cigarette from you late one night on the boat and we talked a bit?"

"Ah, yes. Now, I remember. The American who mingles with foreigners, with Arabs, in the West Bank," he said with some sarcasm, as if the Arabs and I both suffered an ugly, visible disease. "And you are a newsman of some sort, too?" he asked with equal sarcasm.

"Right, at *Vietnam News*," I said. "I see you are still in Vietnam. Don't you miss Israel?"

"Always," said Jabotinsky.

"So how's business? You did mention you were in Vietnam on business."

"I have been busy," he said.

"Business drinks with a buddy?"

"Somewhat," said Jabotinsky, "And yours?" he asked in a pointed, inquisitive tone.

"Somewhat," I said.

"What were you talking about?" Jabotinsky asked, I thought, boldly.

It was really none of his business what I talked to anyone about, but I gave him something anyway: "I'm assisting with some editing a couple pieces for a new magazine. But this might surprise you," I offered. "That fellow's got Iranian blood but happens to have Swiss citizenship. But then I don't imagine Israelis could have a friendly interest in Iranians?" I jabbed. "Ha Noi is anyway full of unusual expatriates."

Just then the Viet man who had been sitting and conversing with Jabotinsky went swiftly past the bar, but he gave it wide berth, and went outside. He did not acknowledge us at all, did not stop, did not even look our way. Perhaps he had been in the men's room. I noted that he was clutching a truncheon of sorts: a rolled up copy of *Vietnam News*. Maybe that was the best use for the physical newspaper I had been working to edit into intelligible English.

"True, I don't care for Iranians," said Jabotinsky, clenching a fist and bringing it down on to the bar with a thud. The fist reminded me of a photo I had seen of a scowling, angry, pugilistic "Bibi" Netanyahu with his fists clenched and thrust forward.

"Nor Palestinians," I jabbed, "but this Swiss fellow is cordial, engaging. He's not enriching uranium anywhere, just trying to publish a magazine here."

"And how did you meet him?"

"Actually, I met a young Viet woman on the *Emeraude*. It was she who eventually suggested I check out the magazine. I did."

"Ahh, one chance encounter pointing to another," said Jabotinsky. "He's your friend?"

"In time perhaps. I don't know. But here's a question for you. Did you meet a young woman that weekend when at Ha Long Bay?"

"No."

"No? Are you sure?"

I knew he was lying.

"Sure," said Jabotinsky in the direct, unwavering way good liars lie.

I felt a surge of satisfaction. I had him cornered, if just momentarily. At any rate, Jabotinsky didn't cow me, even though I felt in my gut that he could easily overpower me. He was younger and stronger, but I doubted he could run as fast as I often had around the lake outside at dawn. There was an advantage with age, however paltry it was: I did not fear stating what I believed, even to the point of inciting anger and endangering myself, because at my age I was already in mortal danger, or a lot closer to it. I'd be felled soon enough and already had lived a reasonably happy, decent life. I had no illusions about living forever, and anyway, I did not want to live if I could no longer, say, run around a location like Hoan Kiem Lake.

"I beg to differ," I said.

Jabotinsky laughed. It was a less a normal laugh than a kind of higher pitched, scornful squeal. Whatever it was he emitted, it was a bit unnerving, but maybe he was nervous then even while I did not imagine he was the sort who ever became unnerved.

"Fuck you," said Jabotinsky in the warmest possible way and very softly.

"Is that the sort of thing an Israeli says? I thought you were of the Chosen People? What? Chosen to be profane? To beat up on Arabs, too?" I asked with equal softness. "But on this matter of this woman, named Tao, we find a new difference."

Jabotinsky was smiling. I thought a bit like Phuc always did.

And then I let him have it: "Yes, I know this young woman somewhat. I did meet her on the boat. But more importantly, you just said you don't know her. But I know you must at least have met her. When I left the boat I was looking for her. I wanted to say goodbye and thank her for her company the previous day. I could not find her. But then, as I was walking on the dock with friends to arrive at the bus to take us back here, I saw her for an instant. She and her son getting into a black SUV with YOU and a couple other men I could not identify."

Jabotinsky was silent. The smile was gone. He was staring at me harshly, and coiled as if he was about to jump off his stool and attack with his hammy fists, but I knew he would not, at least not at Bobby Chinn's. I thought of the lizard at the mosque on Hang Luoc.

"What is this woman's name?" Jabotinsky finally spoke.

"You don't know her name?" I asked with incredulity.

"I didn't catch her name. I had the ride back to Ha Noi and this woman said she had to get back to Ha Noi fast. She had a child. I offered her a ride."

"So you say you don't really know her?"

"No, but for that ride."

"But I was told something quite different. I inquired. I am a newsman, after all. I think we differ yet more!"

Again, Jabotinsky was at a loss for words for fifteen seconds or so, still coiled as if he were about to leap off his bar stool at me.

"Listen, Tao is a friend, or was," I went on. "She's someone special, I have thought. So I do listen to her. She said the vehicle, that SUV, the ride back, was pre-arranged for *her*. But you say this is not the case? You just said YOU had the ride back, and then invited Tao along like some maiden in distress."

"She is mistaken."

"One of you two are definitely mistaken. But if she's not the one mistaken, what were you doing with access to a government vehicle? Tao claimed it was sent to pick her up, and I know she works for the government."

"My business in Vietnam is Israeli business, not yours," warned Jabotinsky. "What is your business now with Tao?"

"We have been friends. I haven't seen or heard from her in a while. I wonder, have you seen ME since I met you on the boat until now?" I had quickly decided to address another outstanding issue between us. I was hoping this would be the last, but this later proved to be a chimera.

"No," said Jabotinsky.

"No? Well, you did. In fact, one evening during the *Tet* weekend I was walking through an intersection 200 meters from here. Maybe that same vehicle you rode in from Ha Long City blasted through the red light and almost hit me. I saw your face. You were in the SUV. Remember that?" I asked.

"Traffic is dangerous in Ha Noi," said Jabotinsky. "It is always best to stay out of harm's way. I advise it. A warning."

"Warning me? Let me warn you. I can put your name in a newspaper, if not here, then in the US, for one thing," I imagined aloud, even as this was definitely a stretch. "That vehicle you were in went through a red light. I was merely crossing the street. Have I jogged your memory now?"

"No recollection. I cannot apologize for what in my view did not happen, if that's what you are after."

Jabotinsky leaned back on his stool, his arms extended, his hands on the lip of the bar. He shrugged. I noted his hammy hands. They were thick and hairy, almost puffy, a far cry from, I recalled, Anh's long, slim, delicate fingers resting on her hips as she spoke to me on the sidewalk outside her café.

"So where do you call home now, Mr. Israeli Businessman?" I asked with some sarcasm.

"Israel."

"I know that. But where there?"

"Jerusalem."

"West or East Jerusalem?"

"Ma'ale Adumim."

"Then you have become a settler, too," I said. "A colonialist. Like the French were here, and somewhat like the Americans were in the south." Goading him was coming easily.

"Judea and Samaria belong to Jews."

"International law says otherwise, but I know, you people don't care. Last day I was in Jerusalem, I spent most of it at the *Haram esh-Sharif*, what you call the 'Temple Mount'. I met the Grand Mufti in his offices there. We discussed the illegality of the occupation."

"He is a terrorist, too," said Jabotinsky.

"He seemed nothing like that to me. Just a gentlemanly old man. He gave me a document of permission to visit the *Haram* anytime."

"Based on what?"

"Because I had been working in Tubas, I suppose," I said. "But shortly afterwards when I left Ben Gurion for the US, your security people at the airport gave me a very hard time. They asked me where I had been and I told them. They didn't like it. They stole some of my things, also illegal, just as much has been stolen from the Palestinians."

"I have no more interest in talking to you," he said bluntly, and just as he had on board the *Emeraude*, he rose from his stool, left some money on the bar and went outside the restaurant, stuffing his meaty, hairy hands in his pockets. I, too, was again soon out the door and headed to work, hoping even to Yahweh that I would not cross paths with him again. Worse was that Tao might somehow be linked with him.

Later, at the newspaper in the evening during a break in the flow of stories to edit, I did a search at my computer to see if the paper had published anything about bilateral ties between Israel and Vietnam. There were several short items of recent vintage, all of which preceded my employment, but in the usual, bland, superficial style about how both countries desired more economic trade, deeper ties, blah blah blah, as if that was newsworthy. I mean what two countries did not desire better relations and stronger, mutual economic benefits as a result, unless one of them was simply intent on making an enemy of the other?

More searching dredged up another story about how a group of Israeli eye surgeons had gone with a Vietnamese team of eye doctors to the far north, to Ha Giang in fact, Tao's hometown, and volunteered their services for a week, helping scores of the People suffering ocular diseases. How nice, I thought, if only the Israelis would offer the same free medical services in Gaza or the West Bank, recalling the title, at least, of Alduous Huxley's long ago novel "Eyeless in Gaza". A while later, on the stairwell landing with Cain, I asked him: "What do you know about Israel's involvement with Vietnam?"

"Not much, mate," said Cain. "My impression is that Israeli-Vietnamese ties may still be relatively weak, but strengthening. Organizations like the PLO derived support from anti-colonial movements that existed in Vietnam, and the PLO, I think, used some of the Marxist-guerrilla playbooks from Nam. Vietnam, isolated after the war, cast itself as the underdog and identified with underdogs elsewhere."

"But now it's all about economic growth here," I said. "The leadership probably does not give a damn any longer about assisting underdogs or identifying with them unless it involves some economic benefit," I said.

"Which may be one reason among the usual ones the Israelis have opened an embassy here."

"Yeah," I agreed. "They aren't underdogs."

"Mossad operatives, by the way, were doing bad stuff in my New Zealand."

"I met an Israeli on the *Emeraude* the weekend I first met Tao," I told Cain. "I've seen him a couple times around Ha Noi since then. He's an asshole colonialist."

"A Likudnik?"

"That or worse, if worse is possible," I said. "I saw this guy by chance at lunch today at Bobby Chinn's restaurant. His name is Jabotinsky. I was at the restaurant with Marcel Mossadeq, who's helping publish the new magazine. This Jabotinsky was initially sitting with some Vietnamese dude at the bar. He saw me and I think pretended not to recognize me. I went back inside after Marcel went off on his motorcycle and spoke to him. We've got issues but not worth mentioning because you already know I'd clash with his kind. But I've got no real idea what he's actually *doing* in Vietnam."

"You never know. I recall a story some time ago about an Israeli humanitarian mission up towards Sapa in the mountains. They distributed clothes, rice and, would you believe, pigs, on that mission!"

"Pigs, too? Anyway, that Jabotinsky fellow hardly seemed like a humanitarian, whatever *exactly* that means."

"Few in this part of the world dislike pork," said Cain. "Nor do they dislike 'pork', to use the word as a substitute for ill-gotten money. Anyway, I read that after the distribution of the pigs the Israelis reported back to the authorities in Jerusalem that they had donated 'domestic animals'. They did not mention pigs."

"Haha," I said. "Pork of all kinds."

"Anyway," said Cain, "there were virtually no Jews here 20 years ago I don't think. Now, they have a presence here in Ha Noi and down in Saigon, but the numbers remain small. The Viets call them *Do Thai*. So you were at Bobby Chinn's for lunch with this publisher? Expensive lunch."

I then told Cain almost everything I knew about Marcel Mossadeq. "I think you'd like meeting him," I added. "I will try to set something up."

"Sounds good," said Cain.

"Anyway, when I went to dinner at his place with Tao, he said something that would whet the appetite of any good reporter looking for a story to investigate."

"What?"

"Marcel claimed he had a source who told him the wife of a Party official got her hands on two million bucks worth of diamonds on a shopping visit to Hong Kong."

"I'm not all that surprised," Cain commented. "But of course, if true, that begs the question: where did the diamonds come from, how acquired? It's not like government or Party officials are *making* money like that to spend on diamonds. They are just directing the flow, and skimming. A couple mil in diamonds looks like a very personal transaction, not just a part of the standard, systemic corruption that the paper won't find or report except in very isolated instances."

"This is the sort of tip that any good newspaper would send a reporter to Hong Kong to investigate. Fat chance. If I can set up a meeting with Marcel, maybe we can learn more about this."

"If it's true, it's hot information."

Late that same night, back at the apartment and on the bed in the dark, I was feeling uneasy about having told Cain of Marcel's revelation about the lode of diamonds. If Marcel knew I had spread the story he told me, even to just one other person, he might have figured I had breached his confidence. Still, Marcel had told Tao, too. Given that he had, I marked that up to Marcel trying to impress Tao with his knowledge and figured he had no serious qualms about mentioning what he had heard.

12

Tao made 60 years gone a bit more tolerable when unexpectedly the mobile phone rang and the voice I had not heard in some time came through: "Happy Birthday, Marshall!"

"Happy Birthday?" I asked. "How did you know?"

"I have an invitation," said Tao, ignoring the question. "I have two tickets to the Ha Noi Opera House tonight. Interested?"

"I'm working today but I think I can get out of there early. I'll say it's my birthday and all."

"Fine. I will meet you on the steps of the Opera House just before eight."

"What's going on there?"

"Vietnam's National Symphony Orchestra."

Things suddenly were looking up, like the kites straining in the winds high above the Long Bien Bridge. Tao still had power to dictate my mood, though because I had not heard from her in quite a while that power had abated some. Perhaps she truly was a friend at least, and I did not take friends lightly, especially as a foreigner more or less dependent on their kindness in Vietnam. Cicero, the Roman polymath, had described it well: *An accord on most subjects human and divine, joined with mutual good will and affection. Nothing better than this has been given to man by the immortal gods.*

"You like classical music?" I asked.

"I think *you* do, and it's your birthday."

"Have you been working? Finding UXO and Agent Orange to clean up?"

Let's not discuss my work," Tao said. "I must go. I just called to issue the invitation. Maybe you should come earlier, like around seven. The Press Club is near the Opera. We could have a drink there before the performance. Have you been to the Press Club?"

"Not yet," I said. "I heard there was not actually much 'press' at the club."

I had indeed heard of the place, but it had little or nothing to do with the media and was largely a dining and wining emporium of various wood paneled rooms spread over six stories catering, like Vines but with more formality and advertisement, to Westerners and their local Vietnamese friends and associates. The Press Club had offered the first free wireless Internet connection in Ha Noi, and I had thought to go there eventually to kill a few hours with my laptop, but already had found a regular haunt over by St. Joseph's cathedral near *Regina Paces'* bronze smile on the opposite side of Hoan Kiem Lake. The Press Club building also housed offices that booked staterooms on the *Emeraude* and vacations at various retreats in Vietnam.

"It's opposite the back side of the Metropole, across the street."

"Okay."

I walked to work early, around noon, that birthday morning, passing back through the Old Quarter towards Hoan Kiem, its labyrinthine lanes like the branches of some ancient tree whose roots lay somewhere in the green muck of the lake to the south. More buoyant given the prospect of the evening with Tao, I took rather more interest than usual in the scene within the Old Quarter, recalling that its inhabitants had often nurtured Vietnamese opposition to foreign control. The formal trade guilds that had clustered along winding lanes named for various goods had been fertile ground for small strikes by workers that spawned independent presses and ultimately Communist cells that united under Bac Ho's leadership in the decade before the French defeat at Dien Bien Phu. This had been Vietnamese turf in Ha Noi, an area of the city dangerous to colonialists before their defeat, but as one from a country that had also been later humiliated and its minions expelled by the Vietnamese, it seemed to me like the best part of Ha Noi. I reveled again in the fact of actually living there.

But when I finally arrived at work I discovered the paper was about to publish a story containing more substance than the usual blather about how the Party was making Vietnam a workers' paradise. Phuc handed it to me to edit. He dropped it on my desk with the usual, strange smile.

"Is this some kind of lead story?"

"No, not front page. Correct errors in spelling, syntax and grammar," he demanded.

The story involved a couple Vietnamese-born US citizens who had been detained and were, the unnamed reporter claimed, going to be prosecuted on charges of helping plot "violence" against the Communist government. Prosecutors had apparently asked some entity called the Ho Chi Minh City People's Court to try the defendants on charges of "terrorism" in an alleged scheme to bomb Vietnamese embassies outside the country. I did not believe a word of it, if only because one of the defendants was an elderly woman, married to an American in 1973, with a landscaping business in a small town in central Florida.

The Vietnamese really did have green thumbs, figuratively speaking, but the story Phuc gave me made no mention of her benign business pursuits or of the location of her home in the US or that she was actually in Vietnam to attend a nephew's wedding. I took my time and filtered that information from another, fleshier story off Reuters on the Internet. For a minute I pondered whether to shoehorn in such information that was absent from Phuc's version, or at least bring it to Phuc's attention, but then I figured it was not worth the effort, recalling Phuc's explicit charge to restrict my handing of the piece. At any rate, I knew that merely *advocating* human rights, multi-party democracy or peaceful reforms in Vietnam was apt to rouse official opposition. There existed in the current Criminal Code a provision outlawing what was termed "abusing democratic rights", which was another way of saying that Party hegemony was being challenged.

Cain wandered over by my terminal and again expressed interest in my earlier proposal that I set up a meeting between him and Marcel. "The chap's nominally Muslim maybe, even if he is Swiss. He should know Vietnam is allowing Muslims to open the country's largest mosque in Xuan Loc, partially funded by donations from Saudi Arabia."

"I don't think he'd care one way or the other," I told Cain. "But I've heard of the town, on the northern approaches to Saigon. It was the site of the last major battle of the American War. South Vietnamese soldiers, backed by Americans, actually made a rather impressive last stand against the push of the NVA into Saigon."

"That's interesting, mate. But the Party allowing a big mosque to go up? I'd bet the authorities must be a bit nervous permitting a more visible, larger Muslim footprint here," said Cain. "I mean, it's gotten to the point where the next thing one thinks of after the word 'Islam' is terrorism."

"The US has been good spreading that propaganda. It's a huge problem. Few Americans see the terrorism unleashed by the US overseas, or that of the Zionists in Palestine."

"I know," Cain said.

"It's infuriating. Anyway, I haven't probed Marcel about his Muslim roots, what his exact orientation may be, except that I gather he's extremely religious about living well materially. Booze and women and baubles -- nice motorcycles and wrist watches and more."

"I'd second that religion," said Cain. "This chap sounds rather worth a meeting."

"What say I propose we three get together for a drink tomorrow evening?"

"OK," said Cain.

"I will try." I then quickly edited the story Phuc had handed over.

I did not tell Cain about the birthday, or about the plans to meet Tao at the Press Club that evening. Telling him would just drill home the gap in our ages, and as a friend, even if the disparity did not bother him, I did not want to shine any kind of light on it. But I did have to tell Phuc, because the plans with Tao demanded that I leave work a couple hours early. I went to his desk and took him the copy about the lady from Florida who had been arrested for allegedly plotting "violence" against the Party.

"Phuc," I said, "it's my birthday and I've been invited to a performance at the Opera House this evening. I hope leaving early is not a problem?"

"Ahhh," he said, "You may celebrate your birthday and leave early. But I should tell you about birthdays in Vietnam." He pulled the half moon glasses off his nose and pushed back from his desk. "We often celebrate birthdays at *Tet*, New Year's Day. Then, it is everyone's birthday in Vietnam. Many do not acknowledge the exact day they were born."

"That's very interesting. In '*My*' it's quite different," I said, using the Vietnamese word for "America". "At home we do celebrate our real birth days."

"Very good," Phuc exclaimed with some glee. "So how old are you by the calendar in *My*?"

"Sixty."

"We are contemporaries," Phuc said, and he reached out and gave my hand a shake. I figured there was something serious about birthdays that drew out some affability, since I had seen squat of that from Phuc after the welcome on my first day at work.

"Thanks. I regret having to leave early this evening," I lied.

"You may," Phuc responded, as if he could have actually prevented me from walking out, but he was evidently trying to be accommodating.

"Here's the story you wanted me to look at." I placed it on his desk.

"I will review it," said Phuc. And with that, for almost the second time since I had begun work, I felt rather better about him. I was not so hardened to dismiss the notion that anyone's life, even Phuc's, might be difficult, and that to survive perhaps one had to compromise or, to put it more succinctly, believe in something, adhere to something, even if that merely served as a sort of anchor, a way to make some sense of the mess that any mortal life often was. As least, I thought, he had something to believe in, the Party, and his role in disseminating its righteous pabulum in the paper.

For myself, my belief system systematically consisted of the sure knowledge I was bereft of anchors, of creeds political or religious, and I could not even find footing in Marcel's enthusiasms for luxury and hedonism -- all apparently to be highlighted in the forthcoming magazine. For me, I thought in that early evening with the newsroom a buzz of activity, hard copy passing around and the tap of fingers on computer keyboards, that there was little for me but the value of friendships. I valued romance, too, but that was much, much harder to find. Cicero's words about friendships came to mind again.

A while later I didn't bother to inform Phuc I was leaving exactly when I did, heading on foot to the Press Club a few blocks to the north. I did not want to give him a chance to change his mind about the early departure, but I waved to Cain on the way out, who was hunched over his computer terminal, and slipped down the stairs and out past the guards in their neon green uniforms onto Tran Hung Dao just before eight.

A thunderstorm had just passed over Ha Noi dumping considerable but intermittent rain, some of which had blown in through the open windows of the newsroom leaving puddles on the floor under the sills. The street glistened and the broad sidewalks of what had been the French Quarter of the city were littered with debris from the various trees along the boulevard, some of that the yellow, confetti-like leaves of the *xoan*, the China Berry.

When I reached the Press Club, just as I came through its revolving entrance door, I spotted Tao. She was sitting alone at a table near the bar on the first floor. She was not dressed in her usual jeans, but in the traditional *ao dai*, the flesh hugging under pants of her garment a silky white, the over garment a severe black, all reaching to her ankles. She was punching the keys on her mobile phone.

Suddenly, I recalled a photo I had seen from a book I had been reading at the apartment. This was the "Asian Journal" of the American Catholic monk Thomas Merton, who called himself Father Louis, published posthumously, recounting his final trip beyond the confines of his monastery, Gethsemani, in the hills of Kentucky while the Vietnam War continued.

Merton, in a photograph in the journal, was wearing his habit, a loose white gown going to his ankles with a black scapular. It looked a bit like Tao's *ao dai* but of course with much looser drape: After visiting other Asian countries on that final journey abroad, Merton wound up in Bangkok and it was there one early afternoon in 1968 that he had taken a shower before a siesta and afterwards, reports speculated, reached to turn on an electric fan. The fan's wiring was faulty and 220 volts, the same voltage of the current in Vietnam, killed him instantly. And ironic, too, was his return home. The American military whose presence in Vietnam he had strongly condemned, collected his body in Bangkok, took it to the huge base at Danang on the central Vietnamese coast, and from there returned him to the US in a military cargo plane.

"You dressed up for my birthday," I said, taking a seat at the table.

"I dressed up for the Opera House," Tao responded.

"Whatever for, I'm impressed. What will you have?"

"Wine? It doesn't matter," she said with some agitation. Something was amiss.

"What's up, Tao?"

"I need a drink. What's with you?" she asked, deflecting my question with her own.

"I edited a story this afternoon about a couple Vietnamese Americans who had been arrested for a plotting against the government, but I'm almost certain they are innocent. It said they were going to bomb Viet embassies. One's actually an elderly lady from Florida who came here to attend a relative's wedding. Have you heard anything about this?"

"No," Tao said and waved her hand, suggesting she was too distracted by something else to focus on any news. And then her phone gave off a beep. She punched a button and stared at the screen.

"Who's that?" I asked, turning to summon a waiter. When I turned back to Tao she was looking hard at me, her visage strained.

"Well?" I asked.

"It's Marcel," she said. "I'm having troubles. He's texting me. A lot."

I was annoyed. Marcel had said nothing about contacting Tao independently. Slick Marcel was deploying his charms towards someone I suddenly wished I had never introduced him to. His charms were considerable, too, at least on the surface -- far more compelling than anything I could deploy, even when I was his age, I thought.

"That doesn't sound so terrible," I lied, but still I was curious. "I had lunch with him at Bobby Chinn's," I told Tao. "He asked me to look at a couple stories he wrote for the new magazine. You having issues with Marcel?"

"I *like* him," Tao said, with the accent falling heavily on the verb.

"That might be a problem," I said, but I was largely thinking it was a personal problem for me, and I wondered if she had ever told anyone she 'liked' me in the same way I fast figured she 'liked' Marcel.

"He's been contacting me. I have seen him, too. For lunch," she admitted.

"He has told me nothing of that."

Of course, I realized then, he would not have told me. In truth, I barely knew him. He was showing more than a merely platonic interest in her, and I imagined he knew I liked her, too. I recalled that he had seemed impressed by Tao during their first meeting at his house over dinner.

Marcel had a much better than even chance of winning whatever attention he wanted from most any woman. He was targeting Tao's affections, and I was sure he had not told Kristen Andre, just as he had not told her much about the Greek siren. It easily occurred to me that perhaps one reason I had not heard much from Tao since dinner at Marcel's, one reason she had been unresponsive to my queries, was because something was in play between the two of them. I was disappointed. I liked Tao's attention, too, but I had unwittingly deflated it by the introduction. It was clear I had surely not attained the composure Thomas

Merton had before the fan electrocuted him, nor that of Epicurus' blissful freedom from desire.

"He wants to see me. I've been trying to say 'no' but it's hard."

"Trying? I presume you haven't. Because you like him, too," I said, with the stress on "like", stating what I feared to be the case in the vain hope she might immediately deny the assertion. I decided anyway to adopt a posture that, if not paternalistic, was fraternalistic. Maybe it was the only recourse I had if I wanted to maintain any contact with her.

"What *could* you be thinking, Tao?" I said with consternation, and perhaps in a way too much like an earnest, protective father to a daughter. "Look at it this way. What's it going to be like if you and Marcel really get involved and then you discover that maybe he's not someone on whom you can count. What on earth do you think he's going to do? Support you and Tung? Settle down with you at Ngu Xa after he's pushed Kristen Andre out of the house and maybe gutted the magazine's introduction, which apparently is a joint venture between the two of them at least?"

"He's very insistent," said Tao in a husky tone.

"For what exactly?" I asked, even though I already knew: her svelte body.

"He wants to meet me again somewhere soon. He even wants to go to Nha Trang for a weekend of diving."

"I bet. *Diving*," I said. "You can play this along as long as you want. But if you use your head, you'll come to no conclusion that makes sense but one: saying 'no' absolutely."

With that, I knew I was overstepping bounds. I had no right to tell her what to do, but I was jealous.

"What should I write back?"

"You can tell him you can't see him. Do it," I insisted. "Tell him to cool it or something. Make it clear you are just a friend."

"I don't know if I can be just a friend," Tao said, but she began punching a return message.

"To me or to Marcel?"

"Marcel."

"I figured."

"Have I upset you?" Tao asked.

"Not really," I fibbed.

"Let me see what you are writing," I demanded, but she had finished and immediately hit the send button and then, with some evident reluctance, a grimace I thought, handed me the phone. The sent message was still visible on the screen.

"I AM BUSY AND I CANNOT MAKE PLANS WITH YOU. PLEASE, DON'T CONTACT ME ANY MORE RIGHT NOW."

"RIGHT NOW, you wrote," I said. "Are you telling him maybe later?"

"What if he writes back right now?" Tao asked, ignoring my question.

"Then just don't respond," I said emphatically. Suddenly, it did not seem like much of a birthday, but then I could not recall any in recent years that had been anything to cheer about. The number was going up, and I had often wondered how grand life might be if one were born old, and lived backwards. The end, if it were possible, would be pleasant indeed.

The waiter brought a couple glasses of wine. Trying to kick the conversation in another direction, I was feeling lost, but raised my glass. A brave face was better than none. "Cheers! So what have you been doing aside from this distraction with Marcel?"

"Working," Tao said.

"I'm still not quite clear what you do and for whom. Care to tell me?" I figured she owed me something, even if I was not sure exactly what, so I was emboldened to press her a bit. I again remembered her getting in the SUV with Jabotinsky the day after I met her.

"I told you on the boat," Tao said laconically. "I am doing some research for the government on UXO and other leftovers from the war. Agent Orange, too."

"I seem to recall that. I hope you get paid well," I said. "So many other people leaving the countryside, leaving their families to take $50 a month jobs in the Chinese motorbike factory, don't."

"I am much better paid than that," Tao seemed to boast.

"Maybe your son's father works, too? Where is HE exactly?" I asked, but the question was more like a challenge. I was irritated but I was trying with faint success not to show it: irritated some with Marcel, but more with the fact that Tao had been wrestling with him affectively and because for some time past she had all but disappeared. It almost angered me how she literally manipulated me at the apartment, not to mention the fact that, improbably, I had fallen asleep and hours later woke up to find her gone.

"He's in Saigon," Tao said. "We are divorced."

"Does he get to see Tung?"

"No. I forbid it."

"He doesn't get to see his father?"

"He doesn't care," said Tao.

"Well, that's clear, finally. I had wondered. I am sorry Tung apparently has a derelict father."

She fondled her wine glass, then took a sip and glared at me. Maybe I was destroying the evening by interrogating her, bringing up a painful marital dislocation and divorce. But then, with some pleasure, I spied Dar Williams strolling into the bar area of the Press Club. He was sporting a tie and coat, and the loafers he usually wore without socks. Spotting him was a relief.

"Look!" I exclaimed to Tao, "Dar Williams! Remember, you met him on the *Emeraude*?" Dar saw us, too, at the table, and almost bounded over to us.

"Marshall, my man!" he said, slapping me on the back, and then he looked at Tao and added: "And you are Tao, right? I remember. The bold swimmer in Ha Long Bay with my buddy."

Tao nodded.

"What are you doing in Ha Noi now, Dar? You didn't call to say you were coming?" I asked.

"I was going to call you later tonight. It's been some time since we spoke. How's work at the newspaper?"

"Frankly, I've about had it with the paper," I said. "It's any good editor's straightjacket."

"Awww," said Dar with a smile, dismissing my negativity with his usual, positive ebullience. I could well understand why the NGO he worked for appreciated his services.

"Tao here invited me to go to the Opera tonight. It's my birthday. The 60th."

"Sounds good," said Dar. "We are getting up there age wise, eh?"

"Unfortunately. But what brings you to Ha Noi this trip?"

"An American company is coming in here to build a billion dollar computer chip plant, and I just spoke with a couple of their reps across the street at the Metropole. You know, they get access to Vietnam's cheap labor and for that I'm insisting they pay for it by donating to a project for the poor."

"Outsourcing," I said. "Meanwhile, back in the States manufacturing jobs disappear, and along with that, it seems, the middle class. Wage arbitrage run amok."

"But we see the eventual rise of a middle class here," said Dar. "I'm happy about that."

"But of course. You are virtually Vietnamese and won't go home again, having made a home here. But it's likely I shall, eventually. So how's the family?"

"Fine," Dar said. "I saw Hung's grandmother earlier today. She's got that shop up beside the Lucky Hotel near the lake selling trinkets to tourists. Doing a good business. Hung is excelling learning English at school, but he's grown a lot, too much laterally, I think."

"That's because you go to dinner too often at Kentucky Fried Chicken in Saigon," I insisted.

"I'm planning to cut that out," said Dar.

"Sit a while," I requested.

"Sorry, I can't. I just came in here to use the computer in the lobby and grab a Tiger beer. Had to check my e-mail. But I'll call you later tonight? After the Opera?"

"Sounds good," I said. "Never without my phone."

Dar barely glanced at Tao. He patted me on the back and left the bar, and I turned attention back to Tao.

"Good to see him," I said. "That's a friend. I've known him for decades."

"Time for the concert now," said Tao.

I paid the bill at the bar and followed her out of the Press Club building a couple blocks to the Opera House, feeling disappointed with Tao as I waded across the street through the traffic, wishing I'd again see Tan and his cab in front of the Opera House, but he was not there. Gone, too, was Tao's enthusiasm when we were aboard the *Emeraude* or when she was taking me around the city to Vines or to the massage, or going to the *Cinematique*, or like when she volunteered to meet me at the apartment after my communion with Vladimir Lenin. I wondered if she had simply felt duty bound to reestablish contact, if just for one evening, on my birthday, as if doing so was merely a banal chore, like getting the oil changed periodically in her Honda. Recompense, I supposed, at least for inviting her to Marcel's dinner at the house at Ngu Xa, for introducing her to him. I could not think of any other reason, unless, of course, she did actually somehow value me. But I was becoming increasingly aware that maybe she did not, I had to admit to myself. Wary I was fast becoming, even though she looked awfully appealing, as appealing as ever, in her *ao dai*.

The performance at the Opera House by the Vietnam National Symphony, an ensemble reconstituted a decade after the war, was as good as any I had heard, and made better by the ambience in which the musicians often performed in Ha Noi -- a scaled down replica of the Palais Garnier in Paris that retained plush rows of wooden, bolstered and stuffed seats on three levels under a splendid crystal chandelier. I had the sense of being in Paris a hundred years earlier amid the baroque décor, or better yet, in St. Petersburg before the October Revolution. But Ha Noi, a city of more than three million, turned out a crowd that filled barely half of the house seats that night when Graham Sutcliffe, the resident conductor, began putting the orchestra though a medley of music. I turned to Tao at the start of the intermission.

"This is excellent," I said. "Let's go to the lobby and have a glass of wine."

"You go," she said. "I will stay here."

"Suit yourself," I said, and when I stood and turned up the aisle I glanced back at Tao and saw her fumbling for her phone in her bag. "Fuck" was the only word that came to mind. Perhaps she was going to text Marcel. She had seemed bored with the music, a Bartok rhapsody for viola and a piece by Paul Hindemith, the fine suite from his opera, Mathis der Maler.

A few tables had been set up in the lobby of the Opera House displaying an array of beverages. I paid for a glass of red wine, and downed the whole of it in a gulp and then I went back into the concert hall and discovered that Tao's seat was empty. I stood in the aisle, scanning round the hall, hoping to catch sight of her, to summon her back to her seat. I returned to the lobby while the musicians filed back on stage and took their seats and began arranging the scores on the stands before them.

The flow was all one way, back into the hall, and the lobby had almost emptied out and there was no sign of Tao. She had disappeared. She had become as thoroughly enigmatic as the written Tao, but I stayed for the last item on the program, for the Stravinsky. And after the music was done and the last rounds of applause had given way to chatter as the audience rose and began to depart, I spotted Jabotinsky at a distance across the hall nearer the exit. More bad luck, I thought, and that once again Ha Noi seemed smaller than it was, like a little village of expats within a huge, bland metropolis. It seemed I could not entirely shake the Israeli settler colonialist son of a bitch.

13

Hailing a cab from the Opera House steps, I was eager to return to the apartment. There were a few things to do before sleep, but in the cab, unfortunately, it was not Tan, the smart, friendly, cabbie and writer whom I hoped to meet again, at the wheel. I rang Tao's mobile phone from the car. I was naturally concerned about her disappearance. Concerned, and also I wanted an explanation. She owed me that much, I imagined. But no answer.

Soon home, such as it had been, I found the two files Marcel had handed over at Bobby Chinn's and took a seat at the table in the kitchen and popped the cork from a bottle of wine. But before I could read the stories, my phone rang. It was not Tao, but Dar, calling as he had said he would earlier at the Press Club.

"Hey, buddy," said Dar. "That was a nice surprise seeing you tonight."

"Likewise for me," I said. "Where are you calling from now?"

"Settled in for the night at the Lucky Hotel. What's happening with you and Tao? You two were quite apart from the crowd on the *Emeraude*. I didn't expect to see her today and certainly not you with her, too."

"Not much is happening. It's the birthday thing. I'm 60. I guess she just wanted to take me to the Opera." I decided not to tell Dar that she had abandoned me there, embarrassing as it was. At least not right away.

"She looked pretty good all dressed up in *ao dai*. You involved with her?" Dar asked bluntly.

"Not in the way you are thinking," I said. "Since I've been in Ha Noi we've done a few things together. A movie, a day around town on her motorbike, a dinner."

"That's good," said Dar.

"You mean that I've seen her some?"

"That's not bad. But what's probably good is that you said you aren't all that involved with her."

"What if I was?"

"Not good, my friend."

"OK, tell me more. Why?"

"I don't know much about this Tao but some caution may be warranted."

"Dar," I said, "if I can manage several months in a Muslim town in the West Bank, I think I can manage here. Try not offending conservative Muslims and also not getting shot at by Israeli troops and settlers. Not so easy."

"How involved are you with her?"

"I'm just a friend of hers, and vice versa, I believe. It hasn't gone beyond that," I lied, if those few minutes I remembered with her at the apartment amounted to anything more.

"Buddy, you are slowly getting sucked in and you don't even know it. She's like a hawk, circling and circling hungrily over your sentiments and then she's going to dive on you," Dar warned, but with some amusement. I figured Huong had done the same to him in some fashion.

"That's a bad prospect? A woman like that? You should know better. Look where Huong managed to get you: married. She already 'dove' on me," I said, rethinking my decision a minute earlier.

"Explain, please."

"Halfway through the concert tonight she ducked out, abandoned me. I went to the lobby to get a drink at intermission and when I went back to our seats she had vanished. I was disturbed by that but the concert was so good I stayed to the end."

"You two argue?"

"No, but whatever she thinks of me, she's more interested in someone I met here not long ago. An Iranian-Swiss fellow who's been behind a new magazine that may soon appear in Ha Noi. Rather unfortunately I introduced Tao to him one night at dinner at his place near Truc Bach. Tonight, I told her to cool it. Maybe she was angry with me. I'm not sure."

"Uphill battle for you, I would guess," commented Dar. "I'm not sure about this Tao."

"Why?"

"The boat trip is good enough for starters," explained Dar. "That blue bikini and the way she hustled you into the water. First the swim and then off in the kayak with her you went. You hardly spoke to anyone else on the boat, and they were Americans trying to live in Nam, too. And you didn't spend much time with Huong and me that 24 hours in Ha Long Bay. Tao had you on a very tight leash."

"Maybe. I'm sorry about that. No offense intended. But, tell me, do you know anything about Tao that I don't?"

"I don't know anything specific, but a couple people have heard of her in Saigon."

"She does have her ex-husband, the father of her son down there."

"I know nothing of her ex," said Williams, "but I have some friends working in the government, not just flaks and bureaucrat contacts. I did ask one of them, a younger man from Ha Noi, if he had ever heard of Tao. He wasn't absolutely sure, but he thought he might have. She may be some kind of floater, doing random, occasional stuff for high ups in the Communist Party."

"She hasn't revealed very much to me, but I have long known about the government connection. Defense Ministry, I believe, maybe quasi humanitarian work like getting a grip on how and where to clean up UXO and Agent Orange."

"Look, buddy, she has to be kind of a special case. Despite her relative youth, at least relative to us, she's been around. She's lived and studied in Washington. Her English is good. She seemed at ease among us expats that weekend in Ha Long Bay."

"Who invited her to join the Amcham group on the *Emeraude*? She's not formally connected with Amcham."

"No one challenged her presence on the boat. I reckon you were a big assist on that score, seeing as how she was alone, except for the kid, until she latched on to you that weekend."

"Well, whatever," I said. "She's been interesting. But in recent weeks things have gone flat with her. Hadn't had any communications with her for some time until she invited me to the Opera House. I tried to call her from the cab when I left the place a half hour ago. I wanted to know why she left me there, of course, and whether she was okay."

"Take it easy, buddy. Take it slow," Dar said. "I've got to get some sleep now but when I come back to Ha Noi maybe we can get together for dinner at the Metropole or something?"

"When?"

"Don't know. Maybe you should come back to Saigon. Lots to do there," Dar said. "You can stay with us again."

"Invite appreciated, but I'm stuck for a while at the paper. I want to have some kind of positive impact, but I don't know if that's possible, before I leave."

"Leave?"

"It has crossed my mind. The job is awkward for me."

"Whatever, I'd miss you if you did leave. You know how to reach me."

Marcel's writing exuded energy and enthusiasm, almost but not quite as much as *Tet* fireworks over Hoan Kiem Lake. That was what the magazine would have to maintain, at least, to find readers and paying advertisers. About all I saw to do to the copy was try to clean up some spelling, syntax and modest organizational errors, which I more or less did but with a pencil since all I had was the paper hard copy. Either piece, I figured, was and would be representative of his output for *Orient&Occident,* and this would have to be balanced by other contributions focusing specifically on locations or art or culture or people in Vietnam.

One of his stories celebrated a fine yacht costing some $40 million that was allegedly plying the waters along the French Riviera with computerized propulsion technology that allowed it to maintain position over any reef without the need for an anchor that might damage the living coral below, though there was not much coral, if any, still alive in the Mediterranean.

The other story celebrated the Porsche automotive *marque* and the various iterations of the Porsche 911 over more than three decades since its initial introduction. I had not yet seen a Porsche in Vietnam, but I did recall hearing that a local businessman, leaping forward with bragging rights over all potential competitors, had imported two new Bentleys and parked them ostentatiously, side by side, by his residence somewhere on the shores of West Lake. It took me no longer than half an hour to mark up the copy and since it was not quite midnight, I decided to notify Marcel immediately that I had done what he asked and also see if I could arrange a meeting the following evening.

I not only wanted to set a time to deliver the edited copy to the house at Ngu Xa, but also see if I could introduce Cain Hamilton. I thought Cain might want to try to earn some cash on the side, perhaps with some writing of his own for the magazine in future, assuming it survived long enough. I called Marcel. He was still up and, he said, Kristen Andre was not there. She had flown off to Singapore to report a future story about tourist attractions there, especially the fine hotels like Raffles. He was grateful for the work I told him I had done on his stories and had no problem with the prospect of meeting a colleague of mine at *Vietnam News*.

All this was more satisfying after what earlier had been a difficult evening: the exchange with Tao at the Press Club about the negotiations between Marcel and her, and then Tao's sudden exit from the concert and my failure to reach her on the phone so I could learn why she left me there. I had spotted Jabotinsky there, too. But, of course, I said nothing to Marcel about any of this regarding Tao. I did not want him to know I had been with her when he was texting, or "sexting", her. Nor did I want him to intuit I was jealous of their communications.

"We can go out with your friend from the paper," Marcel said, noting again that Kristen would not be around to object.

"Agreed," I said to Marcel. "I'll be there after work with Cain. Should show up around nine."

I finished off the bottle of wine at the kitchen table while thoughts returned to Tao. I figured there was at least one item about our meeting and time together aboard the *Emeraude* that did not add up. We had swum in the bay for at least an hour, and climbed into the cave on one of the islands in the bay for the buffet and drinks, and then we had gone out for an hour or so in the kayak. Nothing odd there, but I wondered: what had she done with Tung, her child?

I did recall she had said something about getting a crew member to watch the boy, but this seemed an unlikely arrangement if she were quite conscientious about tending Tung properly, and I had no reason to imagine otherwise. I had to wonder if she had involved Jabotinsky. I could not recall meeting his mug earlier that day -- not until I saw him smoking his Cohiba late and alone. Maybe he had stayed in his cabin most of the time like some troglodyte.

The next day, as often before, I had time to kill around Ha Noi before work, and went out, if for no other reason but that the apartment was no serious comfort, and definitely no pleasure palace, nothing like Marcel's house anyway.

I headed south and across Hang Giay the 100 meters to the Maitre Café where I'd find Anh. I had not stopped by the café in some time. I was mulling over a dream I had had a few hours earlier. It was the equivalent of an old man's nightmare on any man's first night past sixty.

It involved a location never seen, but one read about in a couple of the Vietnam guidebooks: the village of Khau Vai and its Love Market. Up in the mountains near the Chinese border, not more than 50 kilometers from Ha Giang as crows fly over the verdant mountains of the region, lay Khau Vai where, according to legend, a teenage boy and girl suffered unrequited love because they were from different ethnic groups and forbidden to be together. Unable to bear the thought of never seeing each other, they therefore decided to risk a meeting every year on the same day in Khau Vai village.

This rather forlorn tale of Khau Vai, true or not, had allegedly developed into the social event of the year for the region around the village where old and new friends apparently met up, where for an evening there was music and dancing and various performances and food expressing, I imagined, vain hopes of eternal love and requited romance. Fine, I thought, that such a market existed if just for a day each year, except that in my dream I was at first wandering around the village and then spied Tao. *Tao in the blue bikini on her Honda Dream sitting backwards on the seat.* From a distance she waved me over towards her and off I went in her direction, at a fast jog, but each time the distance closed between us, the motorbike, by some magic, sped off and then stopped once again. I continued towards her, but again and again the Honda sped away. Round and round we went, up and down hilly lanes within the village in a frenetic cycle, fomenting increasing frustration and weariness. Fortunately, the noise of the dawn traffic outside the apartment woke me. It had been an exhausting night chasing Tao.

When I arrived at the Maitre Café and waved to Anh, she pointed me to one of the tiny tables on the sidewalk. After a while she came over and I asked her: "Ever been to the 'Love Market' at Khau Vai?"

"No," she said, "I overhear of it a couple times. You go there?"

"Not interested," I said, not telling Anh I had already been to Khau Vai -- if just in a dream -- and been unsuccessful. Any thought of going back to such labors was unappealing.

"You look for love you not find it," said Anh. "It come to people. Chase it not good."

For a split second I thought Anh could read my mind. She was correct, though. I had spent all night chasing Tao.

"Has love come to you? It came to me once."

"Mother of your doctor son?" asked Anh.

"Yes. But what about you?"

"I hope. Someday," she said evasively. "You want coffee?"

"Of course, Thanks."

"Some *pho*, too?"

"Not now."

"Where have you been?" Anh asked. "Not see you around."

"Crazy busy," I lied, because I could have stopped in at the Maitre Café almost anytime.

"You happy? You worried?"

"I'm up and down. Like everybody, I imagine."

"Up and down. Yes, that right. Like everybody," she answered.

"You, too?" I asked.

"It human," said Anh. "Being human hard sometime."

"I know," I said, looking at Anh appreciatively. "And what makes it hard are inhumane people, whom I come across occasionally." I was then thinking particularly of Jabotinsky.

"I not know that word," said Anh.

"Inhumane? It just basically means mean or selfish people. People who do harm to others."

"Understand," said Anh.

The adjacent Dong Xuan market was opening for business with people flooding across the Long Bien Bridge bringing their wares on bikes and motorbikes. The market scene was ablaze with flowers of all kinds, blossoming peach branches and even diminutive orange trees, some of them for sale, some merely for visual pleasure.

Anh sat at the table opposite me on one of the ubiquitous plastic stools. Seated, she put her hands -- those hands that I thought lovely -- on her hips and straightened her back such that she was leaning forward over the lip of the low table: "I tell you something. I a little worried for you."

"What are you saying? Why?"

"While back one day I see you go out of building. Later, men come to street. Truck with two soldiers. Not police. Army uniforms, with Kalashnikov. They go into your building and then they come out maybe ten minutes later. Traffic continues by like always, but me and others here on the street, we stop. We shake our heads. We wonder why soldiers come to Hang Giay. We see police a lot, but not soldiers."

"I can't imagine what that was about," I said to Anh, surprised at her account.

"Now I tell you," added Anh, "some whisper soldiers looking for foreigner. But maybe they just go talk to policeman I tell you living there. I not know."

My surprise shifted to alarm. I had some tendency to paranoia, and I was in Vietnam and it was not Europe, not Western and not even my more familiar Middle East, where I had spent much more time over the years. But the atmosphere of welcome in Nam, such that I had experienced it, had been almost seamless but for the day I went into the newsroom with bared knees.

"What foreigner?" I asked.

"Not many live in Old Quarter like you."

"Are you suggesting they were looking for me?"

"No sure," said Anh.

Maybe she was right to wonder. There were no other expats in my building, at least none I had seen, but then I had met none of my neighbors in the building but for the old Viet man who guarded the gate between the sidewalk and the undercroft. Perhaps I belonged in the neighborhood as securely as anyone, but then maybe I did not, and therefore had literally been a closely scrutinized resident. I recalled what Dar had said: that foreigners, their comings and goings, were watched by Viet security. I was feeling, if not alarm, then some anger that maybe I was living under a microscope, just as I had been in the West Bank, where everyone was.

Anh evidently picked up on my concern. "I think it's just a bad whisper," she said. "I think you should not worry."

"Bad whisper?"

"That maybe people look for you. No worry...."

"Are you sure?"

"If army or police want to talk to you, they come back. They have not come back. It has been long time and you okay. No problem, right?"

"I don't know of any like that so far," I told Anh. "I haven't done anything, except maybe not give you a big enough tip!"

"You good man. I know that. No problem for you."

Anh went inside to fetch me coffee. I was feeling slightly better. I had seen nothing of the police or any soldiers up close. I scanned along the crowded sidewalk and across the street. No one was staring at me, no one was walking by deliberately giving my seat at the table a wider or closer than normal berth. In a word, as I had so far experienced life on Hang Giay, everything seemed normal, as it had been since the day I took delivery of the key to the apartment. But I had not forgotten the night I had walked the long way back from the newspaper, had lingered around the statue of Lenin in the park across from the Army Museum.

I recalled talking to Tao on the phone from there, and inviting her to come with me to Marcel's house for dinner. But I also recalled arriving back at the apartment that same night and for the first and only time before or since discovering that my door was slightly ajar, unlocked, and thinking at the same time with almost absolute certainty that I had never left the apartment without securing the door. I could not forget that night, for that was the one time I had almost gotten quite intimate with Tao.

Anh returned carrying the usual, diminutive cup atop which precariously rocked the usual tin filter with coffee grinds into which hot water had been poured. "Thanks," I said, "but can I ask you another question? Do you have a minute?"

"Sure. I make time for my *My* friend when you come."

"You mentioned the soldiers came to my building. You don't remember exactly when?"

"Some time ago," she answered. "Late one afternoon. Cooler then. They not stay long. Ten minutes."

"Like how long ago?"

"Not know what day. Not remember."

No way, I realized, to pin down, at least with Anh, the exact day the soldiers allegedly entered my building, but the thought occurred that perhaps it was on that same day I had discovered late the unlocked door. Perhaps the soldiers had entered the apartment, but there was no evidence that anyone had. The apartment inside seemed undisturbed when I got back that night and, too, there was no proof that even if the soldiers did go into the building, they had gone to my apartment or were trying to find me or find out something about me. And, according to Anh, they had not returned. I was mystified nonetheless while enjoying the coffee. I waved to her again when I had finished the drink and decided to stroll by the mosque over on Hang Luoc. She smiled warmly and it felt like balm, or the hands of the blind masseuse, but on my very soul. When I arrived at the mosque after a few minutes I found the door leading inside to the courtyard locked. I continued on, later taking lunch at the Moca Café near the cathedral and the statue of Virgin Mary before continuing on to work.

14

Jabotinsky's humorless countenance I kept remembering at the newspaper -- the work was mechanical and barely required mental exertion, so my mind often drifted from the immediate task. His face, I thought, was diametrically at odds with the warmth and mirth evinced by Thomas Merton in the photos in his Asian journal, which I had been reading off and on at the apartment. During a break with Cain, still remembering Jabotinsky, I did not speak of anything Middle East related immediately, but did of Merton and the latest read. After that, I told him about leaving Israel, about the scene and actions of the chief of security at the new Ben Gurion airport terminal near Tel Aviv.

I had hoped to avoid the crowd that would line up to pass through security, arriving at the airport four hours before the departure of a Continental flight to Newark. When asked where I had been, I readily admitted having been in Tubas in the West Bank. Then came an ordeal impeccably orchestrated by the chief security officer at the airport: rapid sequestration behind a locked door at the terminal in a small, windowless room, three strip searches spaced over three hours of incarceration there, the scattering and almost comically microscopic examination and reexamination of all my belongings on a table amid five separate interrogations by five different interrogators who all asked the same questions looking for anomalies or variations in my responses. Finally, the security chief took my cell phone and computer and handed me a boarding pass, saying I could not have the phone or the computer back, that the items *might* be sent along to my final destination at home "in a couple of weeks". I protested the theft, but to no avail, and received no guarantee of delivery and in fact never got delivery. This all cleansed me of any sympathy I might have had for those severe Zionists who were aiming to ethnically cleanse the West Bank of the Jordan River.

"He was probably Shin Bet," said Cain. "They were tagging you as a sympathizer with the enemy. I guess any Palestinian, all of them, are considered terrorists."

"They lived there so I guess they were deemed terrorists."

"Of course," said Cain. "They were Arabs and worse, Arab Palestinians naturally opposed to the occupation and settlements."

"They jumped on me at the airport," I said. "Having nothing to hide, I didn't expect the ordeal, but they really could do little more than take my most valuable things and make the overall departure so uncomfortable that maybe I'd never want to come back. Well, they did not *want* me to come back."

"Instilling fear and uncertainty. That's the nasty game, mate," said Cain.

Despite some vague, unanchored foreboding of my own, I managed to edit the copy the other Anh, the one directing the flow of domestic stories, handed me at intervals in the steamy newsroom. Summer by the calendar had not officially arrived, but summer it seemed: air flicked through the open windows like the hot breath of a slobbering dragon. Cain and I were sweating through our shirts, feeling dirty withal, but I was finding nothing so glaringly amiss that evening to raise objections with Phuc or Anh, which anyway would have been a waste of energy. Anh that evening was again refusing to use the control device for the air conditioning system hidden somewhere in her desk, or in some other dark place, like between her legs -- a location I'd not have suggested to anyone but Cain.

Round about nine, Cain and I headed down the steps into the basement parking area of the building and rode off on Cain's motorbike, a Yamaha, towards Marcel's house. When we reached Ngu Xa, I suggested that Cain park his bike along the street that followed the shore of Truc Bach Lake. The house on narrower Nguyen Khac Hieu was just another block in from the shore, and many residents of Ngu Xa parked their motorbikes on the lakeshore sidewalk.

Marcel greeted us in a pressed white shirt and tailored trousers. He created, as before, an impression of preparation, showing us into the living room on the first floor where he had already placed a tray laden with a fresh pack of Marlboro Lights, a bucket of ice, three glasses and a full bottle of his favorite booze, Johnny Walker Red Label. The Marlboro's were a nice touch: Cain especially had been sucking on the *Vinatabas*, the relatively rancid Vietnamese cigarettes, for so long that I wondered if he had forgotten what a good smoke was like.

"Here's your copy," I said to Marcel.

"You like the stories?" he asked.

"They are energetic. I am looking forward to seeing them in the first edition of the mag with photos."

"Thanks for the help."

I introduced Cain as the New Zealander and editor colleague he was and we three took seats on the sofas.

"New publications sound good," Cain said, aiming to get a conversation going as Marcel poured the booze. "Might be a good medium to report some real news, except I wonder you might be dealing with censors?"

"That's correct," Marcel said. "We must avoid controversial articles for now. I think Vietnam is a shithole sometimes. This has not been a good day. Until you came over, I have been unhappy."

"What has happened, Marcel?" I asked.

"Been trying to extend my visa, for one thing," Marcel said, "but I have a new passport, too." He swallowed half a glass of the Johnny Walker. "Get this. Three days ago I went to the Ministry of the Interior. Looks like something Fidel might have thrown up in Havana. A large room all painted up in special toxic green with long counters and lady officers sporting red epaulettes and yellow stars. I had to see if they would transfer and extend my visa to the new passport I picked up at the Swiss Embassy. I gave one of these ladies my expired and my new passport. I went back today to retrieve it all and this same lady has a funny look on her face. Maybe my shirt wasn't tucked in, maybe I had a spot of food stain on my trousers, you know. She could not extend the visa, she says, adding that she didn't think my new passport was real, but a fake."

"That's fucked up," said Cain. "And a Swiss passport, too."

"I was angry, and showed it," said Marcel. "The bitch, she's all alarmed and grabs a red phone, I guess a Commie hot line, haha, off to the side, and calls her superior. I have to calm down or maybe I'm really fucked. Her boss comes down and asks me all sorts of silly questions, suggesting I have breached some kind of unnamed protocol. He's polite, though. Finally, he says come back in a week, that it will be done then. Nothing I could do but leave. Next time I need something I'm going to give a fat wad of cash to a desk clerk at the Metropole or to a waiter at Bobby Chinn's and get it done the Vietnamese way. But I don't have my passport right now. I feel trapped."

"Get used to it, mate," said Cain. "I've been here a while. Now here's something neither of you may know about yet. A young lady I know from my neighborhood -- she's Vietnamese -- works at the American Embassy part-time. She's a go-fer. By her account it seems like the Americans may declare war on one facet of corruption here. It's about child adoptions by Westerners, often Americans. She says the embassy is preparing a report to publicly condemn some aspects of the adoption system. Something she says she overheard. The government won't be happy with that."

"This would make a good story for the paper," I said.

"Phuc wouldn't accept it."

"Phuc?" asked Marcel, evidently thinking "fuck", too.

"He's something like our boss at the newspaper," Cain said.

"Tell me more about this adoption problem," Marcel said.

Cain described what he had heard: that adoption service providers in foreign countries, and especially in the US, were obliged to pay exorbitant sums to Vietnamese orphanages for children on a per capita basis, and the orphanages therefore sought to obtain as many children as they could to offer for adoption since that meant more income. "They do this by paying off hospital and social workers across Vietnam," Cain claimed. "The parents of many children designated as 'abandoned' children, and thus available for adoption under certain rules, have not actually abandoned them. The children have been stolen. There's a lot of money changing hands up and down the line. This country is a candy shop."

"The Viet elites will do anything for a buck, just like many bankers I used to know and work with," said Marcel, evidently disgusted, but perhaps not so much with the bankers. But whether the result of Cain's report or the Johnny Walker, Marcel was just warming up, and I was a bit surprised that, once again, to someone who was essentially a stranger, he reported the alleged diamond transaction in Hong Kong as he had done to me and Tao when earlier we had all dined together at the house.

"Two million paid for diamonds is not chump change," said Cain. "But diamonds are a girl's best friend, eh?"

"Where do you suppose the diamonds came from? Are they a big deal in this part of the world," I probed worldly Marcel, assuming his source had told him more than he had so far revealed. As a reporter, too, one could play dumb. This could so flatter subjects that sometimes they would open up more.

"Anywhere, diamonds are a big deal, and often useful," Marcel said. "A perfect medium for money laundering, for example."

"Of course," said Cain.

"Let me go on. An example, if you like. In my country not long ago a Swiss court convicted Benazir Bhutto and her husband of money laundering when she bought a diamond necklace for over $200,000 with funds obtained from kickbacks from a government contract with two Swiss companies. This fraud occurred during her second term as Prime Minister of Pakistan," Marcel said coolly. "The necklace was purchased by Mrs. Bhutto at a jewelers in Knightsbridge in London."

"How do you know this stuff?" I asked, shaking my head in surprise.

"You know I was a banker. I was paid well by my bank to be informed so I could make profitable deals," said Marcel.

"What are you saying exactly?" I asked.

"That I was privy to lots of inside information as a hot banker," said Marcel. "You asked how I knew about Mrs. Bhutto."

"Understood," I said.

But I was also remembering Marcel's story about the young Greek siren, the honey pot who had feigned pregnancy, and I was still smarting about the "sexting" with Tao and their alleged lunch, if not more, together. I also was wondered if Tao, not knowing how Marcel had actually lost a substantial chunk of his assets or even that he *had* lost it, was particularly impressed by Marcel's appearance of wealth -- the funding of a magazine focusing on luxury at least initially, the procurement of arguably one of the finest houses in Ngu Xa to lease, the simple but elegant clothing, the gold Breitling, the Russian-made BMW replica motorcycle, the talk of a most expensive hobby -- aviation and airplanes -- and even the fine dinner and wine we had enjoyed at the house. Well, I thought, she hadn't been impressed with my lodgings in Ha Noi.

And then, sitting opposite Marcel as he emptied his glass and reached for the bottle of Johnny Walker, I noticed that the gold Breitling watch was not on his wrist. Whatever watch he was wearing, it was black and the band looked like rubber.

"Excuse me," I said, "but have you given up the flying drug? I see you are no longer wearing that aviator's chronograph, the Breitling?" I turned to Cain quickly and added: "Marcel had an interesting watch for pilots. We both have an interest in aviation," I explained.

"It is lost," sighed Marcel. "Or it was stolen. This is another recent problem."

"Stolen?" I asked.

"I suspect the housekeeper," said Marcel.

"You've got a housekeeper?" laughed Cain. "I'd like one myself, say about 22 years old and who will do anything for a few *dong* and for my dong."

"Thuy," Marcel went on. "An old woman, completely reliable until today. Kristen and I hired her months ago to come to the house twice a week and clean the place up, do our laundry, even pick up groceries. She'd walk over to Fivimart, buy what we wanted and lug it back to the house. She was supposed to come today and clean. Bring food, too. She didn't appear. That's why I have nothing here for you to eat tonight."

"Have you tried to call her?"

"No phone. And I don't know where she lives. Anyway, if she's got my watch, she would not admit it even if I found her. That would be big trouble for her. I'd *make* big trouble for her, the thief."

I thought Marcel was jumping to conclusions, and anyway could have reminded him that many bankers were thieves, too, except on such a grand scale the thefts came off as legitimate and legal. The same could be said for governments and central banks, I believed, but I held my tongue and commiserated.

"You lost a nice chunk of gold, in addition to the time, even if it was just 18 carat," I said. "I'm not a finance guy but gold's real money. Not the unhinged paper that's just printed up willy nilly."

"I agree," said Marcel. "All fiat paper money dies eventually and disappears. Average historical life has been 40 years, in fact. Gold has been used as money for 5000 years. I should know. But look, this watch is more unique, though far less expensive than the Breitling." He held up and twisting his arm about to show off the timepiece. "It's a Sinn."

"Never heard of Sinn, but sin is another matter," Cain quipped.

"It's less expensive than the Breitling and far less expensive than a Rolex. But both those other brands fetch absurd premiums. The Sinn is German, its case made with the same exotic steel alloys used for the hulls of German submarines. It's a relatively unknown watch, but it has mechanics as good a Breitling, just not the obvious, flashy sex appeal," Marcel said.

"That sounds like an item you might want to feature in the magazine? Another quality German product, like the Porsche 911," I commented.

"Perhaps," said Marcel, but his tongue had loosened some and he aimed to return to the subject of the diamonds. "You wondered where the diamonds came from?"

"What do you think?" asked Cain, virtually taking the question from my mouth. He had already emptied more from the bottle of Johnny Walker than Marcel.

"Well, of course, the diamonds actually came from Africa, as most diamonds do. South Africa or Congo. Maybe Angola."

"That's not what we mean," I said. "Who do you think might have owned them when they got to Hong Kong?"

"This is a guess. It's not originally my guess, but I will go along with it because it's plausible," Marcel said. "The diamonds were probably in Israeli hands originally."

"Ah, yes, that's plausible," I said. "The Israelis have been eating into DeBeers' control of the diamond trade for decades. Diamonds are a substantial business in Israel, the center of it in Ramat Gan."

"Yes," added Marcel, "and they've got a growing presence based in Hong Kong for the Asian market. It's also been claimed that al-Qaeda has financed some of its operations with trade in diamonds, so you might figure the Israelis might use diamonds, too."

"What you are suggesting," Cain said to Marcel, "is that the Israelis may be a party to corruption. I mean, if what you say is true -- that someone near the top of the political hierarchy here got paid off for something -- diamonds are certainly a way to grease some deal and stand for good payment. But with diamonds passed through Israeli hands to a Viet who's gone to Hong Kong to close the transaction?"

"Hong Kong for sure," Marcel said. "It's like Mrs. Bhutto getting her kickbacks laundered in London. Maybe it looks innocent enough. A couple goes off to Hong Kong for a weekend on an unofficial visit, like on a short, romantic vacation. Makes contact, gets the diamonds and returns to Ha Noi. The stones don't set off any alarms in airport security. Maybe the lady stuffed them in her bra. Expensive boobs, I'd call hers, if she's got any worth notice."

"Fine, Marcel," I said. "But there are two important question about all this and remember, you first brought all this up by mentioning it to both me and Tao at dinner right after we first met, and now Cain knows -- that I wonder if you can clarify?"

"I brought it up because in truth, I have finally discovered I don't like Vietnam," said Marcel, leaning back on the sofa opposite Cain and me. "What I heard underscored my dislike. What happened today with my passport did, too."

"Okay," I said. "This couple got two mil worth of diamonds. What did they get them for? What was done for them? And finally, who are they?"

"A Swiss contact at the embassy had a hunch," Marcel said. "He would not give the name to me. He wasn't sure anyway. But I can assure you that this man is important here. If such corruption exists at the top, the point is that you can well imagine it's everywhere. The current government exists solely to perpetuate itself and enrich its leaders, with some very minor trickle down to the People."

"Ah, yes, trickle down economics," I said. "I've heard that before. The voodoo of the Republicans in the US. Reminds me of the prime aim of our elected reps in Congress. Not good government, just their own perpetuation and enrichment."

"It's often all BS. I should know. Bankers hand in glove with government. I know banking. The job was simple: screw anybody to reward others. I admit. I enjoyed it. It was a rush," Marcel commented.

"I guess it was a rush, too, for that Greek siren."

"That's why I probably didn't want to kill her," Marcel said. "I actually understood her. We had things in common besides the sex. Well, really, I liked her and yes, I got scammed."

"What's this Greek matter?" asked Cain.

"Just a lady problem for Marcel," I said dismissively. "Let's return to the diamonds. If Israelis were part of this diamond deal, they gained something in exchange for the diamonds. What?"

"On that I have no clear idea," Marcel said. "More access in Vietnam? Arms sales? I don't know. Maybe access for something in the future. That can be important."

"This is a good story from any newsman's perspective, but it's not a story we likely can pursue," said Cain. "Too many dead ends will crop up, not least of which is that if we told Phuc this he'd dismiss us, I imagine. This is precisely what *Vietnam News* is not about. Once in a while the paper will report about some provincial official getting punished for corruption, but it can't turn the spotlight above a certain level, and that level remains low."

"Of course," I said. "Corruption exposed high up would compromise, maybe destroy, the Party's entire image, which Ho Chi Minh from the start sought to create and maintain. It was an image of moral purity. This is what comes through about him, I think. But he was hardly any kind of Gandhi when it comes to ways of throwing off colonialists and uniting north and south in Vietnam."

"The bright Gandhis of this dark world, I am sure, are just too rare, and when they appear, they die a bloody death. Americans had their Gandhi in Martin Luther King. What happened to him? He was shot dead on a motel balcony in Memphis," said Marcel. "But did you two come by to discuss all this? No, I think. We have had our serious conversation. Let's move on. Let's go over to Bobby Chinn's and check out the babes, but first I have to make a quick call."

Marcel hoisted himself from the sofa and pulled a phone from his pocket. "Just a minute, please," he said, and disappeared beyond the foyer next to the living room into the small kitchen where Kristen Andre had prepared the meal for Tao and me weeks earlier.

15

It was near ten when Marcel, Cain and I walked to the shore of Truc Bach and hailed a cab to take us to Bobby Chinn's restaurant. A hot fog, a weather I had not seen in Ha Noi before, enveloped Ngu Xa, and visibility across the lake to Fivimart was impossible. The air also stank of putrefaction, like it had when I had walked back to the apartment to meet Tao after the visit with Lenin, or his statue, near the Army Museum.

I was a third the way to inebriation, exactly at that point where I usually stopped, content enough with thoughts and images that had lost just enough of their borders and definition, had become somewhat surreal, but pleasantly so. Though relieved that neither Marcel nor Cain wanted to ride over to Chinn's on their two wheelers, I rather hoped at some point to get a ride on Marcel's Russian "BMW". Interesting motorcycles were, after all, a poor man's way to get some of the speed thrills inherent in flying small aircraft. I had cruised the entire East Coast of the US, Florida to Maine, at one time or another at an altitude of a hundred meters. At 200 miles an hour in a Mooney, a specific aircraft which Marcel knew of, I found a piece of Heaven or, rather, pushing the envelope like that had given me the perception of being about to break forth into another, far finer dimension of time and space. Anticipating a breakthrough, even if it never came, was thrilling even though, logically, it was called "death", or at least what one might hope death involved.

Marcel evidently was about to partake of another kind of speed, too. I caught him throwing back something, a pill of some sort, and then taking a swig from a weirdly shaped bottle he drew from his shoulder bag in the cab. The taxi pulled away from the end of Nguyen Khac Hieu by the lake, the road around lined with yellow street lamps and coconut palms, the palm fronds hanging so listless they looked like they had been stricken with some kind of nasty virus.

"What's that?" I asked him.

"That's what my attempted phone call was about. Ecstasy. Resupply from my supplier. He also sells snake wine bottled up near Fansipan by the Black Hmong. It's a special concoction, bound to make you hot, and hard to get. The Viet chap has a cell phone he always answers, but this time he didn't pick up when I tried to call him from the kitchen. Never happened before."

"You'd better hope he hasn't been arrested," I commented. "He might point a finger at one of his customers, like at you. Then you'll surely not get your precious Swiss passport returned."

"I must tell you," he said, "I discovered the fellow is a municipal cop. I spotted him once standing in the middle of an intersection, all dressed up in uniform, over by that empty water tower near where you live. He was waving a baton around that looked like a small barber pole, as if he were actually controlling the flow of traffic in the intersection. He was completely ignored, but at least he didn't get run over."

"Welcome to Vietnam!" Cain blurted.

"Like I said, these people will sell most anything," said Marcel. "My inhibitions vanish with this hooch and the pills."

"Marcel," I said, "I truly didn't think you had inhibitions to lose, to be honest. But that stuff?"

"Here," said Marcel. He handed me the small, flattish bottle. "Look at it."

"How about one of those pills?" I asked. I was eager to find out what it was like to be uninhibited, what might happen if I were.

"Sorry, none left."

I did as he suggested and looked at the bottle. Inside amid a somewhat clouded liquid was a baby King Cobra, all of maybe just eight inches long and very thin. "That I won't drink," I said. I handed the bottle back to Marcel.

The driver got on the accelerator when he could, hitting speeds that, in Ha Noi, were possible only late at night.

"Forgive me again for not having some food at the house tonight," said Marcel.

"No. No," chimed Cain. "The drinks were fine. The Marlboro's a treat. I'm not one to overpay for what will kill me. It's been *Vinataba* all the way here."

"Well," Marcel said, "too many problems for me right now."

"Bummer!" shouted Cain, who was listening to Marcel, while he was also lunging out the cab window by the front passenger seat as we rounded the north side of Hoan Kiem Lake headed south, trying to touch young women shooting past the cab on motorbikes. Viet girls in jeans and tight blouses, or psychedelic T-shirts, were buzzing round the lake like exotic bees around a hive.

"Bummer indeed," I said. "Marcel, you've had a run of bad luck. So now maybe you can look forward to a run of good fortune. One follows the other often."

"Tonight maybe for sure," Marcel responded, and the cab pulled up in front of Bobby Chinn's restaurant, which was packed with expats and tourists and a few Vietnamese, too. There wasn't an empty table in sight, but Marcel was undaunted, leaving us for a minute standing near the bar at the front of the restaurant. "I know Cuchi," said Marcel. "The head waiter."

By degrees Marcel's back faded away behind the waves of diaphanous, yellow silk curtains that hung from sturdy bamboo poles demarcating separate but almost identical dining areas. Red rose petals filled bowls at each end of the bar and many thousands more lay scattered and mostly crushed over the polished wooden floor. The rose petals were part of the décor, like a carpet that got restored to new every day. Cain turned to the bar and ordered two Bloody Marys, and as we waited for the drinks and for Marcel to advance from the reefs of yellow silk, waving like inverted corals, I noticed a tall, striking, big-boned blonde who had turned around in her seat at the ebony bar and whose eyes followed Marcel's back. Soon, Marcel returned.

"Cuchi will find seats at the back," Marcel said. "Just head back there and he'll see you and seat you." He left us again and this time went straight for the bar and the blonde. I figured if he had any lingering inhibitions, the snake wine and the Ecstasy had completely eradicated them.

He engaged the woman straight on, his face alight with charm, his brown eyes sparkling. He placed his hands on his butt and churned his hips a couple times. If I had tried that -- at any age -- I'd likely have been slapped hard, but the woman was clearly amused, and almost immediately she was grabbing her handbag off the bar and rising from her seat with some urgency. Marcel turned back to Cain and me.

"What's going on?" I asked, feeling somewhat confused, but then quickly gathered what Marcel had negotiated and I envied him for being able to do it with just a smile and a couple churns. Such were the advantages of youth and his charm.

"I'll be back in a hour or so," Marcel said. "I'm going back to the house with the babe. Back soon, I promise. Wait for me."

"Jesus, Marcel, I couldn't do what you just did, not even at your age. You know the lady?"

"She's the wife of the head of security at the Canadian Embassy. Nice looking babe, don't you think? Has two children, too." Marcel winked.

"I thought we were going to check out the babes, not just one, as you said."

"All you really ever need is just one," said Marcel. "Good luck," he added, and in a flash he was out the door, the blonde's hand in his, as if they were longtime partners.

"Your friend moves fast," Cain said admiringly. "Light speed fast."

"Now you know why I wanted you to meet him. He's amusing," except that I thought not amusing at all to me in his dealings with Tao. "Let's go sit. He'll return. We can wait and enjoy the scenery at least."

Cain, cradling the Bloody Marys he collected from the bar, followed me back deeper into Bobby Chinn's. I did not know Cuchi, but exactly as Marcel had said, a young Viet man in a dress white shirt under a cummerbund strode up to us.

"You must be Cuchi?" I asked.

"Mr. Mossadeq," he answered politely above the restaurant cacophony, "said you were looking for a place to sit. I have seats for you."

"Thank you."

We wound up as far back as one could go and not be out the backdoor at the restaurant, but the location was fine with seats on a divan behind a low table. I could have napped, lying back on the cushions, but Cain, crocked, seemed energized.

"I don't come here, mate. Too expensive, but glad we did," he said, chomping down on a stick of celery he had withdrawn from his drink, casting his eyes about. "Whadduya think Marcel is up to?"

"Do you have to ask? Marcel's got just the right combination of goods to be where he is right now. I have to say he's rather impressive in that regard. So, Cain," I asked, trying to make myself heard over the buzz in the restaurant, "what do you make of Marcel's story about the diamond deal?"

"Sounds plausible," said Cain. "But the Israeli connection is still a bit puzzling, unless you consider that Vietnam has come a long way in recent years by establishing links with the Zionists."

"I'd have presumed the relationship between Israel and Vietnam might be weak. The Israelis are colonialists, after all, and Vietnam had its bloody colonialist problem over and over for centuries. The Viets would not relate positively to the Zionists, in theory at least."

"We've maybe discussed some of this before," said Cain, "but you know organizations like the PLO derived a lot of support from anti-colonialist movements like the one in Nam."

"Yeah, I think the PLO used some of the Marxist-guerrilla handbook as foundations for their efforts starting back in 1965 when they blew up the Beit Netopha water carrier in the West Bank. That was the beginning of military resistance by Fatah."

"OK, and Nam was isolated for so long after the war, casting itself as the underdog, that it sought the same political bed fellows. Supported the PLO, the ANC in South Africa during apartheid back when. Vietnam had even closer ties with Cuba and Castro and still maintains them. But my point is that that overall posture's been fading fast. Can't have the government here supporting the Arab dispossessed and at the same time have their hand out to join the WTO and land business deals and investments from your country, given your uncritical support of Israeli colonization."

"Not my support," I said. "My government's, such as it is, and the 'my' government part is increasingly debatable, not just for me, but for most Americans except an elite few."

"But we come back to what the Israelis got in return for doing the diamond deal, if they did it?"

"We don't know. Hard to find that out."

"Mate, two things. Corruption is part of the overall package. Reporters, Viet reporters, are fucking *arrested* here if they get too enterprising. That's why they don't let us, us Western editors, do much at the paper. They probably wouldn't arrest us, but they'd send us packing if we got ambitious. So their best bet is just to keep us on a short leash and not bother to say exactly why," Cain said. "I heard the government recently charged the one or two good Viet reporters working for Vietnamese language papers with something called 'abuse of power' and put them away. One was a fellow about your age, a popular journalist who had blown the lid off a few small scandals over the years involving low level Viets."

"Cain, shit, I wouldn't have lasted a month if you hadn't been at the newspaper to amuse me, and make me accept temporarily something I cannot change, but would if it were possible."

"No, problem, mate."

"Don't think I've mentioned this. You remember me talking about a woman named Tao?"

"You were meeting her at the *Cinematique* after the fireworks around Hoan Kiem. Right?"

"Glad you remember," I said. "Well, first time I met her was on the *Emeraude* in Ha Long Bay. Weeks ago. That same afternoon I was on deck and there, slipping past off our stern, was a most stunning yacht. Maybe a 100 meters long. I still remember the name -- *Geneva Princess*. I had read that private yachts of foreign registry are not allowed in Ha Long Bay. This one was French. It even had a helicopter on a pad with French registration. Now, get this: I had a pair of binoculars and the Viets on board looked like top Party brass. A bunch of babes in bikinis serving food and drink, too. Maybe the Prime Minister was there, for all I know. This was about the time the Airbus consortium rep here in Ha Noi was working up a 'Memorandum of Understanding' to sell commercial jets to Vietnam Airlines."

"Anything's possible," said Cain.

"The Europeans, with the yacht, with the pedigree chum, they were all maybe greasing the deal. They were having a good time. Who wouldn't, you'd say, if you had seen the *Geneva Princess* and the ladies moving about. But here's the point: I hardly thought much about it. The word 'corruption' did not come to mind right then. I don't know what I was thinking that it didn't. I was naïve," I confessed.

"Chum. That's a great metaphor," said Cain.

"Can you imagine Bac Ho cruising Ha Long Bay on a French yacht like that, with that chummy company? The old man, revered by the Prime Minister and his ilk, would rise up here in his mausoleum if he knew what had become of the sons and daughters of his Communist colleagues, how they had veered off the *siraat mustaqim*."

"The *what*, mate?"

"It's an Arabic term," I explained. "In the *Qu'ran*, it means more or less 'the straight path', something like sticking to the duties and prohibitions incumbent on Muslims. Golden Rule stuff in essence."

"O, I forgot. You know some Arabic. I got the point. Nothing new in any of this," Cain said dismissively. He wasn't much interested in the topic then anyway, and I dropped it.

After a while I caught a glimpse of Bobby Chinn hovering over a table beyond the closest, gentle barrage of yellow silk. His ponytail swung about as he chatted up some diners. He was indeed a local celebrity, and no doubt what diners he deigned to greet might be more inclined to order the most expensive of the expensive dishes at the restaurant. But Marcel then brushed past

Chinn, clapping him gently on the back. He had returned, taking a seat beside us on the divan, looking completely unruffled, exactly as he had before he swooped up the Canadian at the bar.

"You look no worse for the wear," I said to Marcel.

"That single pill did the trick. I don't tire when I have them."

"What happened to the lady? You came back alone, it appears."

"She had to get home to the children," Marcel said with not the slightest hint of concern about what had transpired.

"I guess she had to get home to the husband, too. I would not want to tangle with any security chief at an embassy," I said.

"Nor would I," Marcel said. "It's all under control. She's discrete enough."

"And she doesn't bother with the small talk. Gets right to it. You've met her before?"

"Yes. Actually, at the Metropole. The night I went over to settle things, more or less, with the Greek. She was in the lobby when I arrived there and we hit it off for a few minutes as I was heading upstairs to fuck the Greek that last time. She got in the elevator with me. She said she liked to get a drink now and then here. I took it as a come on up close in the lift, and, you saw, it was. I was not that surprised when I spotted her at the bar. I told her I come here frequently for a drink."

"Amazing Grace," I said, recalling the title of the hymn sung at my son's mother's funeral. I could not think of anything else to say, but the impulse, probably shared with Cain, was to query Marcel about the goings on at his house over the preceding hour or so. Some details, as it was. But I held my tongue, and so did Cain, who was beginning to look a bit glassy eyed.

I suddenly felt a huge ache of nostalgia for time past. The diaphanous, yellow silk curtains fluttered. They separated me, like at least a score of years were, from the happily married youth I preferred to be. An image of the big boned Canadian blonde, naked, flashed in my head like a mirage. The hands of the huge clock outside atop the main Ha Noi post office, lit up and reflected in Hoan Kiem Lake, were closing on midnight.

16

I dozed off on the cushions of the divan at Bobby Chinn's. Marcel's presence had engaged Cain and they talked, the younger men getting to know each other I reckoned. My burgeoning exhaustion was no doubt part the consequence of the cacophony in the restaurant. Noise, attempts to hear any specific voice within surrounding noise, had become increasingly tiresome and nearly impossible: too many hours, several thousand anyway in the distant past, subjecting my ears to the low frequency vibrations emanating from the engines of small aircraft, and I had stupidly never worn noise-cancelling headphones.

I must have dozed for half an hour, but then I was startled by the sound of breaking glass, and then Marcel was shaking my shoulder, rousing me to a scene where no one seemed to care what anyone did as long as they did not try to bust up the place. I had earlier noticed ladies going into the men's room, and vice versa, and sometimes men and women together to either loo. No one cared, and evidently both Marcel and Cain had imbibed more drinks. Marcel seemed to handle the booze well: he was in control, but Cain was flying fast well beyond propriety.

The restaurant had almost emptied. Those remaining were stirring, moving out, a few spectral figures in the low light among the yellow silk curtains, but there was Cain embarrassing himself, embarrassing Marcel, too, and bothering Cuchi and several of his staff. "Noooo, you can't close!"

Cain was shouting, making a scene, sullen vapors and unwarranted outrage exuding from him like a disturbed swarm of African bees.

"I want another fucking vodka! Get me another drink!" he bellowed. But native, quaint brooms of straw bundled with colorful twine were already emerging from closets near the kitchen in staff hands, brooms to sweep up the thousands of bruised, crushed rose petals from the floor throughout the restaurant.

I remembered the city's flower market near the Long Bien Bridge. How many red roses would it take to prepare the scene at the restaurant for the morrow? In another hour or two the place would be cleaned up, the dishes and glasses washed, the trash and the smashed petals taken out and discarded, the place readied for the next day and then the same cycle all over again. Bobby Chinn was nowhere in sight.

Cuchi was exerting admirable control, but then he was half Cain's size, and Cain was tough and looked it -- he had a scar, rather an appealing one, an inch long on a cheekbone, a feature I had not inquired about, but it looked to me like the lingering mark of a barroom brawl in Auckland.

"You mates are a bunch of weasels!" shouted Cain at the Viet wait staff moving to surround him, but they did not have a clue what exactly to do and kept a safe distance, and they weren't interested in serving him yet more alcohol. There seemed no alternative but to try to mollify him myself.

"C'mon," I said to Cain, "let's get out of here. It's late. Let's go back to Marcel's." I wasn't going to jump on Cain, either physically or verbally, for the bad behavior. Better, I thought, just to get him outside, get us all outside. "C'mon Cain, we can get another drink at Marcel's house."

This latter summons seemed to work, but I was lying to him. More Johnny Walker at Ngu Xa seemed insane. Maybe I could get him on his Yamaha and send him home, wherever that was, and I realized how little I truly knew of Cain except that his friendly and informative presence had made the newspaper just tolerable.

"Yeah, mate, let's go. This place sucks closing early," said Cain, flinging an arm across my shoulder, and with Cain sort of attached to me like a remora, perhaps because I had suggested further libations, I moved us towards the bar at the front and the front door. Marcel followed. I looked back and saw him give a hand full of *dong* to Cuchi. He pointed to the broken glass, what had been a tall crystal tumbler, and a pool of Bloody Mary as dark red as the crushed rose petals littering the floor. Cuchi followed along behind Marcel, and when finally Cain and I reached the sidewalk, there was Marcel backing down the three steps to join us, apologizing to Cuchi, who stood in the doorway brandishing keys but looking unperturbed. No doubt he had seen something like this before -- a patron who had imbibed too much.

The hands on the clock above the post office pointed to one thirty. I could not remember when I had been out so late at night, except along Hang Giay briefly, and never before so late around Hoan Kiem. It was a view of Ha Noi's heart my tired eyes had not seen: the traffic was virtually gone but for an occasional cab lurching across the uneven pavement at the intersection. It was quiet, almost frighteningly so. The grassy park bordering the lake across Trang Thi street appeared empty: not yet time for Doris Day belting out *Que Sera, Sera* from a boom box for the dawn cadres of women doing their exercises. And then a cab pulled up and we three climbed inside and scooted off counter clockwise around Hoan Kiem, then directly up past the Dong Xuan market north of the lake, by Anh's Maitre Café, then my apartment building, the French water tower, and after another kilometer, across one of the two small bridges onto the island that comprised Ngu Xa. The cab stopped, at Marcel's insistence, where Nguyen Khac Hieu met the shore of Truc Bach, where Cain, amid 50 other bikes and now maybe 50 more there, had earlier parked his motorbike.

I felt I had to pretend with Cain to make a show of further partying, and anyway hoped the walk to Marcel's house might be just long enough for Cain to collect himself a bit so he could eventually ride his Yamaha home without taking a tumble.

"Marcel," I whispered as we wended up the street, "it's been a nice evening. Thanks for the hospitality. Sorry about the scene at BC's."

"Not a problem," said Marcel. "I had a talk with Cain while you were resting." He turned to Cain. "Right, Cain?" he said and gave him the thumbs up.

"Riiiiiiight, mate," Cain answered, severely elongating the vowel.

"Holy Shit, man," I lied to Cain, breaking the bad news, formulated in the cab, to him. "I completely forgot. I have to go home soon. I have to be up in five hours."

"Whaaaat, mates?" Cain asked.

"I've got to rest. You forget that I'm fucking 60 now. No more partying tonight. Come on, Cain, let's go!"

Marcel looked at me and winked, nodding affirmatively. Even he had had enough for one night. And that had included the Canadian blonde who, I did not doubt, sucked considerable energy from anyone she might depart the restaurant with. Immediately, I liked Marcel more, forgetting about his dalliance with Tao then. He was showing an unusual degree of toleration, given the hour, the circumstances. He had not expressed a word of dissatisfaction with Cain's antics at the restaurant. He had paid the entire bill and then some -- the uncounted wad of bills handed to Cuchi, probably adding up to a million *dong* at least. I shook Marcel's hand and whispered: "Nice night. Hope to see you again soon." Then, I turned around and headed back down Nguyen Khac Hieu away from Marcel's house.

Walking slowly, I figured Cain would follow me, and I did not turn around until I had almost reached the lakeshore and the motorbikes parked there, among them Cain's Yamaha. I turned around because suddenly Cain was ratcheting up the decibels on the otherwise empty, quiet street, and he had not been following me. He was still standing near front of the door to Marcel's house: standing with his pants down around his ankles and pissing in the street and screaming: "Maaarrrrcccceeeel, Maaarrrcccceeelll! Open up! C'mon, mate. Let's have another drink!"

But Marcel had passed inside and apparently locked the door to the house and then Cain, his pants still at his ankles, two kinds of *dong* spilling out in full view, shuffled awkwardly to the door like a prisoner in shackles. Cain banged on the locked door with his fists.

It might have all been very amusing if the scene had not been completely appalling at that late hour, appalling primarily because Ngu Xa was a quiet, relatively upscale Ha Noi neighborhood filled mostly with Vietnamese families and their swarms of children and their shops, somewhat off the main channels of the city, more decorous, and not the place for non-natives to get wild. I headed back towards Cain, scanning the façade of Marcel's house. I saw the lights go off on the first floor, then on on the third floor, then off again.

Marcel, I calculated, must have run up the steps and was probably signaling that he was fast going to bed, that he would not respond to Cain's demands, and then I reached Cain again. "Let's get away from here," I insisted to him. "Marcel's beat and so am I and you are, too."

With that, Cain stopped the shouting and the door pounding. "Sorry, mate. Don't step in my piss. Sorry." He bent over and pulled up his trousers.

"I don't care about your piss or your pissing. But look, if this continues we'll have the police here. Let's hurry to your bike. No one's likely to question us by the lake."

I didn't bother to examine whether I had stepped in Cain's piss. It did not matter because even if I had, I could not have felt any filthier and more in need of a shower, then bed. I had sweated through work a few hours before, and my clothes were sticky and wrinkled. The hot fog still slopped through the area and Fivimart still was not much visible across Truc Bach when finally I got Cain back to his bike. But I saw he was in no shape to ride his yellow Yamaha, and by some stroke of good fortune a cab rounded the shore and came towards us. I flagged it down.

"Can't leave my ride here," said Cain. "Someone will steal it. Long way back to my place, mate."

"It's okay," I said. "It'll be fine. My apartment's just a kilometer from here, not far at all."

"No, I can ride," said Cain. He climbed on to the bike, started the engine, twisted the throttle and then popped the clutch. It lurched off the curb and tipped over and down went Cain, but he was unhurt.

"See, you can't ride now. Not yet. I plan to see you this afternoon at work. Here, get in the cab," I urged. "And look, I'll walk back to my place in a while. I'll stay here for a bit and be sure your bike is not stolen, and then I'll come back later this morning and watch over it. Better, I'll call you from here later this morning, too, and you can come and get it. How's that?" I grabbed Cain's shoulders and hustled him into the back seat of the cab. "Tell the driver where you live."

Cain sprawled across the back seat. I heard him mumble something to the driver, and to the driver I turned and said: "Take him home safely," and I gave him more than adequate fare to drive anywhere in Ha Noi. I was thinking I was glad Tan was not driving Cain home. I thought it might have been embarrassing to me if Tan saw me with Cain in the condition he was in, and the condition I had been approaching.

The cab pulled away and within a few seconds rounded a bend along the lake to the south and disappeared. A half minute later I spotted its red taillights on Truc Bach's south shore road, and then, with a left turn, the cab disappeared into the labyrinth of the city's streets going I did not know where.

"Damn," I whispered. A night like no other yet in Ha Noi. A touch of helter-skelter to it, I thought. It was interesting, but it had been wearing on my aging constitution and not the sort of night I truly enjoyed, aside from any simple camaraderie with friends.

More decorous nights there had been, like the one with Tao at the *Cinematique* and with Talloires -- and *both* Claire's knees -- in full display on the screen. Talloires with its clean streets and trim houses and restaurants and small hotels and French pastry shops banking down to cut green lawns by the clear, inviting waters of Lake Annecy. Heaven in Haute Savoie, I thought, standing alone there by the stinking sump of Truc Bach at almost three in the morning. I was too tired to walk immediately back to the apartment, and savoring the quiet, I sat just beyond the cadres of motorbikes on the stone embankment around the lake, almost invisible in the dark, as perhaps I had been late on a distant evening lingering under Lenin's statue in the park across from the Army Museum, where I had spoken with Tao over the phone.

Nothing stirred nearby, unusual in Ha Noi, not even the slightest breeze through the listless palms. No one passed by for five minutes, and I was beginning to relax, to shake off the dissonance of the scene of Cain pissing and shouting and pounding on Marcel's door. I might have sat there longer, but I still had to walk back to the apartment, and as I started to rise headlights rounded the sweep around Ngu Xa. As the headlights lights came closer, I recognized what appeared to be the same black Chevrolet SUV that I had seen twice before.

The SUV slowed at the intersection with Nguyen Khac Hieu but did not turn up Marcel's street. I ducked down again behind the parked motorbikes, my heart involuntarily pounding and my breathing labored, as I had experienced right after I had almost been struck by the same vehicle by Hoan Kiem. After the SUV disappeared around the next shoreline bend, I stood and headed back to the apartment as fast as I could, feeling nauseated.

Arriving back on Hang Giay some fifteen minutes later, the guard roused himself from his cot and let me into the undercroft of the building. Up the stairs and then inside the apartment, I peeled off my clothes, vomited in the running shower and finally crawled onto the bed. It had been a night to remember, but what I was remembering in the bed was not even a tenth of what I would soon never forget.

17

I was never one to dream often, at least not while asleep, and if asleep, I rarely remembered anything upon waking. One exception was the dream of fruitlessly chasing Tao at Khau Vai, and now I was dealing with a second, even more unsettling dream: by the shore of Truc Bach I had not hidden behind the motorbikes, but had given chase to the SUV as if in my younger years on speedy long distance runs, and with this dream, once more, I was unable to attain my objective -- to catch the vehicle, flag it to a stop, find out who was inside and why they were prowling around Ha Noi well past midnight.

The dream scenario was just as frustrating as chasing Tao had been: whenever I got closer to the SUV, it sped up and widened the gap, and this happened repeatedly. I had to wonder if this might be some aspect of being 60 plus: dreams in which, awake or asleep, one never reached whatever objective existed; dreams marked by frustration and enervation. But Cain ended this dream. He was not, however, to end more wakeful frustration that we both were soon dealing with in spades.

When the ringing phone woke me, my first thought was Tao: she might at last be calling to explain her disappearance at the Opera House.

"Marshall," said Cain. "You must come to Truc Bach now!" He was addressing me, for the first time I could recall, by my first name, not with the usual appellation of "mate".

"Right now? I just left there five hours ago. I put you in the cab. Remember that?"

"Doesn't matter what I remember about that," he said. "It's what I'm seeing now. Get over here!"

"Are you there?"

"Yes. I slept some and then I was worried about the bike. Came to get it. I've had to sober up fast."

"Man, you do seem to have recovered fast. What's the problem?"

"You'll see. It's sobering. Just come. Now!" he commanded, and then he broke the connection before I could respond one way or the other.

I figured someone had tossed his Yamaha into the lake or it was just missing. I was a bit irritated by the summons. I hadn't even had a morning shower or coffee at the Maitre Café, but I managed to find a pair of fresh jeans and a clean shirt and got out the door as quickly as I could.

The strange fog had cleared out and the rhythm along Hang Giay seemed normal. Ten minutes later I was walking down Dang Dung Street, noted for its rows of shops on both sides of the street marketing discarded mobile phones, and had my first sight that morning of the area around Truc Bach: a few municipal workers, women in blue uniforms, tending flower beds scattered along the west side of the lake, Fivimart farther up the shore open for business as usual, the encircling traffic, a couple of pedal boats in the shape of swans heading from their dockage near the grocery, but over near Nguyen Khac Hieu a crowd of maybe 100 by the lake's edge, a couple of crude barricades on the street and three or four police cars with their blue roof lights twirling about. *What's this*, I thought, and picked up the pace. Closer, several men were low on the stone embankment, their bamboo fishing poles poking at something. When I reached the scene, pushing my way past some gawking Viets, I saw what they were poking: a body dressed in a white shirt and dark trousers. At that moment, Cain appeared at my side.

"This is bad, Marshall. Really bad."

Four men with the poles were placing them on the body, face down, in the lake in unison, pushing it underwater until it disappeared. Then, they removed the poles and the body reemerged, floating back to the surface. They did this repeatedly. It appeared they were playing some sort of nonsensical game, and no one was yet to get in the lake and haul the corpse onto the embankment.

On the wrist of the corpse was a watch. It resembled the Sinn Marcel had proudly shown us. The body was Marcel's. My first thought was an image: an alleged fortune telling black 8-ball, a mere amusement with a multi-sided bit of plastic inside which gave random answers to questions posed to it. "Yes" and "No" and "Maybe" and others. How the answers, if one turned the ball over, would disappear into the inky liquid inside the ball, and then how one of them, randomly, would reappear, come up, in the little window if one turned the ball back over again. Marcel's body was disappearing and reappearing in the same way in inky Truc Bach. The Viet men getting some kind of kick making Marcel's body bob in and out of sight in the water. The fucking point I did not understand. Maybe the idiots preferred that he just sink. They weren't doing anything else, like pulling him out of the water.

"This is crazy," I said to Cain. "Marcel? I can't believe this. He'd be the last person to consider a swim in Truc Bach. Not even the Viets swim here. Wade some, but not swim. God only knows the exotic bacteria in this lake."

"I got here twenty minutes ago. Same scene then. I avoided the crowd at first, but then I had to find my bike. You are seeing what I saw when I got here, but the crowd has grown. That's when I called, the moment I realized it was Marcel."

"We've got to do something. Let's get his body out."

"Yeah," said Cain. "I've hesitated. I figured some Viet would be in charge. The police have been running around like a pack of monkeys on that snake booze Marcel had, talking a lot on their handhelds, maybe wondering what to do themselves."

With that, we moved down the embankment to the men poking Marcel's body with the bamboo poles. Cain took over, what with the scar and all plus an angry visage, and with an arm he swept aside one of the poles and it flew out of one of the men's hands into the lake. "Stop that, morons!" he bellowed, and the Viet men stopped the poking and stepped aside, not because they understood Cain exactly, but they understood his intent, and we managed to grab hold of Marcel's trousers and an arm and pull him onto the sloping embankment. But then, once we accomplished that, a couple of the policemen rushed down to us, poking their batons towards us, waving us away, as if we had hauled some long lost State treasure from the depths.

Though I had never seen a drowned body before, I figured Marcel had been in the black soup for some time. He looked ghastly but still the same, handsome face, but just flat dead, the animated charm utterly gone.

Well, in fact, I thought, exactly how a dead body is supposed to look after immersion in foul water. The two policemen finished the job of getting Marcel to the sidewalk and one of them began going through his clothes and pockets, turning most everything inside out. Nothing of the sort police usually want to find there, no wallet anyway, not even any *dong*. But I was close enough to see a woman's thong withdrawn from Marcel's trousers, a thong as red as the rose petals I figured the staff at Bobby Chinn's restaurant probably already that morning had bought from Ha Noi's flower market to set a fresh carpet for patrons to crush later in the day.

I imagined that Marcel had stolen the thong from the blonde Canadian dame and kept it as some kind of trophy, or maybe she had just let him have it as a reminder of an open invitation, of some future hot hour together. One of the policemen stared at the thong quizzically and then balled it up in his hands and tossed it into the lake. So much for adhering to any policy, if such existed, for not further mucking up Truc Bach Lake or destroying evidence. Then a police car moved to the lip of the embankment and a cop got out and opened the trunk of the vehicle.

Cain and I went to the back of the car. "We know that man," I said, but he spoke no English, or he could have but was just ignoring us. With that, though, a Vietnamese dressed in suit and tie -- he would have been a dead ringer for Phuc except that he was skinnier -- strode hurriedly up to us. In another weird flash I remembered the food on Phuc's desk at the paper one evening around *Tet*, the glob of fatty, grisly pork and spices wrapped in a green banana leaf as iridescent as the uniforms by the lake: *this guy maybe doesn't eat that crap.* I knew it was a weird thought, but this was a worse than merely a weird situation.

"And you are?" he asked in an officious tone to both Cain and me.

"We are friends of his. We know who he is," I said.

"Who are you?" he repeated.

I pulled out the best card I had under the circumstances, in fact the only thing I had in my pockets but for the apartment key. It wasn't a driver's license from *"My"* or my passport. It was no real card at all, but a piece of paper, a coupon, entitling the bearer to a free drink at Bobby Chinn's. Perhaps, seeing what I had to cough up, I thought quickly it might be a sort of bribe. A free drink at Ha Noi's finest. But the officious fellow looked at it and simply threw it to the ground. At that point I figured I had to say something that at least *sounded* important, even if it was not.

"We are *senior* editors at *Vietnam News* in addition to being that man's friends," I said, pointing at Marcel's body. I figured the "senior" part might make an impression, whatever that meant except that I was, if not Cain, a senior citizen.

The Viet suit was silent, as if he hadn't heard me. He did not ask us our names, but then I figured if he wanted to learn them and more all he had to do was call or drop by the newsroom where we were captive most every evening and have a chat with Phuc. I assumed he must be a higher-up in the local law enforcement establishment at least, dressed as he was, if not part of some other department of the byzantine Commie government.

He merely waved his arm emphatically, pointing us behind the barricade that blocked off 50 meters of the street. I noticed another Viet, also not in uniform except a suit, snapping photos with a point and shoot camera. He pointed the camera at Cain and me, click, then swung it away from us to take pictures of the crowd lingering at the scene, and then he walked to the lip of the embankment where lay Marcel and aimed the camera at Marcel's body. Click. Click.

"Better do as he says," Cain warned. "You never know what they might do, what's coming round the bend here."

"Agreed," I said, remembering the SUV coming round the bend on the lakeshore road. "You never know. This is crazy shit."

We stood behind the barricade then amid a score of other onlookers, all Vietnamese, and watched two uniformed policemen drag Marcel's body roughly over the embankment and across the shore road and then, I thought, literally dump it, or him, in the trunk of a police car. Marcel was tall, and his body barely fit in the trunk of the car, a Toyota Corolla dolled up with blue lights and stickers. I was outraged.

"Where's an ambulance? Isn't that normal, to have an ambulance come and collect a body after an accident?" I asked Cain. I had occasionally seen an ambulance or two on Ha Noi's streets.

"I would imagine so," said Cain, just as surprised. "But Marshall, I don't think this is an accident. There's nothing normal about this. Did you see?"

"I saw enough."

"No, *did you see?*"

"I'm not getting you, Cain. I'm seeing a lot."

"There was a small hole in Marcel's head. I saw it when we pulled the body from the water, just back from the hairline behind his temple. A small hole, like he had been stabbed with a little pencil that went in cleanly. No blood visible, but the lake water would have taken care of that."

"What are you saying exactly?"

"No accident here," said Cain, shaking his head in dismay. "I think Marcel was assassinated and then dumped in the lake."

"Cain," I said, "whatever the facts may be, this could be the biggest story we've come directly across during my time in Vietnam. Certainly for me because Marcel was a friend, or becoming one. We may be dealing with something macabre, and it's personal: a friend's murder. Maybe we can have a role in getting to the bottom of this horror," I said.

I was thinking that, as an editor who was a senior, I had not yet found anything much to stand up for emphatically during my months at *Vietnam News*, not even my bare knees, and time was running out. I had, however, readily objected to aspects of this or that piece headed for publication in the newspaper, but that was not difficult. Any self-respecting editor faced with the possible murder of another expatriate in Ha Noi who also happened to be a personal acquaintance and with whom favors had been exchanged was big. I was eager to get back to the newsroom and try to stir Phuc into action. He could make calls. Maybe he would be willing to put us to work trying to flesh out the truth behind Marcel's demise.

"I don't know, mate, but let's swing around the block and come down Nguyen Khac Hieu towards the lake. Maybe we should get a look at the house now since we are here," Cain said. "We can't accomplish anything just standing here."

Cain and I, a few minutes later after a roundabout walk to the other side of Ngu Xa, were coming at Marcel's house from the opposite direction on his street. We passed by slowly and got a look at the front door. The police had already been at the house, which seemed strange. We noted a strip of red plastic tape stretched horizontally across the door and the hardwood round door lock had been smashed and splintered. Marcel had already been identified. The man in the suit, I recalled, seemed uninterested that Cain and I could identify the body. He had asked solely who we were, and then when we told him, he seemed uninterested, unimpressed. *Maybe they already knew*, I thought.

The red tape seemed fitting -- the original Bolshevik color. There was no way to know when exactly the door had been forced open, but we presumed someone had broken into the house, found Marcel, perhaps shot him and then dumped his body in the lake. The five "W's" of basic reporting came to mind: Who, What, When, Where and Why. Cain and I had answers to four of them: Marcel, Murder, Sometime in the past six hours, Nguyen Khac Hieu. The last and most important, the why, was the mystery.

Cain and I returned to the lakeshore at the end of the street: already the Toyota with Marcel's body in the trunk was gone and the crowd was dispersing. With the body gone, there was nothing unusual to gape at. Neither Cain nor I had a clue where the body was headed, or might be headed. Marcel was gone: that's all we knew.

"We still have our jobs, if not Marcel," I said to Cain.

"I know. You want us to become real newsmen now. But it's up to Phuc."

"We can go in sooner today. He might assist us. This is serious news," I said.

"We'll see," said Cain. "but I wouldn't count on cooperation even if this is fucking terrible. Marcel and I had a nice talk at Bobby Chinn's when you dozed off some. I liked him."

"Let's do what we can, Cain. I've got a call or two to make and then I'll be at work in a while."

Cain found his Yamaha unmolested. He climbed aboard and sped off and I headed back towards Hang Giay, clutching my phone, aiming to stop by the Maitre Café to sit and collect my wits, to calm my nerves, to use the phone, to grab a cup of Anh's coffee. I wondered when Kristen Andre was supposed to be back from her trip. She had to be notified first. I made a mental note to call the magazine's offices, at least, to try to get word to her, assuming someone was there who would assist.

"You worried," said Anh. She wasn't asking a question, just stating a perception, and she was right. And she was, I knew, perceptive despite no formal education that I knew of, despite her lack of exposure to much of anything but Ha Noi, despite her simple job.

I had some months earlier suggested taking her to dinner. She had smiled and said she was "too busy". She had perceived my loneliness and more then: that I was looking for a fast and easy solution for a loneliness she would have no part in diminishing just for a night, realizing my age, realizing that given our differences I could not offer her what Marcel had failed to offer any woman -- a presence with security and fidelity over many years.

"Yes, I'm worried," I said. "Thanks for the coffee. I need this one."

"You still think of soldiers coming here?" she asked. "I see none."

"No. Nothing to worry about really," I lied.

"Good. I come back," she said, and moved to another table to take an order.

I was worried about Kristen's reaction. Worried about getting to the paper and trying to generate support to start to investigate Marcel's demise -- but I was an employee, after all, and ought to be heard. I kept thinking of the small hole Cain had seen behind Marcel's temple when we pulled him from Truc Bach Lake.

But I wasn't optimistic. I knew that a couple reporters at two Vietnamese language Ha Noi newspapers had recently been "detained" for their work detailing a corruption scandal that had occurred a couple years earlier. The scandal resulted in the conviction of 12 people, all low-level government officials, who had been betting millions in government funds on European football matches and then trying to bribe slightly higher ups to cover up their crimes. They had allegedly embezzled funds from a unit of a Ministry of the Interior that managed major road and bridge building projects with funds partly sourced in Japan and from the World Bank. The two reporters had actually been arrested for nothing more than alleged inaccuracies in their reporting, which hardly seemed criminal. Actually, they had been too thorough in their reporting. The Authorities labeled this "abuse of power".

But Anh, at least, was looking her usual sweet self, trim in a colorful smock, and attentive, making it known even as she moved to answer other patrons at the café that she was aware of my presence, because she soon came back.

"You want *pho*?" she asked. "I cook you eggs if you like better."

"Some other time, but thanks," I said. "Coffee's great, as always."

Anh smiled again, I thought, perfectly.

"I'll never forget you, wherever I am. I will never forget you, *do you understand*?" I said.

"Not forget you, too," Anh responded, but I did not think she fully understood what I was saying: that I adored the purity of her spirit and apparent unselfishness. There was almost a Merton-like harmony about her, and it wasn't just physical like Tao's, but spiritual, too. Something so ingrained in her that she wasn't aware of it herself and I thought then: if all the human world consisted only of Anhs such as she, there would be no need for humans to imagine any kind of afterlife in any kind of Heaven, a concept that also was on my mind that morning.

I was hoping Anh did not see my hand shaking with the coffee cup. Though I felt calm enough -- visiting the café was a brief return to normalcy -- the shaking hands constituted some kind of autonomic reaction to the morning's discoveries. I tried to disguise the condition by placing the coffee back on the low table. I was almost relieved when Anh moved away a second time to serve someone else, and used her departure as an excuse to leave some *dong* on the table and return to the apartment and make the phone call to the offices of *Orient&Occident*. The phone rang half a dozen times and finally someone answered.

"Who is answering?" I asked.

"Trang."

"And you are?"

"I work here. I work in office for Ms. Kristen Andre."

"I think you may have showed me up to the conference room there."

"Who is this?" asked Trang.

"Excuse me," I said. "This is Marshall McLean."

"I have heard your name," said Trang.

"Is Kristen there? I need to speak with her."

"No," said Trang. "She is due back from Singapore tonight."

I had half a mind to ask her for Andre's traveling cell phone number, but then decided not to. Instead I would tell Trang about Marcel so she could relay the news to her boss. I had met Kristen only twice, the last time at the house when I took Tao there, and that had been some time ago. I had not spoken to her since and even then, had barely spoken to her at all.

"Trang," I said slowly, "please listen carefully. I was by the office there weeks ago, as you may know, and met both Kristen and Marcel. Since then, I have become a friend of Marcel's. I was with him at Bobby Chinn's last night. Kristen knows who I am. I have some extremely bad news."

"Oh, no!" exclaimed Trang, but she did not know how seriously bad the news was, and I went on.

"I was near Marcel's and Kristen's house a couple hours ago. He's been found dead in Truc Bach Lake. He may have drowned," I lied. "I am very, very sorry."

It was quite enough, I thought, just to say little. To mention he had been murdered, as Cain surely thought, seemed unnecessary. Death was the ultimate bad news. There was a long silence on the receiver, but finally Trang responded.

"I will go to Noibai and meet Ms. Andre when she comes in. I will tell her," Trang said. Her voice was quavering. "How can we reach you?"

I gave Trang my phone number.

18

I had witnessed death. My parents were long dead. In particular, though, I had seen death come to my beloved son's beloved mother. In her case, it had come slowly over a period of 18 months as she wasted away with cancer and we had savored many opportunities to say farewell and love each other before her last breath.

But I had not witnessed anything so unexpected and sudden like the death of a friend, or an almost friend, like Marcel had been. I was sodden with thoughts of death, and with being 60 and nearer to it, always nearer to it myself with each breath. But I remembered reading a particular written statement by Ludwig Wittgenstein, the Austrian-born philosopher, in Divinity school. He had written: *We do not live to experience death.* Indeed, it was true: with death, no one likely experienced anything. But I was anxious to try and connect the dots to Marcel's end and went on to the newspaper, arriving an hour before I usually showed up for work.

Once in an infrequent while those unknown powers above Phuc in the media hierarchy threw us working stiffs at the newsroom a bone with a bit of real meat on it. In this case it was a buffet, and when I arrived there the staff was gorging on a variety of Vietnamese finger foods in the hallway outside the newsroom. Lunch could be anytime between sunrise and sunset in Ha Noi. Staff had just risen from the siesta sprawls. Cain was among the crowd shuffling in front of the buffet table and when he saw me, he groused: "You'd think they'd have offered us real drinks, too. I can't find any."

"This is not Bobby Chinn's. Never mind. This is more important. I called the magazine office," I told Cain. "Looks like Marcel's girlfriend gets back tonight from Singapore. I told a woman working there about what has happened. She said she was going to Noibai to meet her boss this evening and give her the news. Maybe she's tried to call her, reached her already. I don't know. I merely said he might have drowned in the lake."

"That's good, mate. Don't feel much like the usual work," said Cain. "Food's okay, though. I'm still hung over some, but just a headache. How'd she take it?"

"She was naturally upset."

"Like me, mate."

"Like me, too. Where's Phuc?" I asked.

"At his desk. He never joins the staff for this kind of thing. I think he doesn't want to eat from the buffet because it makes it appear he's not subject to it but only to the one who's served this up for us peons. The Editor. Sets him apart, I imagine he thinks."

"Let's address him now," I said. "The newsroom's almost empty for a few minutes."

"Okay, mate."

"I tell you, I don't know what to do except try to get Phuc's attention on this," I said to Cain as we left the buffet and went into the newsroom.

"Yeah," said Cain, "being on staff here is all we got to ride in on, and we weren't actually witness to anything more than those standing around Truc Bach this morning, except seeing Marcel's body up close."

"I don't feel like doing any work but this, reporting Marcel's death. It's fresh and it may not even be news in a couple days."

"I'm with you on that," Cain said.

Phuc was seated as his desk scanning the previous day's edition of the paper.

"Phuc," I said, "there's food in the hallway."

Phuc ignored the comment.

I supposed, aside from any false posturing about having planned and ordered the party himself, that he had had his lunch, and that probably at home, wherever exactly that was. But I had once overheard he lived alone somewhere three or so miles southwest of Hoan Kiem in a vast district littered with Soviet style apartment blocks thrown up in an earlier era, before the enactment of *Doi Moi* began generating a better economy and better housing in Ha Noi.

"Phuc," I said. "Cain and I have a front page story for the paper if you'll let us work on it."

Phuc seemed slightly curious, smiling as usual, and I went on. "We had an acquaintance here in the city. A Swiss fellow by nationality. Actually, we were out with him last night. Cain left his motorbike over by Truc Bach near his house yesterday and when he went to get it this morning this fellow's body was in the lake. He was dead, of course. The police were there and all, and they took the body away. We don't know where."

"Many have drowned in Ha Noi," Phuc responded. "It's not news."

"But this is a foreigner, and many foreigners here may want to read about this, if we can get to the bottom of it."

"Marshall and I pulled the body from the lake," Cain added.

Phuc was unimpressed, but he said: "Get to the bottom?"

"Listen, Phuc," I chimed in, "we have reason to believe he did not drown."

"Not drown?" Phuc said.

"This may be both an important domestic *and* international story," I argued further. "Yes, we think he did not drown. We think he was murdered and dumped in the lake."

The smile widened. "What leads you to think so?" Phuc asked.

"I saw something," said Cain. "Marshall didn't, but I saw it. It looked like he had been shot. A small caliber wound, no blood, under the hair back from his temple. No exit wound."

"I don't think so," said Phuc dismissively. Staffers were drifting back to the newsroom, some with plates in their hands, and taking their respective seats. "There's work to do now for you."

"This is what we want to do. Work. We want permission to get this story reported and written for tomorrow's paper, using whatever we can find out. You could help us. You know people to call, where to call, like the police or authorities or someone. We don't and we don't speak Vietnamese."

"No," said Phuc emphatically, staring at both Cain and me with the smile back on. "This is not your job."

We were captive in the newsroom, even though the doors were open and the windows flung wide and the sun was visible to the west over Ha Noi's gaudily painted rooftops and a hot breeze was urging a gauzy curtain on one of the windows near Phuc's desk to flutter and billow a bit. Phuc knew it, too, how captive we were, and not merely by our ignorance about how to proceed, if we could. Lose the job if we pushed too hard and we might as well be on the next plane out of Noibai. But after half a minute of silence - - Cain and I had expended what ammunition we imagined we had - - he relented marginally. "I'll make a call," he said. "Do your work." He turned back to the previous day's paper as if he had heard nothing unusual, and apparently also feeling no urgency to pick up the phone on his desk. Cain and I headed to our terminals.

"Know any other journalists working in Ha Noi?" I asked Cain.

"I've met a couple. One is a woman who works for *Agence France Press*. Met her at a couple parties."

"Maybe you should try to get her on to this, too?"

"She's primarily business oriented. French-Vietnamese contacts and joint deals between the two countries. She's no crime reporter," said Cain. "A dead end with her, mate."

Work late that afternoon was not easy and not because of the work. Occasionally, I glanced up between stories to see what Phuc was doing. Once, I could not spot him. Another time he was reading the paper again. But once I did catch him on his phone. He was nodding his head like someone having to listen intently, his eyes focused on something on the floor, like someone taking direct orders. An hour later he sidled up to my terminal.

"Did you make a phone call?" I asked him.

"I make many calls," he said,

"You know what I mean, Phuc," I said. "Did you inquire about the death of my friend?"

"No," he said.

"Fuck this, Phuc," I blurted.

"You will leave now," Phuc shot back just as angrily. He pointed to the door. The entire newsroom fell silent. The tap tapping on the keyboards stopped momentarily, too. The staff likely had seen nothing like this.

"Good," I said, pointing at the terminal screen. "I've been bored as shit with all this." I stood and grabbed my things as fast as I could.

"Go!" shouted Phuc. He had a temper.

"No problem," I said.

With both shock and relief, I headed towards the door. Cain has been watching and almost as quickly, before I got to the door, he joined me. But then he turned around. Anh's terminal was just a couple meters from our newsroom exit. He glared at her and pointed a finger at her face and said: "Here's some good advice for you with your drivel stories: *get that fucking mole removed!*"

With that, Anh's hands flew to her face, covering the mole, covering a look of horror, but almost in the same instant Cain turned and he pushed me out the door and followed fast.

"Damn, Cain," I said. "I did not know you had the same aversion I did to Anh's mole. Glad you told her. I couldn't have. She might have said something to me about getting my knees replaced. Or Phuc might have."

And then together we moved down fast -- past the landing between floors where often we had lit up the *Vinatabas* -- unwilling to wait for the elevator, and out to the sidewalk in front of the building along Tran Hung Dao near the guards' booth. The breeze had picked up into a wind and the yellow leaves were falling, like confetti, from the China Berry trees. From the sidewalk, I looked up and several staffers were glaring at us from the newsroom windows on the fourth floor as if we had scuttled the newsroom with a lode of overpowered *Tet* fireworks. I did not mind getting thrown out and neither, apparently, did Cain, but there we were by the street and suddenly without reason, or without a job, to be in Ha Noi.

"What are you going to do?" I asked Cain.

"Ride my bike home and get a drink," he said.

"What a mess," I said.

"Not a worry," said Cain. "I was going to blow out of there anyway eventually. I can find other work if I want to stay in Nam. Fifty bucks a day can be found."

"But what should we do about Marcel?"

"Not much we can do it seems. The people here in authority don't give a rat's ass about people like us. I'm fast getting the impression -- at least from the cops at Truc Bach and now Phuc -- that the Powers don't want us mucking about trying to find out why Marcel was murdered," Cain said solemnly. "But call me if you learn anything more about all this."

"I saw Phuc on the phone upstairs. It did not look like he was asking questions, as I hoped he would, but maybe taking orders. He also said he had made no calls regarding Marcel."

"Figures," Cain said. "We have to get away from here. Phuc might sic the guards on us. I'm going to grab the Yamaha. You keep walking."

"I'll call you soon," I said.

Cain left the sidewalk and disappeared under the building into the garage where he had parked his Yamaha.

19

For nearly a full day I stayed in the apartment out of sight -- like the ancient turtle in Hoan Kiem keeping his (or her) head down. I slept off and on at odd hours. I was trying to figure out what next to do, and generally what to do after the next thing was done.

Mere tourism was unappealing, at least in Vietnam, given the exposure I had already had. Major, foreign newspapers I was certain would not hire me anywhere: I was too old and most print media in the US were contracting, shedding reporters and editors like dandruff, and closing bureaus everywhere. This seemed, in effect, nothing more than a variation on the same theme where the Commie media were not much interested in probing for, finding and then reporting the Truth as accurately and fully as possible. Well, in my own truth, I really did not want to be either a tourist or a correspondent. Investigate Marcel's murder? Impossible. I did not have the tools, the contacts, the language skills or the credibility to pry. I was no longer at the paper and Cain was out of commission, too. And, truth was, I barely knew Marcel Mossadeq. I had spent no more than half a day total time with him in all the time I had been in Ha Noi. Maybe I'd just have to leave Vietnam: the apartment did not carry a lease, as if that mattered; I had been paying up month to month.

I called Dar Williams in Saigon and merely told him I had left the paper, that I had become too bored with the job to stay. He again suggested I come back to Saigon, but I had neither a sense of mission nor the requisite zeal to help the Vietnamese poor, as he did, and no gift for striking fear of loss of husbands addressing luncheon crowds like those members of the "International Ladies Club" in Saigon -- a fond memory from my first days in Vietnam. I felt no need then to tell Dar what had happened in Ha Noi. He had

never heard of Marcel Mossadeq anyway. At least I hadn't
previously mentioned Marcel to him.

I did not go by the Maitre Café for coffee or *pho* or for Anh's
hospitality and her gentle nature. What would I have told her? That
I had been fired, but then she might have asked why, and I'd have
had no answers she'd have understood, I thought. Around the café,
hearing always the staccato propaganda from the speakers strung
along the street, had to have had an impact, if just a modest one,
on her.

I hoped Marcel had reached the Islamic version of Paradise.
This was a heavenly domain alleged to contain virgins and clear,
flowing streams and gardens of fruit trees and flowers and burbling
fountains. Even if Marcel had believed little or nothing about
Muhammad or 'Ali, the latter the pride of Shi'a's, or the alleged
miracle of the *Qu'ran,* and dismissed its various prescriptions and
proscriptions, that was his most probable heavenly abode, if any
heavenly abodes existed. I had sometimes wondered what
happened to the virgins in the *janna*, the Garden, after they were no
longer virgins. The *Qu'ran* did not explain this. I wondered if,
deflowered, they were removed to a heavenly place of their own,
perhaps one with burbling children.

During that almost full day of seclusion Cain and I scrambled
out of the newsroom, I called the offices of *Orient&Occident* again. I
did not have Kristen Andre's mobile phone number, and was
almost surprised when Trang, who answered the phone, put her
boss on the line immediately.

"Is this Marshall McLean?" Kristen asked. I remembered her
voice, though we had hardly spoken much, and most of that when
I met her at the magazine's offices the first time.

"Yes," I said. "I am very sorry."

"Trang told me. Marcel spoke well of you a couple times. I
believe you met him for lunch?"

"Yes, and he gave me copy to look at for the magazine there,
too. Copy he had written."

"You were nice to help him. What do you know?" she asked.

"I came by the house around nine that night with a friend from the paper, a New Zealander named Cain Hamilton. We had drinks with Marcel. Later, we went to Bobby Chinn's for more drinks. After midnight we went back to the house. Cain was very drunk. Marcel went inside. We didn't. I finally put Cain, in a cab and sent him home. This was past midnight. Marcel went to bed, I assume. I walked back to my place. Next morning Cain calls. He's back by the lake. He had gone back to get his bike. He tells me come fast. I go. We see Marcel in the lake. Lots of people are standing around. Police, too. Cain and I pull Marcel out of the lake. We are told to stand aside, behind a barricade on the street. We have to comply. I tell someone who wasn't in regular uniform we know Marcel. He seems more interested in who we are. I tell him we work at *Vietnam News*. Marcel's body is placed in a police car. Cain and I then decide to walk by the house. We do. The door is barred by tape and the lock is broken. We dared not go inside. That's it. That's what we saw." But I left out some details. I did not want to upset Kristen Andre more. Finally, I asked her: "You got in last night?"

"Trang met me. At Noibai."

"She said she was going to. I called her."

"Trang told me."

"Did you go directly to the house after you got into Noibai?" I asked.

"Yes, with Trang," said Kristen, "and as you said, the lock was smashed at the front door. But there was no tape. I just went inside. I saw the drinks in the living room. The bottle of Marcel's favorite Johnny Walker. Everything looked normal, I think. Nothing seemed to be missing, but then I looked around more after I went upstairs and I didn't see Marcel's laptop computer in his office. That's where he was connected to the Internet, to the entire world really. I couldn't find his mobile phone, either. He usually left all that on his desk at night. But his bag with his wallet inside was slung over the chair in front of his desk."

"Someone took his computer and phone?"

"They weren't in the house."

"Then, who knows, it may be a simple robbery-murder combination?" I conjectured. "But I left out something a minute ago. I didn't see this myself, but Cain did. He claims he saw a small hole in Marcel's head when we pulled him from the lake. Under his hair behind his temple. We think he was shot."

Kristen was silent for half a minute, and I had to be patient, and then she said slowly, in a low tone. "I think he was murdered, too. If it was simply robbery, they'd have taken more, like the money in his wallet. There are other valuables in the house. I have some jewelry, for one thing. That wasn't taken."

"I didn't tell Trang about the wound when I called her to find you. But why?" I asked. "What enemies could Marcel have had?"

"He may have made some. I don't know. I was only with Marcel for the past eight months! After we met, we came to Vietnam within a month. But he did talk about problems here in Vietnam, things like corruption and censorship, especially with respect to our magazine and what it might eventually be publishing. We imagined the high-end lifestyle focus would be a way to start. He didn't like the censorship aspect of publishing a magazine here, the review of pieces we were considering. He wanted to open things up eventually. He got around Ha Noi. He was gregarious and he wasn't one to keep silent about what bothered him."

"I know. He's outspoken. I am, too. When I came for dinner that night with Tao, after I met you at your offices, Marcel spoke about corruption. You didn't hear that. We were up on the top floor outside. You were in the kitchen downstairs. He claimed the wife of an official in the Communist Party was in Hong Kong. He didn't name names but he said she and her partner got their hands on a couple million dollars worth of diamonds. Money laundering. He suggested the diamonds might have come from Israel."

"I heard that story, too, a day or two before you came to dinner with that Viet woman friend of yours. That was the big one on Marcel's mind. If he knew, but I don't think he did, he didn't tell me exactly whom he thought was involved on the Vietnamese side. But it was someone important, or else Marcel wouldn't have been so excited about whatever he heard," Kristen said.

"Well," I said, "one question I have about that suggestion -- that they were Israeli diamonds -- was this: what did the Israelis get in exchange for the diamonds? Did Marcel ever say anything about that?"

"He didn't know, but he did think they were Israeli diamonds. For one thing, he said the Israelis are becoming the biggest players marketing stones in Asia through Hong Kong," said Kristen.

"So, anyway, you don't have ideas about who did this?"

"No."

"Cain and I went to work yesterday afternoon at the paper. We tried to get the Viet managing editor there to let us investigate the story. We pleaded with him. We felt obliged to get this story thoroughly reported. Not everyday that a Swiss expatriate, any expat, is murdered in Ha Noi, you know. Our boss at the paper was completely uncooperative. He wouldn't let us touch it. I think he did make a phone call. Maybe he found out something, but he didn't tell us what it was. I got angry. I was ordered out, fired. Cain left with me. Losing the job didn't bother us, though."

"This just gets worse, I think. Now, you and your friend have lost your jobs!" Kristen cried. She was crying about Marcel mostly, but she was also upset about what happened to Cain and me and I was touched by her concern.

"I was eventually going to leave anyway. Doesn't really faze me," I said. "But what about Marcel's family? Have you told them?"

"Marcel was alone. He had no family that I know of. His father died a couple of years ago and his mother has been deceased for some longer time. They were divorced, too. She was Swiss, his father Iranian by birth and nationality."

"I did not know *all* of this," I said. "Tell me about his father, if you can?"

"Marcel always spoke of him warmly. He apparently learned much from him. I gathered there was great affection between them. He was very sophisticated, knowledgeable, good looking -- just like Marcel. At one time he was rich, Marcel told me. He established banking links between the Persian Gulf and Indonesia, which you know is largely Muslim. But he got into some kind of trouble and was detained in Bahrain for several years. It was a set up. He didn't do anything wrong. Marcel said many Bahrainis don't like Iranians and are scared of unrest among the Shi'a minority there. Iranians are Shi'a and the people in control in Bahrain, the Khalifas, are strictly Sunni."

I had run out of cigarettes and needed a smoke badly. I asked Kristen to stay on the line and told her I'd be back in five minutes. I flew down the steps from the apartment and out onto Hang Giay from the undercroft, knocking over a motorbike on the way. Across the street squatted the old woman with her cigar box filled with random brands of cigarettes, exactly where she was every time I looked, day or night. I bought a handful of *Vinatabas* and ran back across the street to the apartment, dodging the traffic. Kristen was hanging on.

"I'm back," I said to Kristen. "Now, you were saying Marcel's father was detained in Bahrain for a time?"

"Yes. Marcel tried to get him freed, get him out. I don't know the finer details, but Marcel said he escaped to Iran, across the Persian Gulf. It sounds fantastic, and Marcel didn't tell me much, but he did say his father, Hussain Mossadeq, managed to escape in a small boat and, by prior arrangement, he was intercepted at night in the middle of the gulf by an Iranian naval patrol vessel and taken on to Tehran eventually. From there, before he became ill and died, he was in Djakarta. This was years ago. The Indonesian government gave him a passport and citizenship, and afterwards he was involved helping raise money for an offshoot foundation somehow connected with the Aga Khan," Kristen claimed.

"Damn," I said. "This helps. This maybe explains why Marcel was so outspoken about corruption wherever he got wind of it. It touched him personally. His father, after all, and he was an only child."

"I see that, too," said Kristen.

"Marcel spoke about his father being an Ismaili Shiite. I know a little about the history of that sect. The most intellectual and arcane sectarians within Islam during the Middle Ages. The Aga Khan is a descendant of 'Ali, who was married to Fatima, the Prophet Muhammad's daughter. His devotees are descendants of the early Ismaili sectarians. Marcel worked for a foundation before he died and I wonder what it was for, what it was doing?" I asked Kristen.

"Marcel did once say something about that. He mentioned something about his father raising funds and directing them for humanitarian purposes. You've heard of Hizb Allah in Lebanon, which represents a lot of poor Shiites in Lebanon? I know you know about Hamas in Palestine," said Kristen. "Didn't you mention you were in the West Bank not long ago? Something about helping create an American-funded school there for Palestinian children?"

"Exactly," I said, and suddenly, without knowing where this information was headed, I felt instinctively that it might be leading to illuminations.

"You know there's been a lot of news about Hizb Allah and Hamas? Your government, the Bush people, think they are part of the "Axis of Evil" or something like that?"

"Of course," I said. "The US labels anyone who might one day seriously challenge, or just share, US and Israeli control in the Middle East 'terrorists'."

"Well, Marcel gave me some background on the Mideast situation and I recall him telling me once that his father had indirectly gotten humanitarian funds to *Hamas* and to *Hizb Allah*. The both represent almost the poorest of the poor in the Middle East. Marcel was concerned about that. He wasn't really very political himself, but he knew what was going on. He was interested, as you may have found out, in the good life and nice things."

With that, I almost wanted to add, "and pretty women, too" like the Canadian vamp at Bobby Chinn's, but without mentioning the Canadian. Kristen was pretty herself, and, I was discovering, also smart. I could understand why Marcel latched on to her dream of coming to Vietnam from travels or whatever in Europe and starting a magazine focusing on things and places they both appreciated in a country that was not at war.

"Okay, Kristen, did you stay last night at the house on Nguyen Khac Hieu? I don't think you should have. There's not even a working lock on the door."

"I went there coming in from Noibai. Of course, I had to. It was home. Trang was with me and I took some clothes and what valuables I had and left with her. I'm staying at Trang's place. She's very sweet."

"Where is that?" I asked.

"Near the office here."

"Good. And what about the magazine? Have you had time to think of that?"

"I can't. I'm in shock. We were just about to go to press with the first edition. Not now. Marcel was the engine of it all. I was the bells and whistles. It's over."

I thought she might have more accurately said the "*Tet* fireworks" of the nascent enterprise, but it was anyway, under the circumstances, a dumb thought. Maybe Anh and Tao would have said I was thinking way too much again.

"I don't know what to do," Kristen said plaintively. She was crying again and I was feeling very sorry for her and even myself, too, because I had lost a friend, perhaps eventually a friend such as Cicero would have admired and enjoyed.

"Maybe you should go back home to France if you can't manage here on your own?" I suggested. "It's interesting. I read somewhere that the current Aga Khan has a presence in France."

"Really?" said Kristen.

"Really. He apparently operates the largest thoroughbred horse racing and breeding operation in France. It's quite remarkable what that man does, I believe."

"Interesting," said Kristen. "But I think I should go now. Trang and I have things to do."

"One more question, please," I said. "Where is Marcel? Where's his body? Do you know?"

"No. Trang made some calls. I don't speak Vietnamese. She got nowhere. She says there were lots of denials. She said one police official claimed he knew nothing about an accident at Truc Bach. Marcel has vanished."

"God," I said. I was flooded with dismay. It was tough, apparently, being a foreigner in Vietnam and not being able to speak the language at crucial moments, being incapable of mounting an adequate argument to ferret out desired information. But then, Cain and I had been completely unsuccessful with Phuc, who spoke and understood and even wrote English well enough.

I told Kristen Andre to call me if she needed anything, or heard anything we did not both already know, and gave her my phone number. But I also suspected that I would not hear from her again unless I called her with fresh information. I had spent less than half an hour directly in her company, and the dinner at the house at Ngu Xa did not count, because there all she did was make dinner. My sole claim to any notion of talking to her again was that Cain and I had been with Marcel an hour or three before his demise.

20

Perhaps Tao had gone away to do research on UXO or Agent Orange in a remote province where her phone could not get a signal. It was a thought. American-made killing devices were still randomly knocking off hapless Vietnamese in what amounted to delayed murder all over Vietnam, especially near the Ho Chi Minh Trail. But Marcel's murder was different and close at hand and the last time I had been near anything like it was in the West Bank, which reeked of violence with the IDF checkpoints and patrols and the hardcore settlers who imagined themselves God's servants, if not gods themselves. A majority of them were Americans with dual citizenship, acting like cowboys against the indigenous Indians, the Palestinians, living beyond the fences at the fringes of the settlement blocs.

There had been indelible journeys in Palestine like riding to Jenin from Tubas in the northern West Bank with staff from the Palestinian Red Crescent in an ambulance to visit the refugee camp where the IDF had waged war indiscriminately in 2002, killing scores of women and children and the young men -- "martyrs" to their people -- who put up a hopeless fight. It was a slow drive to Jenin over a broken road through scattered towns -- 'Aqaba, Zebabda, Qabatiya -- most of the world would never know, towns set amid bright fields and groves of almond and olive trees. In every town tacked to lampposts were posters of *shuhada*, martyrs to the Palestinians, killed by the IDF or Shabak operatives. One poster, in Technicolor, was most evident -- that depicting Yahya Ayyash -- for a while the chief bomb maker for *Hamas* -- like some matinee idol. He had his head taken off by a cell phone the Shabak had packed with explosives. But at least in his case, there was a body, or burnt parts of one, to bury in Gaza. Not so for Kristen Andre, Trang and Marcel's friends and acquaintances. She had no idea even where her lover's body *was* despite Trang's inquiries, and I had no way to help either of them.

The best opportunity was gone with the position at the newspaper, but I did wonder that maybe the Swiss in Ha Noi should be notified and a while after I spoke with Kristen I called their embassy, which occupied the 15th floor of an office building not far from Bobby Chinn's restaurant. A Swiss employee there claimed she had not heard of any Swiss citizen's recent death in Ha Noi, nor had she specifically heard of a "Marcel Mossadeq". But Marcel had heard informally and off the record about the diamond transaction from someone there.

That conversation could well have occurred amid a few rounds of iced Russian vodka, if not Johnny Walkers, at the Metropole, where Marcel liked to go. But I got nowhere with the embassy and I could not show up and announce: *Hey, I knew a Swiss fellow. But not all that well, and I'm American. He may have been murdered here in Ha Noi. Someone here told him that a top official in the Viet government and Party was laundering money for diamonds in Hong Kong and I wonder would you please find out who that was because I'd like to speak to him or her as well as report my friend's murder to him.* Swiss diplomats in Ha Noi anyway had enough on their hands as some Viet dissidents occasionally sought asylum there, and sometimes Viet soldiers or police carrying Kalashnikovs ringed the building during spells when the government feared a dissident might be heading there.

I told the woman at the embassy that a Swiss citizen had died at Truc Bach, hoping she would help launch an inquiry. But I did not expect to hear more. I was realizing just how isolated I was and had been in Vietnam, relying solely on a few acquaintances I had barely seen enough of or known long enough to cement the kind of friendships with additional friends of theirs that might give my interest in Marcel's case real credibility and attention.

I was not many steps away from being just one of the gawkers watching Marcel's body prodded by the bamboo poles. He had been a drinking buddy for a night at Bobby Chinn's, I had been hosted weeks earlier for a single night at his rented house, and I had fiddled a bit with a couple stories slated for a magazine that had not even gone to press yet -- ever. And, to boot, I was, thanks to Phuc, *persona non grata* at the only tangible anchor I had had in Ha Noi -- the newspaper. I was, in a word, plunged into a Neverland.

In any event, speculations emerged on a linkage between Marcel's death and the conflicts in West Asia. I thought of Jabotinsky on the *Emeraude*, his carriage in the black SUV when I almost got run down in Ha Noi weeks earlier, the vicious talk at the bar at Bobby Chinn's after lunch with Marcel, his punk hard face at the Opera House and then the appearance of what looked like the same Chevy SUV cruising through Ngu Xa after I had gotten Cain in the cab by the lake. Was I clutching at straws? Something like possible explanations were rising from the black muck of Truc Bach, and it wasn't a relative of the ancient turtle in Hoan Kiem.

Some Viets may have had reason to want Marcel gone -- he had been critical of the government whose guest he was, and he was also laying groundwork for a magazine authorities may have feared could eventually aim to expose the rot. And Israelis, Israelis like Jabotinsky (and he was the only one I had met in Vietnam), might also have had reason to want Marcel gone. Kristen Andre had said Marcel's Iranian father had been a known figure in financial circles in the Middle East, and he was almost certainly cited in intelligence archives in Israel as a threat, particularly if he had been involved in channeling funds to *Hizb Allah* and *Hamas*, Israel's most immediate enemies among many made. Perhaps I was thinking too globally, but there was some reason to it.

Marcel's father had passed on, a natural death, in Indonesia, Kristen said. Had Marcel, the former investment banker in Europe, the bright son of another financier in both the Middle East and Indonesia, taken on some of his deceased father's alleged humanitarian efforts in some capacity, I wondered. Had I not thought after I met Marcel that I had seen him before I met him at the end of my visit to the only mosque in Ha Noi? Had he been arranging a contribution to Islam's tiny footprint in Vietnam or, more accurately, a contribution the mosque might pass along, say, to the exploited orphans the US embassy was upset about, or to other needy recipients? Muhammad himself had been an orphan who identified with the poor and disenfranchised in seventh century Arabia, and the *Qu'ran* was in large measure aimed at addressing extant social ills and laying out what a just society ought to look like, *be* like. But Israelis, the prime US ally in the so-called "War on Terror", made few or no distinctions between money for humanitarian relief and money for insurgencies. Money was fungible: worthwhile charities doing peaceful work had been targeted by the US and Israel for strangulation or closure almost everywhere they existed. The assumption was that *any* support was tantamount to support for those who opposed hegemonic designs on parts of Asia.

Late that night, whacked some by liberal pulls on Tiger beers and *Vinatabas*, I was aiming to touch base with the last straw I knew of in Ha Noi, and this was Tao and she worked, she had said, for the government, too.

I also knew she should know of Marcel's murder. Couldn't have her texting a dead man. But another full day passed before I punched her numbers on the mobile phone. I had waited a while, wondering if I might hear from her. I had not heard from her since her disappearance at the Opera House, and failed earlier to reach her by phone. Maybe she did not want to hear from me, but I did not care under the circumstances. Trying to call her once more, the result was the same: the phone rang but no answer. Frustrated, I thought to search for her the next morning in the poor neighborhood over by the Red River where she allegedly lived, across the dike boulevard. It was a neighborhood that, seen in passage before, reminded me of the quarters of an old Arab *medina* -- narrow, winding lanes not wide enough for much of anything but donkeys or horses or bikes, where a stranger could get lost, a bit like parts of the Old Quarter off Hang Giay behind the Dong Xuan market.

I tossed about for another night. The air conditioner was fucked up, too. Some stress no doubt, perhaps some trauma, too, but nothing like the trauma thousands of American boys and girls were suffering after immersion in the wars in Iraq and Afghanistan.

Perhaps part of the insomnia was also a delayed reaction -- stirred up by Marcel's murder -- to distant, stressful weeks in the West Bank. I found myself clenching some on morbid questions centered on isolated historical events: like exactly what kind of hi-tech poison it was that two Mossad agents with fake Canadian passports blew into the ear of Khaled Mesh'al in Amman, Jordan, in September 1997 when he stepped out of a car near his office. I had read somewhere the poison may have been *fentanyl*.

Mesh'al was a leader of *Hamas*, targeted for assassination by the Israeli government, but he survived the attempt on his life when Jordanian police captured the Mossad agents in Jordan and the Jordanians, King Hussain especially, demanded an antidote to the poison for the dying, hospitalized *Hamas* leader. Mesh'al survived. Also, in return for allowing the Israeli agents to go free and back across the Jordan to Israel, Israel released the jailed Sheik Ahmad Yassin, a co-founder of *Hamas* and a blind paraplegic who had been confined by a sporting accident at age 12 to a wheel chair. Yassin went back home to Gaza to live a while longer before he was killed by an American-made Hellfire missile fired from an American-made Israeli helicopter in 2004 in yet another targeted assassination. Still, there had been a body, or parts of one, to bury, and a quarter million people, almost a quarter of Gaza's population, attended Yassin's funeral.

I also seized on the recollection of reading, perhaps in some novelistic thriller, that in the 1970s the favored weapon of Israeli teams deployed to assassinate those who plotted the murder of Israeli athletes at the Munich Olympics was a silenced Beretta pistol loaded with subsonic, .22 caliber ammunition: firing such rounds, the Beretta made quiet pops that could barely be heard across a fair sized room. Cain's description of the small, clean hole under the hair behind Marcel's temple was consistent with a subsonic, .22 caliber round, which would have made just such a hole and not emerged from the other side of Marcel's head.

The next morning on foot I passed by the entrance ramp to the Long Bien Bridge. Half a dozen kites strained above the bridge over the river's main channel in a brisk wind from the north. The air was clearer and fresher than it had been in weeks. On any day before Marcel's death I'd have reveled being in Ha Noi that morning. I turned south on the dike road and walked a kilometer to Quan Bach Dang, the Ha Noi district which lay to the east between the boulevard and the Red River. Serendipity or not, despite the usual congestion in the district on the primary street -- Bach Dang -- I happened to spot Tao on her Honda Dream weaving like a dancer in a crowd through the traffic and turning down one of the narrow alleys towards the river.

She was facing forward; unlike in the difficult dream I had had of her at Khau Vai, and she was going fast. She had not driven dangerously fast around West Lake when she took me to Vines and then the blind masseuse. I gave chase, running almost like a man of 40, and was pleased I still could. Down the alley, down several alleys and some of them blind towards the river she was nowhere in sight, but ten minutes later I came upon her Honda Dream parked in front of a narrow house painted up in peeling ochre. Tao's home, I figured. I knocked on the front door.

After a minute the door cracked open. I had found her: ""Where in the Hell have you been?" I asked.

She seemed shocked to see me, glowering some, perhaps because I was, too, and out of breath, but maybe because I had come on to her personal turf, and she was looking unkempt like I had not seen her before, barefoot in frayed jeans and a stained T shirt. She had apparently swiftly changed clothes.

Beyond the door inside was a foyer from which a steep stairway ascended with almost impossibly high treads. Toys lay strewn about. Lego pieces, too. I heard a voice behind her. It was Tung, babbling in Vietnamese. He saw me standing outside the door and smiled. Perhaps he remembered the hand slapping game I taught him on the *Emeraude* amid the Amcham crowd, or the assist with his Legos. Tao turned to Tung. She ordered him up the steps: "Go to Pham," she commanded, and Tung went up the steps like a monkey using both hands and feet.

"A lot's been happening, Tao. Where in the Hell have you been?"

"Taking care of Tung and things," she replied unenthusiastically.

"Have you been in Ha Noi since the concert?"

She gave no answer and I pushed on. "I came back from the lobby at the Opera House and you had vanished? Don't you think that's rude? Are we friends or what? Friends don't do that."

"I needed to come home and tend Tung," she said. I knew she was at least partly lying, because I knew she could easily have waited half a minute before she left the concert to tell me she had to leave, or she could have found me in the lobby and then gone out the front of the Opera House.

"I've tried to call you. I tried to call you later that night after the Opera House. Not answering your phone now?"

Tao was silent, but she let me in the door.

"Have you heard from Marcel again?"

"You said to me not to answer him," Tao said, as if I was important enough for her to heed the warning I gave her about engaging Marcel.

"Has he tried to contact you again since my birthday?"

"No," Tao said.

"After you left the Opera House I stayed on for the second half of the concert."

"I am glad you stayed. It was your birthday."

"I know. I saw someone there I met late at night on the *Emeraude*. I've seen his face three times since around the city. A man named Jabotinsky. He's Israeli, actually, and seemed misplaced with the Amcham group on the boat. Do you recall him? Do you *know* him?"

"No. But I remember a man from the boat, but not anyone called 'Jabotinsky'. The next morning, after our day together in the water, after breakfast before we returned to the dock I spoke with a man who said he was Israeli.

"Was this the same guy you got into an SUV with after we left the boat?"

"Yes," said Tao.

"He told me his name was 'Jabotinksy'."

"He introduced himself as 'Leiberman' to me, I think."

"The neither of us may know his real name. As for the ride, what was that really about? You said the ride back from Ha Long City was prearranged for you. Was it also prearranged for this 'Jabotinsky/Leiberman'?"

"I don't know," said Tao. She seemed confused, agitated.

"You don't know whether it was prearranged for him? Is that it?"

"Yes."

"But it was in fact prearranged for you?"

"I think so," Tao said.

Tao moved to the adjacent kitchen and placed a kettle on a burner attached to a bottle of propane. There was no refrigerator in the kitchen. I figured she bought fresh food from the local markets and brought things home to prepare each day. I pressed on: "So what do you think he was doing on the boat? He's not American. What were you doing on the boat?"

"I was working," said Tao. "And enjoying your company."

"That's nice, but I don't get the 'working' part. Were you working when we swam and paddled the kayak? That did not seem like work to me. How did you get on that cruise?"

With more reluctance, after she sat down hard on a stool opposite me at a table in the kitchen, she said: "I am not supposed to speak of my work but you know I do research for the government."

"Yes, you said you were studying and reporting about UXO and Agent Orange. Good work like that."

"I do whatever my boss asks. I am paid so I can survive, so I can take care of Tung. So I can have a few nice things like my Honda. My government sent me to America to study, too. The Party has been good to me."

"Yes, you have nice clothes and a nice bike and a nice boy and you seem to have an education, too."

Tao no longer had me under any kind of affective spell. Marcel's murder was so fresh I could hardly feel much but horror, but my mind had been racing for traction since. "How did you get to go on that cruise?" I asked again.

"I was told to go. It was arranged."

"Good," I said. "Thank you. So what were your instructions?"

"The same as they always are. Report back what you see and hear."

"You've done that before?"

"Yes," said Tao. "I am sometimes sent somewhere without any job but to report back to the government what I have seen or heard. It's simple."

"You must be a good reporter. What part of the government? Come on, Tao. Report to me!" I demanded.

"My superior is in the Ministry of Defense. Actually, he's very important, " said Tao.

"Who is he?"

"An important man in Vietnam," she said almost proudly. "He works for the Minister of Defense, for General Phung Quang Thanh."

"What's his name?"

"I won't tell you that."

I understood her reluctance. I figured she thought it was dangerous to give away too much. I assumed it might be, for her.

"Well," I said. "I was fired at the paper because I wanted to do what you say you do: report. A friend from New Zealand, Cain Hamilton, who also worked at the paper was fired, too. I have no job now here."

Tao apparently was not too surprised. "I hear there's lot of turnover with foreign editors at *Vietnam News*."

"Let's address this business about your work more. Are you telling me, because it seems so to me, that you are asked to spy?"

"Providing information is not spying," Tao claimed.

"It would sure seem like spying to me if you told someone at the Ministry of Defense everything we did in Ha Long Bay and elsewhere and what we talked about. That would seem like a breach of confidence to me."

"Did that fellow on the ride back to Ha Noi say what he did? He was riding in a Ministry vehicle."

"Not much," said Tao. "I asked him. I kind of gathered he might be negotiating Israeli arms sales to my country."

At that moment I heard a voice calling Tao from the stairs in Vietnamese. She answered and then said to me: "That's my father. You remember him from the bar at the *Cinematique*? He says he's taking Tung out for a walk. I will go and see if Tung has his shoes on properly."

I recalled the skinny, excessive hand shaker and heavy drinker of rice wine at the *Cinematique*. Probably I should have spoken to him, but I didn't bother. When Tao returned to the table, and I saw Tao's father and child go out, I asked: "Where is your husband?"

"I am not married," she said. "I was divorced when I came back from America. Tung's father found someone else when I was gone. He is Vietnamese. He was intimidated, I think, by my interests and opportunities. When we met years ago I had just come to Ha Noi from Ha Giang. He was working at the Metropole," said Tao.

"This is news to me. I have wondered."

Tao prepared tea and brought two cups to the table.

"So, tell me the truth," I said angrily. "Why really did you leave me at the Opera House?"

"This is my business," Tao said.

"No, it's mine, too. You tell me!"

"My employer from the Ministry was there. He was sitting with the Israeli man. When you left to go to the lobby he got up from his seat and came to our seats. He was disturbed. He demanded that I leave at once. I told him I was with someone, a friend I met on the *Emeraude*, but he ordered me to go out the side door. He said I would not have a job if I did not do exactly as he wanted right away," said Tao. "I was afraid."

"I didn't figure you were afraid of much," I said. "Has he spoken to you since then?"

"I have not been to the Ministry. I have not been called in. He said when I got up to go at the Opera House that I must go home. But I remember something else," added Tao. "I think he was

sitting next to that Israeli we both met, but separately, on the
Emeraude."

"Mr. Mystery Name!" I exclaimed, almost knocking over my
teacup. Tao was putting the pieces of the puzzle together and she
did not even know she was or what the puzzle was all about. "I saw
the Israeli sitting at a distance in the audience. But more questions.
Consider answers a birthday present because you abandoned me on
my birthday," I said. "Did your employer send you to meet me
along West Lake the Saturday I was walking around and then we
went to Vines and had the massages from those blind girls?"

"He ordered that I keep an eye on you and report back. It was
my paid job. I was following you that morning."

"And what about the night we went to Marcel's for dinner? The
night you met him, when I introduced you to him? Was that work,
too?

"I was told to find out about Marcel and the magazine.
Remember, it was I who told you about the magazine in the first
place," Tao said more forthrightly. "I pointed you towards the
offices. That was work and pleasure, that dinner."

"Were you ordered to take me to the Opera House?"

"No," Tao said. "That was pleasure."

"Thank you," I said. "But matters have gotten completely out
of hand." I paused for half a minute and then said: "Marcel is dead.
He was murdered."

"No!" said Tao. "He messaged me at the Press Club!"

"I know that. Tell me what I don't know. That's why I'm here."

But first I told her about the evening with Marcel and Cain, our
early drinks at the house at Ngu Xa, the three or so hours up to
closing time at Bobby Chinn's, how Cain and I left the bike along
the lakeshore after Marcel had gone inside the house. I told her
about finding Marcel's body in Truc Bach Lake.

"Maybe Marcel drowned, fell into the lake?" said Tao.

"No," I said. "He was murdered. I'm certain of that."

"This is horrible," she said. But she seemed more frightened
than horrified.

"Tao," I said, "what did you say at the Ministry about Marcel?"

"What happened, what I heard and saw."

"As you did when we went over to Marcel's together for dinner, when I introduced you to him?"

"Yes."

"Did you say something about what Marcel told you and me about a top Vietnamese official's wife going to Hong Kong and getting diamonds?"

"I reported fully. My job...."

"Do you now understand what has been going on since then?"

"No," said Tao.

"Well," I responded angrily, "your goddamn corrupt boss in the Ministry of Defense whom you last saw at the Opera House apparently knows this Israeli fellow, whatever his fucking name, as you've suggested by now telling me they were sitting together at the concert. I now have reason to believe that both of them are behind Marcel's murder. I have spoken to Kristen Andre, too. She just got back from a trip to Singapore. She's been informed about the murder. But she gave me some additional info about Marcel's background. It's all complex and I won't go into all the details right now because some of them you won't understand, not knowing the Middle East shit, all its mad convolutions, as well as I do. Let me just say that both men may have had reasons, even different reasons, that when combined resulted in Marcel's murder. I think that Israeli bastard shot Marcel with or without help and dumped his body in Truc Bach! I also think your boss allowed this to happen and he may be the person whose wife got the diamonds, and that with funds supplied by the Israeli. The guy is most certainly an agent for Mossad. You are involved in this. *You are indirectly responsible.*"

With that, at first, she just glowered at me. "I love my country. We have suffered a lot. The work that I do is for my country."

"Bullshit," I said. "It's for money. And Marcel liked you and you probably thought he had lots of money, too. I don't know all you did with him after I introduced you to him. You said lunch, and you halted most communication with me until the invitation to the opera. His advances tantalized you. What if it got out that your boss, this so-called party leader, had condoned or assisted a murder and gotten paid off for it? Would he be seen as serving Vietnam's interest? I don't think so," I said. "And what about another kind of loyalty, like to one's friends? Is that not higher than loyalty to country or Party or ideology?"

"I am just a girl from Ha Giang," Tao said plaintively, trying to exonerate herself with a show of abject humility. I wasn't buying it.

"You are that and then more and worse," I said.

"You don't like me anymore?"

"You are acting stupid. But listen to me. No one knows where Marcel's body is now. Kristen Andre can't find out anything, and neither can her assistant. And I wouldn't know where to look. I know I can't poke around here and start making demands, going to the police myself. I'd be on a plane out of Noibai in a flash, my visa canceled. Cain and I couldn't even get the man we worked under at the paper to look into this. We were frustrated and showed it and got shown the door, as I said."

"It's true. You won't get anywhere poking around," Tao said.

"What could you do? Could you look into this at the Ministry?"

"No," said Tao. "I cannot ask. Do you want me to lose everything?"

"You already probably have. You've compromised your self, maybe your soul, if ever you had one. And you unwittingly, I think, aided a murder."

I could not have been more condemning of her, unless I just slugged her. I'd have slugged the Israeli, but not a woman. The guy, I had to think though, had been smart. The General's aide had gotten the diamonds and in return, however it actually had evolved, the Israeli snuffed Marcel. *Quid pro Quo*. And, of course, what agent for Israel, what Mossad agent, would tell anyone his or her real name in the field if he were not tortured to do so? I could no longer believe anything he had said, except that he despised Arabs.

Tao, I thought, wasn't involved with the actual murder, nor did she know it was afoot, but information she provided had helped at the margin to set the murder plans in motion. Her "reporting", she thought, was merely paid service to her country, but she had served no one but her boss and, ultimately, the Israeli. She had told her master afterwards about the dinner at Ngu Xa when I introduced her to Marcel, and what she had largely told him about -- or what stood out and threatened her boss -- were Marcel's assertions about the diamond transaction in Hong Kong. She could not have known that it was, as I believed, *his* wife who had suddenly gotten rich with diamonds that probably were stashed in a safe box at a Ha Noi branch of the state *Vietcombank*. When I got back to the apartment around midafternoon, leaving Tao in tears at her front door, I was eager to check in with Cain and rang his number.

"Where are you?"

"In my dingy place," said Cain. "I've barely moved since we high-tailed it out of the newsroom."

I told Cain all I then knew and imagined, or considered plausible. I connected as many dots as I could. I told him about the conversation with Kristen Andre and about the visit with Tao and Tao's apparent, unwitting role in Marcel's murder. "Do you have any ideas?" I asked.

"The bitch," he said sharply.

"I think, like a lot of people, she just did not understand what she was about. She felt like she was serving her country. She trusted the leaders for whom she worked."

"Naïve bitch," said Cain. "But I've not met her."

"You want to? We could both go to her place. She's not all bitch, in my view. She was finally very upset when I left her place. I think she was realizing how wrong she has been. She's got some feelings. They count for something positive."

"No, I don't want to meet her," said Cain. "I'm a bit scared sitting around here. I rang up Phuc this morning and told him I wanted to clean out my desk at the paper, that I had left a couple personal items there."

"He answered?"

"Yeah, mate. He said I was forbidden to come back to the paper. That was all he said. He hung up on me. I can just imagine trying to get past the guards there on Tran Hung Dao. I bet they've been informed to keep an eye out for me and my Yamaha, and you, too, come to think of it. They know us."

"What about our last month's wages? We haven't been paid. Would that be a valid reason to go back?"

"Forget that, mate. Every payday was just a cash transaction, you know. No contract, nothing, to underscore or secure anything. Easy come, easy go, I suppose."

"So you've concluded we've come to a dead end with this as, well, reporters or editors at least? I guess maybe we have."

"I would say so. I'm sitting here wondering if I'm going to get a knock on the door by some green goons. I have been having bad thoughts about them barging in here and rifling through my things and finding a drug stash in a drawer and carting me off to jail. You don't want to go to jail here in Nam. Something like Hoa Loa still exists somewhere in country."

I knew Cain was referring to the Ha Noi prison where the future Senator John McCain wound up after he was fetched from Truc Bach. In English the name meant "fiery furnace", or better, "Hellhole". The French had built the prison decades earlier to incarcerate Vietnamese political dissidents objecting to French colonial rule. Americans like McCain dubbed the place the "Hanoi Hilton" and when the new, real Hilton hotel went up in Ha Noi the chain called it the Hanoi Opera Hilton to avoid a reference to Hoa Loa. The new hotel stood a hundred meters from the Opera House and it was from there I had gone to board the *Emeraude* -- for what was, in retrospect, one of the most pregnant weekends I could recall.

"You've got drugs there? Like Marcel had drugs when he could reach his supplier?"

"No, mate. Not any baby Cobra hooch. No Ecstasy. Nothing but branded booze, which is legal, but I'm saying they could plant something forbidden and then pretend to find it. I'm seriously thinking of getting out."

"Where to?"

"Don't know yet. Maybe I'll head out to Phuket in a couple days and sit on that beach in Thailand for a while and chill. Really,

I think I'll go back to Auckland in a month or so and see my relations and regroup. There are always other print media jobs in Asia eventually."

"You can go anywhere and start all over again. I can't. This has been my last late-life overseas job, and it's come to a screeching, sudden halt."

"What about you, mate? You can't stay here."

"I reckon I will soon leave, too. Get back to the US. But Cain, I sure would like to make the story public somehow, expose the bastards who killed Marcel."

"No way I see to get the information you need. The Swiss may look into it, but if there's no body turning up beyond Truc Bach, there's no crime evidence, and they won't. And how would anyone like us ever get the real name of that bloke in the Ministry of Defense? How could one back up such a story? I don't know."

"I don't know, either. A dead end, like you said. Tao would not give us a name. She'd put herself in big danger. Maybe she already is. I can understand her. She's got a fine young son to take care of, too. To stay alive for."

"Maybe if Tao left Vietnam she'd open up," said Cain, "and start naming names."

"She's not coming with me. I don't want her or her son dependent on me. She's not deserving of such attention."

I again recalled the widely reported assassination attempt on Khaled Mesh'al in Amman by the two Mossad agents. The world would never have known about the operation if the Mossad agents had not been pounced on immediately, almost miraculously, by Jordanian police. They'd have slipped back across the Jordan River over the Allenby Bridge as if they had never been in Amman, and Mesh'al would have died and left a mystery reportable only as such. As for Jabotinsky or Leiberman or whatever his real name was, I believed he was certainly gone from Vietnam. Probably back at Adumim on another break from distant, murderous assignments. I had been scanning for the black Chevrolet SUV and seen nothing like it since the early morning of Marcel's murder after I had hustled Cain into a cab.

Cain was right: no body examined forensically, no reportable crime, and the gawkers around Truc Bach probably gave the body they saw little afterthought: some foolish foreigner who drowned in the lake, like some pedestrian struck and killed on Ha Noi's streets -- quickly out of sight and almost just as quickly out of mind. Just another gruesome death in a city of such size. Except that any trace of Marcel, unlike a drowned swimmer or a mangled pedestrian, was gone.

"If this were New Zealand," Cain said, "we'd have an environment in which we could make something of this, investigate it. Did I mention that Mossad agents got caught forging New Zealand passports in my country? They were fucking stealing the identities of cerebral palsy victims in Christchurch! They were looking for people who, because of their disabilities, would not have passports and never travel overseas. We suspended diplomatic relations with Israel. The Israelis charged my government with anti-Semitism. It was outrageous, mate."

"But anyhow, we will stay in touch? Right?"

"Of course, mate. E mail anytime."

"You've been grand here," I said. "I have seriously appreciated your friendship."

"Same here, Marshall. We'll be in touch. But I think it's time to move on. After I get back to New Zealand, come visit," said Cain. "I insist."

"I'll consider it," I said, "maybe on the way back home. I want to see my doctor son. We've exchanged some emails but he's very busy and I haven't told him much of anything about my time in Vietnam. Nothing about Tao, too."

"My best wishes," said Cain.

"Thanks. You, be well, too. And lay off the booze."

I thought about New Zealand. I had never been there, but I had seen photos of mountains and high lakes. Beautiful, like Lake Annecy and Talloires, in France. An echo of *Claire's Knee*, too.

I took a shower and then went out, across Hang Giay to the Hapro market for a Coke, and then beyond without any specific destination, rather in a daze, and after a while on the way back from nowhere I realized I had wandered across the street from the an-Nur mosque on Hang Luoc, the Street of Combs, as Anh had told me, and the gate to its courtyard was open. I reckoned I had a few questions I could pose to the Afghan, whose original home was Helmand, and went inside. He was there, and so were five or six men praying in the hall in front of the *mihrab* pointing the direction to *Makkah*.

The Imam recognized me, and a few minutes later, with the prayers done, he came over and we stood outside in the courtyard.

"You were the one with the *fatwa* from the *mufti* in Jerusalem," he said.

"Yes."

"Welcome back," he said.

"I wonder if you can help me?" I asked. "When I was leaving the day we met, a man appeared here. Do you know a Marcel Mossadeq? I think it was he who stopped by."

"I have spoken with Mr. Mossadeq several times," said 'Abdullah. "I had an appointment to talk with him the day we met."

"He came in and left. Did he come back that day to talk with you?"

"He did."

"I must tell you that Marcel Mossadeq became a friend of mine here in Ha Noi and he has just recently died, but I did not know him when I met you."

"He is dead?" said 'Abdullah with surprise.

"A tragic accident. He drowned," I lied.

"This is very sad to hear."

"Did you know him well?"

"No, not well. He came here three times to discuss the possibility of a *waqf* for the mosque."

"You mean he was thinking of creating an endowment, making a donation?"

"I believe. Yes."

"Marcel's father, who passed away a few years ago, was involved with some sort of foundation related to the Aga Khan's. I think he did humanitarian work in his last years. He lived in Indonesia. Maybe our friend was thinking of doing something like that himself here in Ha Noi."

"I am sorry it is too late now. And very sorry for Mr. Mossadeq."

"I am sorry to bring you this news, but you have helped me. After I met Marcel I wondered whether it was he who came here when I did the only other time."

"I will pray for him," 'Abdullah said.

"He would be grateful," I said. "Now, I must go."

"Will you come back?"

"*In sha'a Allah*," I said.

"*In sha'a Allah*," returned 'Abdullah.

With that, I shook his hand and returned to the street beyond the courtyard and resumed the aimless stroll. No reason, I thought, to have told 'Abdullah more than I had. Would I not possibly jeopardize or compromise what standing the *an-Nur* mosque had managed to achieve and maintain, if that merely constituted its existence in Ha Noi, if I divulged the story, the circumstances, of Marcel's death to 'Abdullah Hamadi? Was he not being watched himself in Vietnam? Anh had told me the police had gone there one day. Religious establishments like the mosque, like the Roman Catholic cathedral over near Hoan Kiem, existed in Vietnam, but at the discretion and invitation of the Party, provided they did not become platforms for dissent. And anyway, Marcel might as well have been rocketed to another planet. I wandered around Ha Noi for hours, well after sunset, before I went back to the apartment exhausted and slept some, unaware that my last night in Ha Noi was ticking away.

The next morning, near noon, my mobile phone rang. Surprisingly, it was Tao and she was upset and I did not much care, but I cared enough to hear her out.

"Marshall," she exclaimed plaintively, "what can I do?"

"What's wrong, Tao? What did you do now?"

"After you left my house," she said, "I thought about what you told me, about Marcel, about everything. I went to the Defense

Ministry this morning on Hoang Dieu Street. I was thinking maybe I should go by. Not to bring up anything you told me, but to see if there was anything to learn. They know me there in the building where I worked. I went in and the guards pushed me out. My identification card was taken. I was told never to come back. A soldier pushed me. I fell on the steps leading into my building there."

"You've lost your job. I lost mine, too. So did my friend Cain. But Marcel lost his life! You should not have worked there ever, in my opinion."

"But I did some good things. I helped clean up UXO."

"But you did bad things, too, even if you were not very aware they were bad. Maybe you will be aware from now on," I lectured her.

"But I have now no support for Tung and my father."

"I suppose you could always teach English," I said. But I knew better. Reliable maintenance, her sponsorship, was gone. She had been cast out, had lost favor with the establishment, with the Party. All that it would take was an order from her boss in the Ministry, and I imagined that henceforth she would be under surveillance if she stayed in Ha Noi, because even though her boss probably did not realize she knew that Marcel had been dispatched or even precisely why and by whom, Tao was a possible danger to him because she knew too much. Marcel had told her about the diamonds at least. That was enough, even if her boss did not think she knew the entire story or that he and the Israeli had murdered Marcel. But perhaps he knew I had been by Tao's place the previous day.

"I'm scared," Tao said.

"I am going to leave Vietnam," I told her.

"You might be stopped at Noibai if you go that way. Maybe a hard interrogation or worse. I don't know but anything's possible now."

"Is there any other way out? It would be best if I could just slip away, disappear, but not like Marcel did. Maybe you'd like to disappear for a while, too?"

"Ha Giang," Tao said.

"Ha Giang? You mean...?"

"Yes, my hometown. I want to leave Ha Noi now. I must."

"I don't know. Can you disappear in Ha Giang?"

"At least I can leave Ha Noi. I would like to do that in secret. Would you come with me and Tung and my father? We can go to the little house where I was born in Ha Giang. My father's sister lives in Ha Giang. She has the key and watches the place."

"Ha Giang might work for now."

I was suddenly thinking what Tao might do there, like open a little café and become more like Anh in future. "But I want to get out of Vietnam altogether," I said. "And very quietly, if that's possible."

"You can go to China. There's a remote border crossing at Than Thi just 25 kilometers from Ha Giang right along the river."

"The Lo River you told me about? The Chinese floating goods down it? Your childhood play?"

"Yes," said Tao.

"But I don't have a Chinese visa. Americans need a visa prior to getting to China."

"Not a worry. You have an American passport. Even without a visa you can pay money and get by the border. But it will be costly."

"More corruption, Tao," I reminded her.

I thought about Tao's proposal for a minute. The idea of leaving the police, or whoever might also be watching me in Ha Noi, in the dust was appealing. Suddenly, I'd be gone, less visible if not invisible. Out the back door beyond Ha Giang, and the authorities might know little or nothing. I figured I had been tagged for reasons no one but Tao's former boss even knew, but he did not have to give reasons. The immediate question was how would we get to Ha Giang.

"How do you propose we go?" I asked. "Certainly not on your Honda." I was trying to inject some levity into an otherwise sorry situation.

"Mini buses go to Ha Giang."

But then an idea: Tan, Tan the Man, the friendly cab driver who had recognized me in front of the Opera House after I had ridden with him once before from work, and found him reliable and thoughtful. He said he would be available if ever I called him, and I still had his business card. It suddenly seemed time to give him a call and a job.

"I have an idea, Tao."

"Yes?"

"I must make a call first. I'll tell you later. But I have another question for you. You remember the night you met me at my apartment building and came inside?"

"I remember."

"And you remember massaging me?"

"Yes."

"I fell asleep. You said I was snoring. Why would any man fall asleep in such circumstances? I was surprised I had. Did you have anything to do with that, the falling asleep part?"

Tao did not respond immediately, but finally, she said: "Will you not be more angry with me?"

"No guarantee."

"I put something in your wine."

"Why?"

"I was not then interested in forming a relationship of that nature."

"But you started to."

"I was wanting you to keep interested in me so I could know what you were doing and thinking."

"I'll call you back in a while. Keep your phone handy. Bye," I snapped at her.

There was no need to slam her more. I already had. I was thinking of Tan, found his business card and rang his number.

21

Tan agreed to drive me and Tao, her father and Tung to Ha
Giang, and I arranged for him to pick me up on Hang Giay and
then drive to Bach Dang, Tao's neighborhood in Ha Noi, and stop
just outside the narrow lane that led down towards the Red River
to her house. Better it seemed to drive from Ha Noi near midnight
to try to avoid observation, if any, and the heavy daytime traffic,
and we set eleven as the hour.

We agreed on payment of $500 cash provided, I requested, he
tell no one -- ever -- whom he was transporting and where. That
sum likely constituted his earnings for a couple months. I called
Tao back and told her the plan and she agreed to it and then I
spent the day cleaning up the apartment and packing a couple
suitcases with the few things I had originally brought to Vietnam. I
left a note on the kitchen counter, too: "I HAVE GONE TO
SAIGON FOR A VISIT," it read in bold capitals. Perhaps the
soldiers, or police, would come back to the apartment building and
find the false destination. Anything was possible, as I had been
discovering.

When I finished packing and cleaning, I went out first to an
ATM machine near Hoan Kiem Lake and withdrew $2,500 with a
VISA card, and then wandered back and wound up at the Maitre
Café to try to relax some and enjoy a bowl of Anh's *pho* and a cup
of her green tea. By then it was almost seven -- about four hours
before Tan was to appear with his cab outside the apartment
building. Business was a bit slow at the Maitre and Anh was
standing outside the café on the sidewalk.

"I see you walking up street," said Ahn when she spied me.

"Hello, Anh," I said in greeting. "You see a lot."

"Mr. Marshall," said Anh. "Not see you in days?"

"Busy, busy," I said, as I had sometimes before to her initial queries. I wasn't planning to tell her anything more, not that I was no longer working at the newspaper and about to abandon the apartment and, if I had some luck, be gone from Vietnam into China. But I did wonder if she knew anything about Ha Giang.

"Anh," I asked, "have you traveled to Ha Giang? Have you ever been there?"

"No, I just been to coast. Hai Phong a few times, and to Hue also. Hue farthest I been from Ha Noi. But I heard of Khau Vai Love Market. I told you before," she blushed. "It near Ha Giang."

"I believe so. You want to go to Khau Vai?"

"Maybe I want good man someday," she laughed nervously. For some reason, though, I did not think she cared, or was in no rush. "Very beautiful in mountains around Ha Giang. I see pictures. It best part of Vietnam. Quiet there. Not like Ha Noi now."

If I were younger man...," I said to her. I could not finish the thought aloud, but I really did not have to. If she understood, fine, and if she did not, fine, too. But I still wished I had been bolder and more insistent when, much earlier, I had suggested taking her to dinner and a night out together. Or that I had asked her again after that first time. But it was way too late.

"Someday maybe you will go see it," I said. "I would like some of your *pho* and tea."

"No problem," Anh said, and she went inside the café.

Like any other evening along Hang Giay, the traffic buzzing by, the old woman up the street with her box holding cigarettes for sale, the family that often had done my laundry carrying inside their home the stacks of fake Lacoste shirts and other clothing from the sidewalk, closing up for the night. I was beginning to cheer up slightly: always, in difficult times, the relative safety and anodyne of movement, of going somewhere fresh and heretofore unseen. Like when I had left home to visit Dar Williams. And it was to be to the farthest, remotest and poorest of all the provinces in Vietnam -- Ha Giang Province, which lay some 300 kilometers north after a slow climb on Highway Two towards the area's limestone, jungled mountains between which spread narrow, verdant valleys planted in various fruits, tea and rice by a plethora of tribal people who spoke languages which were not Vietnamese and which had not yet even been written down.

I was also cheered by the prospect of seeing Tan one more time, and this with Tao, Pham and Tung in our common aim to escape Ha Noi.

Anh came back with the *pho* and tea after a few minutes.

"Thanks," I said. "Thanks for all you have done for me here."

"I not do much," said Anh.

"More than you know. I must go away tomorrow on a trip. Would you do me a favor and call me if you see anything unusual on the street, like near my apartment building?" I borrowed her check pad and wrote my number on it.

"Where you going?" she asked with a quizzical look.

"Ho Chi Minh City. To see some friends for a while," I lied.

"You be away long?"

"For a while. If I'm gone too long maybe I can call you?" I asked.

"Yes," said Anh. "You can call me." She tore a blank piece of paper from her pad and wrote down the café's number and gave it to me. "Wish you good trip to south."

"Will you call me if you see anything unusual on the street?"

"Yes."

"Appreciated," I said.

I reached out and squeezed one of her hands. It was the first time I had ever touched her. But I was at a loss for further conversation, for even if she expected me back at the café, I knew I was not ever to see her again. Once gone from Vietnam, I could not imagine wanting to return anytime soon, and even if I wanted to eventually, I figured I might be too old and merely dreaming of an impossible journey.

There was no telling what would happen to her, but I imagined that ten years hence, when I might not even be alive, she might still be where she was that evening -- in the warrens of the Old Quarter serving patrons at the café. Perhaps, too, with a child or children of her own assisting her. The thought was comforting. That she existed anywhere was comforting.

After a while, after I had finished the *pho* and tea, I left $100 on the table under the tea cup and returned to the apartment and lay down on the couch for a couple hours, anticipating a long journey on the highway while riding shotgun beside Tan in his cab, wishing I had a shotgun for the ride.

I wondered if Anh thought the big tip portentous of anything, but I was not going back to ask her what she thought, because she'd have demanded I take the money back. It was all about gentleness and kindness, I thought: the best of Vietnam, an unsung, unheralded heroine of sorts just doing her simple, honest job, being generous with patrons such as I had been, being humble and minding her own business and looking out for others. I loved her for what she was.

22

At eleven I left the apartment. I placed the key in a kitchen drawer amid some forks and spoons and locked the door behind me, carrying my two bags. Downstairs, in the undercroft, the old guard was sitting on his cot amid parked motorbikes watching his crude television.

I still did not know his name, but it had never mattered and had not asked. He waved me by and unlocked the gate but I stopped. I did not have to say anything, but then I wondered that if police or soldiers returned to look for me, he might be questioned. With a few words and gestures, pointing at the bags, I attempted to tell him I was taking a trip to Ho Chi Minh City and would return.

Tan then appeared exactly on time and I put the bags in the trunk of his cab. There was room for more, but not enough for what I imagined Tao would be bringing along. But Tan had thought ahead. He had jerry rigged a rack on top of the car and had several meters of plastic rope to tie things down.

"I hope you've told your family you'll be away for a day or two?" I said.

"I drive tourists far from Ha Noi before," Tan said. "I told my wife and son I'm going to Hue. They are not surprised. They can call me anytime on my phone. Or I call them."

"Very good. No one's to know that you took me or the other passengers to Ha Giang. That's the deal. Okay?"

"Understand," said Tan.

I counted $500 from my pocket and handed it to him. Money -- or something of value like diamonds -- was certainly the universal language: it talked loudly. It spoke of Marcel's murder. Then we were off, a quick right turn and 300 meters to the Long Bien Bridge ramp, and then south a couple kilometers where we turned into Bach Dang and pulled up near the lane leading down a couple hundred meters to Tao's house.

I asked Tan to wait and got out of the cab and went to Tao's house. The door was open and there was Tao with Tung and her father clutching a bottle of rice wine. They had half a dozen packed, battered bags and boxes, one of the boxes filled with Tung's Lego pieces among other playthings.

"On time," Tao said. She looked unkempt, as if she had been doing laundry by hand, in frayed jeans and plastic sandals, but she also seemed to have recovered some faint ebullience. The chatoyance of her moods was evident -- it had only been half a day since she was evicted from the Ministry of Defense and her life support in the city cut. I noticed scratches and bruises on her fore arms. She had claimed she had been pushed down by soldiers or guards at the Ministry of Defense.

"You are leaving much here?" I asked.

"We will lock up. Not leaving much. We are bringing what we need. It's my father's house. People know us here. They will watch over the house, even if we don't come back for a long time."

"Did you tell anyone here where you are going?"

"No," Tao said. "A neighbor wondered and I told her we were going to Ho Chi Minh City to visit relatives, like Tung's father."

"That's good. I left a note in the apartment, if anyone goes in there, saying I was gone to Saigon, too. Come, let's get your things to the cab. My friend Tan is on the street. He's been well paid already. He will do what I ask."

"Thanks for arranging this."

"I did not want to have to arrange anything," I said, "But I get to see Ha Giang. And then something of China and then I go home, I imagine. But maybe I will stop in New Zealand after some time in China."

"New Zealand?" asked Tao.

"Cain Hamilton may be there. My friend at the paper. The one who was with Marcel and me the night Marcel was killed. You never met him but then, in truth, we haven't spent all that much time together."

Tao nodded. I pitied her some, but not much. She was a leper, as far as the Party was concerned, and the Party, personified in her corrupt boss, had been her foundation. Perhaps it was good that foundation had been ripped from under her. Nothing really fine at all about it. Millions like her were riding motorbikes around Ha Noi, doing some cruddy job. I had virtually fallen for her after the day she took me around West Lake to Vines and to the blind masseuse and then the meeting at the *Cinematique*, and after all the text messaging.

Well, certainly I had been charmed. Then, the messages had gone cold: she was focusing on Marcel. He was younger. He looked rich, too, and Tao had discovered I was not, relatively anyway. I was living in a grubby apartment in the Old Quarter; Marcel had a large, clean house at Ngu Xa. But Tao did not even know that Marcel was not exactly what he seemed, was not wealthy.

For a second, I almost thought I might have liked Tao more had she been fully apprised of what was happening and maybe taken a cut of the money her boss laundered with the diamonds. Maybe I'd have marveled a bit at her craftiness. But then I would not have assisted her, as I was. It took two trips out to dark, quiet Bach Dang Street to move all the baggage to the cab and all I could think of was that Tao had been very stupid and naive. And her ordeal was not going to be over after she got to Ha Giang, but I did not know that when we set off.

Tan stuffed what he could into the trunk of his cab and then tied down everything else on the roof and in a few minutes we were moving, Tao and Tung and her father clutching his bottle, cramped together in the back seat of the cab. Tao spoke with Tan in Vietnamese, and with her father, but by the time we were crossing the six-lane bridge over the Red River five miles north of the decrepit Long Bien span, headed north, Tung and his grandfather had fallen asleep and Tao was quiet. I sat back, less anxious than I had been.

Cleaner air was already rushing past and into the open window by my side, and I had a sense of a kind of ascension out of the Hellhole, the Hoa Loa, that Ha Noi had lately seemed. It was a real

night journey, and thinking simply of that term, I recalled the fable
of the journey of the same name when Muhammad had allegedly
mounted the winged steed called Buraq and been taken up to tour
the Heavens, where he spoke with the earlier Prophets and finally
with Allah. In the *Qu'ran*, this was also called the *Mi'raj*, or the
ascension. In Heaven Allah tells Muhammad to enjoin Muslims to
pray 50 times a day, but then good Moses, practical Prophet that he
was, tells Muhammad that prayer 50 times a day is extraordinarily
difficult and urges Muhammad to go back and ask Allah for a
reduction, until finally the commandment to pray is reduced to a
mere five times a day. Though some Muslim scholars over the
centuries insisted that Muhammad's night journey was a physical
one, I was gratified to know that many others considered the *Mi'raj*
nothing more than a dream, as of course it had to have been. But
the ascension towards Ha Giang was anything but a dream, and it
felt promising, almost like a ride to Heaven might. Eventually, I
dozed off myself and when I awoke we were in another world, a
world I had not seen before, four hours beyond Ha Noi and just an
hour from Ha Giang where the air was mountain cool and dawn
was happening and deeply green, forested mountains rose up from
both sides of narrow Highway Two.

We had already driven through half a dozen large towns and
maybe a score of villages along the narrow highway, but I had seen
little of them. I turned in my seat and found Tao and her father
also awake, staring intently at the landscape. Tung lay prone across
their laps, still sleeping. Tan was dutifully, silently, intently watching
the road, occasionally grabbing a plastic water bottle on the floor
and taking a swig from it and then handing it to me. With the dawn
sections of the highway were just beginning to clot up with vehicles
of all kinds and pedestrians, even ox-drawn carts that occasionally
slowed our passage: villagers and other country people, many of
them in tribal garments of bright colors, beginning their day of
labor, going to market or wherever.

"This is beautiful," I said to Tan. Bac Ho was right, I thought:
nothing better than Freedom, maybe in our case freedom from the
big city.

"You will like my town," Tao said. "We will go swim in the Lo River. I have not been home in three years, before I went to America." She was silent for half a minute and then added: "This is a mess."

I looked back at her and nodded my head in full agreement. Tao had evidently thought some about what had happened in Ha Noi.

"I wanted to report and take credit for the story of the diamonds before Marcel was killed, and afterwards, too," I said to Tao. "The Israeli, Leiberman or Jabotinsky or some name we don't know, knew I was a journalist. I told him so on the *Emeraude*. That may well have speeded up the plot to kill Marcel. You are not the only person who screwed up. But you screwed up a lot more."

I did not want to slam her too hard. I was still dependent on her to take care of me in Ha Giang until she could get me up to the Chinese border some 25 kilometers from the town and negotiate a private exit for me.

"You did not know what was coming. Neither did I," said Tao.

"I went to the an-Nur mosque yesterday on Hang Luoc Street and spoke to the official there. He knew Marcel because Marcel had been there. He was apparently thinking of directing a humanitarian contribution to the mosque that might have been used to benefit Vietnamese, or at least Vietnamese Muslims."

"How shall I get by now?"

"I suppose like anyone who's not on some special dispensation."

Tao was still primarily thinking of herself, it seemed. A leopard does not change its spots very easily, I thought, but maybe she was learning something -- the hard way.

"You were paid, too, to help make a mess. And where money passes hands, the question always is: for what? Good or bad? But even so, look where it has brought us -- almost to the Celestial Kingdom, to China. Maybe Ha Giang is more than halfway to a new Heaven, a kind of purgatory on the way?"

"No," countered Tao, "I don't like China. Remember I told you about the invasion of Ha Giang Province when I was four!"

"I remember, and I remember your account of the Chinese floating rafts of consumer good down the Lo. As for your question of how you might live, I suppose if the government doesn't bother you, you will manage. You could even teach English to young people as they, like you once did, probably dream of getting as far as Ha Noi at least."

"I did not learn much in Ha Giang. I am better speaking English now because the Ministry sent me to America. I would go back to America and bring Tung. When I was thrown out of the Ministry yesterday and my identification card was taken, I was told my passport was voided, that it would not be honored if I try to leave Vietnam."

"Yours is not the freedom Bac Ho probably dreamed of." I had a sense Tao might be angling to get me to help her return to America, like a Viet Kieu.

"At least Americans might vote governments out of office," said Tao. "We cannot vote the Party out. The Party considers itself the People. We could only revolt, but the Party coddles the soldiers and they protect the Party."

"And the soldiers get paid, too, one way or another. You are getting it, or beginning to."

I was worried what Tan was making of the conversation. He understood English well enough to realize then that our journey to Ha Giang was actually a *flight from* Ha Noi. I glanced at Tan and he noticed.

"I honor my friends before my government. I want to come to America someday, too, and bring my family," he said.

"You are welcome in my home anytime I am there," I shot back, "And thank you. But America is not exactly as many think it is outside America. You should know that, being Vietnamese."

"I am pleased," said Tan.

"Tao," I asked. "What did you do with your Honda?"

"I pulled it inside the house. Didn't you see it when we left?"

"No, but I guess you can find another ride in Ha Giang."

'It's a small town. I can get about easily on a bicycle, or on foot. You will see," said Tao. "It is a safe place, not like Ha Noi now. My father and I can even make a fresh garden in the back yard. We have a coconut tree and lychee fruit there already."

"You remember Dar Williams on the *Emeraude*, and at the Press Club? When I first got to Vietnam, Dar claimed he felt safer, and that Vietnam was safer, than anyplace he knew. No crimes reported in the English language paper anyway. I never got mugged in Ha Noi. No one stole from me. But now it feels very unsafe in Ha Noi. This is what governments can do -- create a climate of no information or misinformation that instills fear, and coerces people to obedience and to a belief that government is looking after them. You may be much better off just staying in Ha Giang."

23

Tao's birthplace and childhood home lay on a quiet, unpaved street some 400 meters from the Lo River near the edge of town. The house was a rectangle some 10 meters deep, painted a turquoise blue -- the exact color of Tao's bikini at Ha Long Bay -- with a small, screened porch at the back, and beyond that an overgrown yard with a couple coconut palms and a lychee tree.

Tan had dropped us off at the house. He did not linger. He turned around and headed back to the capital, but I kept his business card as a souvenir. Someday perhaps I would speak with him again, but I doubted it then.

I stayed four days in Ha Giang, just enough time to walk all over the town until I had seen enough and become restless, anxious to get to the border crossing. I slept in a hammock on the porch when the barking dogs in the neighborhood went quiet late at night and woke to crowing cocks. Tao's father was hazy with alcohol much of the time and anyway, I couldn't talk to him, or he to me, but he was quiet and friendly and unlike Cain, wasn't pissing in the street.

Tao and Pham tended Tung and she, at first, set about cleaning the place up, acquiring some additional, cheap furniture at a local market, buying some food, a steel bottle of propane for cooking and other basic necessities. Tao's aunt, Pham's younger sister, the one who opened the house with the key after Tan had driven away, came and went and helped out marginally. She spoke no English and I kept out of her way. She acted a bit surprised to see any of us and a couple times I heard her arguing with Pham.

It was at first an unremarkable four days except that my mobile phone rang on the morning of third day in Ha Giang. It was Anh calling from the Maitre Café and I was standing in the street in front of Tao's bikini blue house.

She told me two men, but not in uniform, just identical dark suits and both wearing sunglasses, had an hour earlier pulled up outside my former apartment building in a government marked van with blue lights on the roof and then gone inside. (I could not help suddenly visualizing characters, men from the film "The Matrix", which I had seen, in which all the "bad guys" wore suits.)

Anh then added, speaking from the sidewalk -- and I could hear in the background the familiar swarms of motorbikes buzzing loudly by and the occasional scrape of low plastic stools on the pavement -- that she saw the same two men come out a short while later with a third man and drive away. She identified the third man as the police or security person she had earlier mentioned to me who sometimes came to the café and was not so pleasant and who lived in the building I had abandoned.

"I just telling you," said Anh. "Nothing to worry about. You worried?"

"No," I said. And in fact, this was largely true. I was a long way from Ha Noi. "Very kind of you to call me with this."

I was wondering whether the three men had gone into my apartment to find it empty, and to discover the note I had blatantly left there in bold capitals claiming I had gone to Saigon.

Perhaps the men had also questioned the guard in the undercroft. He had seen me with my baggage, but I had indicated to him I was just going to Saigon, underscoring the lying note in the apartment.

The guard, whom I sort of envied for the utter simplicity of his old age -- a simplicity that was not my Fate -- had not seen me come or go for three days, and if he were questioned, he'd have likely said that and if he remembered, would have mentioned Ho Chi Minh City, too, I imagined. But even while I wondered, I had no way of fathoming what Anh described was exactly about. Maybe it involved me. It likely did, but I could not know with any certainty.

"How are you, Anh?" I asked. "I have been missing you." And this was no lie. I believed I'd miss her, or someone like her, like my son's mother, for as long I lived -- a day, week, ten more years, I had *no idea*, which perhaps was a very good thing.

"I missing you, too," said Anh. "Different when you go away Ha Noi. Even if you not stop by café, I like it thinking you nearby in city. Now, you not. Right?"

"Sorry to say, Anh, I'm not in Ha Noi at the moment," I told her, and that instant I suddenly realized that for some time she had to have been thinking, or feeling about me, in the same way I had often thought and felt about her, perhaps not as strongly, but still warmly. And she was so much younger, yet extremely wise, wiser than I, in her own special way.

The realization was of the existence of something real and sublime between us, maybe just some love, that had somehow been born, though nothing at all had been consummated and I had not even had the pleasure of any leisure time, if ever she had any, over dinner and away from the café, as I had suggested in what seemed like -- there under raking clouds in morning Ha Giang -- eons past.

"I sorry, too, but I keep my eyes open for you. For you to come back, too," Anh said.

"My eyes are always open for you, too. I see you now, there on Hang Giay. Are you busy this morning? Did I pronounce that right, 'Hang Giay'?"

"Yes. This first time I hear you pronounce right I know of. And not too busy. Not so busy I not call you."

"Then I have finally learned something important," I said to her.

I was thinking just then what I had just learned about her feelings, but I could not tell her that this, was most important. But nonetheless, it was also important that I had finally gotten the linguistic tones of her language correct -- at least those tones in correct sequence required to tell a cab driver -- other than Tan -- where I wanted to go, where I had lived.

But it was all too late, what was fine was coming too late, and I choked up on the phone, falling silent with her voice coming to me like that, in the same sweet way my son's mother used to speak during our marriage.

"Anh, I will call you back sometime," I finally managed to say without audible emotion.

I was about to say "someday" but that would have given away the fact that I was not returning anytime soon, if ever. And I did not have the courage to tell her that. Perhaps it was selfish of me. I had been selfish before. I had often been outspokenly selfish. And I rather felt the vain idea that she might be waiting for me, waiting for me for a very long time, as kind of deep ecstasy, and this certainly was not Marcel Mossadeq's kind.

But at least I could say, if just to myself, that I would always be looking for her, waiting for her, or someone like her, to appear again wherever I happened to be. For some reason, I could not be outspoken with her by word or gesture. I most certainly could not have churned my hips the way Marcel had so cleverly done facing the Canadian blonde at the bar at Bobby Chinn's.

"I will be happy when you call, or come back," Anh said.

And then we both clicked off the connection, in perfect unison.

After Anh's call I was rather amused after imagining the police, or whomever it was, perhaps going into the apartment and finding it bare and empty. Maybe they were trying to figure out where I might be in Saigon, but Saigon was not Ha Noi: it was a much larger city, and much easier for a foreigner to get lost in, or to disappear. I stood in the street for a while, in the same single pair of shorts I had brought to Vietnam and which Phuc had emphatically forbidden me to wear in the newsroom, and a while later, Tao came out. There she was, as first I had seen her after a few minutes at first meeting, when she had peeled off her clothes on the deck of the *Emeraude*. She was wearing her blue bikini under a loose, open coat. She had a towel, too.

"Come," she said, noting my shorts and bare knees, but without complaint. "Let's go for a swim in the river. I have done most chores now. You can swim in your shorts."

"Is it safe? Piranha?" I joked.

"Safer than Ha Long Bay," she said. "There really are sharks in Ha Long Bay. The river was safe enough for me to swim in as a child."

"I know about sharkish stuff in Ha Long Bay. I figured that out." I was thinking of her there, but she did not know it.

Above the Lo in Ha Giang on both sides of the river ran a narrow park. Tao urged us there and then we went down -- she like a dancer or a high wire artist with those bare feet of hers -- the steep riverbank on a dirt path from the park and for half an hour we plunged and dog paddled about in the milky water of an eddy where the current was easy and slow. Then we sat beside the river and shared the towel and watched the water swirl by with its curious ripples and eddies.

"Tao," I finally said. "Have you been to Khau Vai village? The Love Market? I know Khau Vai is somewhere not too far away here in Ha Giang Province."

"I have been there, but long ago, when I was a teen," said Tao. "I've not been to the Love Market. It's just for a day and it's silly, I think."

"Silly? You have become so Westernized," I commented.

"I liked Washington, but now I wonder if I can ever go back."

"I don't know," I said. "But I am going to tell you something now about Khau Vai's Love Market."

"You went there?" Tao asked with some astonishment.

"Sort of."

"How so? I don't believe it."

"The night after the Opera House debacle, when you abandoned me there, I had a rare dream. I was in Khau Vai and it was Love Market day and you were there on the Honda and I was chasing you around. You were sitting backwards on the seat and every time I got close, you somehow managed to speed away. I ran and ran after you, and then, thankfully, woke up. It was no fun. It was exhausting. Frustrating."

"That is funny," Tao said with laugh and a smile. "Do you like me? I really like you," she said, and moved closer to me on the riverbank. In the water, she had already been somewhat solicitous, splashing me, trying to get me to splash her, diving below the surface with a twist and flashing the shapely butt I had enjoyed full view of while paddling the kayak in Ha Long Bay.

"I like you, I guess, but I'm still pissed by what you actually were doing in Ha Noi. Angry about what happened to Marcel. And you *did* like him more than me."

"Will you forgive me ever?" Tao asked, and she pressed, almost snuggled, against me, arm against arm, leg against leg.

"It doesn't matter what I feel. I'm going from Vietnam. But I am worried some about you, what you can do now," I said.

"Would you ever want me to massage you again?" she asked, but she wasn't so playful as she had been the night on the couch in the apartment. "I can do better," she added.

"What I might want in a moment of shallow thinking from you or anyone is not necessarily what should be wanted," I said. "No, I don't want a massage."

Tao drew back. She looked hurt, but I could not tell if the hurt look on her still pleasing to see face was real. Maybe she was just feigning it. At any rate, her allure had been diminished by her unwitting complicity in Marcel's death and her apparent naïveté, her blind allegiance to the notion that her powerful boss in the Ministry of Defense was a sincere Communist. That, to me, was the point: Communism as a system was not inherently better or worse than Democracy. What could go wrong with Communism, as with any system, even one that called itself "democratic" in any particular location, even in *My*, as Phuc would have said, was simply what could go wrong, or be wrong, with any particular person or persons given power by *fiat* or vote and who could not easily be dislodged.

Tao dropped her probing in *that* direction and went on wondering aloud, brazenly I thought there by the Lo, if I could pull some strings and figure out a way to get her back to America.

But quite clearly I then told her I had no strings to pull, and at the same time realized, without saying so, the only possible "string" I could think of to "pull" might be one that involved marrying her right there in Ha Giang.

But I could not see that at all. The idea was not remotely pleasing, despite those things I still admired about her. Marriage was revolting. I could not trust her enough and did not have the confidence to assume I would ever mean more to her than a mere vehicle from the bind she was in. I figured she would be stuck with her father and her son for some time in Ha Giang and I was not moved nearly enough by her any longer to try to make a difference. And there seemed nothing wrong with her being stuck in Ha Giang while Tung grew up. It could be stable there for the lad.

When we stood to head back up the river embankment and to the house, Tao was quiet, clearly unhappy. She paused and reached into her coat pocket and took out her cell phone halfway up to the strip of grassy park, some meters above the Lo's flow.

"Who are you calling?" I asked, pausing behind her on the path.

But then she did not answer. She was calling no one. She drew back with a cry, a sob, and heaved the phone into the river.

"Why are you throwing your phone away like that? You just did what the Chinese did: consumer goods in the river. Except the phone is wet and ruined."

"I know more than you. That phone is dangerous now. If the Ministry wants to know where I am, I just thought they might be tracking that phone. I will get another phone and a new number, and if I can, under another name."

I was a bit astonished, but I could see her logic. "Well, okay," I said. "I guess there's a lot of stuff in that river no one will ever see, unless it dries up."

Whatever phone she might obtain, and I had walked past shops in the town, I figured she might get used to a long spell in Ha Giang. It was, after all, home base. And I did attempt to ease her distress some and said that if she could ever get a new number to me, maybe from the Internet café across the bridge on the other side of the Lo, I'd give her a call someday. I was sure she'd soon change her number with a new phone. I also knew I would want to know how and what she was doing, but not for a while.

Even if Tao had brightened Ha Noi for me a few times amid the frustrations of dealing with Phuc and the loneliness that Marcel and Cain and Anh at the Maitre Café had also helped relieve, her priorities had been fucked up. And much more of the freedom Bac

Ho touted, or at least some distance from possible danger, lay beyond the nearby, compelling border crossing for me, I imagined.

"Tao," I said, when we reached the house, "I want to go to the border tomorrow morning."

But when we reached the house, Pham rushed out to her excitedly. There ensued a sharp conversation between Tao and her father, a conversation that put Tao in even more distress than anything I had said to her, or not said, by the river.

When Pham went back inside, Tao turned to me: "Yes, I will show you the border tomorrow morning."

"What was that with your father?"

"A local policeman came by when we were swimming. I guess someone reported the house had been opened up, and wondered by whom and why. No one's been here for three years. This town is a fishbowl," Tao said with disgust.

I imagined she was getting a taste of what it was like to be on the receiving end of the work she had done.

"What did your father tell the guy?"

"He said he had come home to check on things and visit his sister. He did not mention us, he claimed. But then, there was Tung. The man saw Tung. Maybe he wondered if my father was lying. I don't know," said Tao. "The locals here know my aunt, who has never left the province. She has no children. And they do know my mother died years ago. Her funeral was here."

"Well, I'm sure people wonder who, like me for example, was going to and then swimming at the river. Wouldn't people remember you here? You've been out shopping."

"Ha Giang has grown a lot in recent years. New faces. More turnover. People going to Ha Noi. People coming back from all over Vietnam. I don't think people I've passed know me. I haven't recognized anyone directly. It's a fishbowl, but not as tight as it was, and we have no one here but my aunt."

So it was that the next morning, after a mostly sleepless night in the hammock, with the same cocks crowing dawn somewhere not too far away, I closed my bags again and Tao called a local driver to take me to the border. I said farewell to her father and to Tung, hugging them both, and with Tao left the little blue house.

We drove out past a couple of tribal villages set amid rice paddies and duck ponds off the road to the border just outside the town. Up the road at some distance through the valley of the Lo, beyond the border, tall mountains rose up in the distance like mounds of green Easter sugar.

"What tribe lives there?" I asked as we passed two rather extensive patches of dwellings made of palm thatch roofs and wooden platforms mounted on wooden stilts. There were duck ponds all round, too, and some oxen.

"The Tay," and then Tao opened her bag and pulled out what she said was a gift. It was a small, greenish, bronze bell with a forked handle and it looked old.

"What exactly is this?"

"It belonged to a shaman, a Tay shaman. It is at least 100 years old. I want you to have it."

There were over a million Tay in Vietnam, and all of them lived in the mountains up close to the Chinese border, as did many other tribes. I knew this. I had read of ethnic minorities in Vietnam like the Tay and of others like the Black and Red Hmong, and Dar Williams, who had worked among them, had told me more when I was in Saigon. They were Vietnam's often forgotten people in the rush to modernize, living isolated lives and speaking their own languages, just as they had for centuries. They were largely untouched by *Doi Moi*. Maybe they were mixing and bottling the magic drink Marcel Mossadeq liked -- the drink in which a pickled, baby King Cobra resided.

"Thanks," I said. "Are you sure you want to give me this? I think you need it more."

"It's so you won't just completely forget me."

"No chance that's going to happen," I said, "unless I get Alzheimer's and lose my memory. So tell me more about this bell."

"Shamans use objects like this for different ceremonies. For funerals, calling for rain, invoking spiritual powers, fending off evil spirits. It has been in the house since before I was born."

"Fending off evil is good. Maybe I should have had this in the West Bank, too," I said, "I will keep it and ring it to wish us both luck. Okay, here's something for you."

I still had a considerable sum of dollars and I gave her the same sum I had given Tan. Tao was without work. I did not know how she and her father and Tung would hold up if she could not soon find some paid work, but maybe there was some social safety net in place in Ha Giang. I wondered again about Tao opening a café, one like Anh's. But then I knew that was impossible, for to me Anh was inimitable and made her café what it was.

"This is generous," Tao said somberly, but she took the money without hesitation.

"Use part of it to make an offering for Marcel Mossadeq," I suggested, and Tao nodded her head but was then silent and within a few more minutes, with the Lo River flowing by off to our right in the opposite direction back towards Ha Giang, the cab pulled up beside a couple squat buildings. Huge concrete squares blocked the road ahead, barring vehicles, and beyond them I could see a wire fence with an opening in the middle, and beyond the fence a hundred meters farther along, more low but tidier buildings, these well inside Chinese territory.

Tao told the driver to wait and we exited the cab and I took my bags from the trunk of the car.

"Wait here. I will go inside. What money do you have left?"

I counted $1,000 while Tao watched.

"Give me $600," she said. "I will offer $300 to each side to coordinate your private passage," she said. I gave her the $600 and then she went in the building and came out a few minutes later.

"It is arranged," Tao said.

"The Vietnamese way," I said. "So what am I supposed to do now exactly?"

Tao handed me back half the money I had handed her.

"You can take your bags and walk." Tao said. "And when you get to the other side, give the money to the Chinese official in the building beyond the fence. He will stamp a visa in your passport."

"I will ring the bell you gave me. Borders make me nervous."

I was just then conjuring up visions of Kalandia, the crossing between the far northern outskirts of Jerusalem and Ramallah in the West Bank -- the Israeli soldiers, the huge crowds jostling and inching through cordons of concrete barriers and concertina wire that resembled cattle shoots in an abattoir, trying to get across the illegitimate, illegal border in or out of the West Bank while the haughty Israeli troops stood around with their Uzi machine guns and black batons.

But looking forward, there just ahead was nothing like what existed at Kalandia. There, just an empty path north to the open fence and beyond, and the wide, cerulean sky above, and the lush mountains behind and ahead. I gave Tao a hug. I held her for a few seconds and I wished her well, and then started off. Moving towards the fence that spanned the road, I looked back and Tao was still standing beside the idling cab from Ha Giang. She did not look happy, maybe she was crying some but already she was too far away for me to know for sure. I breathed more deeply than I had almost since the weekend on the *Emeraude* and I knew I'd not forget her or that morning in Vietnam's remotest province and the walk across the border into China.

I stopped and put my things down on the cracked asphalt and took from my pocket the Tay shaman's antique bell Tao had given me. I raised it above my head and shook it and it gave off a sweet, sharp ring of just modest volume. It was perfect. I needed some fresh luck. So did Tao. Maybe there was something to ringing Tao's gift, something like an incantation.

I kept walking, but slowly, and after maybe three minutes reached the wire fence and passed through an opening in it and then beyond. Officially, I had reached China. The fence was the exact border. I could no longer be touched by anyone in Vietnam. And having gotten to China, I stopped and put my bags down again, wanting one last look at where I had walked from, where I had left Tao. I took out the binoculars I had deployed aboard the *Emeraude* to get a closer look at the *Geneva Princess* and the *chum* aboard her in Ha Long Bay, and after I drew the binoculars to my eyes, I knew immediately the Tay shaman's bell's ring had not yet become a positive incantation. Maybe, I thought, it would prove to be favorable eventually, just not yet. Through the glass, I could see Tao as if she stood 100 meters away, and actually it was more like 600 meters. She was not alone and the cab was gone. Two police cars, not the local kind, stood parked on each side of her, and in the space between the cars with Tao were three men in what appeared to be military uniforms and one of them was rifling through her handbag and, I thought, taking things from it. The other two men, one on each side, had a hand on her elbow.

I saw Tao hastily look my way. But she could not see me, I thought. I was too far away and beyond the fence. She was clearly distressed, but she wasn't fighting. She had proven to me she could be pretty cool under pressure. She was a survivor, whatever else she was. And there was not a damn thing I could do for her except something I rarely did in any circumstances: pray. And I did quickly wonder whether I should go back, even while I knew I would not. I would not because I had not made her mess, and anyway I'd want my money back and this might get me shot. I was sure both the Chinese on one side and the Viets on the other wanted me to do what I had already half paid for on the Viet side of the border. As for Tao, I prayed that all any authorities, local or national -- under orders from Tao's former Defense Ministry boss from whom reasons would likely neither be asked nor extracted -- wanted was to pin her down, ensure that she was not going to find a way out of the country, where she might speak freely. Tao had seemed like a decent mother and Tung needed her and I wished, at least, she would not be stripped of that job, too.

Made in the USA
Columbia, SC
02 August 2017